A RAGGED MAGIC

BOOK ONE OF THE RUNEBOUND

LINDSEY S. JOHNSON

ARUS
ENTERTAINMENT

BOOKS BY LINDSEY S. JOHNSON

A Ragged Magic
A Tangled Vision
A Jagged War (coming soon)

Published by ARUS Entertainment (Seattle, WA). Originally released by Per Aspera Press.

This book is catalog #ARUS3001, and has ISBNs of 978-1-954394-09-4 (print) and 978-0-996305-96-9 (ebook)

Edited by Jak Koke

Cover art and design by Angie Abler

ARUS

ENTERTAINMENT

www.arusentertainment.com

A RAGGED MAGIC

For my parents, for being there.

For Scott, for believing in me.

*And for 25-year-old me: It took a lot longer than planned, but
it turns out persistence does pay off.*

CHAPTER 1

I am Rhiannon.

It does not mean queenly, or deep river; it means witch. The kirche warrant declares it so.

I am not allowed to glance at the frightened guards in red who surround me; I am not allowed to notice the stares, the whispers behind hands, the frowns of the guildmembers. I am to witness the hanging, and I am only to see the scaffold before me.

My younger sister, struggling in the grip of Deacon Bertram, is held to insure my good behavior. Be a good little Rhiannon. What else can I do?

The side of my neck pulls, burns from the rope twisted there. The scratchy hemp snakes taut to the nervous kirche guardsman who holds my bonds. The warding of the witch with blessed rope: a new torture devised by the inquisitors. I wonder which priest will persecute me. I wonder if that is blasphemy. I wonder how much longer before I die.

There are no duchy guards here – the dowager duchess travels away from Haverston, and will not return for several days. The bailiff refuses to move against kirche orders. I was told when I begged to see her, or to plead before the duchess, that the guilds gave us over to the kirche, for witchery, for breaking the laws of the Star Lord. There is no one to appeal to.

The town square echoes, both hushed and strident, the voices of the gathered people held low so the kirche guards won't single them out for attention. But the square teems with more townspeople than I thought they could round up. I can hardly see the baker's at the corner, or the bookshop's dusty window. I can't see the scuffed dirt of the square anywhere but near my own feet. The crowd leaves a wide space around the guards who hold me, but overflow everywhere else.

The smells of fish and salt air from the bay are overcome by the odors of too many bodies, and fear. The old fountain, empty for the winter, stands a climbing frame, the stained and greening mermaid a prop for children to get a better look at the gallows. Their parents urge them down quietly, tossing wary looks over their shoulders at the guards. And at me.

They hold me near the foot of rickety wooden gallows. Hastily constructed, the platform stands only a few feet higher than the crowd. A wooden plank waits to be yanked from beneath condemned feet. The walls of the square echo with crowd noises and the creaking of the gallows. Already they creak, before even one body hangs from them. I sink slightly on weak knees, but the rope on my neck chokes, pulls me up again.

Soft afternoon light glows off of kirche guards' uniforms — the crimson and white and black wool embroidered with stars and moons, symbols of the Star Lord and Dorei, his lady. I am surrounded by silent, sweating men — sweating even though it is a brisk spring this year, and I shiver in my ripped gray traveling dress, tattered on the bottom and muddy, as are my torn stockings. I lost one boot to the dogs. My shuddering can't be blamed all on the chill.

The crowd behind me shifts and mumbles. Whispers reach my ears.

"She killed the Pastor – "

" – fell in the mill pond, drowned, not a mark on him! Had to have been demons ...."

"Refused to go into kirche training, that one. Refused!"

"Keenan Owen's a priest! They can't hang him, no matter his sister's witchery."

"He taught her to call demons with her power. They brought the Wasting to kill us all!"

"This has gone too far. How can this happen? There wasn't even a trial."

That last is spoken so quietly, I wonder if it was Keenan. I try not to whimper as guards bring out my family, display them on the gallows. Mum and Da and Keenan – Deacon Bertram still holds Linnet behind them. Three nooses swing drunkenly in the breeze. Keenan gazes out at me from behind one of them, hopelessness in his eyes. I have been trying to reach to him for hours, to send to his mind, but he hasn't answered.

You were supposed to run, why didn't you run, he sends, his mind whispering to mine in despair. *Why didn't you go to the seminary? Orrin was going to hide you.*

I wasn't fast enough, I wasn't fast and I got lost. Dorei turned her face from me. They had dogs, and I couldn't run anymore.

He sent to me that day, woke me before dawn, he

knew the Inquisitor's Building had a warrant, guards were coming for me. I told Mum and Da, and they bade me run, get away from the town, stay off the roads. I took nothing but the clothes I wear and some food; a little money tied into a kerchief, running for my brother and the seminary. I got lost in the woods that night. The guards took the money, after they caught me; trapped me halfway up a tree. Dogs and guards and shouting and I couldn't get away. I thought they'd leave my family alone if I ran. So did Keenan.

Tears leak down his bruised face. Light from the cloud-blurry sky glances off his shorn head, the scabs and gouges glistening with the sweat of despair. Orange stubble and olive skin and blood. Gulls over the harbor give voice to aching cries that echo in my heart.

I am so sorry, Keenan.

No, I'm sorry, I'm so sorry, Rhi. I tried to stop this. I tried to stop them.

I tremble harder. What – what can I do? What do we do? They said they'd kill Linnet, and I-

Nothing, he sends quickly. *Don't do anything. I love you, little sister. I – I will watch for you in Dorei's arms. Try to be brave.*

How can I-

I'll be brave if you will.

"Keenan," I moan aloud, and am jerked to the side by my neck, the guard with the ropes is not gentle. People inch further away.

Be brave, Rhiannon. Confess to anything they ask you. It – will go quicker that way. Look to the stars. I will sing you to them.

His dark eyes hold mine as Deacon Bertram, puffed with his importance, nods to the kirche guard to read the warrant. All these guards of a sudden – the kirche doesn't usually have so many here, and none of them from town. The large man intones a judgment of conspiring to murder, and for harboring a witch and consorting with demons. Not one word is true.

I am not on this warrant, as I was caught only this morning. The deacon has to clench his very square jaw to keep from grinning, delighting in our downfall. How many here delight in our downfall?

The guilds turned us over, because I told people at the market to save a man. Because I Saw with my unsanctified Sight the pastor drowning in the mill pond. Or because I Saw who was with him. Mum told me to hush, but he was going to drown if I didn't tell. Only it happened miles away, so I am a witch.

Mum and Da are shorn of their hair, too, standing in dirty gray shifts, stone-faced beside my brother. Linnet wails for our mum, but Mum won't look at her. Her eyes are on me.

A purple bruise swells one of her eyes almost shut, but that doesn't stop her glare. I feel a chill spreading the breadth of the air between us; my heart forms frost from her glare. I think Mum must believe what she's been told; the priests have convinced her that I summoned demons. I wouldn't keep my mouth shut. I have ruined the house of Owen-Weaver.

It is all my fault.

I flinch from Mum's stare, look at Da instead.

Da's lips tremble, but he stands as tall as he can, his back bent from years at the loom. Master Weaversmith, Guildmaster of all the guilds, Rory Owen's dark eyes stay stern and dry. Gray stubble dots his chin, his jaw tight with anger and pride and pain. The bruises look green on his skin. He looks at me, blinks eyes that turn wet, and looks away again.

I should have listened when Keenan asked me to turn to the kirche, go to seminary years ago. I didn't want to go. The Sight is a wayward power, but not dangerous. And I have so little - I was sure the kirche wouldn't care that I didn't dedicate myself to Dorei, that the town would see I wasn't a threat to anyone. I was wrong.

Not your fault, Rhi. It was ... not easy, with the inquisitors. We tried to keep you safe, all of us. We are still trying, even now. But we have to keep Linnet safe. Keep her as safe as we can. They've promised she will live..

I can't help the shudders through my body, the sick aching in all of my joints, my stomach. I can't help the tears pouring down my face. But I am not screaming. It's as much as I can do. My wrists twist against the ropes, and the guards shudder in their turn. So much fear, but I think it isn't really about me, at all.

A carriage at the edge of the square sits with quite a bit of room around it. Everyone carefully pretends it isn't there. I can See a darkness around it like shadows and fog, an ugly gathering of magic and anger festering.

With my eyes, I can see Mastersmith Aman, who looks nervous but gleeful, nod at the carriage. I pull my gaze back to the gallows when the guard reading the charges steps back.

Deacon Bertram scrambles onto the platform, his dignity frayed by the lack of steps. He sneers his way by my captive family, dragging Linnet behind him. Bertram is happy for the opportunity to publicly disgrace my brother, I don't need the Sight to know it. And he grips Linnet to his side like a prize.

His angular face, topped by lank graying blond hair,

turns toward the crowd with a fierce look of triumph. He hands my trembling sister over to an acolyte. A small part of my soul reserves hatred for him, but it is lost in a maelstrom of wailing denials in my head.

Only Linnet's continued life keeps me from flinging myself on the guards. Linnet cries openly – I can't remember the last time I saw her cry. Her face looks bruised, too.

I hear Bertram's speech in spite of myself. "Hear then, oh ye faithful, that the Star Lord judges those of you who leave the path of light for darkness, and banishes the light of your souls from the heavens. Our great Prophet Ashere, the voice of the Star Lord in the holy city of Shovahn, tells us that magic not given into service of the Star Lord is given over to the darkness. Not even in the kirche are we safe from the whisperings of evil. Even Healing must be sanctified by His Holy Light, or else twist into demon sickness."

Shuffles of unease through the crowd cause the guardsman to tighten his grip on my rope bonds, the others to shift and glance around. I gasp and rear my head, try to ease the choking pressure.

Kirche healers are few and far between, and the Wasting is the cause of deaths all over the town. The hospice that the duchy runs is the only place most people can go when they are ill. The recent bout of plague means the people need it more than ever, kirche-blessing or no.

Deacon Bertram glances out at the crowd, sweat springing shiny on his forehead. His speech changes direction.

"The accused conspired to murder a pastor of the kirche, with a witch not sanctified by the Light of the

Lord of Stars, and shall suffer punishment for it. The witch shall also suffer. This is the judgment. Prepare ye the Way of the Light."

"Receive the Prophet in their name," responds the crowd in a half-hearted rumbling murmur.

The drums start, and the crowd tenses. A guard draws a gray hood over my Mum's head, my Da's, but Bertram denies that dignity to Keenan. "He defiles us! Let the people see the death in his eyes!" he snarls.

Keenan stares into my eyes alone, refusing to flinch or blanch.

I swallow and blink, glance at my parents who stand like puppets, my sister screaming with panic.

Linnet pulls ineffectually at the acolyte's hands, scratching, frantic. He yanks her back, her dark dress tearing in his grip, and she sags against his restraint, sobbing.

Bertram turns and slaps her once, hard, and I taste iron on my throbbing tongue. I snap my eyes back to Keenan. The drums pound the last three beats, and stop.

The plank drops, and my family with it. Mum and Da's bodies jerk once to an ominous snap, but Keenan dangles and spasms, his eyes wild. I moan and sink forward, but hard hands yank me upright.

Oh, Keenan. All Gods, Keenan-

Brave, be brave -

I don't know if he's talking to me or himself; the panic crawls its way through both our limbs. His body sways and sputters, twists on its leash. He longs for death, and fights it, twitching in a rhythm like that of the now silent drums. The crowd shudders, violence and fear on its breath. I choke on pain.

Small children are crying – I hear the wails and

hiccups, the gusts of gasps. I feel Keenan's mind slip from mine like a knot letting go. No longer jerking in time to my heart, his body sways and creaks along the length of rope. A shriek rises up from Linnet's throat, but I have been warned, and I dare not grieve.

Instead I feel my mind jerk, once, twice, like bodies on ropes, as it separates itself from me. I watch myself stand staring at my dead family, and I divorce my will from my heart. I must behave, for Linnet to live. That is all that matters.

The guards drag me back to my perch on the old gray horse that I've ridden since my capture. My toes scrape on cobbles, and I'm tossed into the saddle, my feet secured in the stirrups, one booted, one bare, and my wrists looped over the cantle.

Keenan's body still sways, the ropes grunting and creaking. I look only at him. I cannot see the heavy bodies of my parents. I only see the blankness settle over Keenan's eyes. Linnet's sobs tear at me as I'm led away.

The crowds shuffle out of the way of the guards and the witch. We ride toward the castle; its gleaming spires float on the Seely Magan cliffs overlooking the bay, bathed pink in the dying light.

The castle overlooks the town of Haverston in much the same way: above, painted with light. White towers with pretty blue slate roofs gleam, the walls thick and safe and so distant from me now. Gray puffs of clouds meander across the purpling sky.

The road is lined with the sturdy guildhalls and filled with uneasy crowds. Priests and kirche guards abound in more numbers than ever I've seen in Haverston before. I see the yellow brick of the main guildhall from the corner of my eye as we pass it.

The light slants across the gathered people, striping them in gleaming color and shadow. A cold spring breeze lifts hanks of my snarled hair, and ruffles goose bumps down my back. I shiver and choke back a sob.

Dark muttering issues out of the mouths of the anxious people. More than one prayer to the Star Lord snakes through the subdued noise.

My mount plods tirelessly on its lead rope. My hands over the cantle do not even twitch. Only my knuckles are white. The rest of my skin is scratched and bruised, filthy from three days in the deep wood. My clothes fared no better.

The creaking of leather and jingle of harness and bits break over the murmur of shocked voices like waves over sucking waves. Weaver's daughter – wouldn't confess – she stole his learning to summon demons.

The buildings dwindle as we climb toward Haverston castle. I concentrate on clouds and sky. I will breathe, in and out. I will not vomit down this horse's neck.

Either I listen to my will or succumb to blinding panic. My eyes stare at sky, but I see Keenan on the scaffolds. My brother's body twitches to a macabre rhythm, his tongue swelling. I struggle to not faint, not fall in dizzy anguish, not wail and tear my hair, my clothes, my face. Be a good little Rhiannon.

I shudder, breathe through my teeth – the guardsmen tighten their hold and I gag, swallow pain and shrieks and tears together. The ocean of crowd echoes silent, then cautiously jeers louder as the priests call out the judgment. A small child cries out forlornly in the crowd and is hushed.

I close my eyes and think of Linnet. If only I believed

they will not harm her. Priests lie with such calm faces. Dorei, Grace of Night, protect her.

We pass out of the crowds and climb the slope toward the castle. Whitewashed towers looming, we pass leering gargoyles and crenellations. My breath goes ragged as we turn past the barbican, the castle walls, descend a slope.

The Inquisitor's building is squat, brooding in the shadows, nursing a grudge against the tall grace of the castle. The carriage from the square stands in the courtyard, the bay horses pawing at the ground, restless.

My long ginger hair snags across my mouth as the wind shifts, the sun sets over the crimson sea. So I am to be tried in darkness. If I am to be tried at all.

Ah, Keenan, if only I had run sooner, farther. If only I'd kept my mouth shut to begin with, the priests would never have hung you. I can still see your body jerk behind my eyelids.

I slump across the cantle, trembling. A large guard pulls me from the horse roughly. I wobble and fall on my side on the gray courtyard stones. Still warm from the sun, they smell of rain and brine and muddy feet.

The guard yanks me up and slings me over his shoulder like an empty sack, strides into the Inquisitor's building, my bonds slapping down his legs. My head bumps against the guard's back.

The air grows dark and cool, and I shudder in sudden chill. Tightening his grip on my sore and scratched thighs, the guard shifts and jumps me farther up his shoulder.

Pain and nausea blossom, and I nearly let go of my bladder, grunting. My arms hang painfully from my shoulders, but I dare not move again.

I see black flagstone with no pattern, hear the footsteps echo sharply into darkness. Growing dizzy from blood rushing in my ears, I try to focus on our path.

Why? my head whispers. There isn't any way out of the Inquisitor's building but through Justice. The priests have said that often enough.

I hang limp, desolate in the guard's grip.

The air grows dank: the smell of stale water and mold overpower even my fear-soaked odor. We pass through twisting halls, doorways – a torch flares, and the guard dumps me in a corner. Benches and knives and metal spikes dance dully in the light.

I scramble to sit, my bound hands slipping on gritty damp stone.

"So, this is the witch of Weaver's Guild," a nasal baritone declares above me.

My back against the cold wall, I look up into flat blue eyes, no emotion: a boy studying a fly whose wings he's torn off. He bends down to examine me more closely.

"Yes, Bishop Gantry. She is accused of consorting with demons, summoning the Wasting, and of the spell-killing of Pastor Seaton."

"Of course she is. And does she have the Sight?"

"As reported, sir."

The Bishop's hand slowly wraps, long-fingered, around the rope still at my neck. Suddenly he yanks my head toward him, smashing my ear into his knee. "And do you confess, witch?"

Stars dance around my head; my mouth is too dry to answer.

His mouth turns up in a vague smile as he straightens, his dark robe rustling and billowing. Letting go of my harness, he turns to a bench, gestures for the guard to place me there.

Shackles, sullenly picked out in the torchlight, await my arms and legs. Sweat breaks out on my cold skin.

No trial, then. But a while yet before I die.

CHAPTER 2

I don't know how long it has been. My hands burn, my feet shoot pain up through my body, my throat is raw. The questions make no sense, and they will not take no for an answer.

But I didn't say no, not after they skinned the first hand. I stopped saying words after my feet.

"She cannot sign the confession, my Lord Bishop."

"It doesn't matter. Witness it and go."

"Shall I have her brought to a cell?"

"No! No, I will summon a guard to do that. Go back to the town, and tell that guildsman it is done. And tell him I expect his report by tomorrow."

"I can-"

"Go."

"Yes, my Lord Bishop."

I shudder and try not to whimper at the voices. I don't allow myself relief. I am not dead, yet.

Bishop Gantry moves around the chamber. I can hear him when I can't see him. I can't keep my eyes shut – they keep opening to find him, seek out the danger.

But there's no way to avoid him, no way out. His face looms suddenly over mine, and I flinch, cry out.

Without comment or notice, he uses a knife to slice off the remains of my gown. I gasp, sure this is it, not ready, ready, not ready – but he just rips and tears away the cloth, careful not to cut my skin. I weep and shake.

He lights candles that smell acrid and strange, traces symbols in the air. He chants sharp, biting words, hissing words. I do not know this spell, but the air feels wrong, wrong, wrong.

There is a knife. I see it descend. I feel the bite and pull of it on my leg, the sting, the pain. I am screaming, but there is no sound. A throbbing burn kindles deep in my bones. I can't move, I can't speak, I can only weep and suck air in and out.

Out of the air, the symbols he traced begin to glow a pale purple. A kind of smoky fire fills the chamber, shapes writhe and hiss in the air, whispering words it hurts to hear. Gantry's chanting has not stopped, and the shapes surround me, the cuts he is making on my body. Evil eyes glitter, mouths lap at my blood.

I cannot move, I want out, out – why can't I pass out?

He moves me when he needs to, rearranging my body, cutting careful shapes, and I feel my soul leaving me, draining into the growing monsters. Demons, I think and try to jerk, try to do anything.

The knife carves up my skin, all my skin, and I am not yet dead. I cannot stay here, cannot live here. I struggle to move, to die.

My body shudders as the demons come closer to my face. Gantry curses, the ghostly flames surge and I gasp, gulp in bael-fire, choke.

I cannot breathe, I cannot see. I am afraid to die, now

– what happens to my soul? But I don't want to stay here.

Gantry curses and shouts. Ruined! I have ruined something.

A small coal of triumph burns bitterly under my fear. Good, I managed something, anyway.

Gantry rips at my bonds, shaking me.

Bright pain burns everywhere, and still choking, rushing in my ears, I spin away into the dark.

———

My wrists burn, I am panting, pulling, shackled to a stone wall to await further questioning or death.

But there weren't any questions before, only pain, and screeching, and chanting. The knife cutting deep in my body, carving and twisting my skin for an eternity. Gibbering cries fill my mind again and I remember the Bishop's curses, see his blue eyes glow purple as I gasp, inhale the demon bael-fire.

The bael-fire burns, it breaks me. I breathe in screams without noise. My heels drum against the wall as I shudder, remembering, and I pull harder against the shackles.

The iron burns; I feel it in my wrists so aching and cold, the only specific pain. All else melts into a roar of river rushing blindness. Through the roar I hear the tapping blap of water on stone, the scuttling of small things, and my own gasping.

I twist my wrists, egged on by stabs and jumbles of pain from my body. I know I am dying, but I can't just let go. I try to cry out, try to escape, try to live.

Cold water splashes over me, shocks me quiet. I hang

from my wrists, wheezing, staring into the flare of torchlight beyond the bars. Bars. A cell. No demons anymore. Just the pain, and death on its way.

"Shut up, witch!" A broad face with a scowl, broken teeth, a face that warps into whispering demons; dread fills my stomach.

I twist my wrists harder, blood leaking down to my armpits.

The guard laughs, then chokes, his eyes wide and white, twists back from the cell and smashes into the wall, hard. He grunts only once as he slides to the floor.

A gleam of blond hair, a woman's alto voice. "Connor, quick, give me the keys."

"My lady, are you sure this is wise?" A dark figure, a deep tone.

"You threw the guard against the wall. It's a little late to be asking that now."

I cannot see them, not clearly. Shivering, I search the shadows while my hair drips, sticks to my weeping wounds.

The woman steps quickly into the cell as the door clangs softly open. The wavering flames pick out elaborately braided hair, a dark cape. Blue gems dance at her throat.

"Don't just stand there, Connor. Undo her arms, will you?"

The dark figure moves forward. I am unable to move or speak. The flames jump, casting him into sharp relief. Dark hair curls into dark eyes. He is tall, taller than I am. Even taller than Keenan.

The woman hisses as she catches sight of the carving on my body. The blood and burns conceal the patterns they make.

"Oh, my dear, this is monstrous. So many wounds. I'm afraid those will scar."

I stare, confused. Scar? I'm dying. I don't understand the worry.

The lady reaches for me and I flinch, to ward her off. Connor grabs my chin and growls a warning I can't understand, and my head knocks against stone, rings like a bell.

But I See. I See that in those deep brown eyes lies a flame for this lady. I See he follows her and gives her all in his power and grants her his life, if needed. I See he is terrified this hare-brained idea will take that life, and hers with it. I See things that got me named witch to begin with.

"Connor, let her go. She was only afraid. She can hardly stand, much less attack me," the lady is saying.

Connor's hand drops slowly from my face. My head vibrates in pain.

"Quickly, Connor. There's no time!"

Connor shakes his head. He hands the lady the torch, turns keys. The shackles fall away, into his quick, quiet hands. He leans close.

"Not a word, little witch, or we're all so much kindling. Do you hear?"

My eyes narrow, but even that hurts.

He takes my silence for acquiescence, and tosses his cloak around me.

I stumble to my knees as he pulls me toward the door. I am far too injured to walk. I cradle my hands to my chest and whimper. Connor swings me into his arms, not over his shoulder as I expected, and heads out of the cell.

Out in the corridor he sets me on my feet and leans me against the wall.

I sink slowly sideways, panting and hissing as my torn body cries out in anguish. But I cannot stand any more. I bite back sobs and try to force scorched lungs to open. Coughing into a fold of the cloak, I hear a scraping and open my eyes. Connor drags a bloody bundle wrapped in linen into the cell.

"Connor! What are you doing?" the lady whispers hoarsely. She stands halfway down the corridor, torch held high so the shadow flares out behind her and engulfs her head in fluttering darkness.

"This woman died today of the Wasting, and was carted out for burning. I hid her back here after you made it clear you wouldn't be dissuaded. The burial detail will be here before dawn to collect bodies. The guardsman there won't wake before then, and will be assumed drunk. Gantry won't hear of her death until well after noon."

His voice is scratchy, and he scrubs his face on his sleeve. "The bishop will notice if she's missing, my lady. He won't ask questions if she's dead."

He stands from his task and locks the cell door behind him. His shadow looms closer. I'm lifted back into his arms and the world spins as I whimper and shudder. When I can see again, the ceiling shifts jerkily in the light from the flames. Connor strides down the stone corridor and another flight of stairs appears suddenly before us.

My vision shifts as much as the torchlight. Moss on stone, a sprawled guard, and flickering shadows. I think we have descended deeper into the Inquisitor's dungeon: I hear moaning cries, smell death in the fetid air.

At a dead-end we pause, and the lady grumbles as she appears to wrestle with the wall. Then with a dark wind comes the smell of brine. Connor bangs my feet into the wall and I gasp – bite back a cry, and all is darkness.

<hr>

I am on fire. My skin blackens and my lungs ache, the heat gathers around and inside me and I whimper in fear.

Hands, alternately icy and feverish, touch my face, my arms. Pain blossoms at each spot. I try to brush the hands away but my arms are so heavy. Wavering voices above the roar of flames.

"We have to keep her here, my lady. I can't risk bringing in anyone else. You must keep her quiet until she can be moved."

"Connor, I need herbs and things I don't have here. Torture isn't something I've ever had to heal before. My mother is coming back – "

As the hands touch my arms, I bite my tongue but cry out, anyway. Harsher hands hold my head still.

"Listen to me, little witch. Hold your tongue. No noise, do you hear me?" I open my eyes and stare up at a familiar face as I struggle to understand.

"Keenan," I wheeze. "They've killed you, I saw it. They made me watch."

The eyes frown at me.

"I didn't cry, I swear! Don't be angry. I didn't faint or

shut my eyes. Just like you said. I was brave for you, Keenan."

"Be braver still, witch."

"Her name is Rhiannon, Connor. If you're going to pretend to be her brother, you should use it," the other voice whispers.

Keenan's eyes narrow with frustration.

"Be brave, Rhiannon. Don't cry out."

"They're burning me, Keenan. I'm on fire." I gasp.

"Be brave, Rhiannon. The flames are already out."

I stare into my brother's eyes until I am sure, feel the water flowing. A breeze that smells of spring cools my hot eyes, and I relax into sleep.

CHAPTER 3

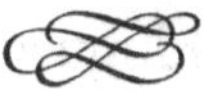

I awake to angry whispers.

" –why you involved Hugh in this!"

"Because you couldn't do it, Connor. Everyone knows you're my escort, and people would gossip if you disappeared and came back with a strange girl. Everyone also knows that Hugh collects strays, and the country estate staff will assume she's from here, and everyone here will assume she's from there. No one will suspect the Duke of Haverston of kidnapping a kirche prisoner. He can easily hide the girl for awhile. And then he can bring her here."

I struggle to open my eyes.

"It's too dangerous to bring her – "

"Ah, Rhiannon!"

I am choking, coughing, blinking through pale morning sunshine and dark blankets.

"You're awake. Water? Connor, fetch me that pitcher, if you please." Her voice is quiet but commanding, and Connor walks to the other side of the round room.

A beautiful woman sits on the edge of the narrow

bed. The bedclothes are soft and warm, and the tall, thin windows on one side of the round room stream with sunshine. The cloak and blood I wore last have been changed for a shift in white linen that smells of herbs and my sweat.

There are bandages on the deepest of the runes that were carved into skin and muscle, bandages on feet and hands, and a splint on my right leg. My hair is gathered in a long braid and laid across my chest, gleaming orange and red in a strip of sunlight.

Back aching, I try to shift my weight to sit. I choke on air, gasping at the pain, and the lady hushes me, strokes my forehead. Waves of throbbing – muscle spasms wash over me. I stare at the high ceiling through a tunnel of darkness and I hear quiet voices telling me to breathe slowly.

My tongue sticks to the roof of my mouth. Slowly air comes back to me, and my sight returns. I blink, and allow an arm to raise me cautiously.

The lady plumps the pillows behind me; her soft yellow hair brushes my cheek in its thick braids, like silken ropes. "I suppose you're wondering who we are, and why we rescued you, hmm?"

I come out of my daze. "Linnet – " I choke out.

"Your sister is safe, I assure you. How clever of you to have discovered just what Connor and I were discussing. I am Princess Julianna."

I twitch, feel like I've been slammed into a wall again.

Her Royal Highness pours water into a ceramic goblet from a matching pitcher, moisture glistening on the side. Her brown velvet day-dress catches the light and gleams. She smiles a little at me.

"Not the usual sort of hobby for a princess, is it,

rescuing witches? Well, I am not the usual sort of princess."

I blink, try to bow. Her hand on my arm prevents me, which is just as well. I spend a few moments panting in pain.

"This is my cousin, the Earl of Dorward, Connor fitzWellan."

I look at the dark man in the dark clothes. His gaze is neither kind nor unkind; only ready to toss me out of a window if I prove a threat. I promise silently to pose no threat at all.

"You're in the north tower of Haverston Castle," the princess continues. "You know I grew up here, that my brother is the Duke of Haverston, yes? Well, this was my favorite spot in the whole castle when I was young. This tower is isolated from the main stairs and looks out over the sea. I assure you that you are quite safe."

My head spins, and I sink back into the pillows. The whitewashed room is bright and comforting, with tapestries of country scenes hanging on the walls, and sturdy oaken furniture. The sheets look like very fine linen, indeed.

Her Royal Highness leans forward to help me to drink. The water slides down my throat, and I feel it pool in the bottom of my cavernous stomach.

The Princess of Talaria is nursing me. I know she started a healing school, hospices all over the country, much to the kirche's dismay and disapproval. But to do the work of Healing herself! I stare at her, a little stunned, as she takes the water away.

"Now I have told you something, you must return the favor." Her deep blue eyes catch mine and hold them. "They say you are a witch, Rhiannon. Is that true?"

I look into her eyes unwillingly. A witch. I See things, yes. But I didn't summon pestilence to the town, or cause boils to form on children, or pray to demons for power, make a man die, as they say I did. Not a witch like that.

"No, your Highness." I press my lips together until they ache.

"Not a witch? Well, I suppose I should have expected as much from Bishop Gantry. He specializes in false accusations. A pity, though. I could have used a witch."

My heart beats faster and all my wounds burn more fiercely. Used a witch? The princess' eyes narrow in an emotion, dark and bloody, and I See.

The vision takes me unaware and it hurts this time. Stronger than usual, I feel like fire burns along and under my skin. Knowledge comes with the pictures, and some words, and I try not to drown in it.

I See that the hospices are targets of the Archbishop Montmoore. He and Gantry are attacking anyone using magic outside the kirche. Some have even been burned as witches. I See that several of them were personal students of her Royal Highness, that the court is divided, that the hospices are not popular. That others are beginning to call her power, magic and otherwise, unholy.

Bishop Gantry points to people and names them witches, calling it the Will of the Lord of Stars. Archbishop Montmoore and others foment rebellion in the courtiers, pitting them against the king, against the princess and her husband the Crown Prince Alexander. They work for the exiled Duke of Torrence, who wants the throne for himself, who promises the kirche more power.

The princess works to curtail the kirche's power. The kirche is on the brink of declaring her a witch.

I swallow, try to clear a throat thick with fear, to clear my mind, stay afloat within this onslaught. These are things I should not speak of: I have at least learned that much.

Connor, Earl of Dorward steps to my side, grasps my chin with hard hands. "She's casting a spell; you can see it in her face." His voice is sharp, cuts my vision in half, and it flutters away in tatters. "What is it, little witch? What spell was that?"

I shudder in his grip, try to turn my head away.

His hand is hard and rough. "She will do you some harm, my lady. You should have left her where she was."

The princess' laugh is low and smoky, and Connor drops my chin to glare at her.

"You do not take this seriously enough!"

"You misunderstand, Connor. I take this all too seriously." She turns to me, and her eyes are more black than blue. "Not a witch, hmmm? Well, I can understand your not wanting to admit it, not after all the trouble it's caused. But now I know something about you. When you are spelling, your face gives you away. You should try not to gasp and stare at nothing."

"Not spelling, lady, Princess, your Highness, not really," I wheeze out, fear shaking my limbs. "I just know things, See things sometimes. I don't control it, or I would have it go away. I swear to you, I never killed a man or consorted with demons or cursed the name of the Star Lord." I paw at her sleeve with bandaged, useless fingers, begging her to understand.

"Of course not. Who ever does?" She cuts a glance at

Connor. "There is nothing wrong with having magic, Rhiannon. Despite what some people say."

Connor only clenches his jaw harder. He wants her safe more than he wants to be right. She wants to be right. More knowledge to keep to myself.

The sun catches a gleam in her eye as she turns to me. "Now then, Rhiannon. What sort of things do you See?"

Connor grasps my face again as I turn my head away. My eyes burning, I know Connor is afraid of what I See, afraid I'll tell her. He glares fiercely into my eyes but I See his heart beating fast, know he loves her quietly, and he would keep it that way. He's afraid I See more than I do, that I am someone's tool, that I will get her killed.

"I See – " but Connor's grip hurts, and I wince away.

"Connor, let her be! She's not hurting me."

Connor's hand tightens, releases, and he turns away. He retreats to the low bench by the table, his lips pressed thin.

"Tell me, Rhiannon, what is it you see?"

"I — your Highness. Sometimes I See things about people: what they want, what they think ... what they've done. I don't do it on purpose; I can't control it. It is not a — comfortable thing."

The princess smiles kindly, the light glinting in her hair. "No, it wouldn't be." Her hand caresses my cheek. "What do you see about me?"

I cannot fill my lungs. Visions pour over me as though willed upon me, and I drown, lost in them. The king, the bishop, men whose names I know without knowing how. A battlefield, a man who smiles too much, secret meetings filled with malice.

My eyes clear to Julianna holding my shoulders, her gaze concerned. I answer as though her grip is the only lifeline in this deluge. Perhaps it is.

"You suspect Bishop Gantry of conspiracy and treason against the king and your husband. You traveled here in secret to try and find out what that conspiracy is. And, and, something about other nobles, and the archbishop ...." The princess has a wicked glint of glee in her eye that makes me wary.

Connor stares. In his eyes I also See that she is here without support. The court is angry, they did not want her to marry Alexander. They did not like her late father, and they do not like her.

I bite my lips, aware suddenly that neither of them want me to know that. Those thoughts whisper quietly, inside walls of other, louder thoughts.

Connor still stares, his eyes narrowed. "You came home to Haverston," he says, "to visit your mother and brother. Or so you informed King Peter. The court believes the king is angry with you."

"Really, Connor. You know how rumors get started." She grins, a mischievous glint in her eye. "But you see, that proves it! She couldn't have known!" Her smile lights the room too bright, and I am forced to look at my disfigured arms, clasped lightly in her dainty hands.

"Now you have proven yourself to me, I shall prove myself to you."

I look up, confused. "I've had to do this in stages, but I think I can complete everything now."

Her eyes grow focused somewhere on my forehead, and my body becomes all pins and needles. I gasp, shudder as the feeling crawls into my wounds and burrows deep. The air around me grows dim as though smoke or broken bits of night dance around my eyes. My breath roars in my ears; the fever recedes and the tide of pain ebbs.

My eyes clear, as the princess slumps into Connor's suddenly waiting arms. I stare in alarm at the pair of them.

Connor is glaring again, this time at the princess. She sighs and stirs, and Connor lifts the forgotten water goblet to her lips.

She pushes it away as she opens her eyes. "No, thank you Connor. Not just yet." Her voice is soft, husky. She lifts herself away from him, and I don't need the Sight to see how his arms ache without the weight of her.

Connor looks at me, drops his eyes and turns away. He busies his hands with the water pitcher.

"How are you feeling, Rhiannon?"

I startle at her words. I feel stronger now, the pain receding, unraveling, pulled like loose threads from a bad weave.

She unwraps my hands where the burns and shackle wounds are. The bandages come away bloody and soggy, but the body underneath is whole. The princess breathes a laugh as I gawk at skin I thought ruined, fingers I knew to be broken lumps of flesh.

The bandages over the rest of my wounds come off next. Connor leaves the room as she pulls the linen from me, revealing pink winding and jagged scars where the bishop carved symbols. The scars travel the length of my body, from chest to knees. Even my arms down past my elbows are covered with ugly sigils.

Her Highness shakes her head sadly. "There wasn't

any way to prevent those, I'm afraid. Whatever Gantry used to cut them must have been poisonous." She presses her lips together, as if still thinking of ways to erase the stain of my torture. "I wish I knew what he was trying to do."

I think of demon teeth and ritual knives, and look away. I try to say "Demons," but I can't say anything. Rolling onto my back, I bite back a sob. I may be hideous, but I am alive. I will have to be grateful for that.

Blood flakes off new skin where a scab used to be. I am amazed by my own body, able to lift my arms and move around with no pain. I smell myself and blanch.

Chuckling, the princess calls to Connor to bring water for washing. As she bundles me back under the covers, he steps in and bows sardonically to her.

"I'll let you in on a secret," she leans forward, a conspirator against the bowing Connor. He glances up at her as he turns to leave, his brow furrowed with worry for her. "I wasn't sure it would work this well. I spent quite a bit of my energy this last week, trying to keep you alive."

Her eyes darken and she grips my shoulder. "I am so sorry for what you went through. Even traitors are treated better. Bishop Gantry is mad. He would never have dared to do this if my mother or brother had been in residence. The kirche may be sovereign to itself, but it does not have the authority to treat Talarian citizens this way.

"Rhiannon, anything I can do to repair damage done to your life, I will do. I cannot bring back your parents, or your brother, but I will make sure you have a life of your own again. That such things could occur in my kingdom makes me ill. I will stop him."

I had forgotten about Keenan and my parents for a moment. I suck in the chill air of the tower too fast, and cough. Wheezing, I hide my grief behind a need to breathe.

The princess grasps my chin and commands me to breathe slowly. She looks into my eyes and I feel a sliding, a quicksilver presence in my body. I blink and the feeling is gone.

"Damn." Her lips pursed, she cups my cheek and cocks her head. "I'm sorry, Rhiannon. It seems that I couldn't heal your lungs all the way. They're still damaged: you can only breathe at about half your normal capacity, I'm afraid. I don't understand why they didn't heal …." Her voice trails off.

I think of chanting and chittering voices, bael-fire scorching my soul, and I shudder once, my eyes closed. The demon-tainted are burned, too.

The princess drops her hand and looks away, her cheeks growing rosy. "I have no right to ask you, but I must, so I will. Will you help me? To stop Gantry, I mean. I could use a person of your … talents." She turns again to me, her smile a little sly.

Connor returns with a basin, towels and soap for washing, and bows out of the room. His gaze burns into mine a moment, worry and anger and compassion mixed.

I shake my head and stare at the princess as he leaves. "Help you, your Highness? What could I do?"

"Are you not a witch? Can you not tell what people are thinking?" I blanch again, and she takes my hand. "I have you at a disadvantage, Rhiannon Owen, and I'm sorry for that, but I fully intend to use you, if I can.

"There is a conspiracy against the king. I believe that

Bishop Gantry is in the thick of it. Rescuing you from death and torture, while the least I can do for an innocent woman, was done in part to foil his plans."

She pauses a moment, staring into space. "He preaches against my hospices, and tries to sway public opinion against the crown. The king refuses to act without proof, which is just, but impractical. I believe this man – among others – is capable of setting this country to civil war. And I believe he intends to try something, to start it here in Haverston. I need to stop him."

Her left hand rests for a moment on her middle, her skin the same color as the pale cream silk stomacher. Then she reaches to push back my hair from my eyes. "I only want to know what he's planning, what he's thinking. I don't expect you to fight him for me, you know. You needn't look so frightened. And you really should remember to breathe."

I gasp suddenly at her words, only now realizing that I need air. My hand clenches in hers.

"Will you help me, Rhiannon? I promise you will be safe; I will hide you, and Gantry will never know you still live."

I sway dizzily and my thoughts chase themselves in circles. What if I am found out? What if I must endure torture again? I can still feel the runes carved into my skin, although soft pink scars stretch the length of my arms now, and my thighs, and belly: not the deep gashes that they were.

I still hear Gantry's sibilant chants to call the demons. I see their purple, ghostly bodies writhe through a hole in the air. I feel them feed on my blood again, their bael-fire scorching. If anyone were to find out that demons had touched me, my life would be forfeit. What if I can be called, if the demons can find me, if they smell my blood on the wind? I must stay here, to hide, in any case.

I nod, slowly. I will help her, if she will help me. I try to open my mouth to tell Her Highness, but no sound emerges. I am still trying to speak when my lungs protest again my lack of air, and I fade into darkness to the sound of the princess's cursing calls for Connor.

CHAPTER 4

I am spending my convalescence in the tower. Julianna comes this morning with a letter from her brother the duke, and reads it to me as I nibble the toast she's brought. Although her healing cured the worst of my injuries, I still have lost a lot of blood, and I feel weak and out of breath.

Rain chills the already damp air, and the sound of waves crashing into the cliffs below the castle vibrates deep beneath the sounds of the spring shower. I wrap tighter in the fur cloak Julianna lent me, my lap covered with wool and heavy rugs.

A tray sits on the table next to the bed as I lie back against the thick cushions, my head and shoulders propped up. Daylight, gray and dim today, is augmented by the fire in the grate and glowsand lamps whose spells are fairly new. Greenish-gold light spills from them in steady streams.

Julianna sits perched on the edge of the bed, her face composed. The lamp- and daylight shine on her dove-gray morning dress. Her blue eyes and gold hair gleam like jewels. I stare at her, rapt, and a little frightened. She is stunning, and I am stunned by her.

She reads the letter from her brother. "They've been staying at Hugh's estates in Berdoral, after a few nights hiding to ensure a clean escape. They should return to Haverston in a few weeks' time."

Julianna scans the letter further, her lips pursed. "Deacon Bertram claims that Linnet committed suicide."

I shake my head. No one would believe that – but maybe they would, with everything.

She pauses, eyes me with sympathy. "It's as well everyone believes it, anyway. No one will look for either of you now."

I nod, but my hands are shaking.

"Linnet is fine, not ill or injured. You'll see her as soon as Connor can arrange for a meeting. Oh that reminds me, I should send a missive to the capitol telling Marcus not to send any of my handmaids …." I put the toast down as she looks at me, a gleam in her eye.

She smiles warmly at me, and already I know to worry. "I've decided that you will be my handmaid. It will work perfectly! And it will keep Mother from foisting one of her guests on me, who would only get in our way."

I stare blankly at her. She picks the toast up and puts it back in my hand.

"Marcus is King Peter's steward. He has some notion that my riding all the way out here away from court with no escort other than Connor stretches propriety.

"Well," she adds, "I did have Nicole with me, but she met up with her husband as soon as we arrived, and is no longer in my service. Mother's been lending me

Sarah for wardrobe, but she's really scullery and much too nervous around me."

I nibble at the toast, feeling a kinship with Sarah.

Connor enters the tower room and bows slightly to the princess. She stands from my bedside, frowning at his carefully blank expression.

Suddenly there is a pale green flash from my skin, and I bare my arms to the elbow, stare at them as the rune scars glow bright leaf green, then fade slowly. I look up to my rescuers, but neither of them have noticed. I feel on the edge of a vision, and fight it — whatever it is, I don't want to know.

"Your Highness, there is a visitor to your brother's castle."

My stomach roils at Connor's words, and the vision fights its way through my blocking. I See a thin face with pale blue eyes, dark hair and a black wool cloak over a priest's robe. Shivering, I drop the last bit of toast and hug myself tighter in the fur.

Connor glances at me, keeping his face neutral.

"What visitor?" Julianna asks sharply.

"The duchess welcomes the Bishop Gantry into her household for an extended visit. She has asked him to assume chapel services from Father Matthew."

"My mother did what?" Julianna's voice rises in alarm. She turns to me, and I am small and shrinking in the bedclothes. She hurries to my side and peels my hands from my shoulders. Holding my hands in hers, she reminds me to breathe slowly. I try very hard not to wheeze.

Connor stands where he is near the door. His face still blank, I see his right hand clench and unclench as he gazes at us.

"All right," Julianna says, "no panicking. We can't very well have mother un-invite him. She did say she wanted to keep a close eye on him, although I did not think she would go this far. But we can make this work for us. He's been staying at the Inquisitor's building, conducting investigations into reports of witchcraft. Since I arrived, he hasn't dared to convict anyone. This must be a move on his part to ingratiate himself with the guilds of Haverston, and get closer to his objective: discrediting me. But we can use this to our advantage, as well."

She takes a massive breath, and expels it, squeezing my hands. "This will make spying on him much easier. No, this is a good thing. We'll get you disguised, and introduce you into my service … we'll have to come up with something plausible as a story for why you're arriving now and not earlier."

She turns to address Connor. "Rhiannon is going to be your cousin, Connor. Daughter of the baron who died in a fire up north, your father's third cousin."

"You mean Baron Wolff. Ste-, we were not close." Connor's right eyebrow raises. His hand is clenched tightly.

"Well," continues Juliana, "Rhiannon here can be your long-lost kin."

It is my turn to raise eyebrows.

As she turns to me, Julianna pats my hands and smiles, trying to reassure. "This will be fine. Gantry thinks you're dead, you know. He thinks you were burned with the pestilence victims, and he'll never recognize you when I'm done with you. Not to worry, this will be fine." She stands after squeezing my hands one last time and walks to Connor's side.

I can't help but think of Gantry's eyes blazing a livid amethyst as he chanted demon fire into my soul. I shiver, remembering screams, the inhalation of bael-fire, the burning. Gantry screamed I was useless. Useless for what? Burning? And if he uses demons in spells, does it matter if he believes me dead? Surely tainted as I am with demon breath and runes he will know me.

Julianna shakes her head at Connor, frowning. He speaks too low for me to hear; I lose myself in worry.

Gantry's presence in the castle is a palpable weight in the air. I fancy I can hear his footsteps reverberate through the walls. Shrinking even smaller in my bedclothes, I try to forget his face, the face of death, Keenan crimson-faced and kicking in the town square. Demons swirl around him and the bodies of my parents, slack like dangling puppets.

"Rhiannon!" Julianna calls my name again. I look quickly at her, the fear plain in my eyes. "I won't let him harm you. Please believe me."

Tears gather in my eyes, but I nod at her command and try to muster enough courage to breathe.

My life is this now. It could be worse. I could be given to demons.

Julianna's plan to hide me in plain sight takes over my every day. She asks me hundreds of questions as she grooms me for a handmaid and changes my appearance. Some changes have already been done for her: scars from torture and fever have left of me much less than I was.

After an awkward girlhood of being short and

sturdy, I shot up to rangy and too tall, but still sturdy. My red hair has always been my only distinguishing feature. Now I look at myself in a silver mirror almost too heavy for me to hold.

Normally faint freckles jump out stark against my translucent skin. Dark hollows in my cheeks explain why Julianna brings me bread and thick goat's milk on trays whenever she visits.

My body feels distant; I don't think of it as mine. I try not to see myself when I wash or change clothes. My fingers feel sharp ridges that aren't scarring, but ribs and hipbones.

I reach my hand up to my hair and pull a short curl slowly through my fingers. Another thick lock drops to join the others on the floor around me. Julianna lifts the scissors and surveys her work critically.

"Did Gantry ever see you before you were caught?"

I feel a little dizzy as the long strands drop. I always wanted short hair. Mother never allowed it.

"No, Highness." It seems silly to cry over hair, after everything else. I opt for tingling giddiness, instead.

"Did you spend much time here at the castle? And stop moving."

The afternoon sun fires glints in another lock as it cascades down my shoulder. I hold the mirror steady, look past it.

"No, Highness. I wasn't involved in guild dealing. My father came here, but on his own, to meet with the duchess. Linnet wasn't old enough. She hasn't even had her coming-out ball yet," I add, realizing it suddenly. That was to be next summer, after her fifteenth birthday. Her fourteenth was just a week ago. With all that's happened, I forgot.

Many things were to happen next year: Linnet's coming-out ball, my marriage to Francis Danwright, and Keenan's ordination were all planned. My life has been stalled, detoured, and all the careful preparations of my family were for nothing. I feel a guilty relief that at least I don't have to explain things to Francis – he never cared to listen much to me. I doubt he feels other than revulsion for me now, in any case.

Julianna steps back from clipping, her face thoughtful. "I haven't come back to Haverston in several years; not since before I married Alexander. Usually Hugh comes to court for the season, but circumstances being what they are ...." She draws a long strand out and snips carefully. "Well, Alexander is at the border of Fanthas, negotiating the peace treaty along with Cardinal Robere. And court has become rather tiresome without him."

I look up, and she straightens my head while she brushes my hair back from my face. "He hasn't visited but once, and was home so briefly that we barely...." She trails off, teasing a few more curls out, to check their length.

I See a charming smile, dark hair, a tallish man surrounded by laughing, smirking faces. The man pulls a woman into his arms, but it isn't Julianna. And I see Julianna frowning at him from across a courtyard. He smiles at her, then down at the woman in his arms, bright and innocent. He doesn't mean either smile.

I shake out of the vision, blink at Julianna. I don't think she'd want me to know that.

Connor enters the tower room with a scowl on his face. He takes a small bag of bread from under his tunic, empties it on the plate on the table and drips honey on it from a small stoppered jar. He bows briefly to Julianna, and then steps back, frowning at me critically.

"Let me look." He walks around me, and I twist my head to keep him in sight. The sun glints off his velveteen doublet, black like his hair. The bronze cast to his skin and his high, sharp cheekbones make me wonder if his someone of his family were from Zohar, or even Indranah.

"Look straight ahead," he commands, and reaches to turn my face forward. His hands on my neck are warm and gentle, and I realize how cold I am without my hair. I shiver and he steps back.

"It's uneven." He turns and grabs a piece of bread. "Eat something." He drops it in my hand and strides to the narrow windows to look out.

"Well, she was supposed to be in a fire. We can say it burned unevenly. I'll have someone else cut it once she's officially here," Julianna says, miffed. "I don't usually cut hair, you know. Perhaps you should do it."

Connor turns from the window quickly. "No, no, it's fine. I am sorry, my lady. I had trouble getting the bread away from the kitchen. The servants wonder what you do up here, and I can't always sneak food quickly." His brows draw together as he looks at the culprit in my hand, and I bite my lips, look for a place to put it down.

"You've told them I requested not to be disturbed?"

He nods.

"Make up something, Connor." She shrugs. "And spread the rumor. I am meditating and praying for my husband to hurry home. It's too cold for walks in the garden. I need quiet to study for a cure for the Wasting. People believe what they will, in any case. And I'm only here for a few hours a day. Surely you can come up with something that will satisfy them."

Connor shrugs uncomfortably. "There is a rumor that you and I are …." He turns away.

I stare at my hand holding the bread, watching the honey drip slowly down the side of the thick bread, onto my thumb.

"They what?" Julianna laughs, her hands over her mouth. "A tryst, you and I? Oh, Connor, how could they believe that? How insane!"

I bite my lips and steal a glance at him. Still looking out the window, his shoulders hunch.

"It is a dangerous rumor, my lady. I think you shouldn't come up here anymore. I'll come on my own, and take care of Rhiannon."

"But Connor …"

He turns, his jaw hard. "She is supposed to be my ward, yes? My cousin? I'll teach her what she must know, your Highness. And in one week I shall present her to you as your new handmaid. In the meanwhile, you should be about your own business. Without me."

Julianna looks stricken. "But Connor, I need you. You're my escort. Whom shall I take instead?"

"One of the duchess' handmaids, for a chaperone. There'll be less gossip about them." His voice firm, he turns from her to me. "Eat that, you need your strength."

I lower my gaze to the bread, and the honey seeping down my hand.

"One week isn't enough time, Connor. She's only just recovered. Her lungs still aren't right, and – "

"It will have to be enough. It's been two months since my cousins perished in that fire, and I'd have found her a place by now. Any awkwardness or weakness can be blamed on the circumstances."

Julianna purses her lips, puts the scissors down on the chest and begins to pace.

"I don't want her here too soon. Gantry can't be allowed to put it all together. And once Linnet arrives, people might recognize them."

Connor sighs. "Then perhaps we should abandon this plan, my lady," he says gravely.

"No," she says. "I will think of something. We can change Linnet's appearance, as well, and change their names. It's been three weeks since the ... hanging."

Connor glances at me, worry in his eyes. "No. Changing their names is too risky. They won't remember them at a critical moment," he says, his voice quiet but firm.

Her pacing quickens. I grow dizzy just watching her, her pale gown swirling and sweeping clumps of fiery hair about. "Linnet is a common enough name. And she'll only be here a short while, before we send both of them on to Corat. Marla's own daughter is named Linnet."

"But Rhiannon is less common," Connor insists. "Even if her hair is short – "

"And brown. When I'm finished it will be short and brown. And we can shorten her name. In the Indrani language, the word for river is Rhia. I've heard the name at court." She turns to me, her gaze locking on mine. "What do you think? Rhia Wolff fitzWellan. Will it do?"

I raise the bread to my mouth, nibble the edge with the dripping honey. It doesn't matter what I think. Her lambent gaze mesmerizes us both, and Connor and I acquiesce. Rhia Wolff fitzWellan shall present herself when the Princess desires, to be the Princess' new hand-maid. She shall be thin, pale, and ill. A bad bargain, indeed.

———

Connor works to ready me for a handmaid. These lessons are so different from my former life. I was a daughter of the guilds, a bookworm, an awkward girl on the cusp of marriage. My mother despaired of my embroidery and told me to stop slouching all the time. Now I am to be a noble lady, ward to an Earl, handmaid to a princess. It's quite a different path than the one I thought I'd tread.

To be a guildwoman, to marry a man in the guilds, that was my future. Or I could have joined the kirche. Keenan begged me to do just that, but I didn't want to.

Now, now I understand what Keenan meant, when he said it would be safer if I joined the kirche. I wish I had believed him. But better a handmaid with a future than a witch with none. I walk around the tower room daily until my weak lungs and legs protest in shivers and shakes. I must be strong enough for this role.

I know Connor fears I won't be. His gaze stabs me with his worry as he drills me in the names and standing of the Wolff family.

The Wolff family was smallish and backwoods. Baron and Baroness Wolff had a son and two daughters, all some years younger than I. But no one here knows that, and they were rather a country cousin to Connor's family.

He doesn't speak of the rest of his family at all. He is an Earl; he is cousin somehow to the princess. He seems to think I should know of him, and I haven't admitted I don't recognize his name or title.

He's my only kin in Talaria, he tells me. I don't know the name fitzWellan, and Dorward is far to the east – but if his family has other, more important titles I would merely have heard the most prominent. I know only the grim way he has of saying "family," and that dark look in his eyes. I remind myself to investigate the fitzWellans later.

My own family looks darkly at me from their graves. If indeed they have graves; Julianna has not said, and I'm afraid to ask. But I feel a ghost of Keenan's mind in mine, or want to tell him something interesting that I'm learning, and sharp loneliness stabs me. The silent spot in my head aches; I reach for Keenan and sob in sudden bursts of grief that he isn't there.

Until I close my eyes. There he stares accusingly at me, with Mum and Da, and they all dangle and twitch as though they're puppets dancing. Sometimes I don't sleep.

I cling to the thought that Linnet is safe. She's supposed to come to Haverston soon, although I'm afraid it's too dangerous. But there is hardly any staff at the duke's country estates when he isn't in residence, and he must bring her back here. I almost look forward to her coming, despite the danger of discovery: I miss her sunny smile.

CHAPTER 5

At last it's the day Connor will present me to Julianna as his cousin. I lift my head from my blankets with effort. The night lasted an eternity, and my limbs lie heavy. Woozily I reach out for the water goblet on the table. Dawn haze shimmers about the tower room; I hear the gulls cry for their breakfast.

Evil dreams and haunts fill my head from my restless sleep. When my eyes close, I see the ghouls again. They reach their hands for me and I flinch, shudder away.

I reach out for Keenan's mind, for comfort and reassurance, and again remember….

Sagging back in the bed, I throw my arm over my eyes. I am too tired for today.

Connor knocks on my door and enters without waiting, as usual.

I wonder if he's this rude to everyone, or just to me. I hear him set something on the table and feel a bundle land on my legs.

"Hurry, I need to get you to the carriage before morning bells."

I lift my arm and look at him.

His back to me, he pulls a black gown out of a long sack. The gown is wrinkled and some the worse for wear. A dark veil of mourning follows the gown, all tossed on the bed along with a threadbare cloak.

He turns, gestures to the clothes. "Get into these, eat what you can, and hurry." He strides out, the dim light making him a shadow among shadows. I hear the door close.

My shoulders, cold from the brisk air, ache as I try to draw a full breath. Muscles stiff from poor sleep protest. I slowly lift the heavy covers and swing my legs over the side of the bed.

More thick bread lies on the table, next to a ewer of goat's milk just as thick. I pour myself a cup of it, although I have always hated milk. It clogs in my throat, frothy and slick, and I shove bread quickly down after it. Connor is right – I mustn't appear too sickly. I can think of more agreeable ways of fattening me up, however.

I dread getting dressed, dread the day ahead. First Connor will smuggle me out of the castle, so that I can enter through more normal channels. Then the charade begins, and my new life. I owe Julianna my life, and my sister's as well. I sigh and put on the clothes Connor left.

The black gown hangs loose through the bodice, the wool gaping a little where it should pull tight. Fortunately that adds some length to the otherwise too short garment. But I suppose I cannot appear in borrowed servant's clothes and Julianna's fur slippers. Connor said he was ordering me a wardrobe, but he couldn't get it into the castle in time. This must be what he could come up with for now.

Fastening the veil takes more time than I thought –

short hair makes the process more difficult. I worry the skirts will show the scars on my legs.

Connor strides in again before I finish with the veil. "Good enough, don't worry about that yet. Get into the chest."

I try not to shudder as I turn to look at the dark wooden chest. It sits innocuously empty in the corner. The linens that filled it lie on the floor beside it, folded neatly. I fear this next step more than meeting the duchess. I fear hiding in that small space, waiting for Connor.

I try to stall. "Where are you taking me?" A question he has yet to answer.

"Hurry, just get in. I don't have time to explain," he orders. I find that's true of Connor in general.

Pressing my lips together, I gather the skirts tightly in one hand and step into the chest cautiously. I wonder if Connor ever has any time, or if he finds it convenient to never explain.

I wobble precariously and he catches my shoulder to steady me. I turn to look at him, his face no more than a few inches from mine. His eyes blink once, twice, and he looks down. He frowns in consternation.

"You'll have more clothes to choose from later today. I'll bring you some shoes, as well," he says as he helps me down into the chest. There's just enough room for me if I scrunch small on my back with my knees sideways. A thin pad lines the bottom of the chest. Connor begins to cover me with the sack.

"And stockings," I add, stalling a little longer. I hold my hands close to my face, keeping the sack from smothering me.

The lid hesitates in its descent. "And stockings," I

hear him sigh. The lid shuts and latches, and I hear straps fastening above me. The only light is through a crack in the seal near my head.

I hold the sack off my face as best I can, keep my eyes on that small splinter of light. Forcing myself to breathe as evenly as I can, I fight off panic that boils through my blood. I am not trapped, this is not a trap, it is a hiding place, I must stay still, I must stay quiet....

I feel the bumps of the uneven floor as Connor pulls the chest out of the tower room. "Don't move, and don't make any noise. I'll let you out when it's time."

I hold onto the rough whisper of his voice, put it between my mind and fear. My eyes lock on my sliver of light.

Footsteps thump up the stairs, and the door to the tower room clicks shut suddenly behind me. Men's voices murmur around me. Shadows pass over my light and I pray silently to Dorei and the Star Lord. Please don't let them discover me.

My small dark world jumps and tips as the chest lifts. Low grunts as they settle the chest, and I hear Connor direct them to his carriage. It is a long way down out of the castle. The chest thumps into the carriage, with a hiss from someone, and the carriage rocks as Connor climbs in and the door shuts behind him.

I feel trembles starting in my legs, and I quietly count my breaths in and out, try not to shudder. My lips and mouth slowly parch.

"Not much longer now. Just hold on," I hear Connor murmur. The carriage leaps forward and I prepare myself for a painful ride.

My mother's face frowns at me from the darkness. A guildwoman wouldn't get herself stuck in a chest, she seems to say. The roof of my mouth begins to pound, and my teeth ache. Ah, Mum, a true guildwoman wouldn't have the Sight, either. Such a peasant's power. Mum always tried to hide her own mother's peasant farmer stock. It's too bad I resemble gran in more than looks.

I jolt from my daze when the carriage lurches to a halt. Drawing a dank breath, I realize that smell is me: sweat soaks my gown in itchy patches. The chest shifts, moves out into the light and fresher air. A small whiff leaks in from my savior crack of light.

A seabird cries, and water laps ships and docks under the noise of people scurrying, calling to each other. The chest shifts so I am at a slant on my neck and head, and my spine painfully protests this treatment. My shoulders bunch. I hear the harsh voices of sailors, thumping of feet on wood. A ship? Did Connor say anything about a ship? Panic gnaws my chest and I shake to be out of here.

The chest steadies, is set down. The voices fade, a door closes. Am I alone? I hear nothing but my own heart, thumping mad in my chest. My shaking turns to fierce pounding. Let me out of here this instant. I rock wildly in my airless coffin, strain with my knees to open and let me out!

The lid flies free, and I tumble out of the side in a wild rush. A hand touches my shoulder. I throw my arm out, certain doom is near, and twist to scramble away.

Connor's cautious face stares back at me, his arms wide and steady. "Easy," he says softly. It isn't the first time he has spoken, I realize belatedly.

My hands shake as I pull at the gown around me, try to straighten my skirts. My stomach twists with fading fear, and I try to control the pain in my chest from straining heart and lungs. I close my eyes a moment, steady my nerves.

"I'm fine," I gasp, clearing my throat.

Connor offers me a hand up, which I accept with shaky aplomb.

I realize that we aren't alone, and freeze.

Implacably, Connor pulls me along and leads me to a seat on a cot.

I tremble with reaction, try to gather my tattered courage.

"What have you brought me, my lord Connor?" asks the older man on the other cot in the cabin.

"Not you, Your Eminence. This is Rhia Wolff Fitzwellan. I told you about her. She begins her position with the princess today."

The man's wiry white hair curls close to his head, and his eyes are a brown a little lighter than his skin. He smiles at me, but has questions in his eyes.

I feel a charge in the air, a slight ruffling inside my head. He's reading me, I think, but I don't know what to do about it. I huddle in on myself, try to appear harmless. I don't understand why there is someone else here.

"Good day to you, young Rhia. My name is Laurent Robere," he says.

I look pointedly at Connor.

"Cardinal Robere is helping us," is all he says.

I continue to stare at him. This is one of those things he might have mentioned before.

Connor looks back at me, expecting something.

I close my eyes, try to pull myself together, my body shaking and my breath loud in the creaking cabin.

"We honor the First Prophet, and give our fear to her for safekeeping," the cardinal murmurs.

"General Sherron at the battle of Kiras," I say, opening my eyes to look at him. Cardinal Robere smiles.

"You are well educated."

I don't know what I should say.

"I have always found that speech to be of comfort," he continues, "when I find myself overwhelmed."

I nod, thinking the battle following that quote wasn't particularly comforting. But I'm sure his sentiments are well-intentioned.

That ruffling in my mind again. I feel a vision shaping, sharp and painful, but an outside source gentles the magic, and the vision melts open without hurting.

Be easy, a voice sends to me.

I See a man who looks like Connor, but older, his face stormy as he listens to papers of a treaty being read. A woman, a queen, shoots him a sharp look, but does not stop the courtier from reading.

I See messages the man writes, in a language I don't know, and the presence in my head tightens its focus. I See Gantry, his face dark with fury, and I wince out of the vision, push the magic away.

When I look up, Robere regards me with an apologetic smile. "I understand terrible things have happened to you, my dear. From all reports, you seem to be a capable young person. And I can see for myself that you are intelligent and composed, and quite strong. Your magic is impressive. I think you'll do." He smiles again.

"Cardinal, you should prepare," Connor says.

The cardinal stands and shakes out his brown robes. Not very cardinal-like, I think.

"I will leave you to recover, Rhia Wolff Fitzwellan. I know you are in kinder hands with the princess and Connor, than you have been. I wish you success in all your endeavors," he says. As he steps out of the cabin, he turns and gives me another long, strange look, and then leaves.

I look at Connor. "You might have warned me," I say.

He shakes his head. "It wasn't as well-planned as it might have been. But Cardinal Robere knows your story, as much as we do. He wanted to meet you. It seemed a provident time."

I shake my head, blinking back sudden tears. "You should have told me something. I'm not just some, some game piece on a board." My hands clench, and I force them open, stare at them. I see him shift out of the corner of my eye.

He sighs, seems about to take my hand. Changing his mind, he stands and paces the three steps available in the cabin. "It really couldn't be helped; he wanted you not to know. Now, we're on the ship Jihansa, and from here out – "

The door opens and I jump, ready to run, only there isn't any escape from the cabin. A woman enters, tall, dark, her bright skirts swirling gaily. She smiles, her teeth a startling contrast to her copper skin.

Connor bows while I stand in a half-crouch, clutching my skirts awkwardly.

"Connor, it is so good to see you. Bhanu told me you'd arrived."

"Mistress Asa Siradhi, please let me introduce my cousin, the lady Rhia Wolff fitzWellan."

I bite my lips and curtsey, catch a warning look from Connor as I glance at him. I try to seem poised, aware of my ripe smell, my rumpled clothes and bare feet. All things that were true in front of Cardinal Robere, as well, I think.

"Please accept our apologies for our hurried arrival," he continues. "Trader Siradhi is indeed a friend of King Peter to come to our aid."

Asa curtseys herself, a graceful movement of layered skirts that float on the slightest breeze.

I watch, mesmerized by the material and rose color. I have never seen so many different shades of red.

"The Indrani Crown is eager to promote trade, your Grace, of information as well as goods." Indrani: of course. The name of the southern empire sinks into my head as I try not to stare. Da promised a trip to Indranah for my honeymoon – as long as I brought back dye. It's several weeks by sea.

Her accent bubbles over Talarian words like spring water over rocks. I try to pay attention to her words, but the meaning gets lost in the sound, and Connor leaves with a curt bow before I figure out what's been said.

Panicked, I stand frozen as Asa smiles at me.

After a moment, she looks a little uncertain. "Are you hungry, lady Rhia? Is there anything I can bring you? Your journey must have been arduous. Connor will fetch your trousseau so you can change." She smiles graciously and gestures to the door. It takes a moment for her words to register.

My tongue sticks to my lips when I lick them. I think longingly of the wash basin in the tower. "Hot water," I sigh, "and soap."

Asa smiles, bows out of the cabin. Sinking onto the cot, I let out a cautious sigh. This all would have been easier if Connor had prepared me. He is so close-mouthed, I complain to myself. And you are so open, Rhiannon.

I'm afraid to speak of the demons. When I try to even hint, I can't speak at all. Demon-taint is not tolerated. I'm not sure how anyone can tell – how do you know if you're tainted? When you run mad? Am I mad already? I think that Bishop Gantry must be, but no one around him in the kirche seems to have noticed.

When the door opens again I am ready for it, and Asa and three men enter. One man carries a round copper tub of a size to sit in. The other two carry large buckets of water. A bath – I hadn't expected a bath. The last time I had a real bath ….

Asa directs them and soon the tub is full, steaming in the spring air. Now that I'm not locked in a chest, the sweat drying on my body chills me a little, and I look forward to the warmth. I try to look like a lady, not fidget, and not hunch my shoulders. The sailors leave, and Asa closes the door after them.

"I brought some water to drink, as well," she says, pointing to a pitcher she brought in, and a goblet. "And I can take your gown and air it and brush it out, at least. I have no proper smoothing-iron, but I can get the worst of your travels out of it."

I nod, thinking that the dress has fewer travels to smooth out than I do. Asa stands, staring, and I realize she's waiting for me to undress, so she may take the gown.

I start to undo the hooks at the neck, and suddenly remember my scars. I hesitate, and she steps forward to help me.

"No," I flinch away from her, and she stands still as stone, her expression concerned. I smell the tangy fear-sweat break out on me. My insides tremble in renewed panic. I can't let anyone see these scars, my disfigured body. I don't want this beautiful woman to look on me in pity and horror and disgust. I can't say anything, can't move. I shudder twice and stare at the floor.

"My lady, I shall bring a screen, of course, and you can undress in private." I can't bear to look at her, but I catch a glimpse of her eyes in the mirror she placed on the bed, with a wooden comb and sweet soap. Her eyes seem worried, and I fear I have acted too strangely already.

I wait for her to leave before shuddering, look around, reach for calm. The cabin is small with a round window and room for a chest against the wall. The cots are narrow, but the blankets are of decent wool. A painting of a mermaid hangs on the wall. A cabin for a traveling merchant, or maybe a minor noble.

When she returns again, I stand anxious by the tub, but she merely smiles at me. The screen is a slightly tattered affair, dark wood frame in three sections with coarse linen hung in each panel. Asa sets it up in front of the tub, which leaves very little room in the cabin for much else.

I remove the musty gown while behind it, almost teetering into the water once or twice, unbalanced by the irregular rocking of a ship at dock. I reach my arm over to hand Asa the gown and hear a sharp gasp.

"Oh my dear! What happened to your arm?" Dropping the gown I snatch my scarred arm back to me, huddling naked behind the screen.

"Nothing! I mean, it," I struggle for an answer. "The fire!" I burst out, remembering my new identity. "The fire did it, when we were trapped ...." I leave it at that, hoping she'll drop it.

"Of course, my lady. I am so sorry," she says, her voice subdued. "I will leave you to your bath," and she closes the cabin door quietly behind her.

I unclench my jaw painfully and cling to the side of the tub with relief. Picking up the soap and comb and cloth from the bed, I step shakily into the water.

The bath relaxes me enough to nearly doze. As the smell of my fear washes away I try to believe this may work. I can be a noblewoman, one who is poor and fallen on hard times. I can be a young cousin to a lord, and a handmaid to a princess. I just have to be strong for Linnet, and all will be well.

I take heart from the thought of little Linnet, alive and unharmed. I need to be strong so she can have a future.

Sighing, I start to unbind my hair from its braid, and remember – my hair is short now: short and brown. I run the comb through it, snarling it on the short curls. They're so unruly now they're cut. Da would throw a fit at a daughter of his with short hair, I think. I bite my cheek and focus on getting the snarls out.

Sitting with my knees drawn up, I sink until the water laps over my head. I stay submerged, letting the warmth tingle my scalp and listening to the strange language of the water as it burbles around me.

I soap myself vigorously and rinse, anticipating the return of Asa or Connor. Drying off quickly and wrapping the towel around me, I step around the screen for the shift that fell to the other side.

Connor enters as I'm leaning over the bunk. My hair drips in my face as I stand frozen, and our eyes meet. His mouth sticks on whatever he'd been about to say.

I whip back around the screen, mortified. As I huddle, miserable and now hot, now cold with embarrassment, I hear him take a breath to begin again.

"I brought your wardrobe, lady Rhia," he says. His voice sounds only a little strained. "I think the gowns should fit, although the princess was right." I jump a little as a dark gray gown of fine damask slumps over the screen.

"Right about what?" I choke out.

"You've gained weight in the last week. You no longer look as though you've had the Wasting." Somehow this doesn't make me feel any better.

I put on the gown, relieved Connor took the time to gather me a trousseau before we set off for the castle. Julianna had Connor arrange it last week, so I wouldn't arrive with nothing.

The gown is finer than I am used to, although my mother often wore this style: a full skirt and high neck with lace at collar and cuffs. It fits well enough; Julianna's measurements were thorough. Black bands of mourning adorn the sleeves, and a black shawl follows.

"I picked out boots and stockings as well, so you won't have to appear barefoot. I'm sorry they weren't ready earlier."

"Thank you, my lord," I say, as I shrug into the gown. My damp body makes the material stick to my arms.

"Just hurry, we haven't much time. We need to get out of here soon, before most of the crew comes back from leave."

"Just what does Mistress Asa – do the Indrani know about me?" I ask.

There's a pause, and I pull up my stockings a little firmer before tying the ribbons on my garters.

"The Indrani believe you to be my cousin Rhia, family lost in a fire and on the run from an enemy. They're helping me because the Indrani family who owns this ship is ... a friend to the royal family. The Indrani sovereign is close to our King Peter, and when Hugh was caught in a difficult situation helping the Indrani with something ... sensitive last year, Asa's family made sure he got home safely."

"Oh." The boots fit a little snugly, and I'm dressed and dry but for my hair, but I don't want to come from behind the screen just yet. "Were you working on that something sensitive as well?"

"Extremely unofficially."

I stand still, collecting my courage in wisps.

Connor goes on, perhaps just to fill silence, although that's not his usual habit. "Officially, I was sent away from court for awhile. In fact, I'm usually not in favor at court. They –" he hesitates.

"They what? Why not?" I realize I have broken in too soon, and his brusque manner returns.

"Just get dressed. We leave at the shift bell."

When Asa returns to bid us farewell, she has some information for us. "Bhanu saw a man following your coach past the dock, who questioned your driver, and tried to question a crewmember of ours. None of our crew, of course, understand a word of Talarian," she smiles slyly and shrugs her shoulders. "He seems to have drifted over to the fish market. Bhanu is keeping an eye on him for you."

Connor presses his lips together as he peers out of the window. "It's time for us to be going, Rhia. The spy will believe you docked here on the Jihansa." He turns to Asa and bows. "Again I've trusted you with precious cargo, and again you've repaid my trust tenfold. I thank you and your family. The goods we discussed will reach you soon."

She smiles. "Our honored guest continues his journey with us to Fanthas, then?"

"I would count it a great favor," Connor says.

"We are happy to oblige, your Grace. I'm sure we will have goods for you when we dock again." Asa curtseys deeply as we leave the cabin.

The ship is strangely quiet around us: the slap of water and cries from the fish market sound loud to my ears. The crew bustles around us without seeming to notice us. Connor hurries me to the carriage.

The gown rustles beneath my shaking hands. I step off the gangplank and the carriage driver bows as Connor helps me into his sleek black carriage. Soon the jolting progress of traffic at the docks becomes the rhythm of half-trot through the town of Haverston.

Staring out the window, I try to calm nerves suddenly screaming to run from here. The streets seem quieter than they should be for a market day, and more black slashes of charcoal, signs of pestilence, mark doorways than before. More priests move purposefully from business to home, as well.

I force myself not to flinch from view. I am supposed to be Rhia Wolff fitzWellan, and nobility does not shrink from windows of carriages. Nor do they carry scars of torture.

We pass the town square and I jerk back. The gallows are gone, but I still see them as they were. I ball my hands into fists in my lap and stare at nothing, fighting anguish. My mind whispers in my mother's voice, a lady does not gape out windows or fidget, either. My stomach roils.

Connor lays his hand on mine. I look up into eyes dark as night, and he squeezes his hand lightly over my clenched ones.

"It starts. You will not fail the princess," he says. His tone is kindly, and perhaps it is kindly meant, but I take no comfort.

Julianna saved my sister and myself. But only to this point, and from here I must fly or sink.

I fear greatly that I shall sink like stones.

CHAPTER 6

I am presented to Julianna and her mother the duchess in Julianna's solar. Duchess Marguerite is a smiling, rounded woman in late middle age, her hair gone to silver and her face softening into comfortable beauty. I have seen her from afar before, but she would not recognize me. She pats me kindly on the arm and welcomes me to Haverston, and her castle.

"Hugh's castle now, surely, Mother," Julianna says.

Duchess Marguerite smiles at her daughter, and I can't help but smile with her. The duchess has been the duchess for some time, and Haverston is hers: Haverston is happy to be hers. If she had been home when – but I won't think of that now.

"I'm pleased to have you here, young Rhia. Do make yourself at home. I hope you can recover here from your terrible ordeal." She's referring to Connor's cousin's fire.

I blink back tears and look at my feet.

Julianna shows me to a small closet room in between her bed chamber and the solar, which is to be my chamber. "Normally I'd set up a handmaid in one of the rooms down the hall, but I told mother you still had fears from the fire, and should stay in here. I think it's better to keep close while Gantry's in the castle." Smiling, she pats my arm just as her mother did, tells me I'm doing fine, and sets me to work at once.

I must keep up her highness' wardrobe, see to her breakfast, which I bring from the kitchen on a tray. I am to write her correspondence and supervise her personal servants, of which she has none here. I am to accompany the princess when she sits and embroiders with the duchess and the duchess' guests, minor gentry staying here in the castle.

I am her chaperone and her companion on outings. These outings include visits to the hospice to heal people, which many in Talaria consider shocking. Those visits also anger the priests, especially, by report, Bishop Gantry. He preaches the strict line about every Healer a kirche Healer, all magic belongs to the Star Lord.

But there aren't enough Healing priests to help everyone who is ill in Haverston, and without the princess, more people would die. People look at Julianna with longing and fear in their eyes.

I do not blame them – I look at her that way myself.

Her highness is like no one I've ever seen, although I have spent my life around some who think quite highly of themselves. But she outshines and outmaneuvers everyone she comes into contact with. It's like basking in sunlight when she smiles, which can stun the unwary. When she visits the hospice, the priests glower from corners.

I hide in opposite corners, holding poultices and simples, all but unnoticed in my mourning clothes. I look in no one's face, and so far have seen no one I know. But the Wasting has mostly struck the poor, and usually merchants can call Healers to their own houses.

With the Wasting has come the rain, and the ground is too wet and cold to plant early crops. The farmers try anyway, only to watch the green shoots rot where they sprout. The market is a dismal affair, and everyone tightens their purse-strings. Duchess Marguerite talks of importing food from the southern counties, and Julianna visits further victims of the Wasting as more of the poor and middling-poor succumb to it.

I know the town far better now than I ever did when I lived at my father's house. The poor quarters are more squalid than I believed, in my large merchant's mansion, with its own large garden and servants to tend to most chores. The dirt floors and vermin-infested bedding of people who haven't made it to the hospice make me nervous, while Julianna seems not to notice them at all.

She works tirelessly to Heal any who will accept her. I drop to exhausted sleep each night in my narrow bed, not even bothering to read the books on handmaid etiquette I'm supposed to study. My family moans from the dark corners of my mind, and the faces of the dying join them.

They all whisper of illness and death and witchcraft, and Bishop Gantry chants in my dreams. The demons chant with him, and I push his hand with its bloody knife back night after night. I sleep fitfully when at all.

Although I have been here almost two weeks now, I have not yet been to chapel for fear of seeing the bishop. Connor informed me this morning that I must go tomorrow morning or raise suspicion. Today has been going much too fast: it's late afternoon, and I'm airing her highness' gowns.

My hair springs out of its band in wisps – unruly curls that refuse to tame. The new short style doesn't quite fit my small face, making me appear even younger than my eighteen years. My gray morning gown swishes as I wander from task to task. The day is cool and damp from the early afternoon rain, and dark with heavy clouds. I remember Julianna left her gloves in her solar.

The room glows with soft gray light, the large windows in the false turret and along the long diagonal wall letting in all the daylight this late spring day has to offer. The furniture sits gracefully in the long shadows thrown by the russet curtains, elegant and brocaded and smelling of Julianna's perfume. Her embroidery sits in its basket by the fireplace, the rose chaise angled to catch the most heat.

As I spot the gloves, there is a knock on the door. My hands clench, and rehearsing the proper lines, I pull on the heavy latch.

I open the door to a face I have only seen inside my head before. I blink, my mouth open.

"Bishop Gantry presents his compliments to her Royal Highness and would like, would like . . . " says the young man, trailing off. His brown eyes widen in his dark face, as he begins to recognize me.

I stare at Orrin in shock. He was in seminary with Keenan. I have never met him, but I look enough like Keenan. And he looks just like visions Keenan sent to me.

His mouth gapes open.

"Would like a moment of her time," says the person

behind him, and I jump at the nasal voice, feel my pulse shatter. Gantry is here as well. With Orrin, Keenan's friend, who I'm sure has recognized me.

My tongue aches, bleeds a bit before I realize I have bitten it. "I – I – she – " I stammer, swallow, fight nausea. "H-her Highness is – isn't, isn't here. She, she is in Her Grace's sitting room, my L-lord Bishop. She asked not to b-be disturbed until dinner." I look at his boots, keep my eyes averted. Let him not look at my face. I sneak a look at Orrin.

He stares at me. The whites of his eyes stand out starkly against the dark brown of his irises, and his darker skin. He seems to be in shock.

Gantry, annoyed, glares at us both.

I rip my gaze from Orrin.

Gantry tries to push the door open. My body freezes and burns in terror of him, of his voice, and I start to shake, pushing back. "I will wait for her here," he says, but I cannot move, and so the door stays where it is, glued to my shoulder and hands.

"I am sorry, my Lord Bishop," I rasp, looking at the ground, trying to disappear.

"I must speak with her immediately. Go and fetch her, and I will wait here."

I hold my breath to keep from panting. I am afraid to leave the safety of my lady's rooms; he is too close, and my knees wobble, threaten to dump me on the floor.

I stammer and fumble a curtsey. "Please, my Lord Bishop, it would be improper," I whisper. I feel his glare; it burns on my body in carved patterns under my shift.

He turns and wordlessly stalks down the hall. I know my face is bloodless as the corpse I should have been.

Orrin stares at me. Gantry, striding away, calls him

sharply, and he winces. "The Star Chamber closest to the doors in the chapel," Orrin whispers. "Directly after dinner."

I shudder, nod. What can I do?

"Please don't, don't-" I choke out, and he touches my hand, draws away.

"I won't," he says, and leaves. What can I do? I choose to believe him. I watch the swirl of their robes from under lowered lashes. That flash of annoyance as Gantry looked past me into Julianna's room — he knows where she is. I know suddenly that he wanted the room empty: he's looking for something.

I shut the door and latch it, lean on it, trembling. Slowly I open my mind, reaching out to the corridor. My eyes close, and I sense the Bishop's thoughts as stray wisps. He wanted in this room – he wants to see her rooms, her things, he wants to try something. Anger and anticipation swirl around him as he moves further toward the stairs and then all I sense is the lingering smell of tansy and swampwort. My fear keeps me from sensing more from him, or his own magic does.

Orrin is a little easier, but mostly I get fear and sadness and a deep shock. Emotions I could read easily from his face, and no help from the Sight at all.

Shaking, I pull awareness back into myself. Julianna has been coaching me, but my power is so strange to me now. I tried to tell her that my Sight is a specious power at best — I can't always tell what people are thinking. I can't always See anything at all.

Or that's how it used to be. I don't know why the visions have been so strong since she healed me. I try to control them, but they rush at me or rush away, and what I do See is a confusion of blurred images and feelings I sometimes have trouble making out. The visions feel like the enemy.

I'm afraid of where this new strength comes from. Why can I sometimes tell what people are thinking without trying, and sometimes not, and why does it always feel like power is running through me? But surely if it were demons, I'd know it. Wouldn't I? My scars glow with a pale green light that only I seem to be able to see. I wish I knew what it meant. I wish I could talk to someone about it. I wish I hadn't heard the bishop's voice today, before I was ready for it.

That voice – I run for the garderrobe in the bathing room, barely make it, retching. That voice that rips through my body like claws through wool. I heave up my lunch, sit on the floor.

I know Julianna is disappointed in my progress: her sighs and moues of impatience when I can't read Connor in the next room are hardly subtle. I know he is fighting my Sight now; he doesn't want me to See his thoughts.

Other times when visions rush at me from others, it's information that I don't understand. My skin burns in rhythms to chants and demon hisses, and I can't seem to tell her that, either. Mostly I wish I'd never had the Sight at all.

I stand slowly and smooth the soft gray fabric of my skirt, remembering that a princess's handmaid does not sit idle. I wash my mouth out with the water in the pitcher in the corner, wipe my face.

I'll tell Julianna about Gantry's visit when she returns, but I'm keeping Orrin to myself just yet. I don't know why I don't want to tell anyone – what if he tells

Gantry? I don't know if I can trust him. But I will find out what he wants, first.

Meanwhile, Julianna's gown must be pressed for dinner. My hands don't seem mine as I open the wardrobe, select a wine-red satin, and heat the iron in the fire.

———————

The chapel is chilly and dark but for a few lamps. The ceiling soars over the altar at the far end of the chapel, and I can hear the ocean clearly against the cliffs. This is the opposite end of the castle from the tower where I convalesced.

I make my way to the star chambers, heart hammering. Tapestries hang in the doorways decorated with the great star, and push aside to rooms little larger than tiny closets. There is a lamp burning in the closest one, shining green-yellow on the stonework.

I don't know what Orrin wants. I hope he hasn't told Bishop Gantry anything.

"Rhiannon," I hear, and I gasp, spin. Orrin stands just inside the doorway. I walked right past him.

"That is your name, right? Rhiannon? Rhiannon Owen-"

"Rhiannon Owen is ... dead," I whisper.

He winces.

I study him as much as I can in the dim lamplight. He's slender, only a little taller than I am. His face is smooth and dark, with high cheekbones and a hint of stubble on his chin. His close-cropped hair is wiry and much curlier than mine. He looks sad and worried.

Owen opens his hands in a helpless way, and I try to smile.

"Rhia. Call me Rhia, here."

"I – I was … close to Keenan."

It is my turn to wince. I turn away.

"He was – he used to talk about you. You look a lot like him," Orrin says. "I miss him very much."

I blink back tears, staring at the wall. "I do, too," I whisper, and I've admitted to treason. Or blasphemy. Maybe both. I am not supposed to be alive. And he's working for the man who thinks he killed me. Connor is right: I am stupid.

I turn back to Orrin. "Please, please do not turn me into the bishop. I really don't – I really don't want to die. And I swear I'm not a witch. Not really."

Orrin shakes his head. "I would not. I – I don't think he should have accused you. Keenan told me – he told me of your Sight. It isn't witchery, not how we were taught."

My eyes sting a little. "I have found that it's dangerous to say such things. You'll have to be careful around Bishop Gantry. He is … not a tolerant man."

Orrin shakes his head. "No, he isn't. He is a very frightening man. I don't trust him. I have written to the monastery in Corat for a transfer, but I don't think I'll get one. And now – now that I know you're here …."

I stare at him, afraid to hope. "If he – you – " I fumble. "I hope you get your transfer. It would be safer for you to go."

"I don't know about safer. Safer for you – I promise I won't give you away. But he makes me feel nervous. I've written to the archbishop. I think Bishop Gantry – I'm not sure he's entirely sane."

I reach out, almost grab Orrin's arm. "Oh, not Archbishop Montmoore," I say, and he nods cautiously at me. I shake my head at him. "You should write to Cardinal Robere. He will help you."

He looks askance. "Why not the archbishop? He is the more direct superior." I can only shake my head at him. "What happened, what did Gantry do to you?"

I open my mouth to tell him something, make up something, but no sound emerges. I feel a sharp tingle along the runes on my body, and I find I can only gasp for air. He takes my arm, helps me to collapse onto the stone bench, and sits beside me.

He sighs, wipes his eyes. "I don't know you, really. Only what your brother said. But I loved your brother," he says, and I feel his heart, See his love, and gasp. Loved my brother. As in, they were lovers. I try not to stare in shock. How did I not know?

I think back to everything Keenan said, or Sent me, about Orrin. Was there more tenderness, extra warmth to his voice and mind? I don't understand how I could have missed it. I grab Orrin's hand, clutching at this unexpected remnant of my brother.

"I will trust you," he is saying. I look in his eyes, try to See more. Although that is probably rude.

"I didn't know. He didn't tell me," I whisper.

Orrin looks away. "I know. I didn't tell my family, either. But he was going to. I swear."

I nod, squeeze his hand. "I believe you." Tears run down my face. "I – I have missed him so much. I am glad you're here."

Moonlight trickling into the chamber through the window catches the glint of tears in his eyes. I struggle with my breath.

Orrin lowers his head. "I miss him, too," he says, and sobs shake him. I pull him awkwardly into my arms, and he clutches at me. His grief rumbles through us both, and I can't hold back anymore.

I feel a deep trembling within my limbs, in my stomach, in my lungs. Sobs break from me, and we are holding each other, tears pouring, raw weeping. It is the first time I've been held since before … everything. I weep for Keenan, for Mum and Da, for my life, holding onto Orrin with something like desperation in my limbs.

It is some little time before I can gather myself together. Trembling, I pull back, wiping at my face. Orrin produces a handkerchief, which I take gladly. "But what about you," I ask.

"I have these sleeves," he says, and I snort, very unladylike. "They're dark, and no one will suspect a thing." I like him already.

I sigh, try to smile. "I will speak to my friends, ask if they can request a transfer for you. They, um, they know Cardinal Robere, so they might-"

"Your friend is the princess," he says, cautiously. And my heart constricts, suddenly worried.

"I am her handmaid. She is, she is-" I flounder. He grabs my hand again.

"I won't tell, I promise. Not a word to Gantry. But I do … wonder."

"Please don't wonder," I whisper, and stand. "Don't ask questions. Don't let – don't let the bishop know anything, or even suspect –" and I can't say anymore. "Please be careful."

He nods, his eyebrows raised, and I retreat. I don't know how I'm going to tell Connor about this.

The damp of the morning seems to seep into my bones as I accompany Julianna to morning chapel. I haven't decided what to tell her or Connor about Orrin, but I'll have to tell them something – he knows who I really am, and that's dangerous for all of us. It would be best if he could be transferred. Safer for him, too. What if Gantry tries another demon spell? Will he try to make Orrin help him?

The chapel in daylight is only a little less daunting. The ceiling rises to an arch that frames the west facing windows with their lacy stonework. Whitewash covers the walls and ceiling beams, and bright murals grace the panels below the windows. Golden wood in fancy cutwork rises to a balcony to the left near the front, and under it a gentry box with padded benches for pews. More golden pews march back from the altar in a short neat row.

The chapel isn't as large as I thought – no more than forty people could fit comfortably seated, including the balcony. Our kirche in town is easily three times the size. But this is a jewelbox of a chapel. I would be charmed, were it not for the service to come.

Julianna greets the duchess and her ladies as we come down the aisle, and there is polite curtsying all around. I find my hands clenching fistfuls of my dark skirt, and try to relax them. Julianna and Marguerite smile and turn to ascend the tiny spiral stair to the balcony.

I find myself suddenly standing alone, awkward, not sure whom to follow. The ladies are filing into the box to the side of the altar, and servants are milling and sitting in the pews behind me. I feel stupid, not sure if I was supposed to go up with Julianna or not.

"This way, cousin," I hear at my side, and Connor takes my arm and leads me to the gentry box.

I let out a shaky breath. "Good morning, cousin," I say, and catch his small smile from the corner of my eye. I realize he's looking meaningfully at me, and the ladies, who are all staring. I let him lead me, fumble for some conversation. "What a lovely chapel. I am so glad to, uh, see it."

"I'm happy you feel up to it today, cousin," he says. The ladies still stare, but my stomach trembles as he hands me into a seat in the back row of the box, and I decide that's enough conversation for now.

Connor takes the seat next to me, which I gather is not usual, as everyone now has to turn and raise eyebrows. Several ladies frown at him, and all of them start to whisper. I find it amazing how little noise six whispering people can make, and yet still echo in open space of the chapel. I stare fixedly at my hands, clenched together.

Two of the ladies turn and smile in a pointed fashion. "Good morning, my lord, my lady," Lady Geneve says. "It is so wonderful you could join us this morning. Are you recovering, Lady Rhia?"

I swallow once, try to find my tongue. "Yes, thank you, Lady Geneve. It is kind of you to inquire," I say, attempting a smile.

She reaches over and pats my hand, glances at Connor, and back again. "So kind of your cousin to escort you today," she says, and I wonder again where he usually sits. With Julianna, probably. I feel a little guilty.

"I could not let my cousin go unescorted, Lady Geneve. She is not used to such a grand castle as this. I wouldn't want her to feel overwhelmed." I stop feeling guilty and instead try not to scowl. True or not, that was just patronizing.

"Your concern does you credit," says the older woman, Lady Charlotte, in a voice that suggests she doesn't expect to give him credit.

I raise my eyebrows, but they turn back around and Connor's face is merely tightly pleasant, when I look.

But now comes the hard part, and I am distracted. Gantry has entered, and the congregation drops silent. He looks out at them, at us, and I try not to feel like a small, hunted thing. He doesn't even glance at me, I try to reassure myself. Orrin follows behind the Bishop, quiet in his brown robes, not looking at anyone in particular. I try not to look at him, either. Connor would notice for sure.

The sermon starts abruptly. Gantry's dark robes sway with his vehemence. His words are rather obviously pointed. I wonder what Her Royal Highness will have to say.

"I hear from my fellow kirchemen that there are

grumblings in Haverston. That the prophet Ashere is leading the kirche astray, that the woman Tejal is the true prophet, and our people should follow the lead of countries like Indranah and Zohar. Even some exalted people have been saying this, all over Talaria.

"I cannot speak for other men. But I know this: Prophet Ashere is the one true prophet. We have and will follow his edicts. And when he tells us that magic not sanctified by light, of people not given to the light, not of the chosen of the Star Lord, is magic bound to the dark, to demons – then he is telling us what is true."

I keep my head down, not looking in his flat eyes, his burning expression.

Connor puts his hand on my fidgeting knee. A jolt of energy shoots up my leg to my spine, and I have to work to contain the startled jump that wants to leap out. I look at him, and find his gaze on me, steady and clear. Taking as deep a breath as I can, I try to relax my limbs.

He leaves his hand for a moment longer, looking forward. I look up before I can stop myself. Gantry faces this way. I duck my head, but his focus is above us, to the balcony.

"We are only as safe as our laws and rules allow. But crude law is not the only power. You must turn to the Prophet, turn to the Star Lord. The edicts are to save you all. No matter the earthly laws, follow divine laws for the sake of your souls. Ignore them, and sickness and death will be your reward."

I don't know what Julianna's face looks like from here, above and behind us as she is. But Connor's face is stone. The kind of stone I would be afraid to come across in the dark. Or the light.

I keep my gaze away from Gantry as he continues,

his voice buzzing uncomfortably, raking along my nerves. I don't know if this is his usual routine, but there is no music, no stop for chanting, no ritual call and response. The congregation is silent and blank faced. There's no joy here. If he is this grim at every service, I am glad the castle dictates chapel only twice a week for devoted attendance.

The service ends abruptly as Gantry raises his hands in supplication to the Star Lord, intoning "The Light and the Path." The congregation fumbles into response.

I mumble "...the Path," and watch, wary, as the bishop stands above us, staring. After a moment, everyone starts to stand, murmur, file out. The normal ceremony of the service is off kilter, and Gantry is happy to have it so. I can feel his grim satisfaction; I don't need the Sight for that.

Lady Charlotte turns to Connor, who is waiting for them to file out. "Did you enjoy the service, my lord?"

"Very edifying, Lady Charlotte," he says, and they smile politely at one another.

I press my own lips into a banal smile and nod at anyone who looks my way.

Connor's hand under my elbow pulls me up, and I try not to flinch at his touch. I feel raw from the service, all my nerves exposed.

Lady Charlotte notices my flinch, anyway, and I can see her filing it away for gossip later. She smiles at me some more, and I smile back, but neither of us mean it. Suddenly I am exhausted.

Duchess Marguerite and Julianna emerge from the stairs to the balcony, and approach the group of ladies.

Marguerite smiles at everyone, then calls out to Gantry. "My Lord Bishop, she says, and everyone left in the chapel stops as he turns and descends from the altar.

"Your Highness, your Grace," he says, bowing. He glances at Connor and me. "My lord," he says to Connor, and now I'll have to be introduced, and I grip Connor's hand on my arm like a vice.

"I present my cousin, Lady Riha Wolff Fitzwellan," Connor says quietly. He nudges me and belatedly I curtsey, keeping my face down.

Gantry bows briefly, but his attention returns to Julianna immediately. I do not like the look I see in his eyes when I glance up. He looks avaricious.

Connor's hand is rigid on my arm, although his expression betrays only bland interest. When I straighten, he lets go and starts to leave. Before I can follow, Duchess Marguerite reaches past me for Gantry's arm. He stiffens in affront, and I am stuck.

"My Lord Bishop, now that you have taken over service for several weeks, I must wonder if you intend to continue with such ... plain ceremonies," the duchess says. "We have many reasons to sing and pray, along with the lectures on holiness." She smiles sweetly at Gantry, who frowns back.

"Your Grace, I speak to the needs of this community," he begins, and the duchess raises her hand to stop him.

Julianna just stands serene, smiling at her mother.

"Lord Bishop," the duchess says, "I understand you have much to impart to our humble duchy. We are a much smaller community than the usual bishopric. Although I believe you have yet to be assigned to this bishopric, my lord? Or indeed, any?"

The duchess sharpens her smile. "And of course, our town has different customs than you are used to. Here, we do not require our citizens to be dedicated to the light. If one desires it, or is joining the kirche, then it is a lovely ceremony. But we have citizens who are Qorial, and those who worship Pavali, as well. As surely there are in Corat, and all over Talaria."

Gantry scowls, but Marguerite smiles sharply and will not let him break in. "And while many of us are indeed dedicated to the light, my children, myself, and my late husband included, I have spoken to King Peter myself on the topic, and he says that he will not require it of his citizens."

"Your Grace," Gantry tries.

"Keep this in mind, Lord Bishop. I require that you keep that very strictly in mind. From now on." She stops smiling, and it is a very chill moment in the chapel.

"Your Grace," he says, and stops.

Duchess Marguerite stares him down. I can only admire her.

"I will bear it in mind," he says, not graciously at all, but she nods.

"Songs, young man. And some of the joyous lectures. Dorei is celebrated for her great love and kindness, after all. And the Star Lord is our heart in the heavens."

"So we are told, your Grace."

"See that you remember it," she says, her smile returning. All of us bow and curtsey as she turns to leave. Most of her ladies leave with her, but several stay, talking just within earshot. They aren't fooling anyone.

Julianna beams at us all. "My mother is a wise woman, my Lord Bishop."

Gantry looks up from his bowing, straightens, and the gleam of hate in his eyes returns. I bite my lip. "She is pious and follows all the holy laws," he says, his eyebrows raised.

"Yes, so she does. We are all of us in love with my mother. Every last person in the duchy and castle, down to the smallest child."

"And yet you yourself are not so beloved by your people, your Highness. It is a pity." He narrows his eyes at her, glances at Connor. "Excepting for some of your favorite pets, of course. I do worry for you so. It has been such a trying several years for you, since your hasty marriage to the prince. It must be good to be home, where you can be sure of a kind welcome."

Julianna raises her eyebrow. "I most certainly can be sure of kind welcome here. Almost everyone can."

I try to edge my way past. Connor waits for me, but Gantry's arm brushes my hand as he gestures. I gasp, my vision goes dim. Sparks travel the length of my spine, all along the scars on my body.

I look up to see Gantry's eyes widen as he turns to me. All I can see are his eyes again. It's over, I know it's over.

"Clumsy oaf!" Gantry exclaims, and I shrink back, panting. I hear a clang and the muffled thumps of bodies colliding.

Orrin sprawls half on Gantry, ceremonial wine spilled and spreading on the floor. The ladies let out squeals and cries of dismay as they stumble back from the spreading stain, and I let them take me with them.

Orrin looks up and catches my eye. I nod to him, almost weeping, and Connor's hand is under my elbow, all but dragging me from the chapel. I hear Gantry castigating Orrin all the way down the hall.

I cannot catch my breath. My vision swirls in sparks

and blurs, and I struggle to keep my feet under me as we hurry up the stairs and all the way to Julianna's rooms.

"What was that about?" Connor demands as he deposits me in a chair. I wheeze, but do not answer.

"Connor, what are you talking about?" Julianna asks, coming in behind us.

"Ask her. She has something going on with that acolyte. Answer me, damn you," he says, grabbing my chin. "Have you been a spy all along?"

"Honestly, Connor. Do you think she tortured herself?" Julianna snaps. He has the grace to wince, look chagrined. "And Robere himself vouched for her innocence, you told me."

But no one told me. My lungs start to relax, but my mind is going in circles.

"There is something between her and that new acolyte, I can tell you that," he says. They both look at me. Julianna trusts that he's right about that, at least. And he is.

"He, he," I gulp. "His name is Orrin. He was a friend of my brother's. He, uh, he recognized me." I say, and Connor swears, begins to pace. "He won't give me away. He promised."

Connor stares at me like I'm simple. Julianna stares at me with pity. I'm not fond of either look.

"He loved Keenan. He wouldn't – he doesn't even want to be an acolyte to Gantry."

"Good. Then he won't object to leaving," Connor says.

"No, he won't. I told him one of you might write to Cardinal Robere, have him transferred somewhere safe." I try to get my breath under control.

"That will take too long. I'll simply take him,

removing him from the castle should be enough." Connor turns to leave.

"What? No! You can't do that!" I cry.

Julianna shakes her head, too. "That would be suspicious, Connor."

He turns to glower at us both. "More suspicious than harboring a dead witch?"

"She's not a witch, Connor! And she's right here!" Julianna yells.

"Yes, here, where Gantry or anyone else might recognize her at any moment. Putting her life in danger again, as well as yours!" He's yelling, too, which isn't like him.

But I've thought of something. "I am a witch, I say, and they both turn to look at me. "Rhiannon Owen was recorded as a witch in the Guildhall by now. A dead witch, as you say."

They both wince.

"I only meant," Julianna says, but Connor cuts her off.

"You are Rhia Wolff fitzWellan. Anyone who says differently will answer to me." His voice and eyes are grim.

"Even you," Julianna snaps.

He grimaces. "Fine. You are Rhia Wolff fitzWellan. My cousin and ward."

"Orrin won't challenge that," I argue. "Is it fair to ruin his life just because he loved my brother? He is an acolyte – he has a calling to the kirche. Should he just disappear? How would the Cardinal ever fix that? You can – I know you can ask him for a favor. If you ask him to transfer Orrin, or even write a letter of leave, so he can go home for awhile – I know he will do it if you ask him."

Connor just shakes his head, but Julianna looks at me, considering. "She's right, Connor. We should move with caution. He might be useful to us, where he is. And I think Rhia could use a friend."

My eyes well up.

"A dangerous friend," Connor mutters.

Julianna smiles fondly. "My favorite kind," she says, and lays her hand on his arm, and he doesn't argue anymore.

"Yes, my lord." I can't help the relieved smile on my face. Maybe Julianna is right. Maybe I do need a friend. I haven't thought of my friends in – not since. Not that I had so many. Most of them have married or … but it would be nice to have someone who knew Keenan. I hug the thought of friendship to myself and pick up my tangled embroidery, feeling a shaky, tiny kernel of happiness in my chest.

He looks at me. "All right. But I will speak to him myself. If I think he's a danger, I will remove him. And don't meet with him too often, or in the open. I don't want Gantry getting any interest in you. Do your … spelling, whatever, from afar."

CHAPTER 8

I head to the Star Chambers after dinner. The chapel is back to shadowed and echoing now that dark has fallen, and I hope that Orrin will look for me soon. It's nerve-wracking in here, with Gantry somewhere nearby. I pray to Dorei and the Star Lord, hoping for grace. Or invisibility: either would help.

Orrin enters with a scrape of the tapestry, and I jump, try not to gasp. "Sorry. The bishop was … displeased with me. I wasn't sure he would let me come to pray privately," Orrin whispers.

I feel my stomach sinking. "Oh, no. Is it because of this morning? It's my fault."

He shakes his head. "It's nothing. Don't worry. I – I was nervous and shaky anyway. He has a disconcerting way about him, and I try to avoid his eyes when I can."

I shiver and nod. He notices the shiver. "Is he, did he beat you? I mean, before the – when you were-" he flounders to a halt.

I can't open my mouth to say anything, to tell him

even a lie. My breathing falters, my heart races, and I am in that room again, with that voice chanting.

I shake myself out of it; Orrin is trying to soothe me, pat my arm. I turn to him and hug him fiercely, and I hear him cry out, flinch away.

"Oh, no," I say, drawing away to look into his wincing eyes. "I'm so sorry," I manage through my wheezing. I touch his shoulder and he flinches further, looks away from me. I notice finally that his movements are stiff, and he holds himself as though injured. "He – he hurt you, didn't he?"

Orrin says nothing. I take his hand. "Is there anything I can do?"

"I'm hardly the first acolyte to be disciplined," he says. "No one can do anything. But I swear, it was more than just discipline to him. It was – rage. He wanted what I couldn't give him, and he was enraged. I thought for a minute – well, it doesn't matter what I thought."

"What did he want?" I ask.

"Information. He wanted," he stops, looks away again. My blood freezes, my whole body aches in panic.

"Information?" I whisper.

"Not about you, or not about the real you. He wants – he's looking for information about the princess. And he thinks I can get it for him."

"Why would he think that?"

"He thinks I should be able to use my Sight to spy on her." He laughs a little. "He's angry because I told him that's not how it works."

Shaking, I ask, "You have the Sight?"

"Not much of it. I don't See much. It's not a very useful magic in me," he says, rueful. "I'm sure Keenan told you about it."

I just shake my head.

"The chicken prophesies?" he says, and surprises a laugh out of me.

"Oh, the chicken prophecies! That was you?" I can't stop a helpless chuckle.

"Even the Reverend Superior made fun of me for that. It's the clearest set of visions I ever had."

"Well, it might have been useful to the cook to know how many eggs were going to be laid each day," I say, relieved. If his Sight is weak, then Gantry can't use him to spy, not really.

Orrin's smile is wan.

"Have you ever had a vision about the princess?" I ask.

He shakes his head, sighs. "Only once, and it was nothing. She was Healing a woman covered in bandages. I couldn't even really see who – I only knew it was a woman because that's the feeling I got."

I can't feel my face; I have no idea what expression is on it. "Did you tell him of that vision?"

"Not all of it – just that she was Healing someone. That threw him into enough of a fit. He wanted to know what, who, where, and I just – I said I couldn't tell anything else. I didn't even say it was a woman …." His voice trails off, his face shocked in the flickering light. "Oh, Lord of Stars, it was you, wasn't it? Oh, I don't – what did he do to you?"

I can't breathe, I can't think – if Gantry figures out who I am, we are all lost, and Orrin is in so much danger, and I can't speak, I can't speak….

"I'm sorry, Rhiannon. Don't tell me. Don't tell me anything. I'm so sorry," he's saying, sobbing, holding and rocking me, and I find my breath finally.

"Rhia," I whisper. "You have to remember."

He breathes a sigh, another. "Rhia," he says, pulling back. "I will remember. I won't even speak it at all, if that will help."

"It might." I wipe at my face – it's wet and sloppy.

Orrin smiles and hands me another handkerchief.

"Oh, dear," I say, and he laughs.

A thump sounds on the wall and we jump to standing, me muffling a cry.

"This is a place of worship, not a trysting house!" a voice shouts from the next chamber. I bite my lips, but Orrin squares his shoulders.

"I am counseling a worshiper. Pray do not interrupt," he says in a voice that is a perfect match for Gantry. I blink, raise my eyebrows. He smirks a little.

"Beg pardon! Beg pardon, Lord Bishop! Beg pardon!" The voice fades as the speaker hurries out of the chamber, out of the chapel.

I start to shake, relieved laughter making me sag onto the bench.

Orrin's smirk turns to a sheepish grin. "Among my many talents," he says. He joins in my shaky laughter.

I can tell both of us feel sick and frightened and want to ignore it. I clutch his handkerchief, wipe my face. "My lord the Earl of Dorward wants to speak with you," I say, finally calm enough. "He is, well, he's-"

"The princess' spy," Orrin finishes.

"Cousin," I say firmly. But he is … concerned."

Orrin nods. "And rightly so. Where shall I call upon him?"

"Oh, I think he'll call upon you. Probably tomorrow. I'll try to be there, too, but he's…."

"A spy," Orrin finishes.

I cluck my tongue. "A very concerned cousin. Who is an Earl." I correct.

He snorts.

"He's, well, he's intimidating, but he means well," I add.

"I will keep my eye out for his approach, then."

"Don't take his ferocity to heart. He won't hurt you."

Orrin raises his eyebrows at me. "Thanks for the warning."

I shake my head at him. "He is gruff. And very rude. But he has her – he has everyone's best interests at heart." I stand. "I should go. I'll look for you tomorrow. I, we're not supposed to meet too often."

"No. We should not." He stands and pats my arm. "Let me go out first. Get some sleep." He smiles at me, worry and pain in his eyes. I know mine look the same as I smile back.

<hr>

Connor finds me the next day on my way to Duchess Marguerite's solar with my embroidery. He gestures impatiently for me to follow him, and I am just as glad to go despite his peremptory behavior. My embroidery skills are weak at best. I was always better with the loom. Not much, but better.

I follow him down the corridor, staring at his brown velvet back. He leads me to the north tower, but down, where the steps are smooth as ice they're so old, and smell of damp. Slowly a steady surge sounds, an undertone of wild rushing.

As my legs begin to ache, Connor grabs a lamp from a wall sconce that I didn't see in the growing dark. He lights it, and we descend further, spiraling into the heavy weight of earth.

The stairs stop suddenly at a heavy wood and stone door. I bump into Connor's back and he grunts, squeaking hinges sound, and we walk out into the misty daylight.

The sea bashes the cliff we stand on; a short wall at the edge of the path is wet from the spray reaching high and wetting my hem and hands.

When I step through, Orrin is seated on a stone bench against the wall, the spring sunshine breaking through wispy clouds and painting the dark contours of his face with copper.

I look up, away from the surf, and see the north tower's tip and outer wall stretching high above.

"When you speak to one another, it might be better to meet here. Or just inside, when the weather is bad," Connor says.

I turn and look at him. I suppose this is his way of approving of our friendship. I stare at him for a moment, raising my eyebrows. Julianna does this to him and it seems to work.

Connor shrugs and points to where the wall ends in more rock and a crude door. "It's an old tunnel, to what used to be the Lord's hall. Now it's the Inquisitor's building." I shudder, looking away. How they got me out, I realize.

"Why not keep meeting in the Star chambers," Orrin asks.

"A pattern will be noticed. Meet here," he says, and closes the door behind him, leaving me with Orrin. I blink a couple of times, turn to regard my friend. Yes, my friend.

"Is he always like that?" Orrin asks.

I breathe a laugh, shrug. "Worse, mostly. I hope he wasn't too … too Connor."

Orrin looks at me at little sideways, starts to smile. "So you call him by his given name? Ah, but he is your cousin and guardian now, isn't he?"

I nod, a little confused.

"And anything else?" he asks archly.

"What do you m – no! No, nothing else. Good grief, Orrin," I say, trying to be repressive, but he grins and I can't help a rueful smile back. "He's just my – he's just my-"

"Connor," Orrin supplies.

"Exactly," I reply, and he laughs.

"Oh, exactly."

"Shut up." I sigh and he laughs some more. I take his hand, and we sit in the sunshine, enjoying the wind and the sound of the waves. I lean on him for a minute, then remember the ladies, and the solar, and the dratted embroidery. "I have to go. But do you want to meet here? I mean, soon?"

He stands and offers me a hand up. "I'll try and come day after tomorrow, after dinner. I'll let you go up first now. We should probably leave separately."

I hadn't thought of that. That he did – and I have a vision of Keenan so sharp, so sweet, that I have to sit down again.

"Oh," I say, just that, and he looks stricken.

"You felt that," he says, and I bite my lips, nod. "Your Sight is stronger than mine."

"You and Keenan – you hid your relationship?"

Orrin looks away. His hands clench on his thighs, and I feel a wave of sadness that isn't mine. "It was an open secret. Everyone knew. But our Reverend Superior believes strongly in celibacy for students and acolytes, and didn't approve. Since there aren't any official rules about acolytes forming attachments to each other, we just kept everything quiet, and he never told us to stop."

He looks back at me, blinking back tears. "After the … arrest, everything changed. Keenan was so loved, and then suddenly he was-" he stops, closes his eyes.

I See angry faces, raised fists, feel the ghost of old pain. "I think that's why the Reverend Superior sent me here, when an acolyte with the Sight was requested. No one else wanted to go."

The phrase jerks me back to myself. Something about Gantry wanting the Sight specifically crawls through my skin, along runes cut by a knife and demon spells.

"Bishop Gantry requested an acolyte with the Sight?" I try to keep my voice calm, but I can hear it going high and quavery.

"That's what he said. I told him it wasn't much, but he didn't seem concerned."

"Oh, no," I whisper. Magic trickles through me, and I See a knife, Orrin's eyes wide and terrified. I shake myself free of it to tell him – but I can't.

"What? What is it you are so worried about? What did he do to you?" Orrin asks, frustrated.

I feel my lungs constrict, hear the demon voices from my memory, and I cannot speak, cannot breathe again. It is this, it is this question – I can't speak if someone asks me about the scars, about the demons, about what Gantry did to me.

I can hear Orrin calling my name, the ocean surf, and my own gasping. I think carefully only about Orrin, that

I am concerned for Orrin, and not why. I pull pieces of myself from the air around me and weave them together with promises that I am not thinking about anything.

"Rhiannon! What is it?"

Gasping, I manage to say, "Do not ask me that question," although I can't be sure he understands me. But he has his own Sight, and I try to send him something, anything.

He stops talking, just holds my arms as I manage my breathing.

"I think," I say when I can, "I think you are in danger. Do not ask me why. I can't breathe when you ask me questions. I can't tell you. But please, please be careful. Be careful with the Bishop. I think he wants to use you." And I can't say any more, but at least I can breathe.

"How can I help you?" he asks, his eyes worried.

"You can be … my friend," I say. "Stay well." I look into his dark eyes, the sun warming them to a deep umber.

He sighs, nods. "I am your friend. And I will be careful. As long as you are, too."

I smile at him, take his hand. I don't think I know how to be careful anymore. We sit for awhile longer, looking at the sea.

CHAPTER 9

His Grace the Duke of Haverston arrives today with Linnet. It's weeks later than he originally meant to arrive. His last letter expressed concerns installing Linnet as a ward in Corat, but did not specify why.

Julianna has warned me that Linnet has been deeply grieving and going through significant changes. I tried very hard not to roll my eyes.

Connor spotted the carriage from the tower, and hurries me down the back stairs to greet them in private. Connor is concerned Linnet will need coaching. I'm concerned Connor will frighten Linnet.

The cracked wood of an old garden door squeals in protest of his rough handling, as I have not, and we rush into the kitchen gardens. Winter foliage begins to give way to early spring green, and the raised beds are fuzzed with small shoots. Chest-high walls surround the small square garden, with statues of saints and warriors set round the top, facing out toward the formal gardens.

The morning breeze raises bumps on my neck and flutters my gown. I watch the sky while Connor paces. Sun teases through wispy clouds and paints the garden in grays, both muted and almost silver. Light gleams off puddles in the beds, and the paths between show hints of green through the brown mud and grass of last fall. A fountain trickles somewhere beyond the gate, in the formal gardens. Over all I hear the crying of sea birds and the ever present shushing of the sea.

A smiling, elegant blond man who must be the duke enters the garden through the arch of the back gate. He guides a thin girl in dark wool by the arm, her face sullen and wrinkled with frustration: Linnet.

I rush forward three steps, and stop, breathless. Little Linnet. Even in these few weeks, she seems to have grown taller, almost to my own height. The dark kerchief tied to hide her hair does a poor job of it, and bright orange strands escape to curl over her hazel eyes. Those eyes catch mine and my heart stops at the rage I see glittering there.

"Linnet -" I start, but her gaze clogs my throat. I feel a power emanating from her that she never had before, and it crushes my words before I can speak them. She blames me for running, for surviving while our family did not. She blames me for Deacon Bertram's rhetoric and cruel words. She blames me for death.

"Linnet, little bird, I'm so glad you're – are you –I..." Her eyes grow colder. I search for a hint of warmth, anything, and I step forward to hug her. She backs away, wrenching her arm from the duke. He pushes her forward again, tells her to behave.

"Don't touch me, witch!" Her magic glows pale green

to my Sight. I can feel her magic calling to mine, her anger fueling it, and I have no idea how to stop it. Hot magic flows through us both.

She has grown, in more than height. I cannot speak for her rage. She never had this power before, and it crackles around her like lightning. I choke, fluttering my hands as her eyes burn into mine. "You're a liar and a murderer, and Mum is dead and it's your fault!" Her lips twist into a sob.

Hugh, Duke of Haverston, dashing in a blue riding coat, steps forward and with a touch her power fades. With a firm hand on Linnet's shoulder, he puts on a determined smile. He looks a twin to his younger sister.

"Connor, well met! And your lovely companion," he says as he bows gracefully at me.

Linnet turns her rage to Hugh, but my eyes are only for her.

"There have been some developments. If you'll bring her to my sister, I'll inform you later. I have to see to things in the hall. Keep all of this –" he waves his hands at us, "quiet, if you can. Best to go to Julianna's rooms quickly."

Hugh turns to Linnet. "Remember, you're safe now. And be a good girl." His gloved hand squeezes her shoulder. She shrugs it off, and he walks briskly away, his bright hair gleaming.

Linnet's eyes look bereft a moment, following his form as he leaves by the formal gardens. I reach for her hand.

"I said don't!" Linnet jerks her hands behind her back.

I am lost, I can't move any way, until Connor sighs

and steps forward. "I am the Earl of Dorward. This is Rhia Wolff fitzWellan, and she is my cousin. You are Linnet Tallys. Keep that straight. We will take you to see Her Royal Highness, Princess Julianna. You will do as you're told and keep your mouth civil. Is that clear?"

Linnet stares mulishly.

Connor is suddenly taller, without moving a muscle. "I said, is that clear?"

Linnet backs a step, frowns fiercely, and nods. "Yes, my lord."

"Well, your tone is civil, at least. See that your expression is as well by the time we present you to the princess." He turns and strides toward the kitchen, motioning for us to follow.

Linnet mockingly bows to gesture me ahead, her face puckered in an angry pout. Her eyes are as cold as Mum's were, that day.

I lower my head and follow Connor.

———

The back stairs are steep and narrow, empty for the moment, and echoing. I climb as quickly as I can to stay close, but Connor is feeling brisk and I tire so quickly. He waits with little patience as I enter the upper passage, his arms crossed.

I feel Linnet's gaze on my neck; sweat slides down my temple as I grow hot. I blink back tears and Connor, who has already reached the princess' chamber door, turns to wait again for us. He looks at me, and at Linnet, and his chin softens a little. I feel a brush of something kindred from his mind, but I am trying not to cry. Connor opens the door to the solar.

I precede Linnet into the room. Princess Julianna sits, rose-colored from the light, in her high-backed chair by the east windows. Her embroidery catches the morning sun, and she smiles as Linnet and I curtsey. Linnet's expression remains uncharitable as we rise at Her Royal Highness' gesture, but she says nothing. The princess rises and steps forward, grasping Linnet's hands.

Linnet backs a step, her eyes wide. Her Highness' smile is dazzling.

"Oh, good, you must be Linnet. Our Rhia has told us so much about you. I'm sure you're exhausted after your journey."

Linnet blinks at Julianna, taken aback.

"Such a lovely face you have. Come sit with me, my dear."

Linnet follows to the chaise with a dazed expression.

Connor clears his throat. "I will meet with Hugh, my lady. He mentioned developments."

"Very well, Connor. Did he explain?"

"Not yet." He bows and leaves, and I am standing in the middle of the room with no idea what to do now.

I pick up the basket of mending, and cautiously settle into the chair Julianna has abandoned. Linnet looks at me, at the basket, and smirks. I feel my face flush again - I am awful at mending, it's true. I try to smile at her, but she looks away.

Julianna notes the exchange, but merely strokes Linnet's hand and continues. "I understand we are changing our plans, so we'll have to find a place for you here. It's a bit of a worry, having you and your sister here as well as the Bishop, but it seems we must. I promise we will do everything to keep you both safe."

Linnet pulls her hands away and folds her arms, slouches back into the corner of the chaise.

"Linnet, be respectful," I admonish, and she glares at me.

"Don't tell me what to do," she snaps, slouching further.

Julianna's smile dims a little. "I know this has been a terrible time for you and your sister. I am sorry that such things have happened in my country."

Linnet stares at nothing.

Reaching out, Julianna brushes back the strand of hair that has escaped Linnet's kerchief. "It's too bad we'll have to change your lovely hair. So like your sister's."

Linnet glowers.

Julianna stands, and I stand also, clutching the mending to my stomach like a shield. Julianna pats Linnet's shoulder. "I have faith that you'll find your footing here soon. But for right now, why don't you get settled. Rhia will help you."

Julianna heads for her bedchamber, beckoning me to follow. I look between them for a moment, set down the mending, and head after her. Linnet stays slouched on the chaise.

"Here, Rhia, hand me my shawl. I'm going to look for Hugh, and then I'm having lunch with my mother." I hand her the shawl from the top shelf of the wardrobe, then her boots when she asks.

She looks up at me as she reaches for them, shakes her head. "Don't worry so much." She pulls the boots from me and sits on the edge of her bed to put them on herself. With them on she stands next to me, pats my arm. "I know it's frightening, but really, you're better off here than anywhere else. Trust me."

I realize for the first time that her head only comes to my shoulder. Her gaze catches mine and holds it by force of will. How can I not trust her?

"Yes, your Highness."

She leaves and I am alone in the apartments with a sullen Linnet. "You can put your things in this chest," I say to her, twisting my hands. I walk through the short hall between rooms into the solar.

Linnet sits where the princess left her, staring out the window. "I don't have any things. The guild confiscated the manor when the priests came."

The news punches me low in the stomach; but of course they did. The manor, the looms, Mum's gardens: all of it confiscated at our family's shame. The manor was to go to Linnet: her inheritance.

"Oh, Linnet."

"It was quite a fight. Deacon Bertram was extremely angry. He understood the land was to go to the kirche. Guildmaster Aman persuaded him otherwise."

"Aman is Guildmaster now?"

"He took Da's place while they carted everyone away. He said the manor was his now." Her voice struggles toward emotionless, but snags on bitter. Her hands roll the edge of the kerchief she pulled from her hair.

I touch her shoulder, and allow a small flicker of hope when she lets my hand stay. I close my eyes and listen to our breathing, unsteady and loud.

"That must please Melisande no end," I say, feeling a little bitter, myself. Melisande is Geoffrey Aman's daughter. She and I dislike one another, but she always was jealous of our social status.

"Melisande is stupid," Linnet snarls.

I shrug – Melisande isn't stupid, but I'm not going to take up on her behalf.

"Francis showed up right away, I heard, and Aman passed all the waiting journey folk to master without even looking at their master works." Linnet glares out at nothing. "Da would never have done that."

"No, he wouldn't," I say, feeling even more bitter. Francis is – was – my betrothed. He's been passed over for master three years running: his works have always been terrible. I guess he wanted master status more than he ever admitted to me. "So Francis and his father must be pleased, too."

"Francis is stupid," she says.

I can't refute it, although a part of me still wants to try. I let it go and try to think of anything else to say to her. Anything at all. We were never as close as Keenan and I were, but Linnet was always laughing, always happy. And she always had a smile for me. I don't know how to deal with this angry Linnet.

"Did his Grace treat you well?" I try, and she shrugs my hand away, angry again.

"What do you care? What do you care about anything but yourself! You ran off and left us to die!" She shouts at me, standing, gesturing, and suddenly I feel choked on power – rushing through me, filling the air, coming from everywhere, but mostly from Linnet.

I don't know how to react to her power. I didn't even know I could feel magic like this, and my heart starts to pound.

"Linnet – this – what is this? Do you feel this?" I ask, as cushions and papers rattle and shuffle from her anger. "This - you have magic now."

"I know! And I hate it! What am I supposed to do with this now? Now it's too late to do anything with it."

"You, did you ever … before?"

She glares at me, but finally answers. "Yes. Some." The papers settle, her power bleeds away, unused. "Not this much. But after – after. And then that stupid deacon – anyway, he was surprised. More surprised than I was." Her mouth quirks, but her eyes are savage. "He's convinced we're a huge family of witches, now."

"He – what did he do?"

"What do you think," she snarls. "Deacon Bertram likes to hit people. He said beating the evil out of me was his duty. I persuaded him otherwise, with his own whip." She tosses her hair. "And choked him with his robe."

A flash of rage through my limbs. I almost forgot about Bertram. "Good," I say, feeling savage. "I hope he was terrified." I try to reach for her hand, but she snatches it away.

"At least his Grace showed up when he did. Nice of you to send him along."

"I didn't send him. He – the princess, and the earl and the duke", I take a breath, try again. "They rescued me – us. And they want me to help them."

"I know you didn't send him. I know all of it. His Grace told me. So you don't have to go on about it." Her agitation grows, and she starts to pace. Small items in the room start floating to follow her.

"Linnet," I start, but she ignores me.

"Now I'm stuck in this – this situation, with no friends, no family – you don't count," she throws over her shoulder. "And I'm cut off from my whole life! My education, my weaving, my reputation in the guilds – all vanished!" She spins to face me. "And it's all your fault! If you had just stayed put! You didn't have to run off like a coward and leave us like that!"

"Linnet, I had to run. Keenan told me to run! They were going to take all of us – I thought – we thought, if I ran, they would just –"

"They took all of us anyway! And look what happened!" Her face is a livid red, and tears pour down her cheeks. "You left us there, and you didn't stop any of it! You and your stupid Sight, and your stupid cowardice! I hate you!"

Her shouting and temper cause the items to swirl around us both. With the temper comes a spike in her power, and it draws something in its wake.

Around us I can hear a sibilant chanting, hissing voices, and the skin of my body starts to sting and burn. Linnet and I stare at each other as this new magic filters into the room, and the paper and things in the air float or thump down as Linnet's magic releases.

"What is that?" Linnet asks. I can feel my skin trying to crawl off of my bones, and my body starts to tremble. The demons have found me.

I try to scream at Linnet to run, to get out, to find Connor, anyone, but my voice is silent.

Linnet stares at my gaping mouth, my gasping, shaking form. The susurrous whispers of the demons slither through the air, and all I want to do is run and run.

"Is that some other magic? For pity's sake, Rhiannon, don't just stand there like a baby! Do something!"

But I can't do anything except try to breathe through damaged, spell-scarred lungs, and gesture at her to run.

She does not. Confused and angry, Linnet walks over and shakes me. "What is going on?"

There's a wrongness to the room. The whispering and pressure increase – now it is not only me who can't speak. Linnet grabs at the fireplace poker, ready to do battle. I don't think the demons will find it much of an obstacle, but I admire her determination. So this, now, is when the demons will take me. I take heart from Linnet's bravery, and make myself stand up straight, draw breath. I will fight, too. If only I knew how.

Something tugs at me, trickles along my scars. I scramble for what Keenan taught me; how to make a barrier, how to push things away. The creeping feeling of the magic fills the room. I can feel it testing me, tasting the air. Linnet and I stand back to back, both of us trembling.

The door from the hall flies open, and the duke and Connor rush in. His grace chants something, grabbing Linnet and me by the wrists, and I feel suddenly muffled, cut off from the noise and the weight of the magic. The lightness in my head staggers me, and I sink bonelessly into the chair.

Duke Hugh chants and weaves his magic into the air, and the wrongness in the room dissipates. Within moments, it's as if nothing happened.

Except for the agitation and presence of two very upset men. Connor prowls the room looking for anything to fight as the duke berates Linnet.

"Where are your barriers? We're right on top of the largest power-well in the province, and I still felt your lack of control half the castle away! Don't you remember anything I told you?"

"Gantry," I gasp, and both of them look at me.

Hugh runs his hand over his face, glares at me. "How did that spell get in here? This room is shielded. What in Dorei's name were the two of you doing?"

Linnet glares and is about to reply when Connor holds up his hand. "We don't have time. Others will be here any moment. You two," he says to Linnet and me. "Get in your room and stay there until you're told otherwise."

"Too late," Hugh observes, as the door smacks open again, and in rush several kirche guards and Gantry. Orrin steps in behind them, his face drawn tight in fear.

"Treason!" Gantry yells. "Unsanctified magic! It was-" He looks around. "Where is she?"

Connor looks murderous. "Are you speaking of Princess Julianna?" he asks, his voice quiet and menacing.

Gantry snarls something about treason again, and I can feel his magic crawling around him, beginning to crawl around the room, searching.

I don't know what will happen if it finds me, so I just go with an instinct that I hope isn't disastrous. "Intruder!" I cry, standing suddenly.

Everyone stares at me.

I'm shaking, and tears leak down my face. I'm sure I look frightened enough. "My lords, there was a man in here – or – or someone! They ran back out? Did you see them? I – there was such a noise! I don't know what they wanted. We were so frightened, oh," I say, as everyone continues to stare. I stare at Linnet.

She blinks for a moment. "Oh! Oh, my lords," she says, breathless. "Please go and catch them! What would have happened if the princess had been here! Oh!" she cries, and pulls her apron up to cover her face, the way our old cook used to do. She wails, and I join in the carrying on.

"Oh! The princess! Is she safe?" I know Julianna is with her mother, but likely they do not. "Oh, my lords, where is the princess? My lady, Oh!" I cover my face with my hands, lacking an apron. I hear Connor start to bark orders to the kirche guards, the confusion and counter-orders from Gantry.

"What is going on in here?" Julianna's voice carries over the din.

With a quick glance at Linnet, I hurry to her side, pushing past all the men. Orrin winces when I look at him. I frown at him, and keep wailing. "Oh! Your Highness! We were so worried! An intruder! Someone in your rooms! Are you quite safe?" Now Linnet is with me, both of us pulling Julianna further into the room, fussing, getting her closer to her brother and Connor.

"An intruder? Here? Are you certain?" she looks around at the men, standing at staring. "Then why is no one searching for this person?"

"I will summon the castle guards, Highness," says Connor, and he starts to leave, raising his eyebrow at me as he passes.

"This should be handled by the kirche guards. There was unsanctified power used here," Gantry insists.

Connor ignores him, brushes by.

"When the intruder is found, my Lord Bishop, I am sure we will consult with you on how best to handle the matter," Hugh says. "Right now, I trust the castle guard and my cousin to begin the search. I think your kirche guards can go back to the Inquisitor's Building, at present. Come with me, my lord. Tell me what you felt."

Hugh leads the rest of the men out of the room,

leaving Julianna with two seemingly hysterical young women. They mostly seem happy to go, although I catch a wry look from Orrin as he closes the door.

My hysteria is not entirely feigned. The close call, the spell, the demons, the fight with Linnet – I feel my heart has hammered a hole in my chest.

"Well, now," Julianna says. She settles herself on the chaise, gazing at us both.

I take a deep breath, but Linnet starts before I can. "There was some kind of strange magic, and it was crawling all over the room. And Rhiannon just stood there, and then his grace and that earl ran in and chased it off. After that those other men came in here shouting about unsanctified power, and—"

"That was Bishop Gantry," I say.

Linnet stops, glaring at me. "So what? He didn't seem that scary to me."

"It was his magic you found scary enough just before that," I snap, angry now. "And since it was your lack of control that brought his spell here in the first place, your unsanctified power he was talking about."

"Rhia," Julianna breaks in. "You're sure the spell was from Bishop Gantry?"

I nod.

"And it was Linnet's magic that – summoned it?"

"It – yes." I can't say anything else about it. I know I can't, so I don't try.

"It might have been anything that brought it! I didn't do anything. How do you know it was me?" Linnet yells.

"I just do. And the duke did, too, he said—"

"You're just mad because it showed you up a coward again. I wouldn't trust her, your highness. She has a tendency to turn coward and run."

"Linnet!" I think I'm more upset at her rudeness, although I feel my eyes sting.

"I think that's more than enough," Julianna says with reproof.

Linnet flushes, but it's hard to tell under the flush of anger she already has.

"Why don't you retire for now, Linnet. It would do everyone good to calm down."

Linnet shrugs, sullen. "Fine." She turns to go, then turns back. "Where am I going?" she asks neither of us in particular.

"The door in the little hall there," I say. She starts to go. "Linnet – ask pardon first," I say, surprising myself in how much I sound like Mum.

Linnet's gaze leaps to mine, but she turns and curtseys. "Your Highness, I am sorry. May I go?"

"Yes, Linnet." Julianna watches her go, her eyebrows raised. When the door closes she turns to me. "Quite a morning, Rhia."

"I'm sorry for Linnet's behavior, your highness. I don't know – she never used to be so fresh, or so rude. Our mum would never have allowed it."

"She is rather high strung at the moment. But I suppose it is understandable behavior, considering." Julianna draws me down beside her and strokes my hand. "So the intruder: your idea?"

I swallow, nod. "I hope it doesn't make things worse. I just couldn't think of anything else. And it seemed as though the bishop was about to maybe – " I swallow again. "Recognize me, or figure out it was Linnet. And I couldn't let him just accuse you of treason, so I just, just-"

"It was quick thinking. I don't know what we'll do

about the intruder. But you managed to turn a very ugly situation around." She smiles and cups my cheek. "Well done, Rhia."

I feel myself blushing.

Patting my face, she sits back, rubbing her chin. "She should have more training. Magic schools are thin on the ground in the region – and closing, or being closed, due to Prophetic edicts. But Hugh was trained by our Grandfather for many years, and could probably keep teaching her. He wrote me he's been showing her the basics."

"His grace is a Healer, too?"

Julianna chuckles. "Oh, no. No, Hugh is a magician. He can cast minor illusions, speak into other's minds, and call Light. His training was different from mine. I don't know how much he can help Linnet. But it's worth a try. I'll speak to him about it after dinner."

I rub my neck, nodding. I am exhausted and sore, and the day is not yet done. Julianna rises, gestures to me.

"Why don't you stay up here with Linnet while I go and see what Connor and Hugh are up to."

I nod gratefully and watch her leave. Traversing the short hallway between the solar and her rooms, I stop outside my door, listening. The only sound I hear is the beating of my own heart.

I enter my small room — now our small room — with some trepidation. Biting my lip, I ease the door closed behind me. The light of a rainy spring day through the small window does little to illuminate anything. I turn the knob on the lamp beside the door to activate the spell and bring the light up.

Linnet lies sprawled on the bed under the window, face down in a pillow, asleep.

I step quietly to her, and ease her boots from her feet. The blanket is stuck under her knee, and I can only imagine the crick she's going to have in her shoulders when she wakes up. But I can't bear to wake her and relive the accusations in her eyes. I slip a blanket off my bed to cover her. When she's sleeping I can pretend that the only family I have left doesn't hate me.

CHAPTER 10

The walls of the long room seem to glow of their own accord, the bindings of the books shining in the morning light from the high windows. I turn slowly, craning my neck to peer at the upper gallery and see more shelves, packed tightly with more books than I've ever seen, apart from the monastery's library. And that I saw only once when we visited Keenan.

Breathing in the musty smell I love, I hug myself tight to keep from touching any of his Grace's books. One thick brown tome lies open on the long table before me, and I can't help leaning over it to see if I know the author.

"I thought I was the only one who liked Perrine around here," a tenor voice sounds behind me.

My hand over my mouth, I whirl to see the duke ensconced in a window seat, the shade drawn behind him. "I-I beg pardon, your Grace. I didn't see you."

"Not to worry. I often lurk." He smiles and stands from the window and approaches me, leaving his book on the seat. Sweeping a bow, he takes my hand in his and passes a kiss over it, as if I were a true lady.

I blush, flustered.

"Come, please sit. I'm glad you could take some time for me today. Julianna tells me that you and Linnet need a teacher."

Blanching, I look around wildly to be certain no one has heard him.

He chuckles mildly as he guides me to a chair. "Don't fret, Lady Rhia. I know this castle, and its denizens. I know when I am being watched, and when I'm not. It's perfectly safe to be frank." Sitting next to me in a brown leather chair, he smiles and leans back.

I try not to gaze helplessly into his eyes — he's as charming as his sister, and as beautiful. Women must fall into his lap.

And men too, I realize as a fleeting vision passes through my head. My cheeks burn fiercely, and I try to pay attention to him as he begins to ask me questions.

"How long has Linnet shown signs of this power? I noticed while traveling with her that she didn't have much control. In fact, I was going to suggest to Julianna that she get some training in it."

"She never had it before, your Grace. I mean, she says she did, a little, but kept it hidden. We're – the guilds are wary of magic in mastersmiths. I didn't know about it. But after – after...." My mouth freezes over the words 'our family' and 'hanged'.

The duke takes my hand and strokes it as I catch my breath, washed over by memories and pain.

"Keenan had magic, and I the Sight, but Linnet was the weaver of the family. And she never showed anyone any magic," I manage to whisper after a few moments.

Hugh continues to stroke my hand. I think I should pull back; it is a liberty, after all. But he seems to mean nothing by it, as if he were comforting his sister, or a child. And it is comforting, and I could use the comfort.

"I think I see. Nevertheless, she should have some training. And you, Julianna says. I'm surprised your family didn't do that for you," he says.

I shake my head. "It was never very strong. I mean, before. It's been stronger … since."

"Since Bishop Gantry?"

I nod. I don't look up to his gaze, but I feel it. He tugs at my sleeve suddenly, and I pull back, startled. My wide eyes meet his friendly but too determined gaze.

"I would like to see the scars, if I may. I might be able to tell something about them," he says.

The edges of the lowest scars peer from beneath my sleeve, pushed nearly to my elbow. Shaking, I pull it back down as I stand and back away.

"My dear, I'm sorry to distress you," Hugh says. I can feel my skin freezing and burning by turns as I tremble. I clear my throat, try to speak, but I can't. I'm not gasping, but I still can't speak.

"I can see that this is too difficult. No matter: I have seen the drawings Connor made."

The what? I stare at him, feel my jaw open, the air rasp in my lungs.

Hugh nods slowly. "Ah, he didn't tell you that. Well. They're your scars; I think you should know. Connor thought they might be a spell of some sort. Or part of one. He made drawings while you were ill enough that Juli thought you might not recover. I don't recognize them. I thought if I saw them more fully – No."

I am shaking my head and backing away. I stop myself and stand firm.

"Cardinal Robere didn't recognize them either. He's going to try to find out more about them, from what Connor sent him. But as he's far from Corat at the moment, it will be difficult. I'll look through our library here, of course. You needn't worry, Lady Rhia. I shan't force you to disrobe." He tries a smile, and I nod, wary.

"As for helping you and your sister with your sudden magical prowess, I'm not exactly a teacher, but I remember the exercises Grandfather taught me. And I'm the best we've got, right at the moment." He catches my eye and smiles again. "I'm not very powerful, not like Julianna is in Healing, but I'll do my best to give you and your sister guidance."

"Thank you, your Grace," I manage to breathe.

"You most definitely do not need to thank me, young lady. You and your sister are people of my duchy, and I owe you both an impossible debt, for not being here to stop the kirche in the first place," he says, his face grave. "I will do my best to make it right." Hugh bows to me, and I curtsey as he takes his leave.

A binding catches my eye as I look across at the shelves: Tamarin's History of Kiras. Da promised to bring me that one in the next wool shipment. I find myself staring at it, tears dripping down my face.

A hand on my shoulder makes me gasp and whirl.

"I didn't mean to startle you," Orrin apologizes. "What's the matter?" he asks, when he sees my face.

"Oh, nothing. Just – memories," I say, wiping at my eyes. "What are you doing in here?"

"Looking for you." He holds out his handkerchief,

and we both chuckle. "I really need to start carrying more of these," I say.

"I've begun keeping three in my pockets." He grins at me.

Our meetings have often been watery as we grieve together about Keenan. But I see tension in his face under his smile. "What is it?"

He takes a deep breath. "I'm going away for awhile."

Relief and regret rush through me. "Oh? Did Cardinal Robere write to you?"

"No. The bishop is taking me on a trip with him."

I find all the relief has drained away, leaving a rushing through my scars that bodes ill. "Where is he taking you?"

"He won't tell me."

"You can't go with him. You have to find a reason not to go." I grip his hand and pull him to the chairs with me.

"How am I supposed to do that? I am the Bishop's acolyte. I have my duties. I'm a junior member of the clergy: I can only do as I am bid. And anyway – this way he's away from you, and maybe I can find out what he's planning."

I shake my head, and he nods his. "What do you mean, what he's planning?" I ask.

"I know he's planning something; I think something dangerous. I don't know what it is, but it's going to be even more dangerous now, since yesterday, after that spell, and the intruder," he stops, raises his eyebrows. "There wasn't an intruder, was there?"

"Of course not. But I couldn't think what else to do!" I sigh and shake my head again. "How did he even end up at Her Highness' chambers, anyway? And those kirche guards with him. What made him come up yelling about treachery and spells?"

"I'd like to know that myself," Connor says from behind us, and Orrin and I both gasp and jump.

"My lord!" I gasp out.

"I thought I told the two of you to meet at those stairs," Connor says.

Orrin bobs his head. "Of course, my lord. Beg pardon, it was my fault." He starts to leave, but Connor grabs his arm, his expression exasperated.

"You're here now, and I checked the hall. There's no one about for the moment. I would like to hear an answer to Lady Rhia's question."

Orrin looks uncomfortable, shrugs. "I'm not sure of the answer. The guards came because he requested them of the Inquisitor's when we rose yesterday. He's been muttering about the princess for days. I told you he's been attempting to spy on Her Highness, my lord."

"I know," Connor says. "Do you have proof beyond your own observation of anything he's doing?"

"No, my lord."

Connor turns and paces a few steps. "What kind of spying? How do you know he's spying?"

"I – I was supposed to use my Sight to find out things. But I think he has other means, I haven't been able to tell him anything – and I've been lying to him about trying. I promise!"

"I believe you, Orrin," Connor says. "But there must be something else he's doing. Or you wouldn't have said so."

"I think … I think he has a watching spell on her rooms. It isn't anything I recognize; nothing I've been taught. But he was certain there was magic, and he was certain of where."

"Her Highness' rooms are shielded," Connor says flatly.

"I know. He's very angry about that. He wants to know what she's hiding, and he thinks he can find out. He's certain she is hiding something. He won't tell me what his plans are, but he rages about her – about her use of magic outside kirche doctrine – I mean, what he considers doctrine. He says she flaunts her connections. Um, meaning you, my lord. And that she's working against the kirche, against the archbishop. That, that she has too much power. That she should not have married Prince Alexander." Orrin trails off, uncertain.

I put my hand out to Connor. "I have tried to See Gantry, to find out his plans. But it – it is hard. He is ... he has strong barriers." I don't try to say demons, and I keep my breath, if barely. I must try to find a way around whatever keeps me from saying it. I must figure out a way to warn them. But I also have to breathe.

Connor is regarding me, and I flush. It can't help him to have someone who panics all the time.

"Gantry wants to take Orrin away with him. We can't let him go, Connor. It's too dangerous." I reach for Orrin's hand, grip it.

Connor looks at our hands. "Where is he going?"

"He says we are to meet some of the laity, do some charity work," Orrin says. "It would be for a week, perhaps two." He shrugs. "So he says. He's being very secretive – I mean, more than usual."

Connor's gaze sharpens, which I thought was impossible. "I see. And he insists you go with him."

"I am his acolyte."

"Of course."

I shift unhappily. "I have a terrible feeling about this. Something really awful is going to happen if you go; I can feel it. I wish you would find a way not to go. Don't you feel the danger?"

Orrin shakes his head. "I feel nothing but a dread of traveling with that terrible man. But maybe I'll learn more of what he intends for her Highness. And – and it gets him away from you. And your sister."

Connor's look is inscrutable. "Could you recognize her?"

"Yes. I knew she was coming, though."

"Maybe it is best you are gone while she settles here. Fewer opportunities for mistakes. She may be sent away before you return, in any case."

I shake my head. "He is planning something terrible. It might be a move against the princess. But it feels focused on you, Orrin. I – that's all I know. It isn't any more clear than that. I think he will hurt you." I turn to Connor, pleading in my eyes.

Connor looks gravely at Orrin. "I could take you somewhere safer tonight. You'd be forsworn from your vows, and I can't guarantee the Cardinal can intercede for you later. But you'd be away from Gantry, and I can guarantee that he won't find you. It's your choice."

Orrin regards us both for awhile. Shaking his head, he sighs. "No, but thank you. I will go with him. Perhaps I will learn nothing. Perhaps he will beat me more. But I will not give up on my vows so easily. I feel the Star Lord and Dorei have called me to this. I will do what I can to stay safe, Rhia. But I won't run away."

I blink back tears of frustration and worry. "This is a mistake, Orrin. I feel it."

"It's not your mistake, Rhia. I'll take my chances." He smiles at me. "Use the handkerchief."

"It's not funny," I mutter, but wipe at my eyes.

"I'll be fine, Rhia. I promise," he says.

"I'm holding you to that," I say fiercely. I glare at him, and then Connor. "And you, too." I shake my arm free of Connor and walk away, before I embarrass myself further. I promise myself that I'll try to find out more about Gantry's plans tonight. Maybe I can learn his plans before something awful happens to Orrin.

CHAPTER 11

Morning drizzle curls and frizzes my hair as I stand on the castle wall. The carriage driving away down the coast road carries Bishop Gantry and Orrin, leaving behind a castle full of dazed servants and not slight disarray. Gantry started his morning with shouted orders that the staff hadn't anticipated. It seems the only people informed of his plans to leave were Orrin and the kirche guards riding with him.

One of whom, I am informed, will report back to Connor. I don't know which one. And the guard can hardly interfere, if Gantry hurts Orrin again. Fear churns in my gut, but there is nothing to do but wait and hope. Hope that the nightmares I had last night about Orrin are only that.

Nightmares of blood, and the demons I can't speak about, and Orrin's terrified face. I wish I never had the Sight. I wish Orrin weren't leaving with this monster.

Father Matthew is to return to giving chapel service here in the castle. I walk down the steps of the inner wall and into the yard, heading for the front hall. On my way to service, I see more servants are heading that way than normal. The services have been thin on attendance since I came. I suspect some have gone into Haverston for kirche instead of suffering through the Bishop's disconcerting stares.

But Father Matthew seems nervous, as well. Not that I knew him before. We do sing a song, one of penitence, and his homily – "Be thou vigilant" – seems shakily given. I don't know what orders the bishop gave, but I see Duchess Marguerite shaking her head when speaking to him, afterward.

I excuse myself from the midst of her ladies. Lady Geneve smiles absently at me, but most take little notice. The six of them are from neighboring minor estates, and are of minor nobility. Since my assumed rank is of a minor family from the north, and they have some resentment I don't understand toward Connor, they have, for the most part, snubbed me.

I am content to let them.

My duties for Julianna are few, as she wants her freedom here at her childhood home, and not chaperonage. And she wants me to concentrate on honing my Sight, and keeping safe. I attend her in the morning, bring her breakfast and help her to dress. Now that Linnet is to be her personal seamstress, which was decided late the night she arrived, no one will suffer from my uneven stitching and poor seaming.

My other duties for Julianna consist of making medicines with her in the herbarium, and bringing them to the sick. Julianna uses her Healing for those that need it most, and gives simples and medicines to others. The people of Haverston seem thankful, but the kirchemen follow her with wary eyes.

The weather is still cold, spring hardly emerging from winter. I am relieved; I can keep my hood up as we ride through town in Julianna's carriage. Haverston seems bare and grim; few people walk the streets, and most of the bright shops look faded, and haven't been repainted yet. Guild members snipe loudly with each other outside the guildhall when we pass, and I keep my head ducked low.

Linnet speaks little to me, and is snappish and sullen by turns. I left her today with the mending, and designs for new gowns and cloaks. Julianna wants to set up a small loom for her in the tower room. Linnet seems resigned to her new role, and ungrateful. But it's hard to be grateful when your life is ruined.

I'm only grateful because I almost lost mine.

Now that Linnet is here, and Hugh has discovered our lack, we are to have lessons, which consist of beginning magics such as Keenan was taught at monastery: shielding of mind and thoughts, sending thoughts to others, drawing magic from wells that gather the wild magic and tame it to a more manageable source. This last Hugh has only a little skill at himself. He mostly uses what is in himself, or is shared with others.

I knew some of these things already, although only in theory, as I was never very strong. Keenan always did most of the magic before. But now I feel power dance along my senses all the time, and Hugh says I should be able to draw from some of the stronger lines of magic.

There is an ancient tale of the First Prophet Dorei blessing these cliffs for hiding her from her enemies, and as she stood and called on the Star Lord, the magic pooled here under her feet. The cliffs in the old language were called Seely Magan, or blessed power. The castle has always glowed a little to my Sight.

The well under the castle is so strong that Hugh says it is difficult even for strong mages to sense magic workings here: the power from the well masks it. Hugh says that our magic was only noticeable when Linnet arrived because of the combination of spells plus our magic. Normally, magic is so imbued in the stones of the castle that one cannot feel most spells.

Hugh is obsessed with barriers, however, and now so am I. I will not be caught and used again. I still don't understand why I can't speak about what Gantry did to me: is it fear only? Or is it part of the spell? Since I cannot ask, I've decided to spend my free time pouring over books in the library. Hugh commends my study habits. Linnet glowers and says unflattering things about bookworms. When I say she never minded before, she glares and denies that I was one.

Today, Hugh sits in front of the tower's narrow windows, resplendent in a dark blue doublet of silk. It's been more than a week since Orrin left, but there has been no word of him. I try to concentrate on Hugh's words about magic flowing, and not the thoughts running in circles in my head.

Also the fact of Hugh's unconscious beauty and conscious charm is distracting enough. I think he knows it. His smiles flirt without meaning to, and his manner is familiar for a duke speaking to daughters of the guilds. But our rank has changed, as he keeps reminding us when we stammer.

Linnet is discontent to be the orphaned daughter of a knight, as Hugh is presenting her – the child of a dear friend, killed in battle. Which means she ranks below me, as the orphaned daughter of a Lord. This is still considerably higher in the instep than our parents' births. We chafe under unknown rules.

I worry we will betray ourselves as imposters, or sisters. We certainly fight like sisters – more than we ever did before. I worry we'll fight in front of strangers. I worry about Linnet's anger and grief. I worry about Orrin. I worry about my magic. I am exhausted with worry.

"Lady Rhia, do pay attention," Hugh says.

I snap my gaze back to him from the window and paste a smile on my face. "I'm sorry, your grace. What were you saying?"

"I want you to let your barriers down just enough to receive a sending from me, and then raise them again. But don't lower them until you feel me ask."

"What does that feel like?" asks Linnet. She can't send yet. Hugh thinks she might be able to, but it isn't something she's figured out. I feel some relief at that.

"It feels like an internal nudge," he says, and then I feel it. Although to me it feels like a tingle, a shiver, a plucked thread puckering in my mind. Keenan's sends were softer, but I knew him better. I lower my barriers from the tight lockdown I put them in, after Hugh showed me where I was leaking before. I need much tighter barriers than I ever used to.

Hugh's sending comes to me as a feeling – expectation – along with the words from a children's rhyme. I snap my barriers shut again – I feel so much safer with them shut – and recite the rhyme back to him.

"Very good. I know you used to do this with your brother. But you and I should get used to each other, if you're to help Juli and me out. Why don't you send me something back. Anything is fine."

Linnet mutters something about showing off. I roll my eyes and ignore her. I decide to send Hugh a memory of Linnet throwing a tantrum when she was a baby. For perspective, I think. Although she outgrew them after toddlerhood – until recently – she was a champion tantrum thrower in her day.

I lower my barriers again, and try to nudge Hugh the way I would have Keenan.

Hugh rocks back in his seat, hands to his head. "Not so hard, Lady Rhia! That hurts!"

I pull back on the power, but it seems to push at me. It pushes harder the more I pull it back, and suddenly I'm in a vision that rolls through my lowered barriers, rolls through my mind, and takes over.

Orrin lies strapped to a table in a dark room. Above him, Bishop Gantry chants sharp words that tear at my memory, tremble through the vision. Gantry holds a knife. Orrin's eyes are bleak and empty, and I am frantic with fear for him.

I have to get him out, stop this. I come to myself, yelling, trying to run out of the tower room. Hugh holds me hard by the waist, and Linnet pulls at my arm.

I go limp, panting in Hugh's grip. He stops his own shouting, and turns me around.

"Rhia, where is that? I got some of it, is it a true sending?" His hands clench hard on my shoulders. "Do you know where that is?"

Shaking, crying, I can only shake my head. I need to find Connor, Connor must know where they are.

"I had to shield myself from most of the vision; you were wide open and sending. I shielded the entire room, just in case. Your Sight is that powerful, I thought the whole castle might feel it if I didn't, Lady Rhia."

I shudder, sick with reaction and fear. "Don't call me that," I say, suddenly tired of pretend, tired of everything. I want to lie down on the cot. I stumble toward it, flinching away from Hugh and Linnet. I want desperately to be alone.

"Don't call you lady?" Hugh asks. "Lady – Rhia. It is your title now. You-"

"Well, she doesn't like it," Linnet snaps. "Just leave her alone." Her face is tight and angry, which means she's worried. I feel a little grateful she could be worried for me.

Hugh's mouth sets in a grim line. "It doesn't matter if she likes it. That's her title. She needs to get used to it. As do you," he says, then he sighs. "But it isn't important if we're alone, I suppose. It's not as though we're following the rules of strict propriety in any case." He sits gingerly beside me on the cot.

My breath is coming easier and with less pain.

Linnet glares at us both. "Well, what did you See? I didn't get any of it," she says. "I felt you being scared, but I didn't see anything."

"Rhia, can you tell the whole vision?" Hugh asks.

I close my eyes, wipe my face, try to gather my breath. "Orrin is in trouble. The Bishop-" and I can't breathe again; I can only shudder and cry.

"I saw him strapped to a table," Hugh says quietly.

"Who is Orrin?" Linnet asks, her voice sharp.

My eyes fly open. I didn't tell her yet.

Her eyes narrow when I look at her, feeling guilty.

"He's a friend of your sister," Hugh starts.

I open my mouth to tell her about Keenan, but she erupts in outrage.

"Your friend? You made a friend here already? After our parents were killed because of you, and Keenan too, and you're up here making friends?" She is yelling fit to rouse the castle. I hope Hugh shielded this room for noise, as well.

"Linnet, he was Keenan's friend first, from seminary, and he-"

"So you thought you'd just endanger everyone by making friends with him too? Or does he not know about you?"

I can't take her tone anymore. "He recognized me! I was going to tell you, but he left two days after you got here, and you've been sulking and not talking to me, so when was I supposed to mention him? It's not like you want to listen to what I have to say!" I yell, overcome with everything, with the unfairness of it all. "And the important thing is we have to go rescue him! Not how hurt you are!"

She stands a moment, her jaw grinding in fury.

Hugh tries to make a soothing noise over our harsh breathing.

Linnet shoots him scathing glare. "Like you rescued me?" she snarls quietly, and storms out of the tower.

Trembling, I fight more tears. My head and eyes ache, which is becoming very familiar, I cry so often now.

Hugh pats my back, tries to speak to me, but I'm not listening.

"You have to tell Connor," I say. "He has to find them. He said he would know where they were. I knew this would go wrong, I told Orrin not to go."

I hear the tower door open again. Looking up, I see Julianna framed in the doorway. She takes in the scene – my pinched face, Hugh's attempts at comfort, and shakes her head.

"Hugh, why don't you find Connor and tell him what happened. Rhia is right about that." When we look at her in surprise, she smiles. "I caught Linnet on the way down. I sent her to your room, Rhia, so she can calm down. She told me some of it."

Hugh stands after patting my back again. "I hope no one else heard her," he says, furrowing his brow.

"Not today. And with Gantry gone, I don't fear spies in the corners so much," she replies.

"We should." Hugh raises his brow at her.

She shrugs. "We'll have another conversation with her about discretion. Do send Connor to me once you've had a word," she says, a clear dismissal.

Hugh shakes his head as he leaves. Julianna sits where he vacated.

My breathing is better, but I snuffle into Orrin's crumpled handkerchief. At this rate, I should carry more than one.

"My poor Rhia. Magic hasn't been so kind to you lately, has it?"

I shake my head. "It's not me we should worry about right now. Orrin –" and I take a breath, fight the paralysis that creeps onto me. "Orrin needs help. He's in so much trouble, your highness. Please, please send Connor to help him."

"I promise we'll do what we can for him. Can you use your Sight to see anything else? Anything that might help Connor find Bishop Gantry. Or help us to convict him, when it comes to it." She looks steadily at me. "I need proof of his actions, Rhia. Moreover, I need proof of conspiracy. If anyone else was there, is helping him in this – if you can help me prove it, I can stop him all the sooner."

I let go of my barriers a little, but the power whirls around me like a top, and dizzy exhaustion drops over me. I drag my barriers to me again with what energy I have left, feeling bruised. "The visions won't come now," I say. "What I saw, what I saw was … ask Hugh. But there wasn't anyone else there. Just the bishop and Orrin. And the room is dark, and I can't tell you anything else. I'll try later, I will, but Connor said he'd know where they are. He had someone with them. He promised."

Julianna shakes her head. "He told me a few days ago – Bishop Gantry sent the guards away after one night. When Connor's man tried to go back later, they were gone, and we don't know where."

"What? Why didn't you tell me?"

"Hush, now. I told Connor not to tell you. I knew you would only worry. Connor has someone looking – discreetly – for them. But we can't break down doors or invade kirche yards in the search. We can't tip our hands like that."

I curl my hands into fists, stare at the floor. "We have to be careful, Rhia. But if you See any hint at all, let one of us know right away."

I can only nod tightly, my lips pressed together. I want to yell that she should have told me, but she is a princess, and I am a dead witch.

Julianna pats my shoulder in sympathy, and gets up to leave. "We'll do everything we can for Orrin. Why don't you rest for awhile, then come down for a meal.

Some food will help your headache." I look up at her, and she smiles softly. "Healer, remember? Come down in time for lunch." She leaves.

I stare at the tiny window, seeing nothing, consumed with worry. Gantry is using Orrin in the same spell he tried on me. If it isn't happening now, it will happen soon. Even if he weren't my friend, it is an evil spell. I have to find them.

CHAPTER 12

The light dims as I round the corner from the chapel to this back corridor. Dark stone reaches high and damp above me, and only one lamp persuades away the darkness. Gantry's rooms are here, the door to the apse only a few strides away. His essence permeates the air like a hissed invective – poisonous and painful, for all he hasn't lived in the castle long.

I can't feel Orrin in the air at all. My stomach lurches at the thought of my intentions, but I steel myself to the task.

If I have any hope of finding out where Gantry took Orrin, I need to do this. Linnet suggested searching his rooms. Connor, of course, has already done so, and he said he found nothing. At least, nothing relating to Orrin's whereabouts. I hope my Sight can provide more information. Julianna and Connor did not say yes, but they did not say no, either.

I take a determined, if shaky, breath.

Putting my hands on the door, I let the essence of the rooms wash over me. Turmoil, anger, pain: nothing definite. Opening my eyes, I press the latch. It doesn't budge.

"It's locked," I hear from behind me.

I gasp and whirl around.

Linnet stands tucked behind a pillar further down the hall. "I checked already. I almost had it open when you interrupted me." Her tone is annoyed, but her eyes betray her nervousness.

I let out a shaky breath. Strangely, I feel less sick with her here.

"Well, let's open it now, then," I whisper.

Linnet raises her eyebrows for a second, then rolls her eyes and stalks to the door. She mutters to herself as she holds the latch, which glows slightly. Sweat breaks out on her forehead and her arms shake.

After a bit, I put my hand on her shoulder, thinking to tell her to ease up. From my arm, I feel a sharp pull and a dizziness, and the lock flares bright green and clacks. Both of us jump a little.

Linnet shrugs off my hand, and we look nervously down the hall. She reaches for the door and I reach to stop her.

"Wait," I breathe.

"Until someone else comes?" she asks, her tone derisive. She pushes open the door, breezing into Gantry's chamber, and I freeze, certain some horrible trap will spring. An eternity standing there with my breath held, until she whispers, "Don't just stand there like a ninny!"

I wobble with nerves. Little jogging steps rush me into the chamber, and I push the door closed behind me.

Linnet stands in front of a long table, looking at jars with painted runes in brown and red and black.

"We have to be careful," I say as I look for something

to focus on, for a vision. So far I only feel nervous and unhappy. Not as helpful as I'd like.

"I know that. I looked for trap spells, the way Hugh told us, before I even opened the door. I'm not stupid."

"I didn't say you were stupid." I roll my eyes at her.

"Started seeing things yet?" Linnet asks drily. She pushes past me further into the rooms.

I move in front of deep shelves stuffed with papers and tomes thicker than a man's thigh, dried animal skulls and mysterious, dusty things.

Daylight filters through the heavy brown drapes on the west-facing window, highlighting clean swept slate floors, an immaculate writing desk, and a door to the bedchamber. I am nervous about touching anything, but I start looking through papers and scrolls in the bookcase. One of the scrolls looks ancient, and when I peer at the writing it's full of swirly script in a language I don't recognize.

For a moment I See the guildhall, figures walking, hear voices. One of them is Gantry's, he is asking about provisions, pointing at maps. Before I can make anything out, I fall out of the vision. I try to pull it back, but the magic is jagged in my veins, agitated. I open my eyes and look around.

The door to Gantry's sleeping chamber is slightly ajar. I leave the scrolls to peer into darkness, heavy curtains covering the windows of the smaller room. But I can make out a large bed next to one wall, the curtains drawn around it as well, and a pallet on the floor at the foot.

Slightly glowing runes surround the pallet. In the darkness they glower a faint amethyst, sickly and sinister. I feel a pull on my soul, as though I had no choice but to lie down there.

I shiver and start to back away.

"This room feels funny. Surely you're getting something from this place." Linnet pushes me a little, moves me into the bedchamber. She turns and looks at me, her eyebrows raised. "Try it. Come on."

I sigh and close my eyes. Pulling my magic into my center, I lower my shields just a little. My unease expands into a deep horror and a desire to run. I See the room with Gantry in it, chanting, painting runes in what looks like blood around the walls. Demons curl through the room as a vaporous menace, chittering in a language I half-understand. I feel myself backing away, shutting down. I yank my shields back in place and open my eyes.

Linnet stands near the wall where I saw Gantry drawing the runes. Idly she levitates a piece of marble in her hand, lets it drop. She looks up in question at my gasping. "Well, what did you See?"

"Come away from there," I snap in panic. I can feel a gathering power in the room, shadowing the now invisible runes on the walls.

"Why?" she looks around, starts to straighten.

"Linnet, there's a trap!" I say, and it springs. The air goes still and muffled, like underwater.

I can see the spell moving inward from the walls, and Linnet is engulfed by the first wave. I reach out to her as I back away – I can't stop myself from backing away – but she is stuck, immobilized.

I send to Hugh as I watch her wide, frightened eyes – *Help me! Help now, Gantry's rooms.*

The wave moves toward me as I shuffle backward,

amethyst and blood red streaked and weaving darkness. I pull power from the well beneath me with rough abandon. It burns as I push against the weave, the runes. I don't know what they mean, I don't know what the chittering means, but I can almost tell how they're woven together, how they're holding Linnet in a web of stillness.

I throw my will against the spell, snatch at the rough places, the trailing ends. Hands out, just outside the spell, I can feel the spell warp like ripping fabric. I catch at the fraying edges of the runes, attach my magic to the raveling threads, and yank carefully. I'm not certain what will happen when it collapses, but it has to be better than letting it alone. I hope.

"Just a moment, little bird, just hold on a moment," I whisper, concentrating. Linnet's face tells me I'd better hurry.

I hear the door crash open, and people, but I can't look away from what I'm doing.

"Rhia, what's going on?" Hugh appears beside me. "No, no, not like that. Like this," and I feel him slip his magic into the work like adding wool to a spindle, start to direct it, although the power is still mine. It feels a little like our lessons, except the amount of power – and the amount of terror I feel – are so much greater.

The spell collapses with a sound like breaking glass and a smell of burned hair, and Linnet is free. I wobble where I stand, panting, until I'm whiled around to face Connor.

"You little fool! What were you thinking? I told you I'd searched these rooms! What did you think you could find?"

I hear Linnet snuffling, glance over to see Hugh

checking her for injury, holding her face in his hands. "I thought it would help me with a vision. If I See something, I can help you find Orrin."

"And I did find something," Linnet grates out. "Here." She hold out a piece of vellum – an invitation, it looks like. Connor snaps it from her fingers.

"An invitation to a party – several months away, I might add. I saw this already," he says, his face severe. "This tells us nothing." He stalks to the desk, where Linnet must have found it.

"We should get out of here," Hugh says. "Take the girls to Julianna. I'll … try to deal with this. I might be able to repair the spell…"

"Don't bother. Just make sure he can't trace any of it to us. We might have to ban him from the castle. Let me know what we need to do." Connor glares at both of us.

My head spins, and my knees tremble with reaction. My lungs hurt and the scars on my body hum like pins and needles. I look at Linnet. "You're all right?"

She shrugs, nods, and starts to walk away.

Hugh looks at me. "How did you even begin –" he stops, narrows his eyes. "The amount of magic you used to pull this spell apart, Rhia. Where did it come from?"

I don't understand this question. I used the power he showed me how to use. "The power well under the castle. You said to use it, since I could."

"Yes, but – but this much! Rhia, that is too much magic to handle safely! You have to be more careful."

Linnet turns, sneering. "I thought you knew she was a witch, your grace," she says. "Isn't that why you're keeping us?"

"Linnet," I warn, but she isn't listening.

"Aren't we just doing what you wanted? We're here for your amusement, and aren't we amusing?"

"You're here by the generosity of Her Highness," Connor snarls. "So watch your tongue when speaking to her, or to his grace. And you," he says, turning to me. "I no longer wonder how it is you managed to land in so much trouble in the first place. I now wonder how you stayed out of it for so long!"

I draw in a sharp breath, angry tears pushing at my eyes. But before I can retort, Linnet does.

"That's not fair!" she shouts, and we all stop and look at her. She flushes a deep red. "Well, it's not." She folds her arms.

Connor folds his as well, purses his lips. "Perhaps not." He takes a deep breath. "My apologies, Lady Rhia. Let me escort you to your rooms." He gestures and offers me his arm.

I am too shaky to manage a stiff curtsey, so I stiffly nod my head. Both of us clench-jawed with anger, I place my hand on his arm and allow him to take my weight. Partly because I am too tired suddenly to walk so far without help.

Hugh and Linnet follow, muttering to each other.

When we get to Julianna's rooms, we find her at her writing desk in the solar. She looks up at us, her expression quizzical. I'm sure my expression is sour: I don't bother to look at anyone else's.

"Is something amiss?" she asks us.

Connor deposits me in the nearest chair and bows slightly. "It seems these two took it upon themselves to check my work, my lady," he says. Which isn't fair – I was trying to help.

Linnet sulks in the corner. Hugh stands next to his sister and shrugs.

"What do you mean by that? I felt a surge of power a little while ago. But I thought you were working on lessons again. I was going to speak to you about shielding, Hugh. If I can feel these things in a shielded room – and I know at least a few staff have small magics..."

Hugh shakes his head. "Not lessons, Juli. Rhia and Linnet broke into the Bishop's rooms, and fell into a trap spell."

"They what? What happened?"

"Rhia managed to pull enough power to slow it down until I got there. I didn't call on you since no one was hurt."

Julianna's eyes seem to take up most of her face, but the rest of her expression is stern. "What were you girls even doing in there?"

"You wanted me to use my Sight to find out more. I was trying to do that," I say quietly.

Everyone stares at me.

Shrugging one shoulder, I look away, pick at the embroidery of a pillow. "Someone has to find Orrin."

"And did you?" asks Julianna.

"Not yet. But I Saw a map."

"What map? What was on it?" Hugh asks.

"I don't know, it wasn't clear enough." I stare at my hands, refusing to look at anyone. Anger and humiliation burn in my gut. And fear – for me, for Linnet, for Orrin. For all of us. I wish I knew what I was doing. And this spell on my body, I wish I knew what it was, and why I can't tell anyone anything important. It's becoming very hazardous to my health, and everyone else's opinion of me.

"Why would the two of you go in there on your own? Why wouldn't you just come to me?" Julianna reaches out a hand to me, but it's Linnet who answers.

"You would have just said no. And anyway, no one got hurt."

"You might have been seriously hurt, or compromised everyone's safety!" Julianna snaps. "I don't know what you were thinking. And what do you expect from us? We've taken you in, hidden you from harm, provided for you-"

"As long as we're useful," Linnet snarls.

I bite my lips hard as Julianna looks taken aback. I stand and walk over to Linnet, take her hand. She pulls away, but I stay next to her.

"Orrin is in trouble," I say, emphasizing each word. "I wanted to try for a better vision, for information. Linnet was helping me. You weren't."

Connor steps toward us, his shoulders stiff. "I've been searching everywhere for information that will help him."

I flush and look away.

"I will not compromise everyone's safety to do it. And I can't find him if I don't know where to look! If you want a vision of him so badly, then you come to me. I can take you into Gantry's rooms safely. Do not – under any circumstances – take such an action again without checking with me first!"

Hugh clears his throat. "Or me, or Juli, of course. One of us."

Connor shakes his head. "No. Check with me. You two are almost as bad. The lot of you are going to get us all killed, and endanger the crown."

Julianna and Hugh both look shocked. Her eyes narrow first. Linnet and I both step back.

"I had no idea you felt so ill used by me, Connor. I thought you agreed to help me when we arranged to come here, which by extension helps the crown; the crown of our king, Peter. Or is it Alexander you're so concerned for? You remember the prince, my husband?" Her voice is quiet and cutting.

Connor's back is already straight, but his lips go gray. "My duty is first and foremost to the crown and country of Talaria. As always, your Highness." He bows deeply and leaves the room, and not a one of us breathes until he is gone.

Hugh stirs. "That was unkind, Julianna." He sighs and walks to the door. "You should be more careful. I'll talk to him. But you will have to, as well." He leaves.

Linnet turns and leaves the room as well, just walks back into the hall and is gone. Still feeling weak and wobbly, I contemplate heading for my room and taking a nap. But Julianna pins me with a look, and I don't think I'm going to get out that easily.

"Oh, sit down; you look like you're about to fall over," she says. "I don't want anyone saying I don't take care of my ladies. You should probably eat. Did you even get lunch?" She gestures to a tray.

I shake my head and sit down.

Julianna surveys me from her seat. "I'm afraid Connor is right about some things. You can't just take these actions without talking to us first. We have plans in place that you know nothing about. That we can't tell you about, to keep you safe. But we need you to keep us safe, as well. Do you understand what I'm saying?"

"Yes, your highness," I say. "But I can't just leave Orrin in danger, if I can help it."

"Rhia, we don't even know if your vision was a true one."

"Yes, I do know it. I can tell! He-" and I can't breathe again, I'm gasping and my skin burns and I can't find a way around this spell that keeps me from telling the important things.

Julianna gets up and comes to my side. "There, you see? You're overset. And I can't blame you. But we have to be realistic, my dear." She sits next to me, pats my back while I work to regain my breath.

Tears pour down my face, and I am astonished, when I look up, to see tears in hers. "I do want to find him, and help him. I do. But the safety of everyone is here is paramount. Especially those who are entirely innocent. Like yourself, young lady, and your sister. And..." she trails off, one hand on her belly.

I blink at her a few times.

"I need to stay safe, as well. For the sake of my children, Rhia. For this child in particular."

Shaking my head, I put my hand over hers. "Your Highess," I whisper. "I didn't know."

"I know." She smiles at me, cups my chin. "I haven't told anyone, yet. I wanted to be sure it wouldn't - my powers don't really work so well on myself. I have miscarried before." She sighs, shakes her head. "I'm keeping it quiet for now.

"Everything is in such an uproar. And my husband ... it's best if when I do tell, I'm seen being very quiet at my family's estate, for the duration. I must seem modest and retiring."

I open my mouth, shut it, and she smiles more. "I

know," she says, "But it must appear so. So please, when I ask that you take care, know that I want you to take care for all of us. But I'm feeling very vulnerable, too. Please, Rhiannon, help me to take care."

I let her stroke my cheek, and I lean into her touch, tears leaking out of my eyes. "I will, your highness. I will."

CHAPTER 13

Another week goes by. Julianna doesn't want to tell anyone about her pregnancy, not even Hugh. But now that I know, it seems obvious – she has been tired, and her gowns are getting tight. If she weren't already curvy and pretty, it wouldn't be a secret at all. When I point out that everyone will figure it out sooner or later, she waves me away and tells me to go learn something useful.

I worry she is pushing herself too hard, but I don't know enough about it. I wonder if I should tell Hugh. Or Connor, or her mother. But it is her decision, not mine. I can't bring myself to betray a secret she seems so determined to keep.

I tell Linnet to let out her gowns a little, and I think she guessed. But being Linnet, she just shrugs and rolls her eyes, muttering to herself. Probably insults.

I've decided if I can't make them out, then I don't have to respond. It helps. And snide comments about my lack of sewing skills are old habit from my family.

Easy to brush off. Da made the same tired joke every time I got near unfinished fabric.

Linnet adds the gowns to her growing pile of mending, while on the sly making a tapestry, which is Julianna's family present for the Solstice celebration in a few weeks. Julianna is avaricious about using Linnet's talents with cloth while she has access to them. She's planning several elaborate gowns and gifts.

This morning Julianna rushes around her rooms, getting ready for her ride to the hospice. Normally I would go with her, but today she wants me to stay and work on my Sight. I think she just doesn't want me to nag at her to take it easy while Healing.

"Just find my gloves for this riding outfit, Rhia. And don't tell me to eat again. Those eggs turn my stomach, and the oatmeal has gone cold."

"They're good for you, your highness," I try.

But she shakes her head. "Then you eat it. Bring me my riding boots, please."

"At least eat the oatmeal."

Julianna shudders. "Not cold."

"It wouldn't have been cold if you'd eaten it when I brought it up." I stare her down. "And the goat's milk, as well. You made me drink it."

She scowls.

"Fair is fair," Connor remarks from the doorway.

Both Julianna and I startle, although I at least don't squeak. Julianna scowls at him.

"Connor! You can't just come in here without knocking."

"I did knock. You didn't hear me. Possibly because of all the noise you were making about cold oatmeal. Rhia has a point, you know. About it not being her fault that it's cold."

"You did not knock, you liar."

"I'm a royal liar: I only lie for the crown," he says.

She sticks her tongue out at him, and he makes a face back.

I stare at the both of them, taken aback.

"Julianna, eat your breakfast. What would your mother say," he teases.

"You wouldn't tell my mother."

"Watch me. Rhia, I need to speak with you when you have a chance."

He winks at Julianna and leaves.

"He'd better not tell my mother," Julianna says darkly.

I hand her the boots. "Did he – did he just make … jokes?"

Julianna plops herself down in front of the breakfast tray. "I hate eggs. What? Oh. Yes – he is capable of it, you know. He used to be a lot less stern before … before we all grew up, I guess. We used to have such fun."

She smiles fondly. "He used to come up with the best pranks. But that was a long time ago. I suppose he has become rather serious recently. And you haven't seen him under the happiest of circumstances, either." She plays with the cooling oatmeal, sighs. "Can I get some that's hot, at least?" She makes eyes at me, and I roll mine. "Please?"

"Fine, I'll go get more. But don't you dare leave before I come back." I step out of her bedchamber.

Connor waits for me in the solar, staring out the windows into the gardens. When I walk in he turns to me, an almost happy expression on his face.

"I wanted to tell you first. Gantry and Orrin were spotted late last night on the road back to Haverston." He nods when I open my mouth. "He seems healthy, from a distance. He's getting in and out of the coach by himself, and speaks when spoken to. He's quiet and keeps his head down, but that's normal for him when he's with Gantry."

I feel dizzy with relief. "Oh, Connor, that's wonderful to hear! Thank you," I say, my smile hurting my cheeks, it has been so long since I felt one there. "Oh, I could kiss you!"

He blinks at me a couple of times, starts to smile.

I flush and stammer. "I, I mean, uh, thank you, my lord, um-"

"I'm glad to give welcome news for a change."

I nod, and he takes a deep breath. "It seems unlikely that your vision was a true one, given his evident lack of injury."

I hadn't thought of that. But I'm glad, even if it means my visions can't be trusted. "I'd rather Orrin is safe, than be right," I say. I reach forward and grab Connor's hand. "Thank you for telling me. That was kind of you." I feel his hand warm in mine.

He looks at them, our joined hands, and I realize I'm staring, too.

I whisk mine away, clear my throat. "When, when are they expected back?"

"Sometime late this afternoon, most likely. They broke their journey late at an inn. My informant rode into the morning to bring me the news."

"Did he know where they've been?"

He shakes his head. "It's likely they went to an old monastery up the coast. I have people checking it out.

We're looking for any evidence of what may have happened, anyone they may have met. But they are coming back."

"I'll keep an eye out for them. Thank you my lord!" I smile at him, my shoulders feeling more loose by the second, even with Gantry returning to the castle.

Connor smiles back, and I curtsey, practically skip to the door.

I have to force myself to remember what I was doing. Oh, yes. Oatmeal for Julianna. I'll beg some spice, as well. I'm so happy I could sing, but I know I'll be out of breath just going down and up the stairs.

I don't care. Orrin is safe. I shake my head at myself. For the moment. But it's a moment I'll take.

The clatter of hooves on cobblestones snaps me out of my reverie; I've been standing on the castle walls, staring at the road out of town for some time. Only I guess I've let my mind wander.

A carriage rumbles into the courtyard below. I try to seem casual as I make my way down the inner stair near the stables.

Gantry steps out of the carriage first, waving irritably at the castle guards. A kirche guard makes his way over, and Gantry begins gesturing, speaking to him. I hang back, eyes on the carriage door.

After a few moments, Orrin makes his way slowly out. He stands behind Gantry, head down. I keep hoping he'll look up, but he doesn't. I don't know how to catch his eye without catching everyone else's, too.

He looks exhausted. His dark skin seems papery

and gray, even at this distance, and his shoulders slump. He grips his own hands as if he were holding himself together. Whatever happened, it wasn't pleasant.

I start walking quietly past the stables, toward the courtyard. He doesn't look up.

I'm not looking, either, it turns out, as I bump into Connor.

He steadies me, then offers his arm. "Shall we stroll, cousin?" he asks. I venture a small smile.

"It is kind of you to walk with me, cousin." Our strolling near the stables is a little odd, but no one seems to be paying attention.

Orrin still doesn't look up, even when the carriage is led off behind him.

"Something is wrong," I murmur.

"Give it time, Rhia. You don't know what part he's had to play these last weeks." We continue our stroll into the gardens.

I sigh with frustration when I can't see them anymore.

Connor shakes his head. "Give it longer than that. In fact, wait until dinner, then wait at the tunnel stairs. He'll likely look for you there."

I look at my shoes. "I will, but something is wrong; I can feel it."

"Maybe. But until we know what that is, there's nothing we can do. I'll have people keeping eyes on them. Try to use your Sight, if you can. But fretting about information you don't have won't help anyone."

I resist the urge to scuff my feet, but only just. Scowling, I admit he's right. "Fine." I'm not very gracious about it.

"Go on inside. If you can't be discreet, go wait at the stairs now."

I let Connor's arm go with little grace, and head indoors. After half-heartedly wandering around the library for a time, I head for the stairs. I wait for hours, but Orrin never comes.

———

I wait for Orrin at the rendezvous stairs for hours every day over the coming weeks. I wait in vain.

Connor shakes his head when I ask him if he's spoken with Orrin – but Orrin is almost never out of Gantry's presence these days. And Gantry almost never leaves his rooms, except to go to the Inquisitor's building. Father Matthew continues with the chapel services, telling us Bishop Gantry is preparing for the Solstice celebration.

Connor's people report to him that the monastery is abandoned and crumbling, but it's obvious people were staying there recently. They found remains of food and charcoal in a fire pit. And a lot of dried blood and bandages. My heart sinks when he tells me.

Time I don't spend waiting for Orrin I spend in the library, or in the Star Chambers, trying to delve into Gantry's mind. Sitting underneath the feet of the statue of Dorei, who smiles benevolently at me from her voluminous cape, I push my power to show me something, anything, of Orrin, or Gantry. I spin my power into thin threads, trying to wind Gantry's thoughts around skeins of my making.

But all I catch are his vague mutterings of self-right-eousness: he is ordained, the Star Lord speaks through him. Who is this witch to thwart him? I get no sense of what he plans, or if someone is planning for him. Only that he believes Julianna a vessel of true evil that must be removed from power.

I can't sense Orrin at all.

Other visions contain themselves to glimpses of the past, or Gantry reading old books in languages I don't understand. It isn't helpful, as Julianna points out. She can't remove Orrin without proof, although she did write again to Cardinal Robere.

"We have to do these things properly, Rhia. Wrong moves could ruin so many of our plans. The kirche is very powerful, in this country and others. We cannot risk offense."

I don't think she's right: how could leaving Orrin in such danger be right? But I bite my tongue, try to find something.

Connor wants more information, as well. He wants Julianna safe. But Julianna waves him off, too. She doesn't want to warn Gantry, and thus the rest of whatever conspiracy may be working against us, that she might be aware of them.

I push myself to headaches, all for naught. If I could only speak about the demons, that would be evidence enough, I feel sure. But something keeps me silent on that score. I'm afraid I've been cursed or tainted by the demon magic, and I don't know how to find out. I've been looking for what the runes I bear mean in the library. So far I haven't found anything that tells me. Maybe it's a demon language. I pray to Keenan to intercede with Dorei for me. I pray not to be cursed.

Meanwhile, the servants whisper speculation on Princess Julianna's Healing powers. She Heals the sick, but they often become sick again. Can her powers be for the Light? She is no ordained priest, but she is noble. Nobility is ordained by the Star Lord, some argue. But with so many turning toward a harder form of worship, Julianna's Healing looks suspicious. Dark looks follow us on our outings to the hospice and away again.

I wonder what those people would think if they knew an ordained bishop was summoning demons.

The morning of the summer Solstice dawns dreary and cold. I can hear Dawnsongs being sung in the courtyard – I did not observe dawn services, and no one asked me to. Connor was going to go.

I curl into my blankets, not relishing the idea of today. What with the extra, outside services, and the feast later, it will be a long day. I hope it doesn't pour rain all day.

Linnet isn't in her bed – she either rose to go to Dawnsong, or she went to work on the tapestry for Duchess Marguerite and Hugh. Julianna wants to present it this evening, after dinner. It will be her family present.

I asked Connor for some pocket money, so I could find something for Linnet. She's my only family, now. It's the summer after her fourteenth birthday, so she should be getting something special. I couldn't go into the shops to look – too afraid someone would recognize me. So Connor brought me a lovely little star pendant for her. Thinking of it, I rise and rummage through my drawer, find the linen package.

After washing my hands and face, I'm pulling on my

dress when I feel a surge of magic. It dances along my nerves and chitters like demons. The whole room seems to hum with it, and I hear a cry from Julianna.

Tripping over my feet, I rush to Julianna's bedchamber. I find her huddled in her bed, clutching her middle. She looks at me through tangled blond hair.

I can still feel the spell humming.

"Rhia, call for Hugh! I can't – I need all my strength. Quick! Help me – help me fight this off. I have to concentrate on the baby." And she curls further over.

I can see a blue aura surrounding her, through a haze of brown and purple fog that seems to be seeping into the room.

I start to send to Hugh, to work with the shields on the room as he taught me, and find those shields in tatters. I can feel the ends waving loose, the foreign spell charging through. My sending is not gentle. I feel him jump, start to run, his questions in my head.

What happened? Who is doing this?

Gantry. It must be, I send, and I'm sure I'm right, but I have no proof. When he asks how, I try to send some thought of demons, but my mind blanks and I can't breathe, and I'm holding the doorway for balance.

Julianna glances up. "What's happening? Where's Hugh?"

"Coming," I gasp, and concentrate on trying to weave the ends of the room shield together, make a barrier for Julianna, push the demon spell out. I don't know what I'm doing, but I work on instinct, which Hugh always tells me is my friend.

The demon spell circles Julianna, surrounds her, fills the room. And the castle, I realize, seeming to come from all around, although Julianna seems to be the focus. How did he make a spell so huge?

I grasp at the power-well beneath the castle, feel it burning and strong, like scalding water, like rope burns. Panting, I gather a little of it into a swirl and pull at the spell, spinning it like a spinning wheel, making it all into my thread, and not Gantry's.

It hurts, all this power. The magic fights me, aims for its purpose. Whatever that purpose might be, it can't be good, as it sings in its horrifying voice, sounding like ice storms, like fire on the water. It wants to bind Julianna, but I can't tell to what, and I keep pulling, keep spinning, creating my own spell thread. I unravel the danger as best I can.

I feel Hugh beside me now, feel his power reinforce mine. His power feels so small next to demons and power-wells, fighting all this chaos. But he is like a perfect knife: he knows what to cut and where. He disables the spell as I unravel it, and it falls apart. A deep, bone shaking snap, and the spell is gone.

Hugh and I both stumble toward Julianna on the bed. He reaches her first. She still holds onto her Healing, now in a trance. He puts a hand out, and I watch him try to sink in with her.

I'm not sure what to do next.

Hugh opens his eyes, finds me. "I don't know what's happened, but she's dealing with it as best she can. Go find Connor. Tell him what happened. Tell him – oh, great Lord." He closes his eyes again, shakes his head, his face pale and drawn. "Tell him about the baby," he says.

"You know?

"I do now. And from the spell, so does Gantry. If that was him. And it was, wasn't it?"

I raise my hands – I have no proof, he knows that.

He rubs his free hand over his face. "You're good with Connor," he says, which is news to me. "Try and break it gently. And get him here sooner than later. I need his help."

I turn to go, but he puts a hand on my arm. "Later, you and I are going to have a discussion about a few things."

"Like the baby?" I ask.

"Among other things," he says. "Also how you managed that much magic. And where you sent it."

I shake my head. I don't have any words for him. It just went. I don't know what I did, or how.

Feeling shuddery and cold, I run to Connor's rooms, which are empty. Lungs and legs aching, I hurry through halls that are starting to fill with servants and others, coming in from Dawnsong, heading to their duties. All of them look perturbed, but I need to find Connor. He must not have come in, yet. I head for the west barbican, and see him at the far wall overlooking the water.

The wind is brisk against my skin. I didn't bring a shawl or a cloak. And my feet are only in wool stockings, which are now sodden on the bottom. It's a poor solstice dawn, cold and wet and the smell of a storm out at sea. We should have kinder weather by now.

Connor turns when I pass the fire pit, waits for me to reach him. He doesn't give me a chance to catch my breath. "I think Gantry might try something today. We need to try to get to Orrin. It's clear he can't get away from the bishop right now. I watched closely during Dawnsong. Orrin was – he looked very wrong. You were right, Rhia. We need to get to him."

"He – he – spell," I gasp out, and Connor grabs my arms.

"What spell," he asks. "Rhia. Breathe. What spell?"

"Up – Julianna. She – we fought it off. Hugh is with her." I try taking deeper breaths, and the chill air feels like tiny teeth all down my throat. "Go – Hugh –"

Connor starts to fire off rapid questions. "Who fought off the spell? You and Hugh? Julianna? What kind of spell?" I can only nod or shake my head.

Snarling, Connor shakes me a little. "Is she hurt?"

I steady myself as I can, put my hand on his arm. "Connor, she might have lost the baby."

His face goes blank. He stares at me like a man lost, like salvation is too late. "Baby? There's a baby?"

"Yes. I don't know. She's in a Healing trance."

He straightens, waving off my hand, waving me away. He turns to leave, stops, turns back. His eyes are narrow as he growls at me. "Find Linnet – keep her with you or send her to Hugh. Just make sure she's out of the way. Safe. Find Orrin. Find out what happened. Report to me."

And he's gone, his walk rapid but still seems normal. I watch him walk through the great hall doors, pushing a piercing grief that isn't mine from my head. He wouldn't thank me for prying.

CHAPTER 14

I find Linnet in the crowded kitchen, grabbing breakfast.

A good idea; I reach for a bun, myself. "Linnet, there you are," I cry, a little too loudly. Everyone looks up.

"What," she says, surly. Well, she's always surly in the morning. Her hair, blond from the dye, falls into her eyes as she looks over her shoulder at me. There's a little gasp and cluck of tongues around the room, and the servants lean in, eager for gossip.

Linnet only just manages not to roll her eyes. "I beg your pardon, my lady. How my I help you, my lady," she says.

If only her tone weren't a shade too sarcastic. But we don't have time to be nice, so I just raise my eyebrows at her and gesture for her to follow me.

"Tcha, if you'll pardon me for saying so, but you ought to take that one in hand," says Marla, the cook. Her hands on her hips, she shakes her head at me, her long face stern. "Gently bred or no, she shouldn't have such a mouth on her."

Linnet's face is murderous. I can't speak to her tongue, which likely will say something inappropriate in a moment.

"It's fine. She's fine; she's sorry," I say, just trying to get us out of here.

"Can't let her get away with these things now. She has to learn," Marla mutters, going back to her bread.

"Yes, you're right, of course," I say, now shoving Linnet out the door.

"Stop pushing, my lady," Linnet hisses, and I sigh and push harder.

"That one's going to get a slap," I hear behind me.

"I'd like to give her some kind of slap," a male voice jeers, and I look behind me to see a few guards at the back table, gulping breakfast. One woman smacks the man who spoke on the back of the head. I glare as they laugh, and shove Linnet up the stairs and shut the door behind me.

"Stay away from those guards," I tell Linnet.

"I'm not stupid. Anyway, he'd be sorry if he touched me."

"Yes, he would," I say, and she turns and stares at me. "But I'd rather we didn't have to manage that, too, on top of everything else."

Linnet looks carefully at my face. "All right, you look pinched and frantic. What is it? What's gone wrong now?"

But there are more servants coming down the stairs now, shoving around us with irritated glances and murmured "pardon, m'lady" on their lips. I see two maids pause behind Linnet.

I smile brightly. "Oh, nothing! Nothing is wrong. That is, there is a problem with the princess' gown."

Linnet groans. "Don't tell me it's too small," she starts, and I squeeze her arm hard, determinedly not looking at the maids. "Ow!"

"I tore it," I almost shout. "I stepped on it and tore it, and we need you to fix it right away." I push Linnet up the stairs past the maids, who stare without staring, and are much better at it than I.

Linnet goes with little grace. "Piffle. Even you are not that clumsy," she says.

"What is that supposed to mean?" I push a little harder, and we exit the stairs into the upper hall. But I'm not going to Julianna yet, and with a frown and a shooing motion for Linnet, I pass the door to the solar and head toward the chapel.

"Where are you going?" she asks, and starts following me.

"Linnet, go to her Highness," I say between clenched teeth. She shakes her head and keeps up with me, which isn't hard, as I'm tired and out of breath again. I give up on eating the bun and hand it to Linnet.

"I can tell something is going on. You are really slow," she says, and I scowl at her. "You should have come to Dawnsong. It was surprisingly entertaining. The Bishop didn't speak for too long, and the singing was lovely. Your friend Orrin was there. He looked like death, by the way. I can't believe Keenan was-"

"Will you shut up. All right, come with me then. But keep quiet."

"Are you going to see Orrin? Good. I'd like to meet him."

"Now might not be the best time," I say, heading

down the main stairs. Fewer servants; good. The chapel isn't too far, now.

"If you had your way, never would be the best time," Linnet snaps. "But he really didn't look very healthy. Everyone kept edging away from him. And gossiping. Duchess Marguerite wasn't there, either. Your earl was the only person of rank out there.

"The gossip was pretty racy, though. Some of them are fighting about the princess and her magic, about how her Healing isn't helping the poor folk in the hospice as it should. But they still love the duchess, and they think maybe it's those nasty Corat courtiers who've led the princess astray. They don't much like Bishop Gantry, most of them, so that's good."

I should be happy she's chatty, I think. She's been giving me the silent treatment for weeks. But now really isn't a good time, and she isn't as quiet as she thinks she is.

I shush her again, but she keeps whispering. "I do think the bishop did some kind of spell during the service, though," she says, and I stop in the hall just outside the chapel, and stare at her.

"A spell," I say, and look around. I drag her behind me to a pillar outside the chapel, but she comes willingly enough. She seems smug to have gotten my attention. There are some people praying inside the chapel; I can hear chanting coming from inside.

"Tell me about this spell," I whisper. "And keep it down. We are supposed to be hiding, by the way."

"No one pays any attention to you," she says, and I roll my eyes.

"They will if you keep making them want to. No

one's supposed to pay attention to me," I say. "Now tell me."

Linnet glares at me. "Fine. It was during the singing. Bishop Gantry grabbed Orrin's arm, and I felt some kind of magic starting, like the air was shaking. It sounded weird, too. I mean, over the singing. And Orrin's face looked awful, all crumpled and pained. So I knew they were doing something."

"Could you see it, the spell?"

"I can't always see magic like you can," she snaps. "No, I didn't see anything. But it was barely light, since it was dawn. For Dawnsong. Remember?"

"But you did see it – you could tell they were doing magic. Could anyone else tell?"

"How should I know? The lord Earl was there. Maybe he saw it."

"But-" and I think it won't be proof enough – Julianna won't want to talk about the baby, or the spell against her. And if no one knows what the spell was, or what it did, or even if Gantry did it, what good does it do us to accuse him? I grind my teeth in frustration.

"Don't get mad at me!"

I sigh. "I'm not. But what did-" I stop. Voices coming from the chapel, heading out. I pull Linnet further behind the pillar just as the door opens.

We're still visible, but Bishop Gantry isn't looking at us. He has Orrin by the elbow, dragging him down the hall and around the corner. "Do not speak unless spoken to," I hear Gantry say.

"Yes, my Lord Bishop." That must be Orrin, but I almost can't hear it.

Linnet pushes at me, but I wave her back. I hear a loud smack, and a soft cry. The sound makes us jump, and we hurry forward, but I stop at the corner, biting my lips. Linnet shoves at me, but I don't move.

"I said don't speak! You are not as useful a tool as I need," Gantry says, and I wince for Orrin.

I peer around the corner, and see Orrin leaning against the wall, his head bowed.

Gantry shoves him toward their rooms. "Get in there, and don't come out until I send for you. I have preparations to make."

He's heading back for us, and I hastily yank Linnet with me as I hurry toward chapel doors, so it will look like we were just coming from there, or going in. Arm in arm, we open and let fall the chapel door behind us as Bishop Gantry rounds the corner.

He doesn't seem to really see us, just calls for a couple of kirche guards. I start. What are kirche guards doing inside the castle? Since the intruder incident, Connor insists they stay off castle grounds all together, the better to keep watch for outsiders.

Gantry disappears down the corridor toward the great hall, and Linnet and I look at each other, run down to Gantry's rooms.

Orrin isn't in the hallway any longer. He must have gone inside.

I knock quietly on the door.

"Knock louder than that. He won't even hear you!" Linnet urges.

"Well I don't want anyone else to hear me, either," I hiss at her over my shoulder. She kicks my foot, and I remember I still don't have shoes on.

"Ow! Stop that!" My hisses are getting too loud, so I glare at her and knock again.

Linnet reaches around me and knocks harder. There's no sound from behind the door.

"Let me open it again," she says, but I hear footsteps and men's voices from the chapel, and push her away from the door just as two kirche guards round the corner.

The look on their faces is already not friendly. "What are you doing here," the taller one asks us.

I stand as tall as I can. "I need to h-, to, uh, speak with Father Matthew. Regarding tonight's banquet." I stop explaining. Don't explain, my mother would say. And I'm not sure what I would need with Matthew in any case. I glance at Linnet, who just looks grim.

"These are Bishop Gantry's rooms at the moment. You're not allowed back here. He's had some trouble with people going into his rooms."

"You wouldn't know anything about that, my lady." His sarcastic emphasis on the my lady party isn't heartening.

"Or you, girl. Girl. Why are you here?"

Linnet shrugs and glares, never at her best with demands.

I can feel her gather magic, and I feel a faint pulling sensation with it. I kick back with my foot a little, to warn her. We can't be seen doing any magic at all. We'll be caught for sure.

"You're that Dorward's kin, aren't you?" barks the shorter guard. "Dorward, hah, changed names don't make for changed states."

I draw myself up to my full height, which is a bit taller than he is.

"The Earl of Dorward is my cousin," I say, trying for haughty. "If Father Matthew is not here, then we shall seek him elsewhere." Grabbing for Linnet's hand, I attempt to sweep past them.

They have other ideas. "Why is it you're looking for Matthew here? He's been living down at the 'Quiztor's for months. I think you're up to something. My lady." The taller guard – he looks like a ferret – blocks our way back out of the hall, and the other end of this hall is a dead end.

"We have business to attend to," I say, "and we aren't any of yours. You will remove yourself from my path."

Linnet looks at me sidelong, and I look back. I thought it sounded noble.

"I'm not so sure we will. I think you are our business," guard the second – goat, I think – reaches out and grabs my arm.

"Unhand me!" I shout, fear making my voice shake.

I feel Linnet's growing anger and panic, and her growing magic as well.

Desperate to keep her under control, I glare sideways at her while pulling at Goaty's grip. I try to wrest control of the magic at the same time, which leaves me dizzy. When I stop tugging at the guard and focus, the magic flows to me like water down a stream, and Linnet gasps, outraged.

Goaty's hands are hard, and so are his eyes. "I want to know the true reason you're back here," he says, shaking me. I wrench my arm free and stumble back, so he catches hold of Linnet, who was pushing me sideways.

"And I told you our business, you useless goat," I snap. "Unhand my s-, servant!"

Linnet glares at everyone and kicks Goaty in the knee.

I see him wince and move to strike her. If he hits her, I will let her have her magic.

Ferrety advances on me. As his hand shoots out I duck around him and kick Goaty in the other knee. He howls and lets her go, and now they're both coming for us. But I've maneuvered us around so escape is behind us.

"Go," I motion to Linnet, but she rolls her eyes at me and stays put.

I get ready to run.

"What is the meaning of this?" Connor's voice comes from behind me, and I half turn, keeping the kirche guards in sight. Connor's face is blank and dark, like polished wood, and about as forgiving. "Are these guards offering you violence, Cousin?" He walks to stand before us, looking only at the guards. They have straightened, no longer advancing, but their hands stray towards their knives. Connor's hands, I notice, are loose at his sides.

"Look here, Dorward,"

"Earl Dorward. And commander of the castle garrison here at the moment. Do I have reason to call for the castle guards? I'm sure they'd love to speak to any of you fellows privately. Or is that not necessary? For what reason could there be for such behavior toward a lady, toward my cousin and ward, toward a handmaid of the princess? It is unaccountable." Connor's voice is low and menacing. As usual, but I don't know if the guards know that.

"Pardon, my lord," says Ferrety. "They should not be here, and my Lord Bishop has had trouble with people breaking into his rooms."

"We were not breaking in," I say flatly. We might have, but we didn't. This time.

"There. You see? My cousin is working hard to help with feast preparations, and is entirely innocent. She doesn't have time or inclination to petty thievery. So what remains is the matter of your behavior."

Ferrety snorts. "Any relation of yours isn't entirely innocent," he mutters.

Connor's stance does not change, but the chill in the air feels deeper. I think Ferrety has made a mistake. Another one. I See a flash of a face like Connor's, older, angrier. Bloodier. A battle; dead soldiers; broken oaths. I yank myself back to the present.

"Is that so," Connor says. He turns to look at us. "Ladies. Princess Julianna requires your assistance."

It's a clear dismissal, and I'm eager to take it. I can tell that Linnet would like to stay and blister everyone with magic or words, whichever. But I drag her off with me, and hurry us to the front hall.

"I can walk on my own," she says, and yanks her arm free. "And why didn't you let me use my magic? I could have done something. And we might have saved Orrin if you'd let me. Isn't that what you wanted? To save your friend? I was trying to help."

"Not here, Linnet," I hiss, and march up the stairs.

"Fine." She marches faster, and sails ahead of me, all temper.

Julianna's rooms seem unaffected by the bustle in the rest of the castle. Hugh shifts bonelessly in one of the chairs in the solar. Linnet stands with her hands on her hips, and waits until I shut the door behind me. Hugh just looks at us both, apparently too tired to do more.

"Well?" Linnet asks.

"Well what?" I say, which seems to be the wrong thing. I really just want to lie down.

"Now explain to me why you didn't want to rescue your friend."

Hugh sits up a little, blinks in confusion.

"What would you have me do? Break the door down? Kill those guards? Endanger the princess?"

"Well, we can't just leave him there!" She yells at me.

"I know!" I cry, tears in my eyes. "I don't want to leave him there! I want to break that door down, fight people, whatever it takes! But what would happen then? What if those guards overpowered us? Gantry could hurt you."

"Hurt you, you mean. You're just a coward! You're abandoning him just like you abandoned me!" She spins and runs to our room.

I stand hunched over, like I've been punched in the stomach. Like all the air was sucked from the room, and all that's left is a ringing in my ears, and my own panting.

Hugh slowly stands up, shaking his head, as though he can't quite figure out what happened.

Neither can I. I stagger to the chaise as he approaches, and collapse into it, shuddering. I can't even cry.

"What was that about?"

Connor steps into the room and closes the door. "Yes, tell me what happened. Did you even get close to Orrin? Was he able to speak to you?"

I can't speak, I just shake my head, tired beyond words, drop my face in my hands.

Connor and Hugh speak to each other, and I tune them out, concentrate on breathing. Hugh drops onto the chaise next to me, pats my shoulder. Connor pulls up a stool in front of me.

"I need to know what happened, Rhia. Look at me."

I look. "Did you speak to Orrin?" I shake my head no, and he curses.

"I – I'll try again later," I croak. "The guards came as we were knocking on the door. Gantry-"

"Having his rooms guarded. I know. We'll have to separate them tonight, get Orrin somewhere safe. Yes," he says when I look up hopefully. "Yes, I'll get him out of the castle. We'll just have to sort something out with Cardinal Robere later. And I don't know what we'll say about his disappearance, so don't ask me."

I take as deep a breath as I can, lean into Hugh's side a little. "Thank you, my lord. Thank you. I know Gantry is hurting him. The spell – Linnet saw the spell this morning. She said you did, too."

"I saw no spell. Before the service?"

"The Dawnsongs. She said you were there."

He stands and starts pacing. "He used the ceremony to cover up a spell? But why do it there?"

Hugh stiffens. "He wouldn't," he says.

"Wouldn't what?" asks Connor.

"There's a way to use a group like that, in a cere-mony, to focus power, and draw on all of them. But it takes a tremendous amount of power to begin with, if it's not willingly shared. Where would he even get that kind of power? It blew through years of protection spells."

"I think that question is for later. That he did seems to be true. Can he do it again?"

Hugh and I look at each other, sick with fear. "Evesong, before the feast," Hugh says.

"Then we will have to disrupt it, somehow," Connor says.

"If he's having Orrin focus the spell for him while he pulls energy from the crowd – keeping Orrin away from him would disrupt it." Hugh's voice is scratchy with fatigue.

Connor looks at him, at me, and how we're drooping. "The two of you need to rest. Is Julianna still sleeping?"

"Should be. She came out of the Healing trance long enough to tell me the child should be all right. So she tells me, anyway. But it took a lot out of her. I think she'll sleep until this afternoon."

Connor glances toward her chamber, his face carefully blank. "I'll walk you to your rooms, Hugh. I want to ask you about the ceremony. Rhia, send to Hugh if anything happens while we're gone. I'll be back in a short while. Then you can rest."

I nod, and when they leave, I slump over onto my side. I want to rest for a moment. Then I'll check on Julianna, see if Linnet has calmed down. Maybe if I give her the pendant…. I'll just lie here moment, then I'll start again.

When I fall asleep, I'm still telling myself to get up. I'm a terrible listener.

CHAPTER 15

Julianna's voice wakes me, and I flail a moment, sit up, groaning. A thick blanket falls to my lap, as I blink and rub my eyes.

"Rhia, we have to get ready," she says. I look up to find her standing by the window, looking out. The lamps reflect off of the deepening gloom.

"Is it dusk already?"

Being Solstice, dusk is late indeed, which means I've slept for hours. The feast tonight will last past midnight, so I won't have been the only person to take a nap, but I wasn't planning on it. The color of the sky outside is a wet stone gray, deepening to charcoal.

"It will be soon enough. Go and wash up and change. I just need help with my hair, and a few buttons."

Standing makes me feel woozy, but I notice Julianna seems extra pale. "Are you feeling all right, your Highness? Maybe you shouldn't attend the Evesong."

"I have to attend. And I'm fine." She turns and smiles, attempting cheerful. "Don't worry about me, or the baby. I've done a thorough check, and everything is normal. We're fine."

I don't think she's nearly as sanguine about her health as she seems, but she'll only become stubborn if I push her. I nod and head for my room.

It doesn't take me long to dress. I bring a shawl to put under my cloak. It's chilly and rainy today, colder than it should be for Solstice. But the storm that's threatened off shore all day makes the wind brisk. The last few days have been wet and miserable. The weather seems unlikely to change tonight.

When Julianna and I are both ready, I realize Linnet still hasn't made an appearance. "Do you know where Linnet is?" I ask.

"I sent her to fetch the tapestry. And to calm down – she's angry about something again. Did something happen?"

"Connor didn't … didn't, um. He didn't want me to tell her something. She'll get over it," I say, thinking maybe I won't burden the princess with today's events just now. She'll hear about them eventually. But we need to just get through tonight. "Did Connor tell you … what the plan is?"

"He's taking care of keeping Orrin away from Gantry during the service, if he can. He'll cause a diversion if anything seems awry. But I think that with all of us there, Gantry won't be able to try anything new. Not tonight. But we need to figure out a way to catch him, publicly. If he does go after me tonight, we'll have that. But Connor doesn't want to risk it."

"What if Gantry just says that it's your own magic that's causing his spell? He'll find a way to twist it."

"That's what Connor is afraid of." She sighs. "We

have to find some sort of proof of the whole conspiracy, whatever the conspiracy is. And whomever it implicates," she says darkly. I nod, subdued, and follow her out, out of the rooms, through the bustling great hall, to the courtyard of the west barbican.

The wind bites through my cloak. At least this time I have proper boots on.

Bishop Gantry enters the courtyard behind us, causing me to start and glance behind me. He's followed by Orrin, who does not meet my eyes, and a group of kirche guards. I see Ferrety from earlier. He seems to be limping. I bite back a slightly hysterical laugh, try to focus on walking without tripping.

I look back again. Orrin's face is ashy and drawn. He keeps his head down, his dark curls glinting with rain in the torchlight. I can't see his eyes.

Gantry moves to stand on the small rise before the cold firepit, and Orrin stands behind him.

Castle denizens gather in murmuring groups around the pit, huddled together against the cold. Duchess Marguerite and her ladies make room for Julianna and me, and we stand against the chill wind, blinking in the near-dark. I don't see Linnet or Connor. Hugh walks to stand next to his mother, smiling genially at everyone, his eyes roving. I nod when he sees me.

The ceremony begins when Gantry raises his arms and starts chanting. The crowd startles and joins in belatedly. I keep an eye on things, but the only magic he's called so far is fire for the torches, and then the firepit, which sputters to reluctant life in the spitting drizzle. The songs begin.

"Praise to the Lord of Stars, praise to the light. Praise for a harvest bounty, praise for all life." Not the most eloquent of the lighting songs, but at least it's short. Gantry's face is puckered with concentration, and I feel a surge of power building. He reaches back to grab Orrin, and I grip Julianna's arm.

A glow starts around them, and then is cut off when Orrin falls sideways, pushed over by a stumbling castle guard.

Gantry makes a strangled noise, and Orrin cries out, as the guard clumsily, drunkenly it looks like, lifts Orrin to his feet.

The guard apologizes, patting Orrin down, pushing him further from Gantry, keeping himself in between them.

"So sorry, so sorry, please finish, yer lordship, sorry, sorry, go on," the man says, and I feel Julianna breathe a sigh of relief. Connor must have set this up. I glance at Hugh and meet his tense smile with my own.

Gantry's face is a frozen mask of fury. The crowd of castle folk draws back a little further from him. He looks around at everyone for a moment, then raises both hands for the benediction again, the power buildup gone.

I close my eyes and reach out with my Sight to try for a vision, look for knowledge or emotions. But all the people crowd out any specific person, and I can't isolate any one feeling. They batter at me; uneasiness, boredom, irritation, unhappiness, giddy anticipation. The latter seems mostly people who are looking forward to romantic, or at least passionate, pairings after the feast. Solstice is the night for it, traditionally.

There, there is a thread of abject terror and misery, that I think is Orrin. Before I can follow it more closely and find out, I'm jostled as the crowd turns, starts back indoors. Gantry must have cut the ceremony short. No one seems upset by this, especially as the rain starts coming down in earnest, and thunder rumbles out at sea.

I look back and see the sacred fire hiss and smoke, sputter to nothing. A poor omen for the coming harvest. It's supposed to burn all night – and the priest in charge of lighting it is supposed to make sure it does. Murmurs around me suggest I'm not the only one to notice.

Inside the great hall, voices bounce off of the walls as people mill, shaking water from hair and clothes. The steward looks miffed that we're all milling around and tracking in water.

Duchess Marguerite smiles and pats his hand, then heads over to Bishop Gantry. I can't hear all of her words, but I do hear "sacred fire" and "someone else." I think she's telling him to find someone to re-light the fire.

Gantry's face isn't happy. I can't see Orrin's face, but neither can anyone else. He looks only at the floor.

Julianna takes my arm and pulls me along with her. "Let's hang these wet cloaks up and change out of our boots. The banquet will begin soon, and I'm hungry." She smiles thinly at me, and I comply.

We enter the solar, shaking off our cloaks. Julianna is dressed in her gold and russet satin, and light bounces merrily off of it.

Linnet comes from the chambers, holding the tapestry. "It's finished. I'm heading to the banquet, since

I can't tell anyone I'm the one who made it." She glares us and storms out, slamming the door.

Julianna and I blink at each other. I sigh.

Connor comes in a moment later, staring critically over his shoulder. "What is it this time?"

I just shake my head. We're all tired and out of sorts today.

Julianna sways into me a bit when I reach out for her, and I murmur "You should be in bed."

"Don't fuss. I have a job to do, and I'm going to do it."

"Does the job include fainting in front of everyone?" I ask.

"I don't faint," she snaps. "Leave it be."

I look at Connor, and he frowns at the both of us, but keeps his own counsel. I guess he already had a go at her.

"Hello everyone! Are we ready to go down?" Hugh steps into the room, smiling brightly. "Do you have Mother's present ready? Where's Linnet?"

"Already left."

"Here it is," Julianna says, draping the tapestry over the back of the chaise.

Everyone stares in appreciation, and even Connor looks impressed. It's a light silk tapestry, for a doorway in summer to let the air flow. In the center, a rampant lion in scarlet stands triumphant in a field of bright blue. The motto "Strength in Adversity" is cleverly woven in scarlet and gold, twisting around the lion's feet. It's the Haverston coat of arms.

I feel a sting of pride. I can see Da's teaching in her handiwork — the even weave and the lion's mane are his style. But she adds her own flair in the twisted banner around the claws. Linnet's work has been sought after since she was eleven.

"It's lovely," Connor says, and I smile at him. He blinks at me.

"Mother will adore it," Hugh says, and rolls it carefully. "We'll give it to her at dessert. He tucks it under one arm, and bows to his sister. "I think, my dear sister, it is time to descend."

Hugh offers his arm, and Julianna reaches to take it. "Shall we, my favorite brother?"

"I'd say I'm your only brother, but I'd be your favorite anyway." And they sweep out the door ahead of us, teasing each other.

Connor smiles a little, offers me his arm. "Shall we, cousin?" I smile back and take his arm, and he escorts me to the banquet.

There is a magnificent view of the great hall from the short staircase in the entryway. The white marble pillars, high pointed arches, and scarlet and blue banners hanging from the gallery seem fitted to a king's palace, even though this is a duchy. The walls are bathed in flickering light from the lamps and fireplaces, the sound of rain on the high window mostly masked by the voices below.

There haven't been many formal dinners since I came to the castle, or reasons to use the great hall. Most dinners are served en famille, in their own rooms, or small groups. The duchess keeps country traditions and rather prefers the informality.

We walk to the side of the hall and make our way to the high table, the duchess having come in before us. Julianna stands by her seat next to her brother. Hugh smiles at his sister and mother from behind his chair at the center of the head table. Julianna's seat is to his left, as his mother's is to his right. Connor is to Julianna's left, and I am to his.

All the people at the high and low tables, their rich robes and gowns glowing in the light, sit at the duchess' gracious nod. The talk resumes, and soon echoes from the ceiling; a cacophony of voices.

I catch a hint of Linnet's green dress among the duchess' ladies and their companions at one of the middle tables. When I glimpse of her face, she looks small and alone.

Musicians in the gallery above us strike up a tune I've never heard, the strings jumping sprightly from note to note, and Marguerite waves to the steward, Gervaise. He bows low and turns to the kitchen doors. The platters of food enter on the shoulders of servants.

I keep an eye on Bishop Gantry, on the other side of the duchess. I see Orrin's robe bob back and forth, as he pours wine for the Bishop, and serves his food.

Connor catches me watching and takes my hand, smiles at me. "Don't stare too often. But watch for an opportunity to follow him."

Just past Connor, Julianna's color looks better than this morning, but her hands shake as she lifts her goblet, and both Hugh and Connor keep their arms close for her to lean on.

As the first course is cleared, I stand to make my way to the back hall. I'm going to follow Orrin. I stumble as I get up, bumping into Connor so that he spills some his wine. He catches hold of me with one arm and steadies me. Warmth from his hand on my waist seeps through layers of velveteen and linen.

He smirks a little. "Not a bad plan, but aim for your

quarry next time."

I roll my eyes and turn to follow Orrin as he leaves the hall for the kitchens. I catch up to him in the corridor before he reaches the stairs. No one else is here at the moment. I run and pluck his sleeve.

"Orrin!" I whisper. "Orrin, come and talk to me. Where were you? What happened? Are you all right?" He turns and stares at me, his expression blank. I reach out to touch his arm, and he flinches. "Orrin?" I say, feeling helpless.

"May I help you, my lady," he says, but he doesn't look at me, only at the air past my ear.

"Orrin, it's me. Don't you, don't you know me?"

"Should I, my lady?" He still will not look at me. I can't tell if he means he should not know me, or he does not know me.

"Orrin, if you need to leave, to get out, Connor says, he says we can do it. Tonight. We'll take care of everything. Whatever he's done to you, we can fix."

This time he looks at me, and I reach for his arm again, but he moves back. The wine in the pitcher he's holding sloshes.

"Let's go somewhere we can talk for a moment. Orrin, let me help you."

He shakes his head. "I don't know you. I don't know you, and you can't help me," he whispers. "Just stay away from me. Stay away, do you hear me? I can't know you." His eyes are fierce.

I hear people coming, and I reach for him again. "Please just come with me," I beg, and then he does move closer, and I feel a spark of hope.

"I'm sorry," he breathes, and then wine pours down the front of my dress as he tips it, stumbling, looking straight into my eyes. "My lady, I am so sorry. So sorry. Please, my lady, please forgive me," he's saying, and I don't know what's happening until I see red out of the corner of my eye.

Gantry's red feast robe glitters as it billows around him, as he grabs for Orrin's arm. Orrin's brown sleeve slides up a little. I see patterns in angry red and white, runes to match my own.

"Clumsy!" The Bishop shouts as he shakes Orrin. "Look what you've done!"

Orrin begs pardon in a dead voice, his head low.

"I am sorry, lady. My acolyte has ruined your gown."

I curtsey low, feeling Gantry's eyes burn into the top of my head, and sweat drips down along my own carved patterns.

I glance up to See Orrin's scars glow a pale amethyst for a moment, see him flinch and gasp.

Servants are coming through the corridor now, bearing food and drink. I choke on words, then stammer, "My Lord Bishop," I say, and stop. What do I say? "Yes, the gown, I, I will go and change," I say, and hurry down the corridor to an exit, any exit. I end up in the front hall, and then run to Julianna's rooms, my lungs and eyes burning. My hands grip the wall, the stair rails, to keep me upright on my shaky legs.

I was right. The vision was true, and I was right. I start to shudder and cry when I reach the safety of my own room. Oh, Keenan, help me. Help Orrin.

I will have to tell Connor, after the banquet is over. But for now, I just want to hide. I crawl, wine-stained, into my bed and huddle in a ball. Another sacrifice to demons, but his runes burn purple. I remember to breathe just in time to pass out.

Julianna is shaking me. "Rhia, are you awake?"

I see her through a milky haze, prop myself on my elbows. She stands next to my bed, a glowsand lamp in her hand. The shadows from her arm darken and shift, and I blink again.

"What? Um, yes?" My heart pounds and I tremble all over from waking suddenly. I shake my head, suck grit from my teeth. My stomach growls sullenly. I didn't eat much today. "Do you, um. What?"

"Rhia, what happened to you tonight? Here, don't wake Linnet, come with me into my chamber." She helps me to stand and I follow, towering over her like a scarecrow. She sits me on the brocade chair and I slump, licking chapped lips, blinking and shivering in the dim light.

Julianna settles gracefully across from me, her gown rustling. She gazes at me, her left eyebrow raised. I realize belatedly that she waits for me to say something.

"Yes, your Highness?"

"Don't 'yes your Highness' me. What on earth happened tonight? Why didn't you come back?"

I try to organize my swirling thoughts. I think with a shudder on Orrin's arm, his gasp, and the runes glowing demon-purple. I want to try to explain about the demons again – maybe if they could understand what I See, they'd realize the danger better.

Connor stands at my side and I jerk, gasp in surprise. My poor lungs labor a moment from the shock: when did he come in? He stands in front of me, takes my hand and examines my gown. "It's not hard to explain, my lady," he says. "This gown is covered in wine. You tried to get Orrin alone?" he asks.

I nod. "He, he wouldn't come with me. And Gantry caught us talking, so Orrin spilled wine down my front. And I – I didn't know what to do. He, he," and my throat closes on the word 'runes' and I can't breathe. Tears leak out of my eyes, and I bow my head.

"Oh, Rhia. We'll figure something else out. But tomorrow. I am so weary."

Connor clears his throat. "I think we should let you rest," he says gently.

Julianna lays her head back on the chair and sighs. Creases mar the perfect line of her mouth, and gather on her forehead. "Very well, Connor. See to everything, will you? I think it is past my bed time."

Heartily agreeing with that, I stand wearily to help her undress.

Connor starts to exit but I catch his hand while Julianna stretches her arms over her head, her back to us.

He gazes at me, and I get a rush of confusion from him. I See the two of us from his perspective: Julianna, shining and golden and perfect, remote from him as if surrounded by crystal; and me, my eyes wide and clear and my hand warm in his.

I blink, and I see from my own eyes again. His gaze is unchanged, but I draw back my hand and motion to the solar with my head.

He nods, and takes his leave as Julianna turns back.

"Good night, Connor."

"Good night, my lady."

Julianna turns to me after he's gone, and grasps my hands in hers tightly. Dark shadows line her eyes, and she sways a little, as if she were on a boat.

"Poor little Rhia. I wish I could help you more. Things aren't what you bargained them to be." Her eyes are so deep and blue; I nearly weep for the weariness in them.

"Please, your Highness. Just go to sleep. I'm all right."

Julianna shifts to let me unbutton her gown. I help her get ready for bed and bring her a goblet of water from the pitcher on the table. She looks small and pale and ill, now that she no longer has an audience.

I resolve to be more careful of her health in the future as I ease the covers over her. She is nearly asleep already. I douse all the lamps, and walk into the solar.

Connor paces across the heavy carpet by the windows, his hands clasped behind his back. He turns when he hears the door close.

"What is it?"

"Shh, not here. I don't want to wake them."

Connor nods, strides to the door and opens it for me, then heads toward the north stair. "This way."

I follow him closely, and he grabs a lamp from the stairwell and heads up the stairs to the third floor of the castle. Out into the corridor, the lamp swings wide and casts eerie shadows along the walls and statues in nooks, the vases on pedestals. He strides to a door halfway down the hall and ushers me in.

A fire dies in the grate, smelling of pine and chimney-draft. Connor hooks the lamp on the wall sconce and lights other a few more. A large oak bed dominates the room, its burgundy bed covers neatly made and pulled back by some servant or valet to show snowy sheets.

I realize belatedly that this is Connor's bedchamber, and that handmaid or no, ward or no, I am supposed to be conscious of my honor.

Connor closes the door behind me and motions me to sit on his brown leather couch. I hesitate, and he sighs. "No one knows you're here."

He's right. I smile a little, and sit gingerly in my rumpled velveteen. I put a hand to my hair, suddenly aware of how ghastly I must look.

My hair tumbles in knots on my head, and one curl has been in my eyes since I woke up. I push it back behind my ear again, but it's not quite long enough. I fiddle with it a few moments, trying to work up my courage to try again. I don't like it when I fail: it hurts when I can't breathe.

Connor, impatient with my fidgeting, sighs again. "It's late, Rhia. What is it?"

I clear my throat, unwilling to start.

He sighs more dramatically, the mahogany wisp of hair above his right eye drifting up with his breath. As I begin to wring my fingers, Connor sits next to me and grasps both my wrists in one large hand. Laying them on my knee, he grips my chin with his other hand and makes me look at him.

His bloodshot eyes glare into mine. "What," he growls.

I pull my chin away and slip my hands out from under his. Slowly edging up my sleeve to my elbow, I expose scars that shine in the lamplight.

"Orrin has these." I whisper. So far, so good.

Connor stares at my arms, his lips in a thin line. "They glowed purple when Gantry grabbed him. I was so cloaked from him — I shut down barriers so tight I couldn't have seen any visions or heard any thoughts, but Orrin gasped in pain."

Connor stares at me, his eyebrows raised.

"Mine glow green when I See visions, or use magic."

Connor lifts my exposed arm in his hands. With one finger he traces a rune and I shudder; the strange tickling travels up my back as well. He glances at me from under dark lashes, and away, dropping my arm.

"So your vision was true after all, then. What is it he is doing with these spells, and why did he need you, or Orrin, to do them?" He stands and begins pacing before the dark windows in the west wall. The curtains haven't been drawn, and the lamplight reflects off the surface in eerie patterns, following his shadow.

"I can't, I can't ..." He stops pacing and stares at me. "I can't say it. When I try, the spell – something stops me," I push out through labored breaths. I grow tense as Connor continues to stare.

He walks to me and grabs my hand, tugs me behind him and I follow helplessly as we traverse the halls again.

"My lord," I pant, but he strides around the corner, dragging me behind. "My lord!"

He turns his head and holds a finger to his lips, and we wind around to the south side, where Hugh has his rooms. Connor doesn't bother to knock and we barge into Hugh's empty outer room. Connor drops my hand and I stumble to a stop on a rich dark carpet while he pulls open the bedchamber door.

"Hugh," he says, "I —" And he stops abruptly. I catch a glimpse of a man's bare backside before Connor shuts the door, his face carefully blank.

"Your Grace," he calls through the door, "we need to discuss something. It is a matter of great importance."

Muffled curses drift through the door, and after a short while a dark haired young man rushes out, bare-chested with shoulders hunched, clutching a lawn shirt under his arm. He looks only at the floor as he passes us, and Connor has pushed me toward the far corner, in shadow. Only one lamp burns in its bracket in Hugh's retiring room.

I blush. I've never interrupted anyone's tryst before. Certainly not a duke's. I feel embarrassed, a flush creeping over me. I've never even had a tryst before. I pull my barriers down tighter; I really don't want to pry.

Hugh joins us after the outer door closes behind his paramour, his face sour. He shrugs into a rich brown silk robe as he walks into the room. It's the only thing he's wearing.

I feel my cheeks flush even warmer.

"What the hell is the matter?" he snaps, then his eyes light on me. His jaw drops. Cinching his robe tightly, he stalks to a low couch and sits, arranging the silk haughtily.

Connor shifts in place.

Hugh glares at the both of us. "Well. This should be interesting. Pray, why are you here right now, Connor?"

Connor's mouth twitches, and he walks over to sit next to Hugh. "I thought you should have some company tonight. Happy Solstice." Connor shrugs and smirks a little.

Hugh stares at him, then laughs quietly, clapping Connor on the shoulder.

I stand, fidgeting, in the corner.

Hugh looks at me and sighs. "I suppose this has to do with Orrin."

Connor sobers and turns to me. "Come here, Rhia. Show him."

I swallow those tumbling mice again and walk slowly forward. Connor holds out his hand for mine. I ignore it, and stand before Hugh, pulling up my sleeve. If I don't think about it, I can show him. I look away, pull my sleeve higher.

"Your scars? I –" he stands and grabs my arm. "Connor, light more lamps!"

He pushes my sleeve up as far as the thick material will allow and turns my arm over in his grasp. As more lamps add to the light, he grabs my other arm and does the same.

I shiver at the intensity of his gaze.

"I just saw this rune, the one below your elbow. It – this one isn't finished, I think."

I stare helplessly at Connor, who stands at Hugh's side again.

Suddenly Hugh spins me around and pulls at my collar, peers down my neck.

I jerk away from him and turn, panting, to back away

from him. I stumble over the edge of the rug and fall backwards.

Hugh reaches forward and I flinch, warding him off with hunched back and raised arms.

"Please!" I rasp. After a moment, I hear no sound but my heartbeat, and my panicked breath. I lift my head.

Connor stands before me, his hand outstretched and open. Hugh hovers behind him looking worried. I look into Connor's eyes, and see only calm.

Trying to breathe normally, I slowly accept Connor's hand, and he helps me to my feet. Hugh stays put, and I feel relieved.

"Rhia, I —" Hugh closes his mouth after a moment.

Connor guides me to the couch. I sink gratefully from my unsteady legs. Connor sits next to me. "She says she can't talk about them. Something stops her. And Orrin has the same scars on his skin now, which she can see glow with her Sight. Her scars glow when she's spelling."

I'm dizzy, I put my head down on my lap.

Hugh says something, and I look up at him. "That rune, the unfinished one – it translates to 'silence,'" he says.

"What about the others? Do you still have the drawings I made?" Connor says.

My eyes sting and my back prickles with sweat. The fact that drawings exist of these scars makes me feel ill. I do not want them. I don't want anyone to see them. And I can't tell if that's me or the spell wanting that.

"I found a book of ancient Indrani carvings and runes. It's a book of legends, but it has some of the ones you drew. It would help if I could look at the runes directly."

I look only at my hands, clenched in my lap.

Hugh sits on my other side, and the musky smell of the two men overwhelms me. I feel smothered and too close to them. Before I can launch myself like a nervous deer to the door, Connor puts a hand on my knee.

I jump and yelp, and he loosely takes hold of my arm. "Rhiannon."

I clench my hands and stare determinedly at the floor.

Connor tries again. "Rhiannon, look at me."

I pull my arm from his grasp and stand slowly. Remembering to breathe, I start toward the door. I can't stop myself, I want to stop but I keep walking.

"Rhiannon, please."

I stop, gripping the door handle painfully, sobs pushing at my chest.

Hugh tries next. "Rhia, is it the spell now? Does it make you move as well as keep you silent?"

"I don't know," I whisper, miserable.

"Talk to me about the weather," Connor says abruptly.

I breathe in, turn to look at him.

His eyes hold mine. "It's quite cold for this time of year, isn't it?"

"Yes, my lord," I whisper. "And wet."

He nods, and I let go of the door. He stands and walks toward me. "It's terrible for the farms. And so muddy."

I keep my eyes on his, nodding.

"Are your boots warm enough?"

"Yes," I say.

"And your cloak?"

"Yes."

"Do you have enough blankets at night?"

"Yes."

"Does the spell make you report to Gantry?"

"No," I say, and blink.

"Are you linked to him?" Connor stands in front of me now.

"No," I whisper. "I don't think so."

"Can he control you?"

"No."

"Can he control Orrin?"

I shake my head. "I don't know. Maybe. Orrin didn't – he refused to come with me. But it was, it was as if he didn't recognize me. Or pretended not to."

"Gantry gave you these," Connor indicates my scars.

I nod, I don't trust my voice.

"And Orrin. Your vision was true."

I nod again, sniffling a little.

Connor leans forward a little. "I trust you, Rhiannon," he whispers. "Trust me."

I feel tears leaking down my chin. He puts his hand up, brushes some away. "Tell me what the runes do."

"I – they – he – d-" but I can't form words again, and it's too late. There is a green glow around me, and my vision blurs. "No." My voice is dark with power.

Hugh swears loudly in surprise.

I turn, feeling power course through the air around me, and visions pour through me. I See Orrin on a table, me on a table, Gantry's flat pale gaze, knives descending again and again.

Faintly, I hear the men cry out, and I try for control, pulling power back into me, winding it around my hands like the warp around a spindle. But the magic is hot and wild, and I still See.

I See Orrin curled in a ball on a thin pallet. I See Bishop Gantry kneeling in the chapel, swaying and chanting. He calls out the names of demons, demands they do his bidding, demands they only do his bidding and stop calling to him. I See a swirl of amethyst-gray and ruddy brown smoke surround him, hear the faint chitter of their language. I See the bishop open his mouth in a soundless scream.

My lungs burn, and the power burns along the runes. I push the power away from me, and the visions end, leaving me on my knees.

I open my eyes to a room that seems dim after such hot power. Hugh weeps openly, gasping.

Connor's eyes are closed, his jaw tight.

I sit on the floor until Hugh wobbles to his feet and stumbles toward me. He helps me up and pulls me close, his hug warm around my suddenly shivering shoulders.

"All right, Rhia. Enough. Enough." He rubs my back and helps me to the couch. Hugh sits next to me, still moving his hand absently across my shoulders.

"I'll need to study the drawing some more. I think, from what I've seen of them, that they're runes to call power. That, that's a lot of power." His voice is bewildered and sick. And they don't know about the demons, yet.

Connor walks to stand in front of us. "She was glowing," he says.

I'm afraid to look at him.

"If you had the Sight, you'd have seen power pouring from her like a fountain. And outside of the castle, it would be blinding. With the power-well under Haverston, the wild magic hides her normal glow. Even with the Sight, I can't find her magically here –

maybe not anywhere in town. Except when she does that."

Connor walks to stand in front of us. "Would Gantry be able to see that?"

"The dead would be able to see that. And if I hadn't shielded the rooms before bringing Randal here, the good bishop would be running for these apartments with a log and a brand, ready to set fire to us all. Which – Rhia. We're going to have to make you stronger barriers. We'll have to test them."

"I still c-, can't talk about," I stammer, and stop.

"I know. The rune for silence – that is probably why. It's lucky – I think you're lucky he wasn't able to finish this spell," Hugh says.

"But he did on Orrin," Connor says. He crouches in front of me. "Whatever he meant for you, he did to Orrin."

I keep my eyes down.

Connor touches my face, and I look at him. "Rhia, I don't think we can help him."

"We have to," I say, my voice rough.

Connor shakes his head. "I don't want to leave him. But we don't know what the spell does. We can't be sure he's not linked to Gantry now. And he said he won't come with you willingly." He holds my eyes, his face as solemn as I've seen it. "We have to stay away from Orrin." I start to protest. "For now, we have to stay away from him for now."

"I'll write to Cardinal Robere," Hugh says. "Perhaps he's found more information." Hugh hugs me to his side, and I sag, so tired. "We'll figure something out. It just might take awhile."

My lungs burning, I stand up to leave. Connor

reaches for my hand, but I draw away and place my feet carefully, open the door. I hear "Let her go, it's nearly dawn," behind me.

As I walk the dark halls I hear early morning birds sing loudly for the sun. Sun which doesn't seem likely to come, from the sound of the rain pattering. My body aches and quivers with exhaustion, and power ebbs and throbs along the channels in my skin to the beat of my heart. Drawing breath shakily, I resolve never to let the runes so overwhelm me again.

I shudder to think what the completed spell might be for. A spell to call power, carved into a person. I wipe angrily at my face as I think of Orrin, strapped to that table, demons feeding on his blood.

I weep for me, too. For my own hideous, glowing scars, and for my family. And what does Gantry want all this power for, anyway? That he would risk his sanity and his soul to use demons to get it? I must find a way to tell everyone about the demons. They'll have to stop Gantry, then. They'll have to just kill him. And I want him to die, for what he's done.

I reach Julianna's rooms and shut the door to the hall behind me, panting in weariness and receding fear. I'm tired of being so frightened all the time. The weight of the day descends upon me, and I stumble my way across the solar.

Linnet lies sleeping. The package I meant to give her lies on my table. I open her clothes chest, lay it on top. It wasn't much of a celebration day for our family, but a person's fifteenth summer should be recognized. Miserable as it may be.

I undress quietly, listening to Linnet's breath, and slide slowly into bed and sleep at the same moment.

CHAPTER 17

The next several weeks hurt – I hurt all the time, as I push myself harder to have visions, to find a way to stop Gantry, to save Orrin, to speak. My lungs burn, and my scars, trying to force words past this spell. My spirit feels bruised. And the visions I have aren't any more helpful, as I still can't speak of demons.

Julianna is concerned. Linnet is angry. She hasn't spoken of the necklace, or much of anything to me.

"Stop that gasping! You're just trying to get more attention," she snaps, and storms out of the room.

Julianna pats my back, gives me water. "I think you're trying too hard," she says gently.

When I get my breath back, I ask why she doesn't order Gantry arrested, just on what she does know. It isn't quite a demand.

"Because we don't have enough actual evidence, Rhia," she says, tired, pushing her hair back from her forehead.

"But wouldn't the king believe you?"

"It isn't the king we'll have to convince," she says

darkly. "It's the kirche leadership." She looks at me, sighs. "Bishop Gantry was handpicked by Archbishop Montmoore. Montmoore has many supporters, in this country and out, and a good part of our own court is behind him. He's … charismatic. And the kirche has its own authority and army outside of any country's jurisdiction. I can't just remove Gantry, and I can't order any moves against any of the Archbishop's faction, without some kind of verifiable proof of treason."

What she doesn't say, what I See in flashes and feelings, is that the court is deeply divided, and closer to civil war than anyone wants to admit. Closer than even a few months ago, and the factions are bitter and angry. Many mutter about the exiled Duke of Torrence, and his claims to the throne. Those who favor King Peter mutter back about broken oaths. But none of them look with favor on Haverston right now.

The old duke, Julianna's father, drove a deep wedge between certain parties, working to pass the laws he favored. Julianna's marriage to Prince Alexander was not popular, outside this duchy.

The hospices are that wedge. No matter how favored with us here, they are not so with the court. Healers have traditionally been family appointments, or wandering clerics. The hospices and schools make people nervous. The old duke wanted safer places for Healers, and safer places for the sick. Hugh has carried on his work – partly for the woman in front of me now.

Julianna leans back, rubbing her belly. Her pregnancy must be the worst-kept secret in this duchy. I don't know who she thinks she's fooling anymore. It's beginning to look like she's smuggling a melon in her dress.

"I think letting Gantry stay free is a mistake," I say, but without hope.

"I know you do. But we have a plan, Rhia. Help us make it work, and he won't stay free for much longer."

The days are long and gray and frustrating. I can't get near Orrin – he won't look at me in chapel. He goes nowhere else, and is always with the bishop. I stare at him during service, trying to convince my Sight to show me anything that might prove Gantry's treason.

The visions are getting stronger. And the thoughts I hear are angry, and full of vengeance and violence. But nothing proves him treasonous. The last time I tried so hard I fell forward in my seat and Connor steadied me while I gasped.

He dragged me out, telling others I was ill. "Do not try that in chapel again," he said. He glared at me until I promised.

I haven't, but I might.

So it comes to this. I will mix a poison, and give it to Bishop Gantry. I will poison him and he will die.

The herbarium is dark and cool, sharp with the mingling smells of different herbs. The short staircase down the hall from the kitchen leads to a long, low room with shelves and hanging racks for drying along all the walls. Another staircase leads to a thick wooden door to the herb garden.

Three tables down the center of the room hold tools and stone jars for storing the herbs in all the forms Julianna needs – fresh, dried, infusions, decoctions, oils, ointments, and tinctures.

The work is constant and tedious, and not my favorite. The gardener leaves bunches of the herbs – whatever has managed to grow this wet season – on the tables to be sorted, dried, or whatever else for medicines and potions and teas.

I reach for a stone jar on the shelf labeled in a steady hand. Foxglove. Julianna told me that it's poisonous if too much is taken, although useful in very small doses for dropsy and such. She says it stops the heart. I think that will be a fitting end to someone who has stopped mine.

Foxglove leaves look a lot like comfrey leaves, but are bitter. I have an idea to keep the taste from being noticeable, but first I need these leaves. I grind a handful into powder, and wrap it in a packet of linen.

I hide the packet behind some unused jars. I don't want Linnet to find it in our rooms. I'll have to wait for a time to use it. Or I'll have to make a time.

I must end him, for everyone's sake.

Cots line up in neat rows along the whitewashed walls of the hospice. The building breathes with moans and retching, pleas for surcease. A brown robed priest with a blue surplice murmurs prayers and spells of healing over the diseased, passing benedictions over their twisting forms. The Wasting is worse in Haverston of late, and everyone is worried that it will spread further.

Julianna precedes me into the room, stopping at the bedside of a wispy-haired man who groans and clutches his stomach.

I stand behind her, clutching the bag of simples.

A young, sandy-haired priest stands when we enter and hurries to the front of the room, scowling. The salt breeze flutters his pale red surplice as the heavy door shuts behind us, and the stench of the dying overwhelms even the strong smell of herbal potions.

"Your Highness, I thank you for your presence, but we have no need of your Healing. As you can see, there are priests with Healing magic here, and you put your soul in jeopardy ...." He trails off at Julianna's stare. The young priest clears his throat to try again, sweat breaking out on his pale brow.

"I am not here to Heal. I am here to offer succor and comfort to the ill." Her arch tone and expression leave no room for him to argue.

He awkwardly bows out of the princess' way and she bends over the old man next to us. I walk through the dark room to the kitchen to fill a bowl with cool water for the herb-filled cloths. The sharp smells of vervain and swampwort drift up from my bag of simples.

This hospice was the first one in our duchy, and Haverston has always been proud of it. We've had Healers of all faiths, and no particular faith, working here together. Now none but priests of the Star Lord remain, and not enough of them. Not with so many people getting sick.

Stains mar the wood of the floor near the kitchen doorway. A long counter stands next to it, and medicines and supplies have been laid out along the top. I pull a clean bowl from the varied and chipped stack, and bring the water bucket to refill.

The kitchen itself is large and airy, with soup kettles on the fire, and a door into the yard. A tall table stands next to the pump for the sink, but the well water has been brown and murky because of flooding and rain. Barrels placed outside all throughout the town catch clean rainwater, and that is the only good use for the rain that I can see.

Out the back door of the kitchen a young boy wraps bodies in coarse shrouds. His lank hair sticks to his forehead in dark snarls, the rain plastering his gray tunic to the sharp blades of his shoulders.

I stand under the eaves and dip the bowl in the barrel there.

Now that more Healing priests have finally arrived, there should be some relief from this plague. The kirchemen claim their prayers have more weight with the Star Lord than heretic powers, and claim it as proof of the Prophet's words. But the hospice is too full of people, if the priests are doing their jobs. A job Julianna dare not do anymore.

After Solstice, and her weakness since Gantry's spell, Julianna decided she should scale back on her Healing work. She's concerned for her baby now; despite telling us everything is fine, I can feel her worry. And lately her Healing is backfiring – people coming back more sick than before.

All of those she Healed of the Wasting in the last weeks came down sick, again failing of the same disease, only stronger this time. Several of them died. I stayed up with her all night two days ago as she worked to try to save one woman, to no avail. She fears – we all fear – that the spell did something to her magic.

She announced after chapel service yesterday that she bows to the Star Lord's wishes and will not Heal here any longer.

Gantry smiled grimly at the announcement, and intoned a prayer that the Star Lord grant her Highness guidance and wisdom in her choices.

I blink, shake my head from woolgathering. Gantry isn't here, and I have work to do. I look out at the boy in the rain, and wonder why such a young boy works with the dead at all.

He looks up at me as I start to turn back, and I gaze into hopeless gray depths. His belly strains at his ragged shirt, bulging, although his arms and legs are little more than bone. The Wasting has him too. If someone doesn't help him, it won't be long before he is wrapped in a shroud for burial.

Why is he so ill, surrounded by priests to say spells over him? I've overheard rumors from the servants that the priests ask for donations or they will not Heal. With the new crops rotting and failing in the fields, there are many who can't spare even the smallest coin. And Healing has always been free for those who come to hospice.

Even more disturbing are the hushed whispers that follow Julianna about her Healing powers, that they bring pestilence wherever they go, priests or no. And that anyone desperate enough to go to hospice now has little hope of ever seeing the outside of it again.

I take a deep breath. Maybe I can help this boy. "Boy, hello," I call out.

He stares at me listlessly with his sunken eyes, and I walk out into the rain. "Are you here alone? Isn't there anyone to help you?"

He just stares at me, his gaze taking in my warm cloak, my dry clothes, which become heavier with rain by the moment.

I clear my throat and start again. "What's your name?"

His eyes fill up with tears, and I realize he's even

younger than I thought — younger than Linnet by several years.

I reach for his arm and draw him away from the bodies in the yard, toward the kitchen. "Come with me, and we'll fix you some hot tea, all right? We'll get someone to Heal you, and you can go home to your family."

He bursts into silent, choking sobs.

Alarmed, I sit him on a stool by the high table and feel his forehead, pull the kettle from the stove. "What is it, what? Are you afraid? Are you supposed to be working? I don't think you'll get into trouble — I promise I won't tell anyone you had tea. Please, don't worry. Please tell me your name." I plead quietly with him as he shakes inconsolably in a pitiful huddle of dripping rags and mud.

"P-Petey," he whimpers through a sob. "Can't go home, me mum and da're out there." And he points out the door to the pile of bodies, growing slimy in the muck. I drape my cloak about his shivering body and wipe his nose with my handkerchief.

"Why haven't the priests Healed you yet, Petey?" I fear his fever has gotten too high for him to answer me coherently, but he shrugs and sniffles and does his best.

"Wasn't my turn. Can't heal me afore it's my turn," he says, his words slurring.

I hand him a mug of hot tea and wrap his hands around it. "Hold this and stay here until I come back for you," I say and stand up, clenching my fists.

I try to stem my anger. There are at least ten Healing priests sitting in the Inquisitor's building, staying in fine inns near the town square, but no one could help this boy. Here, where the worst cases of the Wasting languish, where babies wrap up their parents in linen and shiver from fever and cold, there are only three priests tending to the ill. And only one, I realize belatedly, who has the Healing blue surplice.

Marching into the large sickroom, I see Julianna arguing with that priest again, near the large stone hearth. At my entrance, they turn, and I hurry to them, drop into a curtsey.

"Your Highness, I ask your help with a matter in the kitchen," I say.

Julianna's glance at me is not amused. "I have a matter to discuss here with Deacon Bertram. Pray do not interrupt."

Grinding my teeth in worry and frustration, I back off and glance toward the kitchen.

Julianna is in high temper, and insisting now will only bring more attention to me. I stand behind her and listen to her lecture. "Now then, you shall tell me why this patient's illness hasn't been dealt with, when there are a plethora of priests taking their ease at the Eagle Inn?"

The priest hesitates and grows red. Pulling at his collar, he attempts to answer irate royalty as if he were perfectly within the right. "You see, your Highness, the stricken here must wait their turn for treatment. There are others ahead of them who must receive the healing spells first —"

Julianna cuts him off with a sharp gesture. "Do you mean to tell me that here, where I can see very severe cases of the Wasting, there isn't a need for priests to Heal the sick?"

The man's upper lip shines with sweat. His face, though red, keeps its blank expression, and I have to admire his control. "The priests with Healing training must conserve their strength for the worst cases, your Highness, and —"

"In case you haven't noticed, these people are the worst cases. I demand you send for more priests immediately and have them begin to Heal all the sick, not just those with money in their pockets."

I know Julianna itches to heal those around us herself. She hates the constraints she has put on herself, that circumstances put on her. It shows in her voice.

A commotion outside distracts us: the voice of a crowd of people talking, and Gantry sweeps into the room. Surrounded by young priests and wealthy merchants, he plays to the horde. Although his rich patrons are damp, none pay any mind to the mud and dreariness of their surroundings. His charismatic eyes draw the young man talking to him into gushing, stuttering adoration. With sickening panic, I recognize Francis, my fiancé. My former fiancé, rather, fawning over Bishop Gantry.

Dropping further back, I nearly fall over Petey, who stands just at my elbow. My cloak droops around him like a massive rain cloud, dragging water on the floor. He leans exhausted on a cot where a young man lies, both unaware of the commotion around them. Their eyes are empty and hopeless with fever. I wonder if I will always see Keenan's face in my memory with eyes like that: hopeless.

I stay behind Julianna to keep out of Francis' sight, and tighten the barriers around my magic, just in case. But even to my shielded mind there is a bright glow to the room beyond me, and I look for the source.

Behind Gantry stands Orrin, silent and expressionless. Magic glows around him like moonlight through storm clouds, turbulent and murky. His eyes look empty, too. Bishop Gantry has many eyes to answer for.

The crowd around Gantry stills as one by one people see Julianna quietly waiting. Many drop to deep obeisance, with a hasty "Your Highness," on their lips. A few around Gantry do not, and I try to note whom.

Gantry smiles benevolently, but his eyes turn me cold. "Your Highness, here you are in the hospice again. I had hoped not to find you here today." A lie — I can sense how he wants to play to this crowd.

"Ah, Bishop Gantry, you wound me. And here you are just the person I hoped to meet. How fortuitous for me that you have dropped by." Julianna's voice purrs over the mob, delicate and charming. She moves around the cots, drawing Bertram forward with her without seeming to try.

Gantry jumps in before she can speak, eager to defame her before these rich merchants. "Your Highness, I fear I must caution you yet again that your soul is in danger from these repeated attempts at Healing without the Star Lord's blessing. I ...." He trails off as he looks into Julianna's eyes, his smug look dropping as she draws herself into full regal stance.

"But my Lord Bishop, you did not allow me to speak my part," she says mildly as she comes to stand before him. She holds out her hand, and he must bow over it, by custom and rank.

His eyes narrow as he rises. "Your Highness," he intones, but his voice sounds less supple, more nasal, and I feel sweat pour over my body at that sound. I remember that sound. Struggling to breathe in quiet rage, I clench poor Petey's hand until he whimpers in pain.

"I am not, as you say, Healing without the Star Lord's blessing. I merely offer comfort to the suffering, and such simples as will ease their pain. If my power does not truly heal, then I shall leave that duty to those who can do so. But, as you can see, my Lord Bishop," and her voice rings off the walls, "those who can Heal are not.

"I have a dozen priests taking their ease at the expense of my mother's coffers, here to combat this pestilence. And yet there is only one priest here, where the worst of the Wasting abides, where people suffer and die for what this priest describes as waiting their turn. Did you know of this, my Lord Bishop?"

A subtle shift in the room. More of the merchants listen to Julianna, and worry for the town and their own people. And mentioning Duchess Marguerite makes everyone want to help her. I feel a stir of hope.

"Your Highness," Gantry begins, unsure of himself as I have never seen him. "I assure you that is merely an oversight. I am here to correct it. A grievous error indeed, if it has cost lives, but of no malice intended." His bow, while perfectly executed, is not deep, and there is a twist to his pale lips.

"Well, then correct it, my good Bishop! There are ill townspeople surrounding you. Heal, sir, and be an example to the people."

Gantry steps back, a hand to his chest. "Highness, I—"

"You have the gift, sir, or am I mistaken?"

I did not know Gantry was a Healer. I cannot fathom it. A true Healer should not be able to do what he does.

But Gantry is searching for words, and Julianna searches for a patient.

Looking at me, she pulls Petey forward. He whimpers when his hand leaves mine, and a wash of dread films over me. Julianna brushes his hair from his head, and smiles at him.

"Here, my Lord Bishop. A young child, deep in the fever. Do you Heal him, with the Star Lord's blessing, and let the priests under you know there shall be no slacking in any bishropic you would consider."

Gantry's head snaps up from contemplating the boy. With a barely controlled sneer, he grips the boy's wrist.

I hear a harsh gasp from behind Gantry, and I see Orrin's hood drop back from a face grimaced in pain. Purple sparks jump from him to the Bishop, and Gantry's eyes light with power.

I feel a pulling, a rush of power. Orrin – Orrin reaches out with his magic, and mine answers. It hurts, and I gasp, too. Gantry fills with our combined power, and he gestures to Petey with a dramatic flair.

But as he gestures, panic fills his face.

I can feel it go wrong – too much power, he can't control it. The Healing is awry – Gantry is not a good Healer, or he would stop the spell.

I try to break off my power but I'm drawn in. I sink to my knees slowly, trying to fix it. I See a nimbus of amethyst haze surround Petey and Gantry. It darkens to ashes, and Gantry's face pales as the Healing burns too hot, burns us all.

Petey cries out weakly once and falls from Gantry's grip, limp. I sway on my knees, try to find balance as I finally break the tie with Orrin. Julianna sweeps down in front of me; my view is blocked by her skirts.

"My lord!" I hear the horror in Julianna's voice, and I sink further down behind her, hidden in a warren of cot legs and ragged blankets. "He is dead!"

The shocked voices of the crowd drift louder. A small hand, outflung and half open, is just visible next to Julianna's kneeling form. I reach out to touch it, but Julianna's skirts swing over it, and I let my fingers drop, numb, to my side.

"I — he was too weak, alas, and dying. The Star Lord willed his small soul to the light. I could not keep him." Gantry's voice shakes, and I hear the crowd mutter at his explanation. Poor child. Killed by the Wasting.

The murmurs around me rise and fall. I clench my hands uselessly in fists and jam them to my temples. Peter's limp hand flops as Julianna lifts his body from the floor. Her back blocks out the sight of everything but his arm, resting on her billowing skirts. Another priest bends and takes the prone form from her.

It is my fault. Gantry would never have touched him if I'd only left well enough alone. If I'd only kept him behind me when Gantry came in, or gone to the kitchen with him to make more tea. Julianna was taking care of things. I didn't need to interfere. And now a boy with hopeless eyes lies dead because of me.

I look up to see Orrin's face – his hopeless eyes. He stares at me, the rest of his face blank as a death mask. He turns away as Gantry's hand fastens on his arm.

I drop my gaze, huddle behind Julianna. My cloak lies on the floor in a puddle of sodden wool. The air buzzes in my ears. I glance up to catch a glimpse of Gantry's face, closed and tight lipped, and the priest's, frightened and backing away from the bishop. My head pounds; I can't stand up, but I wish I had a weapon. I think, if I had the energy, I would kill him now, and consequences be damned.

"The shock: it's all too much for her. Have my carriage brought, and send a message to Lord Dorward. He'll meet her at the stables." Julianna pulls me to my feet.

Hands and arms bundle me out of the inn, and into the waiting carriage. My hands still press in fists to my temples. I stare at nothing, dry-eyed, trying to make a sound, any sound at all. The carriage lurches forward, and I curl into the velvet seats as I bounce toward the castle.

It was my power that turned the Healing too hot. My untamed power that filled Gantry. I don't think he'd have helped Petey much without me, but he might not have killed him, either. I trail ruin behind me like a cape.

The cold of the rainy day brushes in, and hands lift me bodily from the carriage. My legs don't work, and I'm carried from the courtyard to the castle. Jumbles of voices buffet me, but I know Connor's voice, and I curl into his embrace as if it could save me from my sins. Such carnage, empty eyes and broken necks, and I didn't stop it.

A sharp slap snaps my head sideways, and I look up into furious hazel eyes. I sit slumped on my bed in our room, my body aching, tense and cold. Linnet's glare burns into my consciousness as I return to reality.

"Linnet, what are you —" but she ignores Connor in favor of shaking me.

"Don't you dare! Don't you dare turn tail and run again! You coward!"

My neck aches from the force of her shaking, and I

reach up one balled fist and uncurl a finger to touch her cheek.

She rocks back as if I slapped her.

"It's my fault he's dead," I whisper

"It's your fault Mum's dead, too." And she is gone, sweeping out of the room like a thunderstorm.

Connor stares after her, his face a granite mask. His arms are raised, as if he were about to grab her. He drops them, and steps to my side, lifting my chin. I can feel the skin rising from Linnet's slap.

"You needed to snap out of that, but I'd hoped to do it more gently." His lips press into a pale line, and he turns to bring a tray over to my bedside. Tea and steaming towels lie on it; the one he hands to me, the other he applies to my face himself.

I feel tremors start deep in my stomach.

"Breathe, Rhiannon." My lungs creak at the reminder, and I drag in gasps and try to swallow my tea. He takes the cup from me. "One at a time. Breathe. Now, drink." He nurses me as gently as Julianna, only with dark eyes and no smiles and a bleak look to his mouth.

When I have drunk all the tea, I feel a weariness fall over my limbs, like a potion, and I curl into a ball and ignore him. Connor covers me with a blanket and darkens the lamp as he leaves.

My head pounds in rhythm with the burning along my scars, and my heart rages. The dead are mounting, and I fear there will be more. I must plan the death of this Bishop, to add to my crimes. This one I will do on purpose.

CHAPTER 18

My resolve to end Gantry's life lies smothering on my soul, a dense weight of stones. I wake in the morning to Linnet's light snores, and a head on fire, my eyes gritty and burning. The gray light of another wet summer dawn does little to illuminate the dark corners, but this morning I like the dark.

I slump out of bed, pull a gown out of the chest and struggle listlessly into it. The water in the bowl on the stand is cold and stale, but it shocks some of the cobwebs from my mind. I grope my way in the dark to the bathing room and water closet. I touch the lamp and a soft glow lights the room so I can see to relieve myself. Everything is quiet, and I try to think.

Gantry has to die. The words rise up from my heart and choke me. He cannot be allowed to continue. He called for the deaths of my family. He signed the papers. He tortured me. He tortured Orrin. He called demons, and he is probably fomenting civil war. He used demon spells. I don't care that he's a link in a chain, that the kirche is too powerful. I don't care that he isn't even in charge. He needs to die.

I make my way to the herbarium in the mostly quiet castle. Dawn is breaking, and some servants are beginning their days. I hear noises in the kitchen. My cold bare feet make soft sounds as I pass the door and head down the short flight of stairs.

The packet I made a few days ago is where I left it. I put it in my pocket and start making simples in the glow of the lamps. I may as well be useful as long as I'm awake so early. I make myself tea from one of the restoratives, which helps my aching head some.

I just need a way to get close to Gantry. To his drink, specifically. I'd rather not get caught – but if I am caught, after he's dead, I will have done one thing right.

I feel Linnet's mind try to send to mine, and then Hugh's, but I strengthen my barriers and ignore them. Linnet is easy to ignore yet – her sendings still aren't very strong. Hugh is more insistent, but I have more power. I keep working.

Several rounds of tisane later, the stairs creak and I look up to see Linnet staring back at me. I am straining an infusion of chamomile and elderflower into a storage jar.

I speak before she can. "Is the princess awake?" Steam from the infusion wisps around my face, making it hard to see how far I've filled the jar. I blow lightly across the top of the jar to clear it, then fill it the rest of the way.

"Everyone's up and looking for you. His Grace can't even find your shining magic glow," she snaps, glaring.

"I'm sorry if I worried anyone. I woke up early." She

rolls her eyes and turns to look at Hugh, who's walking down the stairs behind her.

"I told you she didn't run away," he says to her, and she shrugs his hand off her arm and runs up the stairs. He watches her go for a moment, then continues down to me. "That child is far too angry."

"Who isn't?" I say under my breath, and he sighs and pretends he didn't hear me. I wipe the jar dry and turn to put it on the shelf.

"Rhia, I came to check on you, see if you're recovered. From yesterday."

"I know what from," I say. He puts his hand out to me, but I dodge him. "I'm tired, but nothing permanent."

"Do you know what happened? Could you tell?"

"Gantry over-reached. He's not a good Healer." Hugh raises his eyebrows, but nods. "He over-reached, and caught me. It burned too hot, and the magic was too much for Petey."

"Who?"

I stare at Hugh, and he flushes. "The boy's name was Petey? I didn't know. I'm sorry, Rhia. That must have been terrible."

"Gantry has no dearth of crimes laid at his door," I say, and I catch the worried frown on Hugh's face, try to dial back my bitterness.

"Did it harm you? I mean, magically?"

"I think I'm … sore." I don't know how to describe the rest of it – the certainty of wanting to kill a man, the cold center of my chest. Is that a result of being exposed to demons? Am I losing my mind as much as Gantry? Does the magic have me as much in its thrall? These are questions I can't ask aloud. I don't know if I would, even if I were able.

Hugh watches me pour another jar full of tisane. "I'm glad you aren't more hurt. Do you think you could help me with something tomorrow, then?"

I look up at him. He regards me with a wary expression, as though he isn't sure he trusts my assessment of myself. Fair enough. "I can try," I say. I reach for another jar.

Hugh touches my arm, and I See him frightened, yelling, something about death, his face a mask of fury.

I gasp out loud. "What is it? Did you burn yourself?" he asks as the tisane splashes.

"No," I say, blinking. "No. I just – I guess I am pretty tired." I reach past him for some rags to mop up.

"Do you think you'll be recovered by tomorrow? I would like – if it's not too soon for you – I would like it if you'd be nearby while I have an interview with Bishop Gantry."

"An interview?"

"We're going to discuss the hospice, and what recompense might be made to families who've lost anyone due to neglect." He grimaces. "I don't expect it will be a pleasant meal."

"You're serving dinner?" I feel a sick chill in my stomach. This might be my chance.

"Luncheon, tomorrow. We'll have something light, most likely. I won't be very hungry, I'm sure."

"Of course I'll help you. Where will you have it?"

"In the lesser hall. It's nice and impressive. It's useful for intimidations and such, if Bishop Gantry is capable of being intimidated."

I toss the damp rags in a pile with some others and turn to Hugh, trying to seem nonchalant. "Where will I be?"

"In the small pantry, which should be close enough to hear. There's a spot to hide." He grins suddenly. "It's a great hiding place, really. You'll love it."

I look at him, not trusting that grin. "We'll work out how your barriers should work for this, so you can listen in without giving yourself away. I think you're almost there."

"If someone discovers me, I'll have some explaining to do."

"I used to hide in there all the time as a child: no one ever found me. And anyway, we can figure out something plausible. But I don't think it will be a problem."

I think he's being too blithe: he's worried about something. But I want to do this. This could be my chance. "All right," I agree, and Hugh smiles and leaves me to my tisane.

The vision of Hugh shouting washes over me again. But I can't tell what he's shouting, why he's so angry. If it's because I'm successful, I will live with it, I think. It's too vague to be sure, anyway. I brush it off. If my magic wants me to know something, it needs to be more specific. I pour the last jar of tisane and clean up, tired again. But a dark determination fills me – I'm going to see this finished.

* * *

The lesser hall is next to the great hall, and overlooks the west barbican, and the cliffs by the sea. The long dining table takes up much of the room, and there are twelve chairs around it. The dark wood of the surface gleams in the lamp light as rain patters on the windows, and gulls cry outside.

Hugh shoos me into the pantry, off the side of the room. A counter and cabinets and one giant wardrobe take up the small space. Two place settings lie on the counter, rimmed with gold and with the duchy seal on them. One goblet is almost encrusted in gems, and the seal is quite large.

"Oh, good, Samuel has brought out the intimidation-ware," Hugh says.

I raise my eyebrows at the goblets. "I know, they're hideous, but they do remind people that I'm a duke." He smiles at me, a wry grin. I suppose I do forget, now and again. He wants people to, I think.

"What is this wardrobe even doing in here?" I ask. It is ugly, and huge, and any wall space that might have existed is more than taken up by it. It covers part of the doorway to the corridor. The carvings all over the front look like sea monsters.

"There's nowhere else to put it," he shrugs.

"But – there's a whole castle? With …" I let that go. "If you don't like it, why keep it?"

"Oh, I like it. But no one else does. And it is pretty ugly, I admit. But I like it where it is. I think my mother put it here in a fit of pique over something – my father brought it home from travelling somewhere. I don't know where. And Mother was not best pleased, although I can't remember why."

"And so it just … stays here."

"I'm probably the only one who remembers it exists," he says. "In you go." He opens the door, which creaks, of course, and a musty smell comes out. Some of the top shelves have linens on them, but mostly it's empty.

"You and any servants who have to squeeze past it," I say, not wanting to go in there.

"Well, yes." He looks over his shoulder. "We don't have time. Just listen, try to See how Gantry responds to my questions, and specifically try to learn if he had any instructions to have priests charge at the hospice."

He half shoves me into the wardrobe and shuts the door before I'm all the way in. I yank my arm in and stick my tongue out at the door.

There's a gap where the door didn't quite shut. I shuffle back so I'm not in the light coming in, but I can still see the pantry, and the open door into the lesser hall. I stifle a sneeze.

Someone shuffles past the wardrobe, and I can see Hugh's servant Samuel standing at the counter, pouring wine. I watch avidly, hoping for a chance. When he walks away, I push the door open a little more, one hand on the packet in my pocket. No one is around for now. Slipping out of the wardrobe, I rush to open the packet of powder. My hands are shaking.

I don't know if this dose will be noticeable in this wine. I hesitate, then dump the dose in, spilling some. I make sure to use the goblet that doesn't have the ostentatious ducal seal on it. I stir it with my finger. The spilled powder I brush from the counter, dusting my hands off, wiping them on my dark gown.

A rustling makes me jump, look up. Orrin stands next to the wardrobe, staring at me.

Heart pounding, I stare back at him. I don't know what he saw.

Biting my lip, I hide the packet behind my back, try to think of something to say.

Orrin stares at me for a moment, then proceeds into the hall.

I swallow, nauseated, slip back into the wardrobe. He

probably knows I'm in here, but I don't know whether he saw the poison. I don't know what he'll do about any of it.

The view from my little crack in the door is limited. I can see the counter to my left, and the open doorway across from me, and part of the table. I can't see anything much beyond that with my eyes.

Hugh passes the doorway, then Connor. Gantry does not. I can hear the rustle of cloth, and clanking – did the guards bring swords? I can't tell this way.

Samuel passes by the wardrobe again and I flinch, only just stopping myself from gasping. Heart pounding, I settle a little farther back from the door, and close my eyes.

Reaching out with my Sight, I try to get a picture of the room from someone. Hugh is easiest – we've been practicing this. He's looking at Gantry entering the room, and the four guards he brought with him. The light from the window glares with that mid-day high gray, the sky and the sea and the rocks below all the same color and it makes the windows look like blank and empty eyes.

Hugh is thinking the guards are overkill.

Connor's mind is, as usual, too tightly guarded for me to get more than impressions. He doesn't like the placement of the guards, he wishes Hugh had made them stay outside, he watches Orrin closely, he watches everyone closely.

I get nothing from Orrin at all, as if he isn't even there. The only hint of him is the dull throb of magic that flows between him and Gantry all the time, now. What spell does Gantry have going that takes that kind of power? But I can't tell. And Gantry's mind is more closely guarded than Connor's, most of the time.

The guards are bored. One of them has a sore knee. That one thinks that Gantry is a scary, scary man. But he doesn't trust Hugh, either. The others are thinking of lunch, and resenting this duty, which they, too, think is overkill.

I hear the door open, and everyone startles. A new person comes in. "Good afternoon, gentlemen," says Duchess Marguerite. I feel everyone staring at her. I can See her from Hugh, from the guard.

From Gantry. I can See in Gantry's mind, at this surprise. He looks at her, he makes his face smile, but he wants her dead. He wants everyone in this room dead, only he's not supposed to do it. Yet.

Yet.

Not supposed to kill them yet. But he dreams of it, the deaths, so like the queen's, so like so many others. There is power in death. There is power to give and to take – the demons whisper of it to him all the time now. He makes his face smile at the duchess, but he thinks of the power in her death to make the smile real.

Sick, I pull back into myself. Oh, great Lords, he has plans to kill the whole family. And the only thing stopping him is that someone told him he's not supposed to. Yet. He killed Queen Cecily.

He killed Queen Cecily. I can See it – the spell, the demons, the sickness that came upon her. Oh, my sweet Dorei. What do I do?

The sound of my gasping snaps me to awareness. What are they saying in there?

"Mother, it is kind of you to offer, but I think it best if I…"

"Are you saying that my input – after I have spent the last thirty years overseeing the business of this duchy – my input is unnecessary?" Her voice is pleasant, but the steel behind it is not.

"Of course not, Mother." Hugh sounds a little strangled.

"Then you're saying that I am too old to have anything useful to contribute?" Hugh is silent, wisely, but I can feel his dismay.

Gantry breaks in. "I do not think this discussion is any place for a woman, your Grace. These are not delicate topics."

I center myself, bring myself into the room again, find the guard with the sore knee. The guard is thinking that Gantry may be scary, but he can't be very smart.

"You are saying, my Lord Bishop, that my place as a woman and as a duchess and as a leader of my people, is not here, to discuss how your priests have been stealing from my coffers, ruining my hospice, and killing children of my duchy?"

Everyone freezes. Gantry has not been accused of murder before this. But the duchess is doing it now.

"You dare," Gantry says.

Hugh cuts him off. "Mind how you speak to the Duchess my mother," he says in a strained tone. "My Lord Bishop. Mind what you say to her. And mind what you say to me. My tolerance is wearing thin."

From the guard's eyes, Hugh seems taller than usual. But the colors are flat and wrong, and I cannot read anyone's face. This guard is near-sighted and colorblind.

"Your tolerance," Gantry hisses, glaring.

Hugh slaps his hand on the table, interrupting. "My

tolerance, my Lord Bishop. This is my duchy. The arch-bishops and the cardinals may grant you a bishropic here, but it is me they must court if they want it confirmed. It is me they must court if they want the monasteries and the newly built cathedral in Jervaulx and Villeur Temple lands to stay in kirche hands. Those lands aren't paid off, my Lord Bishop. To me. I own them. The lands you have your buildings on. Up to and including the Inquisitor's building. Did you know, it has been in my family for generations. My forebears built it and lived in it and owned it. We still own it."

"This is outrageous-"

"That the rents are so low?" Marguerite breaks in. "Yes, I think so, too. I didn't before, but now I believe that they are, in fact, far too low. And that is beside the fact that you, Bishop Gantry, owe the families of the dead a death geld."

My head is spinning from the emotions in the room. Gantry is bleeding power – I'm sure Hugh can feel it, but he ignores me when I send him a mental nudge. He's looking at his mother, and I can feel his fear for her, getting involved, and his exasperation with her as she steals his thunder. Through his eyes she seems a pillar of stubborn righteousness and strength. But what I feel from her is fury and fear for her children and people. I've never felt that from her before.

Maybe I wasn't paying attention.

"Ah, Samuel. Perhaps you would be so good as to give me one of those goblets," Marguerite says. "I'm quite dry." I freeze for a moment, too long, my lungs stuck to my spine in shock. I hear Samuel moving.

Don't let her drink! I shout in my head, send it to Hugh

as hard as I can, I think I might be heard out loud, and I fling back the door of the wardrobe to run out.

The noise of the door is slightly overshadowed by a loud crash, and my heart leaping out of my chest, and raised voices in the dining room.

Stay. Put. I feel more than hear Hugh's mind, and I halt, one foot out of the wardrobe. A moment later Connor rounds the corner and promptly pushes me back in without even looking at me.

"I have some towels, and I rang for someone to come up," he says, and the door of the wardrobe closes shut – fully this time. I hear it click.

My head is full of Linnet asking questions and Hugh's rage and Connor's very tightly controlled fury and everyone else's confusion.

"Are you hurt?" I hear out loud. Marguerite's voice. But I don't know whom – I struggle to push myself back into any awareness in the room.

The guards are around Gantry, the one guard is pretty sure that they're going to have to kill – Orrin. They're all staring at Orrin, who is staring at the floor, at Samuel, who is lying in the remains of the wine goblets and some plates and a tray. Samuel is groaning, trying not to put his hand on any broken pottery or glass or … whatever the goblets were.

"I beg your pardon," Orrin says in a dead voice, near whisper. I only hear him because I'm listening for it from the wardrobe, and the guard sees his lips move.

"What is the meaning of this," demands a guard.

"Be quiet," snaps Gantry, and everyone looks at him. He glares at Orrin, his lips pressed flat. Orrin does not look up.

Marguerite kneels to help Samuel, but she pats

Orrin's hand as she does. "It was an accident," she says, in a cheerful tone at odds with her sharp thoughts and feelings, which I can't quite catch, but they aren't cheerful. "Accidents happen. Oh, Connor, hand me that towel, there's a good lad." Everyone stares at her, and she smiles as she stands. "It's only plates broken, Samuel's all right."

Connor helps Samuel to stand. Marguerite puts her arm around Orrin. "Don't be too hard on the boy. Growing boys are all arms and legs at this age – well I remember. Why don't you come with me, now, and we'll see if you were cut," she says to Orrin, who doesn't move.

"No," Gantry snaps, and now it's time for everyone to look at him. The guards have stepped behind him – I can't See his face. "No, he'll come with me." Gantry stands. "Your Graces, I will pay the death geld. And there will be no charging of money from the kirche, for Healing in the hospice. But do not think to challenge me on kirche Laws. The hospices are not to be re-opened by any lay Healer."

He gestures sharply and the guards fall away. Orrin shuffles toward the door, and Gantry allows him to open it, and get into the hall, before he yanks on his arm and starts to stride away. The guards follow them out, and I let go of the guard's awareness reluctantly.

Silence falls on the room, finally broken when Hugh speaks. "You're all right, then?"

"Yes, your Grace." Samuel.

"Why don't you go clean yourself up. I'll have someone else take care of this. You're sure you're not hurt?" he asks.

Samuel must nod, because I don't hear him answer,

although I do hear a rustle as someone brushes by the wardrobe.

What's going on? What did you do? I can feel Linnet getting closer.

Stay out of this, I send, but I don't think she'll listen.

"Mother," I hear Hugh say, but she doesn't let him speak.

"What was that?" she demands.

I can't get a clear read, everyone is too upset.

"Mother,"

"What was that? You planned to have this meeting without me? You planned to somehow harm the Bishop? While he was under my roof?"

"My roof," Hugh says.

"That wasn't the plan." Connor says, but Marguerite isn't finished.

"It was someone's plan. And it was poorly carried out – that boy, what's his name, Orrin. He didn't want anyone harmed, so that's something. But I think that child is in serious trouble."

"Yes, but Mother,"

"And so are you, and don't pretend you aren't. I know exactly why you're here. I know why Julianna is here. And I know she's pregnant again, and trying to hide it."

"You know?"

"Of course I know. I don't know who you think you're fooling. Everyone knows. The king knows. He wrote to me. I know all about the impending troop movements and the border raids from Fanthas and that the king's cousin Queen Esther is angry about trade, and is harboring Stephen. I'm sorry, Connor, I know your brother isn't a happy subject for you."

Stephen? I think.

"I am aware of my brother's location," he says. Connor has a brother?

"The king won't ask you to do anything to him, if it is his influence behind all of this," Marguerite says, her voice kind.

"He may not have a choice. And if it is Stephen, I will not need the king to ask me." Connor's voice is – not kind.

"Listen, Mother,"

"I'm not as stupid as you think, Hugh. And I know when my children are in trouble. I know when my country is in trouble. You think I only rusticate here in Haverston, and only mind duchy business? Duchy business is country business, and my children are involved in plots and civil unrest."

"We're not-"

"Whatever side, it's civil unrest. And I have been staying clear so as not to disrupt any plans you have. But do not think me simple. And from now on, you are going to tell me when you're going to kill a man in my castle."

"My castle," Hugh says, but after a moment he sighs. "Yes.

"Yes, your Grace," Connor says.

"And let that child out of the wardrobe, Hugh. She's probably suffocated by now. You should get rid of that horrible thing."

"Good day, Mother."

"I suspect Julianna will be along in a moment. Tell her to come see me."

"Yes, Mother." He sighs

"Don't roll your eyes at me. All right, I'm going. Come to me for dinner."

Silence descends. I push on the wardrobe door, but it's stuck. I'm trembling, every part of me is shaking and sick, and I can't feel my face. How did that go so very wrong?

CHAPTER 19

"Rhia!" Hugh shouts. I flinch back from the wardrobe door. "Get out here!"

The door still won't budge, and my arms don't have any strength in them. After a moment the door opens; Connor regards me, his expression blank. I look back. I don't know what my expression is. When he turns to go into the dining room, I follow.

"What were you thinking? What was in that goblet? How could you do such a thing?" Hugh's voice buffets me, inside and out, and I stagger, ward off his mind with my hands.

"Oh, for the love – barriers!" he snaps, and I try, but I've been working too hard and they're weak and wobbly. "Rhia," Hugh warns, and I turn to snarl.

"I'm trying! Stop pushing at me!"

"Stop pushing – you just tried to kill my mother!"

I shake my head, back against the wall. "She wasn't supposed to be here," I mumble.

"Do you think that would absolve you if she'd been

harmed in any way?" The rasp of his shout grates the air, and I stare at the floor, try to build my tattered barriers.

Linnet flings open the door from the hall and runs in, fear and rage clear on her face.

"What did you do?" she yells at me. Behind her, Julianna enters a little slower, but in a hurry still.

"What happened, Hugh?" she asks. She stares at me, too. I feel pinned to the wall.

"Rhia almost poisoned our mother, that's what happened. She seems to think the fact that it was meant for Gantry is a good enough excuse."

Linnet throws her hands up in the air, as Julianna just stares.

"What were you thinking!" Hugh yells again. My stomach feels like an avalanche, and my eyes burn, and I can't get my breath.

"I was just –"

"What could you possibly – how could you –" and I find my voice.

"That he murdered my brother! My parents! That he's killed how many others! That he killed Queen Cecily! Yes, I finally got something concrete from him – he killed the queen, and he's glad. And he'll kill all of you, too, as soon as he gets the go ahead from someone."

Everyone is silent, staring, except for Linnet. She crosses the room, broken goblets crunching under her boots. "So you get to poison Duchess Marguerite?"

"No! She never even touched the goblet. The poison was for Gantry!"

"What poison," Julianna asks quietly.

"What?"

"Which poison did you use, Rhia?"

I look down, away from everyone. "Foxglove."

"How much?"

"Does it matter?" I snap.

"How much foxglove powder was in the goblet that my mother didn't touch?"

I stare at the ground, shrug. "A little less than a one of the small packets."

"A little less?"

"I spilled some."

"How much?"

"I don't know! It spilled, I brushed at it, I had to hide! I was in kind of a hurry."

"To poison a goblet, you were in kind of a hurry. Because you didn't want anyone to find out."

I don't answer. The next question will hurt more.

"You didn't want anyone to find out, because you knew it was wrong. You knew you were wrong, Rhia, and you did it anyway."

"Did anyone see you?" Connor asks.

I don't look at him, either. "Orrin might have."

"Orrin saw you put poison in the goblet? And you didn't tell anyone about any of this?" Hugh snaps.

"He didn't tell anyone either, did he? And he spilled the tray over only after the duchess asked for wine, so I don't think his intentions were to stop me before that."

"You don't know that! What if he was supposed to spill it? What if he had plans to poison me instead?"

"That doesn't make any sense."

"None of this makes any sense! What were you thinking?"

"He's a murderer! He killed my family! He's killing more people, he's going to kill your sister, and you don't care!"

"Don't you tell me what I do and don't care about,

young woman! How dare you jeopardize people's lives like that? You don't know what you're doing! You could have killed someone!"

"I was trying to kill Gantry!"

"And it failed! Spectacularly! What are you even doing right? Nothing, so far!"

As I reel back, hurt even more than I thought, I hear Connor move. He puts his hand on Hugh's arm. "Enough."

"No, it's not."

"Enough, Hugh. I'll talk to her. You calm down. We'll – we'll figure out what to do next."

"This-"

"Enough. Go. Take Julianna to see your mother."

"Gods."

"Tell her." Connor says.

Hugh glares at me. I glare back, but I'm fighting tears. Finally, Hugh stalks over past Julianna to the door.

"Come, sister mine. We'll have so much to chat about with Mother."

Julianna stares at me, her face a mask. I keep the glare, but I know it just looks sullen to them. I don't understand why they don't understand. It's not like the duchess even touched that goblet.

When they are gone, the only ones left are Connor and Linnet, and the mess on the floor.

And me.

"Why did you do it that way? That was stupid!" And now not only is that man not dead, but you just hurt the only nice person in this entire castle!" Linnet yells, her arms gesturing wildly.

"I didn't hurt the duchess! She didn't even touch the goblet."

"I was talking about Orrin!"

I shake my head, annoyed. "You don't even know Orrin. I was trying to help him."

"Well, you failed. You left him with that awful man, and you're just standing here while he's probably beating him right now! Don't pretend it's not true – I saw it in your head that he beats him!"

She clenches her fists and I feel my own temper flaring again, as she accuses me over and over again of something I can't fix.

"You're so selfish!" she shouts. "You don't care about anyone! You think you're so special, you play martyr all the time, and I'm sick of it!"

She leaps toward me, her hand raised, but I too have had enough.

She raises her hand, but I am faster. I grab her shoulder and whack her hard across the face, and then Connor pulls us apart, our hair locked in each other's fists and neither of us able to breathe for sobbing. I wrench myself from Connor's hands and throw myself to the other side of the room, choking on my breath and my rage and not caring who hears this time.

Linnet slaps Connor's hands away too, and runs out of the room. When she's gone, I can only lean back against the table behind me, gasping. Connor stands where he is, his feet crunching in the crockery, and regards me.

"Just say it," I snap. Or I try to snap – it's too watery, and I can't stop the hiccupping sobs.

"What would you like me to say?" he asks, his voice quiet.

I won't look at him. "Whatever it is you've been holding back. Whatever lecture you have waiting – I'm selfish, I'm stupid, I can't do anything right, I'm horrible, not to be trusted, evil –"

"I would never say any of that. None of those words describe you."

I turn my head then, trying not to pant, failing. "What words would you use, then."

He leans one shoulder on the wall, oblivious to the clinks and crackles under him. "Words that describe you: loyal, brave, impetuous. It was you being impetuous that brought you to Gantry's attention to begin with, wasn't it?"

I shake my head, shrug. It didn't feel impetuous. "I don't know. A man was dying – I made sure people knew about it. I couldn't not – Mother was so horrified. It never occurred to her that I could See something like that. She thought it was embarrassing." I bite back another sob, half-laugh. "She wanted me to back down. Say I was mistaken."

"I think she was probably afraid for you."

"Maybe. Maybe. She didn't – she never understood me."

"Rhiannon – I can't speak for your parents. But you frighten me on a regular basis, and I do believe you've been rather less exuberant than your old self, since I've known you."

"I'm really quite shy," I say, and he shrugs.

"Shy maybe. Stubborn is another word I'd use to describe you. Honorable. Intelligent, but not always smart."

I stiffen. "Fine."

"And you have a temper."

I glare at him. "Who doesn't?"

"Fair point. Here's another. You do not have the

knowledge and skills to assassinate a powerful man and get away with it."

I suck in a breath. His tone hasn't changed, but his eyes are quite dark. "So now the lecture."

"Lecture, if you like. Facts. Rhiannon –" he sighs, runs his hand through his hair. His shirt is rumpled under his gray brocade waistcoat. I stare at his chin. "Rhiannon, there are some things you and I agree on. But you'll have to bow to my age and experience."

"You aren't so much older than I am," I say.

He barks a laugh. "Oh, so much older.

"Eight years isn't so much," I say, because I heard Hugh say they were of an age, so I know.

"I've been dealing with assassinations and political plots since before I was born. I am so many more years more than eight older than you." He sighs again, levels a look at me. "If you are sure about Queen Cecily," he starts.

I fold my arms. "I am."

He nods. "Write down everything you can remember, every piece of information or picture that you gleaned from him. Then we'll discuss all of it. This –" he gestures to the mess beneath him – "this isn't the solution you're looking for. Trust me to keep you, and your sister, and everyone else as safe as I can. Let me do it. We'll find a way to save Orrin yet."

I look away, press my trembling lips together. But I nod as more tears fill my eyes. I lean my head back, look at the ceiling.

Connor turns to go. "Rhia," he says, turning at the door.

I look at him.

"If you really mean to poison someone, make sure you're in charge of the vessel the entire time."

I feel my eyes widen a little.

He stares at me. "If I didn't need him alive, he'd be dead already," he says, and then he's gone.

CHAPTER 20

Despite his words to me after the poison fiasco, it's apparent that Connor doesn't trust me anymore than anyone else does. I gave him my description of what happened to Queen Cecily, but we haven't discussed it.

Julianna and Hugh are still furious with me, and stay tight-lipped and coldly civil whenever I am present. Linnet refuses to speak to me at all.

When Connor does see me, he shakes his head sadly and says to keep a low profile, stay away from Gantry and Orrin. I'm forbidden chapel services even, and the herbarium. I spend all of my time in the library, avoiding everyone.

Days pass slowly, but it seems the weeks fly past without my notice. Summer is ending, without ever really appearing at all. Everyone talks about how cold and wet it's been, that it's the worst harvest in decades.

Duchess Marguerite develops a pinched line on her forehead that never goes away, and the talk is that the hospice is more full than ever. Although none of us go there anymore: Julianna sends her simples by messenger.

Julianna has announced to the castle that she's pregnant, with her mother's urging, and everyone graciously pretends that they are surprised. The ladies in the castle gather in her rooms to embroider and sew baby clothes, and exclaim over her.

I sit in the corner and mend stockings, badly. I know the tension between us is noticeable, if only because of whispers about fitzWellan blood are louder. I still don't know anything about Connor's brother, but I know he is a villain in their eyes, and so now I understand what they mean. I keep my eyes on my work and ignore everyone.

I miss Keenan, and Orrin, and not feeling like a monstrous mistake. The castle is full of people who ignore or despise me, and I am so lonely and afraid. If they won't help me, I'm going to have to do something else. Something drastic.

In my spare time, I'm pouring over all of Hugh's magical texts, mostly left to my own devices in the back corner of the big library room. I've found the book of runes Hugh was talking about. The text is very old, and smudged in places. It's written in ancient Indrani, and I only know a few words.

There's an incomplete Indrani lexicon, and I translate what I can onto papers of my own, that I keep with me and study later, trying to decipher the meanings. The grammar is the hard part. Indrani sentences are backwards and inside out to ours, and trying to parse what the author meant takes me a lot of time. I don't ask for help.

But I've found two of the runes, I think. One, on my

arm, is the rune for silence, with intent mixed in. Another, that appears several times on my legs, calls the magic. I don't know what any of the others are, yet. Not for sure. I'm afraid to find out.

My dreams at night are not happy. I know they disturb Linnet, too, because she smacks me awake with her pillow. All she says is "wake up, stupid." Then we both lie in the dark, listening to my harsh breath.

This morning is no different, and I feel more lost than I ever have. Dawn finds me in the library, alone, with a guttering candle and a spent glowsand lamp. The text wavers in front of my tired eyes, but I blink the runes into focus. There. That rune, that rune means free, it opens bindings. It is almost the same as the one for silence. I think – I think I have a plan.

I pad into the kitchen and make a tray as if for an early breakfast. Bread, honey, oatmeal, and I surreptitiously slip a sharp knife onto the tray. The kitchen maids and guards at the back table ignore me but for a few murmured "my lady's" as I bustle about. I know I look half-crazed lately, and they give me a wide berth.

My pulse tingling with anticipation, I bring the tray up to Julianna's rooms, and leave it in the solar. I head to the bathing room, taking the knife and the rune text with me.

The room is tiled in a pale green and blue pattern, with suggestions of fish in the tiles. I latch the door, hands shaking. I don't remember what Gantry chanted: I don't think I want that spell, anyway. But Keenan had a spell to focus power, and I think I can do that. It is just a little spell, but I don't want to mess with a big one. I think Keenan would approve.

I take off my clothes and toss them at the hook on

the wall. The tub is a tiled rectangle, with thick ledges on the sides. Slender pipes jut out from the wall, coming from below the kitchens, where some symmetry of magic and genius brings water at the pull of a chain.

I sit on the edge, my legs in the tub, the chill tile biting into my flesh. I can't catch my breath. Closing my eyes, I chant the words of the focus spell in airy puffs, rest the edge of the knife on my right arm. The text is open on the floor next to me.

I feel my runes, my skin, my body fill slowly with power, like waking a hibernating monster. I haven't used it in the last few weeks. Everything feels sore and rusty, even though not using my power has hurt, as well.

It's hard to keep my hands from shaking, and it's my off-hand that will do the … the cutting. I take a deep breath, shuddering, and press. After the first resistance, my skin parts, and it hurts, it stings, and I push power into the wound as I try to re-draw the rune.

I'm trying to be careful not to go too deep, but it's so hard to tell what's working – if anything is. My arm burns, then all my runes, and sweat runs into my eyes and between my breasts and down my back, and I'm shaking from trying not to shake.

I chant the focus spell again, and I turn the knife again. I part more skin, and tears fall onto my arm and into the tub with my sweat and blood, and I want to finish this. I have to finish this. But I'm afraid I can't. I turn the knife again.

The door bursts open. Linnet stands in the opening, and I know she's yelling. Her eyes are wide, her mouth is wide, but I hear only the roaring in my ears, the power in my skin trying to turn, change, pull me forward. I press too hard and the blood rushes over my arm, and I can't see the runes anymore.

Julianna runs in, her belly a hard ball under her nightgown, her hair a fierce halo of wisps around her head and braid. My hands can't hold the knife steady, my mind can't hold the spell, and I shake as she nears me. The spell is too hot. She should not come near me.

Rhia, what are you doing? Hugh sends me, but I can't answer. His power slips into mine to hold the spell steady, to keep me from dropping anything else, as my legs give way and I slide down into the tub with the blood and the sweat. Even I can hear Julianna and Linnet cry out, but I manage to not stab myself with the knife.

At impass, Julianna and Linnet stand halfway into the room, unable to come closer because of the focus spell, or the magic I put into it, or maybe shock and disgust, because I am so awful. And I'm not done; I feel the power lurching off-kilter through my body. I was always off-kilter, I realize, always not quite balanced, the spell was always a little wrong. Now it's wrong in a new way, and a lot.

It hurts, this new way. Or maybe it's always hurt, and I only now recognize it. I stare at my bleeding arm and feel dizzy. Am I dizzy from blood loss or the spell?

Both. It's both, honey. I feel Hugh in my head, see him kneeling next to the tub, and he weaves himself into the spell. He looks down at the book beside him, then at me again, and there are tears running down his face.

Give me the knife, he sends, and puts his hand over my bloody one, but I can't let go. He sucks in a breath, nods, and leans forward to kiss my forehead. *Then let me guide,* and my shaking hand follows his lead. He grimaces, his face close to mine. He takes my hand, the knife, and makes the last two cuts to finish the rune. I feel a surge of balance, a blast and release. I cry out, and so does Hugh.

The silence after the roaring is a pressure suddenly gone. The room is filled with gasping and sobs, and I don't know whose is whose.

"There. We did it," Hugh says softly. "You can let go of the knife."

Only I can't. Julianna walks over, lowers herself to the tub ledge.

"Let Hugh have the knife," she says, reaching for my hair, to smooth it back, or pet it, or something. I flinch, and she draws back. "Rhia, let me help you," she says gently, brokenly.

Hugh lets go of my hand and stands back. Maybe he can tell how crowded I feel. He backs up, but then Connor is there. He looks at Julianna with his warning look, but his attention is on my arm. Just my arm. He sits where Hugh was and wraps a towel around it tight.

"Keep pressure on that," he says to me, and I start to put my hand over his, but I have to put the knife down, first.

I look at him.

"Rhiannon, hold this tight on your arm," he says again, his eyes on mine now.

I feel my hand spasm, unclench, and the knife clatters into the tub. I grab at the towel, which is beginning to soak through. He nods at me, picks up the knife, gets up. "Let Julianna help you. We'll be outside." And he turns and walks out of the room, taking a quietly sobbing Linnet and sober Hugh with him.

Julianna brushes back my hair, places her hands on

my shoulders, and I feel more magic moving through me. A quieter magic, I remember how this feels, like pins and needles, like summer sun and campfire smoke, like swimming in a storm.

I open my eyes to Julianna turning the water on. The pipes groan a little, spit out hot water. "Let me take that towel, Rhia." Her eyes are kind on me, but I can't look back for long. Her nightgown has blood on it. Her face is wan and tired. And I am broken, again.

"Let's clean you up," she says, and she dips a washcloth in the water, hands me soap. I look at my arm when she takes the towel away. The wound is a shiny scar now, under the blood. As she wipes it clean, the scar shows white on my skin, like the others. Pinker, newer, a little ragged. But it is a scar, and not a wound. The skin feels burned, and I hiss when she rubs soap on it.

"I know. It'll be tender for a few days. You remember." She bites her lip, hands me the washcloth. "When you're clean, why don't you drain the tub and refill it, have a soak. I – I'm just going to sit over in the chair, and wait. I'll help you out when you're ready."

"I won't drown myself," I whisper. "I didn't do it to hurt myself, or anyone. I did it so I could tell – could tell you – " I try to talk about the demons. But it didn't work, the rune didn't work, and I still can't speak. I don't know what I just did to myself, but it didn't even work. Sobs wrack me and I just lie there and let them. All of that, for nothing.

Julianna kneels by my side and hugs me, rocks me while I cry.

Connor and Hugh are waiting when Julianna and I emerge from the bathing room. The solar looks the same as I left it; the forgotten breakfast tray sitting on the table, the lamps half lit and the fire crackling the morning chill away. I guess it is still morning. It seems as though days have passed.

Julianna leads me to the chaise and then heads back to her chamber for a robe. It should be me doing that for her, I think as the cushions engulf me. My limbs feel as if lead lines my marrow, and I sink into the soft corner, staring at nothing.

Hugh gingerly takes a seat next to me. "How are you feeling?" he asks. I turn my head to look at him, and it hurts to do it. He has the grace to grimace. "I mean, the spell; did it help you? Did it do what you wanted?"

I squint to keep from crying again. My eyes burn enough already. I shake my head slowly, keep silent. I don't trust my voice.

"What did the spell do, then?"

I don't know. I shrug, turn my face to the cushions. Nothing. I accomplished nothing. Again.

I feel Hugh take my arm and I flinch, gasp. He lets go at my glare, holds his hands up. "May I take a look at the rune again, Rhia?" I close my eyes for a moment, then pull up my sleeve to show him.

He examines without touching this time. "This rune is for release, peaceful works, or unbinding, I think."

I nod, shrug, shake my head. Maybe. Maybe it is. He traces in the air above it. "I believe it is. Did you think the other runes were binding you to something? To Bishop Gantry?"

I take as deep a breath as I can. "To d-, d-, silence," I manage, but the roaring in my ears and my own gasping show them my failure as much as my words. But it doesn't show them enough, and I slump back in my seat, defeated.

"There's something else," Connor says, breaking in. "Something we need to know, something about Gantry. Something immediately dangerous."

I look up at him, nodding – maybe he will guess. But who would guess demons? Who would guess any of this? Only a madman would call demons.

Connor paces in front of us. "Gantry poses an even greater threat, somehow, than you've been able to say. You have information that means our imminent danger. That's what you're so desperate to tells us."

I nod again, close my eyes.

"That spell is danger enough," Julianna says from the doorway. "Whatever he wants all that power for, we know it can't be anything that will help us." She sighs and moves to stand by the window. Her voice, usually melodic, sounds rough, and her hand rests on the roundness of her belly under her robe. "I'll write to Alexander and King Peter," she says.

"And the Cardinal," Connor says.

I roll my eyes. "He doesn't know anything," I mutter, my voice a rough rasp.

"Then he will find out," Connor snaps.

I cover my face with my hands and lean forward until my head rests on my knees.

"So those marks, those are scars?" I hear Linnet say.

I sit up with a start.

Linnet stands just inside the room, holding onto the wall, her face half covered by her hair. "All those marks, all of them are scars."

I look helplessly at her, at Hugh next to me. "Yes," I whisper.

"Who did that?"

I feel my mouth weld shut with emotion, maybe with the spell. I cannot answer her.

Julianna answers for me. "Bishop Gantry gave your sister those scars after he had her arrested, Linnet. He wanted to use her in a spell, and when he made a mistake, he left her for dead." She says it flatly, but her face is kind.

I stare at Linnet, but Linnet won't look up. Her hair moves as she nods several times. Hugh grips my hand with his, a warm offer of support.

"No one ever told me," Linnet says. I close my eyes.

"No, Linnet. No one told you," Connor answers her.

Linnet peaks out from behind her hair, regards us all with narrowed eyes. I don't know what her expression means, but she nods and turns and leaves again.

A choked rasp breaks from my throat as I try to say something, anything. But she is gone before I can make my voice work.

Hugh pats my shoulder. "I'll go talk to her," he says.

"No, let her be awhile. I'll speak with her later," Julianna says. "Right now I'm going to send for a proper breakfast, and then everyone is going to take a long mid-day nap. After that, you can tell Rhia about our next plan." She walks over from the window, stops next to Connor.

"We'll trust you, Rhia. I know this has been … I know it's been a nightmare. I'm sorry for that." She regards me for a few moments, her eyes dark with fatigue.

I nod. I don't know what else to do.

She sighs and heads for her bedchamber. "Hugh, come help me."

"Help you what?"

"Just shut up and come help me," she snaps.

Hugh sighs and stands to follow her. He turns back for a moment, puts his hand on my shoulder.

"If you get anymore sudden spell ideas, Rhia, just … please, run them by me first. I promise to listen. Even if they seem strange. Especially if they seem strange. I want you to live. We all do. So for mercy's sake, just – just let me know, would you?"

I stare at my hands, at my arm, and nod. He sighs and pats me like he does Connor, only more gently; two pats and a rub. Then he follows Julianna.

Connor stares down at me. "We did send for information on those runes. Cardinal Robere thinks he has some texts, but he has to get back to Corat first. And I asked another trustworthy source." He frowns. "I'm still waiting for information. We didn't forget about you."

"It felt like it. No one talked to me, tried to help me; you all just left me in the dark." I struggle to stand up, to walk away, but I'm so tired.

"Don't be ridiculous. We've been here for you at every moment. We saved you from that lunatic, the princess healed you – twice now. And we gave you a place, I made you my ward –" His voice is rough, but I don't look at him, and I feel vicious.

"Yes, my lord, and thank you, my lord. I'm grateful, my lord. Your servant, my lord. That's all I am, your servant, your tool. Grateful for whatever scraps of information you might toss my way, grateful to be allowed in your presence. Grateful to be a pawn in your plans."

"Wait just a moment –"

I glare up at him, and he closes his mouth. "I am grateful. But I can't hold onto grateful when everything is falling apart. I have to survive, and I can't live every moment feeling only grateful feelings, never noticing any of the thoughtless things that any of you do. And sometimes, my lord, you are very thoughtless indeed."

"We're thoughtless? You –"

"I'm very tired. I just want to sleep." I push myself to my feet, holding back a whimper, holding back tears, holding back more words. I shuffle my way toward bed.

"You need to think about the definition of thoughtless. Since you were the one who nearly killed yourself just now to make a point."

I slap the doorway with my hand and grip it. "It wasn't to make a point," I hiss. "I have done nothing since this started just to make a point! I am trying to survive, and keep everyone else alive in the bargain. And I am terrified of what I don't know." I look over my shoulder at him. "And you should be terrified of what you don't know. Because what if you find out I was right?"

He stares at me, his lips pressed thin. "I cannot operate without knowledge. And I cannot commit certain acts without official approval. Neither can you."

"That may come too late. I can't tell you what I know. But Julianna is in danger, and so is everyone else. I'd think you'd act to save her, at least."

"I have to have official sanction," he grinds out. "It must be lawful. For me, more than for anyone else. Find a way to show me what the danger is, and I will take care of it."

We stare at each other for a few moments, our

breathing and the crackling of the fire the only sounds. He turns and leaves.

I lean my head on the doorway and press my eyes shut. My head pounds, and I pound my head on the wood. It doesn't help. I trudge to bed, feeling beaten and awful.

CHAPTER 21

Julianna wakes me up to make me eat. "I hope to have better luck with you. Linnet refused altogether."

I do what I'm told, and drag myself to the table, hair in my eyes. There is an awful lot of food. "You were expecting the castle guard?" I ask, and she throws back her head to laugh. I blink at her, wary of this development.

I notice that tears are running down her cheeks, and I realize that she is crying, too, and I push awkwardly at my chair to get up to go to her. She waves me back, away. "I'm fine," she sniffles, still watery. "It's the baby, and the stress. I don't usually let it overcome me so, but today has been … difficult."

I wince as I sit down again, from her words as much as my own soreness. Gingerly I pour myself some tea.

"I want you to understand, Rhia, that we have all come to care for you very much. You and your sister both."

I nod, stare at my teacup.

"You are a lovely person, but you are still very young. And you have so much power that you don't know how to control. Your recent actions concerned us. But we never meant," she takes a deep breath, "we never at all meant for you to feel as though you were all alone in this. You can come to me, Rhia. With anything. I know that at times it hasn't seemed that way. And perhaps it feels like everything will be awful forever. But I promise you we are working to change that." She smiles and wipes at her eyes. "With you to help us, we will most certainly triumph."

I stare at my cup some more, nod.

"All right, Rhia?" She sounds wistful, and I sigh.

"Yes, your Highness." It all sounds so reasonable when she says it. I spoon up some oatmeal, eat slowly. It does make me feel a little better.

Julianna begins to talk about what they want to do next, to try and prove who the conspirators are, find out what they're doing. They want to get Hugh and Connor into a party at the Guildmaster's manor. It seems Aman is throwing an engagement party for his daughter, Melisande.

I choke a little on my tea. She's engaged?

"Do you know her?"

I nod. I know her. She's a lot like her father; greedy and mean.

"She's engaged to Francis Danwright, the jewel-smith's son," Julianna says. I put my tea down away from me entirely.

"Francis?" I say faintly, feeling odd. "Melisande and Francis Danwright are engaged?"

Julianna looks at me. "You know them both, I

suppose. You likely know everyone involved. I haven't met Francis."

"I have. He was my fiancé," I say. I think my voice is flat. I don't know how I feel about it.

Julianna bites her lip. "I'm sorry, my dear. Were you in love with him?"

I start to laugh, real laughter. I feel a little hitch and release in my spine. "In love with Francis? He, he is," and the laughter leaves me gently. "He was my parent's choice. I agreed…" I trail off, and shrug. "I agreed."

"Is he kind?" she asks.

"He's not unkind, or he wasn't unkind to me. He wasn't much of anything to me." I know she is hoping for more information. I play with my spoon. "Our families wanted an alliance. The Weaver's guild with the Jeweler's guild. Da was trying to –" and I take a breath. "He was trying to keep the guilds strong, build them up, get political power. He had plans," I say, and feel rue pull a smile from me. "Some of them were very good plans. Not all. But he sees – he saw the kirche trying to erode guild rights, erode guild wealth, and he wanted to fight that.

"I thought master jewelsmith Danwright agreed with him. But if he's allying with Aman, then he probably just wants power. Francis mostly does what he's told. I doubt he knows much about it either way."

Julianna regards me. "Like you mostly did what you were told?" she asks.

I laugh again. "Oh, no. I almost never did what I was told. I was just very quiet about my rebellions. And I … I was frightened of the kirche, when Keenan went for a priest. The prior at the monastery – Keenan swore they weren't all like that. Keenan wanted me to…" I don't want to talk about that. "Anyway, the prior went on and on about bad blood, because of Gran. Everyone knew Gran had the Sight. It frightened me."

"Keenan wanted you to join the kirche?"

"More than anything. He thought I would be safer. But I didn't think so." I shake my head. "And it was, it used to be such a little thing, my magic. I could talk to Keenan because Keenan was so strong. I had visions, but not so many. Not so you could count on them. Not like Gran. And Mum always said it wasn't very useful, and it would be best if everyone just forgot about it."

I startle when the chair beside me moves, and Connor sits down. "She was afraid for you," he says.

I look down, shrug. "Maybe. Anyway, Francis and I weren't any more interested in marrying each other than in marrying anyone else. I'm not jealous. It just surprised me, that's all."

"It won't be an issue for you to see them together, then," Connor says.

I shake my head.

"Good. I think we can use you closer in than we were planning. Hugh has an idea. Dinner tonight, to work it out. Bring Linnet; we'll need her, too."

"You actually want us both to help?" I ask.

Connor walks away. "Hugh has a plan," he says over his shoulder.

"That's what I'm worried about," Julianna sighs.

"You should get some rest," Connor says as he leaves.

She sticks her tongue out at the closed door, but she's leaning back in her chair, rubbing her abdomen. "That's not a bad idea. I don't know where Linnet went. If you see her, tell her about dinner. I'll wear the green gown later. It's easiest, and you won't have to do much to get it ready."

She stands up and groans a little. When she looks at me, her face is grave. "You should get some more rest, too. I hope," she says, then walks over to put her hand on my cheek, sighs. "I hope you are feeling better. Let me know if the new scars bother you," she says. She gazes at me for a moment, then leaves.

I pull the bell rope so someone will come clear the breakfast dishes on the way back to my room. I crawl into bed again, stare at the wall, thinking about the guilds, and Mum and Da and Keenan. What is master Aman up to? And Francis? I stare at nothing and worry, and ache, and finally fall asleep.

Dinner in Hugh's rooms is unusual. Mostly we dine with Duchess Marguerite and other castle guests in the Blue Salon, or even more informally in Julianna's chambers. Julianna sent word to her mother that she had another arrangement for this evening, and we make our way to Hugh.

An elegant but simple table stands near the fireplace in Hugh's outer room. A damask cloth drapes over it, and the white porcelain plates have gilded edges. The crystal goblets sparkle in the lamplight; not the intimidation ware, I note, although I don't say that out loud. Samuel is nowhere to be found. No doubt he prefers to be absent from any further serving opportunities for Hugh's guests.

Linnet had to be cajoled into coming with us at all. She hasn't spoken much today, although she isn't glaring at any of us, either. Sometimes during dinner I catch her staring at me, but mostly she stares at her plate, not eating. I know because I watch.

Hugh and Julianna and Connor discuss how we're going to get into the Guildmaster's manor, disguised as traders or guild members from out of town. Aman is inviting as many traders and guild members as he can fit into the manor, which will be quite a lot. It's a large house, added onto over the years. It has been – had been – in our family for almost a century.

Hugh asks us questions about who is likely to attend, and where are the best hiding places, and where our father's office is. Was.

I answer quietly, my chest aching and my eyes scratchy, but I don't cry.

Linnet never says a word. She nods or shakes her head, shrugs. Her eyes stay on that plate. Nothing interesting is happening on it.

The other three serve themselves, each other, and plot. They wave forks of meat, sauces, and their goblets with grace and animation as they talk, never spilling or spattering themselves or one another, which is a neat trick.

Linnet and I sit quiet, more cautious with our words and our food. We can't be sure of our grace or our graciousness, I suppose. I ache in all my corners, and remembering all our childhood spaces is a weight on my neck and chest. I answer questions asked of Linnet, so she doesn't have to.

Connor notices, and stops addressing her, but his eyes narrow, looking at me. I'm not happy with him, either. Soon we're in a glaring contest.

"Linnet, you haven't touched your dinner. Are you

too upset by all of this? I thought you'd want to help us plan things," Julianna says.

Linnet doesn't look up. I reach over and touch her arm, and she startles, jumping back from my hand as if I'd burned her.

"Linnet," I say, but she stands quickly.

"I'm sorry, may I be excused, your Highness, your Grace," she whispers, and leaves before anyone can answer.

When I turn back from watching her leave, the three of them are staring at me. "Has she been like that all day?" Hugh asks.

I shrug.

"Yes," Julianna says. "I tried speaking to her earlier, but she just nodded and kept with her sewing. I'm not certain she was listening." She sighs. "I'll try talking to her again."

"No," Connor says. "It's my turn. She's going to listen to me." He stands from his chair to stride after her.

"No, you don't!" I rush to block him, knocking over wine and tripping over my skirt.

He tries to brush me out of his way. "I'm tired of her scenes and her unrelenting temper. This behavior is unacceptable. She's going to endanger everyone if she doesn't straighten out." His hands squeeze my arms, but I stomp my foot down and refuse to budge unless he drags me.

"And who is going to straighten her? Straighten how? Are you her father now that ours is dead? And all of you sit here at this table and discuss our lost home as if sneaking into it is some sort of game! How do you think she's going to feel?"

"No one thinks this is a game!" He roars. "The two of

you, however, are playing something dangerous if you let us walk in there blind, and if you aren't prepared for what we'll find. Did you want to just show up and pretend you still live there?"

I reel back from him, my blood rushing in my ears, lungs constricting. I feel punched, although he stands there, no longer touching me. Wincing.

"Connor, enough," Julianna says. She touches his arm, and he stiffens slightly, stands straighter.

Hugh appears at my elbow and draws me to the table, which is now sopping wet with spilled wine.

"Oh, drat," I say, and start to mop at it with soaked napkins.

"Never mind, Rhia," Hugh says, and has me sit in Linnet's abandoned chair. Julianna pushes Connor back to the table.

"You both have a point," she says.

I open my mouth to protest, but close it again. Connor's jaw clenches and I see muscles jump.

"Linnet is a problem, acting this way," she continues. "She needs to be prepared for what's going to happen. And she needs to treat you better, Rhia. She needs to control her temper. All of us do." She looks down at Connor.

He moves to stand, but she prevents him with a light touch on his shoulder. "I will speak to her. And she will listen. And neither of you will interfere. Is that perfectly clear?"

I study the table full of spilled wine. "Yes, your Highness," I say. There is no sound from the men.

"Very well. Why don't the three of you discuss better barriers for Rhia, since she still glows so much to the Sight. The party is only a few weeks away. It would be nice if she weren't a small sun when Archbishop Mont-moore arrives." She leaves, her skirts swishing around her swaying form, and Connor and I glare at each other across the table.

Hugh clears his throat. Neither of us acknowledge him. "Well, then. Rhia, we should test a few things out with your new ... configuration. Have you noticed any significant differences today in how your barriers feel?"

A muscle just below Connor's right eye spasms in time to Hugh's pacing. My teeth ache from clenching them.

"Gantry can't detect you or he would have already – at the hospice if anything." Hugh clears his throat again. "But Montmoore has the Sight, so we'll need to reduce your aura to something reasonable. Some sort of illu-sion to cover some of it that won't raise suspicions."

Hugh paces faster, and I see his arms gesturing out of the corner of my eye. But Connor still stares at me, his lips tight, and I can almost hear him thinking that I am a stubborn fool.

Hugh barks at us to pay attention, but I am not a stubborn fool, and Connor can't just think that at me.

I glare harder.

I hear a sigh from behind Connor, and Hugh's blue silk-clad arm comes into view as he taps Connor on his left shoulder.

Connor glances to his left, then right, as Hugh bends down to meet Connor's face with his own, kissing him squarely on the mouth.

Connor jerks back, surprised.

Hugh smiles sweetly at him. "Hello, Connor dear. Do I have your attention now?"

Connor narrows his eyes again, making them almost

disappear. Then his eyebrow lifts, and he offers a twisted smile. Hugh snorts. He gestures with his head to the door, motioning Connor to leave.

Glancing at me, Connor says "My apologies, Cousin." I snort a little, as well; I don't believe his tone. He bows slightly in my direction as he stands, then walks away.

Leaving me unaccompanied in the duke's rooms. I'm supposed to have a chaperone, but as I'm a dead witch, and we keep dispensing with niceties such as chaperones or days without bloodshed, I suppose it doesn't matter. I try to calm my temper, but I still grip my hands together till they ache.

"Rhia," Hugh starts, and I jump.

"Forgive me, your Grace. You were saying?"

He sits beside me, his smile gentle. "She's rather a fire-brand, your sister. Hard to keep up with. And her temper!" He breathes a laugh. "She is too hard on you, Rhia. And it takes its toll, doesn't it?"

I rub my hands over my face, shake my head. "She is very young, your Grace."

"Yes, she is young, and stubborn. And things have been very horrible for her. But she's not the only one. She needs discipline, Rhia, not forgiveness."

"Not for this. She didn't do anything wrong at dinner, she just didn't speak to anyone. She was upset, but she didn't yell. Yes, she does have a terrible temper, and she is angry with everyone, especially me. But maybe she's right. I did leave her behind when I ran.

"She lost everything: her birthright, the mastership, our family. She has enough talent for any three master weavers. She would've been Guildmaster before she turned 30 if she – but not now.

"Maybe I am a coward. Maybe Keenan was wrong telling me to run. If I hadn't, maybe…"

"Maybe you'd all be dead," Hugh says, and brushes a stray curl from my eyes. "You are very brave, Rhia. Never let anyone tell you otherwise. You don't know what your staying put might have done. But it doesn't sound like Aman was willing to leave your family standing. He turned you in to Gantry, and he got the town upset about witchery. And no one ever did find out what happened to Pastor Seaton, although I had the bailiff look into it. She says it looks as if his heart gave out, but no one is certain.

Aman and Deacon Bertram might have stopped a witch hunt, even with Bishop Gantry coming. But Gantry wanted a witch, and Aman singled out your family. No, you were right to run. I'd've run."

He shakes his head as I shake mine. "Don't be so hard on yourself. And don't let Linnet be so hard on you, either. Although, maybe this morning – you shocked all of us. But maybe your sister most of all." He puts his arm around me, rubs my shoulder, two pats and a rub. "Let's wait and see how she handles it, then. Maybe you're right, maybe she's just still processing. She is young, but she's not stupid."

He sits back in his chair and regards me. "Now, let's work out some new tests for those barriers of yours," he says, and he starts discussing spells and changes and runes until I am too tired to think any more. When I leave to go back to my chambers, it is very late, and the only thing I can do is crawl into bed. Linnet is already in hers, sleeping, or pretending to. I turn down the lamp and try to do the same.

Nine days since Linnet has eaten much of anything, and she grows tired and gaunt. Never a fleshy girl, now her cheekbones seem to stick out like a mask, and she half-faints standing from chairs. I make sure she drinks water at least, but she hardly speaks to anyone and stares listlessly at nothing.

Julianna is at her wit's end trying to reason with her, and both Connor and Hugh have shouted uselessly at her. I just bring her food and beg her to eat.

She hasn't done her chores at all today: she nearly fainted when she tried to get out of bed, and didn't try again.

I bring up a luncheon of broth and sweet carrots freshly peeled. She refuses tea or milk, so a pitcher of cold water sits next to the broth. I didn't add bread, fearing it would be too much pressure. I lay the tray on the chest in our room, and sit next to her.

"Please, dearest, eat something." Her face, pale and drawn, faces the window and not me. "Linnet, you must eat something. It's only broth, it won't make you sick. It's chicken broth. You like chicken broth."

Her eyes stay fixed on the window.

I clench my hands.

"Hugh asked about you today. He's worried about you. Everyone is."

She blinks, but otherwise shows no interest. I lay my head next to her still form in despair.

Fighting sobs, I try begging. Again. "Little bird, you have to eat. Please eat. You'll get so sick if you don't. I can't bear to see you like this." My nose and throat are thick: I can hardly speak.

"I can't lose you too, Linnet. I've lost everyone else. I can't lose you too. I'm half mad already — I'll be raving if you die. You'll join all the other eyes that haunt me and you won't touch me any more than they will. And I will have failed again. Oh please, Linnet. I can't bear it." My words muffle in my fists, wet and staccato with gasping sobs.

I feel a touch on my hair. I start up, and she looks at her hand, a kind of desperation in her eyes. "She didn't look at me."

I can barely hear her. Trying to stifle my snuffles, I ask her breathlessly, "Who?"

"Mum. She didn't look at me. Not even to say goodbye. And Da was so busy trying to look proud. Keenan only looked at you. No one said goodbye to me. And they died, and then it was too late."

Tears start to trickle down her temple. I reach for her hand and she doesn't pull away. I grip it, and feel how frail her bones are. It stays limp in my grasp, but she lets me hold it.

"Mum looked at you, I saw it. And Keenan looked to you. I waited for you to save them, but you didn't. You stood there, staring back at them, and they died. And you never moved. I waited for you to save them."

"Oh, little bird, I couldn't, I was —"

"I waited for you to save them, so I didn't. I didn't do anything. I let them kill my family, and I didn't do anything. And I didn't save you either. And look what they did to you. I just waited, and did nothing."

Like a blow to my stomach, the revelation of her rage. She blames herself as much as me, and now that she knows I was tortured, she blames only herself. It's too much for one soul to bear. I grip her hand tighter and kiss it, hold it to my cheek.

"You couldn't have saved any of us, Linnet. You couldn't have saved me from Gantry. He wanted a person with the Sight for his spell. And Da was unpopular with the guild, or someone would have spoken for him. All you could do was stay safe. That was your part. To stay safe so there was hope. That's all the hope I had: your safety.

"You aren't to blame for their deaths. I swear to you, the man that is, we'll stop him. Julianna and Hugh have a plan, and we'll stop him. I swear to you."

She sighs and turns her face to the window. But she lets me hold on to her hand, and she falls asleep later. I try to look on that as a sign.

CHAPTER 22

Aman's party is in a few days. Linnet is eating better, although I'm worried it's not enough. She won't talk to me about it, but she is trying to control her temper more. She's still sarcastic and angry, but it's not as pointed in my direction. Most of the time.

We've been working with Hugh to create illusion spells for us. They're getting complex, and I can't follow all of the theory behind it, although Linnet seems to pick it up pretty quickly. But it's my power they use to run them. I'm learning how to share it with everyone, in a slow and steady stream.

I've noticed that since the new rune, it's easier for people to just siphon magic from me whenever I touch them. It worries me, but I don't seem to be able to talk about that, either. I knew I bled magic, but now that it's been described, I can feel it happening more and more often. Linnet doesn't even have to touch me.

The weather is, as usual, abysmal – the servants whisper the talk in town is of rationing this winter. The crops are bad. Fishing, however, has been extremely good. I don't think anyone will starve. But we might get very tired of cod.

Water fills all the dips and smudges of the castle grounds, and everything is a muddy mess. The carpets in the main entry were removed completely, and servants can be found every day scrubbing at steps and flagstones with harsh brushes. All our boots are muddy, and the hems of gowns, too.

Not that we are traveling anywhere off of castle grounds. Julianna hasn't left the castle since she revealed her pregnancy. Walks around the garden or the castle walls in the rain are the only change we get. Connor is glad; he's been worried about the outings, and someone recognizing me.

I have to do something, or I'll go entirely mad. And mending towels doesn't count. I decide to sneak off to chapel service. I haven't been in weeks, not since I tried to poison Gantry. But I need to see Orrin, to check on him.

The chapel is half-empty. I sit still in my seat, trying not to stare at Orrin. I am still not to contact him, but no one said I couldn't look. He looks thinner, and his dark skin seems oddly shiny, as if he's sweating. His eyes don't look up from the floor.

When I use the Sight on him, he is murky and swirling, and his magic pulses in muddy hot colors. I can't sense anything from his mind. It's as though he's behind a wall; I barely sense his presence.

Gantry preaches against witches and evil magic. He rants about people turning to the dark, about the country turning to the dark, about lack of leadership. "There are those leading our land onto dark paths, where the Star Lord cannot shine. Do not think to follow them, or your soul will be lost! Only evil awaits such wanderings. Beware such purpose as they have for you. A kind face can hide a dark heart."

The congregation shuffles in their seats, uncomfortable. His ranting against Julianna and the duchess all but overt. With the kirche in town a longer walk than some servants have time for, there are still some who attend services here. And ranting against evil feels almost normal now. But Bishop Gantry has forgotten Haverston's larger truth: everyone loves Duchess Marguerite. She has been Haverston's guiding hand for several decades. Insulting her will not win him any converts.

Gantry stops abruptly, and walks away from the altar. After a moment, the congregation stirs and starts to leave. His sudden exit stirs no comment: we are starting to know the bishop's tendency toward abruptness.

Orrin stays where he is after Gantry walks out, and I stay in my seat, as well. The people empty out of the chapel, and it grows quiet but for our breathing echoing lightly in the tall room. Orrin hasn't looked up. Taking a breath, I push to a stand, turn and head for the Star Chambers. I look back over my shoulder, but he doesn't move.

Brushing back the curtain, I stand inside the first chamber, staring at the stone wall, and listen to the quiet in the chapel, the sound of rain and ocean waves outside. I hear a swish of footsteps coming closer. I close my eyes, and hope.

A body bumps into me from behind, and I spin around. Orrin grips my arms, stares into my eyes. I grab him back.

"Orrin," I say, "I hoped you would talk to me."

"I need," he rasps, then stops, panting.

"I'm trying to figure out a way to get you out of here," I say. "Hugh is working with the Cardinal to figure out the – the –" and I can't say it, silence closing off my throat. "Connor swears we'll just take you if we have to, but they're afraid the bishop will be able to find you."

His hands are hot: I can feel the burn of them through my sleeves. His face is hot, too, and his eyes look feverish. The spell is drawing too much power through him. Bishop Gantry is drawing too much power through him. He leans his head down and rests his forehead on mine, his body trembling.

"Please, I need … I need you to kill me," he whispers.

I gasp and start to pull back.

He grips me harder, stares in my eyes. "Please. Please just do it. I can't – I can't –" and the spell closes his throat, too. We stare at each other in mute mutual horror and enforced silence. Finally I force my voice to work.

"I swear we'll get you out. Somehow – somehow we'll get you free of this. I don't – I don't know – I don't want you to die."

"Dorei," he cries out, "I need you–"

"Orrin Beaudreau!" A roar in the chapel. Gantry.

Orrin puts his hand over my mouth and pushes me back into the dark corner of the chamber. He stares into my eyes, his own a message: be quiet. He twitches himself through the curtain and steps out into the chapel, silent.

"What are you doing in there? Come with me this instant!"

I stand huddled in the corner, shaking, listening to their footsteps, to Gantry's angry harangue. I wait until I hear only silence outside the chamber. I wait longer, my whole body itching and aching and trembling. When I creep out, the chapel is empty. I look up at the statue of Dorei and make a sign of supplication. Please. Please help me. I have to find Connor.

The corridors are mostly quiet, with servants bustling about their duties here and there. No one comments on my face or stops me. I try to look as normal as I can but my face is frozen, and tears leak down my cheeks.

I send out magic in searching tendrils, hoping Connor is nearby. Flashes of minds, bits of vision pour through me, and I run blindly up stairs, down the hall, pulled by a faint feel of his mind. My weak lungs ache and strain, and black edges creep around everything. I thump into Connor's chamber door, feel him beyond, pound on it, gasping.

He yanks the door open and I fall forward into him. Grabbing me, he stumbles back. "What are you doing? What is it?"

I shake my head, try to form words, but mostly I can't.

"What happened?" he asks, pulling me into his room and shutting the door.

I bend over, coughing, my hands on my knees. He tries to help me up, but I lean back against the door, wheezing.

"Is it Julianna? Did something happen to her?"

I shake my head. "Orrin," I gasp. "He said, he said he wants," but I don't know how to say it. I pull in more air, force my body to accept it, to calm down.

"You spoke to Orrin?" Connor asks, angry.

"He came to me. I mean, I was, he, we spoke to each other."

Connor starts to shake his head.

"I told him we were trying to find a way around the spell, that we'd just take him if we had to, that you-"

"Dammit, Rhia. I told you not to speak to him. It's too dangerous. We don't know if he's compelled to tell Gantry-"

I shove off of the wall and then shove Connor, my hands against his chest. "He asked me to kill him," I spit, furious. "He begged me, Connor. He wants to die. Whatever else is going on, he is desperate, and we have to help him. We have to – we can't just leave him there!"

Connor closes his eyes, bowing his head. After a moment he rubs his forehead and nods. "Yes. Yes, you're right. I'll – I'll work out a way to get him out of the castle."

I suck in a breath I hadn't realized I needed. "Tonight?"

He rubs his hand over his face. "Maybe. I'll have to contact some people, and I have to wait for a chance to get to him, or create one. He's almost always with Gantry now. We'll have to figure out a way…"

"But you'll do it?"

"Yes." He looks at me, and I wipe my sleeve across my face. "Come on, come sit down." He puts his arm out, guides me to the couch across from the windows. Sitting next to me, he pats his pockets for a handkerchief, hands one to me with a little smile. My breath comes in little hiccoughing sobs. His hand settles on my back, rubbing small circles.

Gray light filters in through the windows and

curtains, and I hear the steady, unending sound of the rain. The warmth from his hand seeps into my muscles and I feel them ease, feel the bands around my chest give so I can breathe a little better. I rest my head on my knees. Relief and panic and sour anger roil in my stomach still.

"You should kill Gantry," I say to my knees.

His hand leaves my back, and I feel him tense, hear his frustrated growl. "I can't just do that. I have to have just cause, it has to be sanctioned by the law."

"You'd kill Orrin if you had to," I shoot upright, accusing.

"If I had to kill Orrin, there'd be repercussions for that, too. I would only do that if he were immediately endangering everyone."

"Gantry is endangering everyone!"

"I don't have any proof of that," he snaps. "I of all people cannot take the law into my own hands and play with it like a toy. I must obey the letter and spirit of the law, and the law says I don't get to just murder people because I don't trust them."

"What does that mean, you of all people?" I ask. "You keep saying that, and I don't see how-"

"Because of who I am, Rhiannon! My father, my brother."

I just throw my hands up in the air. "Who is your father?" I shout.

"Was. My father was the Duke of Torrence."

My mouth stays open, but no sounds emerge.

He nods, his mouth twisted into a parody of a smile. "I see you didn't know." His eyes close, and he sighs heavily. "I apologize for adopting you as a cousin without making that clear."

I feel my head wagging, my mouth open, try to control both. "Then, then Duke Valcourt, the exile…"

"Is my brother Stephen. He and I … are not close."

I shut my jaw with a snap. The former Duke Valcourt of Torrence was exiled four years ago after he tried to stage a coup. He nearly killed Prince Alexander. The king and prince personally escorted Stephen's routed army to the border of Kantir, leaving them without supplies in the mountains in winter. Not many survived.

Duke Valcourt did, and vowed revenge, they say. Revenge for that, and for his father.

The king's brother. Gerald, Duke of Torrence. Executed for treason.

Connor, nephew of a king. Son of a traitor. Brother of a traitor.

Oh.

That explains some things. I stare at my hands. "Wait, but Valcourt's half-brother is the Duke of Lussier -"

"I don't use that title," he says. "I relinquished that title back to the crown, along with the ducal lands of Torrence. And I took and older family name, fitzWellan, instead of Valcourt."

He relinquished a duchy. He relinquished two duchies. I don't know what to think about that.

"Stephen was always ambitious. And bitter. So bitter after Father was executed. He changed his coat of arms to battle axes, did you know?"

Fifteen years ago, King Peter had his brother executed by battle axe at Torrence castle. Gerald had tried to raise an army in Fanthas to take the Talarian throne from his brother. That was his third failed attempt. King Peter was furious, and murderous, it turns out. But then he required public mourning for six months after. The apprentices wove in black for what seemed like ages, I remember. I was very young, but I remember that.

"I didn't know," I say, about the axes. About all of it. The windows reflect in his eyes, until his lashes sweep down and he looks over at me. I never noticed the light brown flecks in his irises before. I lean forward, to comfort him, to say something, but then catch a waft of my own fear sweat from my clothes, and I lean back again, look away.

"I don't talk about my family much."

"I noticed. I'm sorry about your brother." I hesitate, put my hand over his on the couch. A thrill runs through me that is not magic.

He looks at our hands, turns his over and grasps mine. Gently pulling, he draws me into his side. I rest my head on his linen-clad shoulder and he puts his arm firmly around me. I close my eyes at this human contact, feel my stomach muscles clench. I try not to think about that thrill.

My left sleeve is pushed up past my elbow, baring pink and white runes along my arm. Connor picks up my arm in his left hand, pulling tighter around me, against his chest. He begins to trace the runes slowly with a fingertip, his chin in my hair.

I shiver again, and my heart beats strangely. Gently I pull my arm back, and he stops the tracing. But he does not let go. I feel very aware of my tongue.

"It's strange, isn't it?" he says, his voice soft near my ear. "I was the forgotten son of a traitor when Julianna found me. We were about thirteen. My father was dead a year, and I was sent to live with Stephen in Torrence. My mother had died by then, too. I fell ill with a fever, and the king was feeling remorse about Father, so we were allowed to return to Corat.

"I was feverish and delirious, and had managed to get lost in the castle halls. Julianna found me, and even then her magic was strong. She Healed me as best she could, and took me to Alexander and demanded I be tended to by the royal Healers. She was the one who made King Peter reverse the attainder against Stephen and me."

"I thought that was her father, the old duke."

Connor snorts. "No. He was busy … elsewhere. Julianna and Hugh were the ones who took me on as a cause. One of their many causes." He snorts again.

"No wonder you are so loyal to them."

"Like a pet, you mean?" His voice grows harsh, weary.

"Like a champion," I counter. "Like a friend."

"I'm not a champion," he says. "But you might be."

"What are you talking about?"

He shifts, turning me toward him "You're quite a champion, in fact, fighting for everyone else."

I stare into his dark eyes, our faces close. "Fighting? I don't fight," I whisper.

He shakes his head. "Every day another fight, another person to stand up for. You take them on like a hero in a story, each one getting all of your zeal and attention."

"Linnet is my sister,"

"And Orrin-"

"Orrin is-"

"And Julianna, and Hugh. And me. Are you taking me on, now, as well?" His breath is intoxicating, and I find myself watching his mouth.

I look up again into his eyes, and see a question there. I stare a moment longer, then brush his mouth so softly with mine it is like feathers. A shock runs through me and I gasp. His mouth joins fiercely to mine, his arms tighten and I turn into him, closer. I feel his hands in my hair, on my back, his muscles under my own hands.

My mind says *you are kissing Connor, Connor is the king's nephew,* and abruptly I pull away from him, extricate myself and stand, my hand over my mouth. I stare at him, and he stares back, out of breath.

"Connor, I, we-" but I'm not sure what to say.

He sits up slowly, a guarded look in his eyes. Opening my mind, I find his locked down: all I see is Julianna's face, kind but pitying.

"I did not mean to press you."

"No, it's not – I mean – Connor. You are not-"

"Enough?" he snarls.

I shake my head. "Mine."

He stares at me, and I back away. "I have to go. Linnet is…"

"Yes." His face is carefully blank.

"About Orrin,"

"I said I will take care of it."

"I know. Thank you. Tell him – tell him goodbye for me," I say, and whirl around to yank the door open and run into the hall. This time it is to run away from him.

CHAPTER 23

Archbishop Montmoore has arrived from Serramonte on his way back to the capitol. He comes here from the Fanthas border, where he was working with Cardinal Robere and Prince Alexander on new treaties with that neighboring country. Montmoore's retinue arrived in the afternoon, and is settled into the Inquisitor's Building. He is to present himself to Hugh and Duchess Marguerite tomorrow.

Julianna thinks he's the one pulling Gantry's strings. If there is a conspiracy against the throne, it's likely Montmoore at the center of it. Although now I realize everyone thinks it's the exiled duke – Connor's brother.

Connor stole Orrin out of the castle this afternoon, and has yet to return. After midday a message came for Bishop Gantry from the Inquisitor's Building, likely about Montmoore's impending arrival. While he was gone, Connor took Orrin from his rooms.

When Gantry came back from the Inquisitors, I sat in the chapel, listening with my mind and my ears. I expected rage, shouting. I expected him to call for the kirche guards, who were curiously absent from their posts in his hall.

But instead I felt a spike of panic, abject terror, and he locked himself in his rooms. And now, even through his barriers and under the onslaught of the power well, I can feel magic, pulsing with the feel of demons. I fear he's searching for Orrin, and I fear he'll find him.

Hugh and Julianna are worried we haven't heard back from Connor yet. I tried to See where they went, but I have trouble Seeing Connor most of the time, and Orrin has been a blank space for me since he returned from that trip with Gantry. I could feel Connor's anger and his concern, and then I couldn't.

I wasn't able to keep track of him or Orrin with my Sight after they left the castle. My magic is more powerful than it used to be, but it doesn't have a lot of range, which irritates Hugh. He'd like a nefarious spell that we've commandeered for ourselves to be more impressive in our favor.

Julianna rolls her eyes at his irritation and pats my arm. "I'm sure they're fine," she says, standing with her hand on her back. We wait in Hugh's rooms. "Give me the letter, Hugh."

Hugh has a message from his spy in Montmoore's retinue, and Julianna wants to see it.

"I don't think that's a good idea," he says.

"Pish-posh. I will read what my husband has to say."

"Juli, it's in code."

"Don't worry, Hugh, I know this code. I made this code, remember?" She walks by him and grabs the paper from his hand, grinning at him. She opens it, and as she reads her smile broadens. "We have him! Well, one of them. Montmoore has made an error; there is a letter he sent to Guildmaster Aman that may have what we need to break this conspiracy. And news from Corat,"

Julianna's face goes white and still, and I rush for a chair for her. She folds into it slowly, her hand on her mouth.

"Your Highness, what is it?" I ask her gently.

"Someone tried to poison Princess Eleanor. There's a faction that is claiming I did it with my witch magic. The court is even more divided, and some are heading to their homes to prepare for civil war. If – if we can't find proof of who did it, Alexander fears some will force Peter to try me for attempted murder." She stares at the letter, but she isn't reading anymore.

"Rhia, bring me the letter."

I take it from Julianna's unresisting hand and give it to him.

Hugh scans it quickly. "Alex wants proof of Stephen's hand in this. He's sure he is the one behind it."

"Stephen," I blurt, and Hugh glances at me.

"It could be Stephen, but poison isn't really like him," he says, and keeps reading. "More of the hospices have been forcibly shut down. There were some casualties." He shakes his head. "We can't let the hospices be the cause of more death, Juli. But closing them down will cause death, as well.

She slumps and sighs, wiping her eyes. "I don't know either. I just don't understand what the kirche wants with them, or what they get out of closing them. And what good does poisoning Eleanor do? She's still just a child."

"Poison," I say. "Are you sure it was poison?" The room washes in and out in front of me, a vision spiraling down on me. "I think it was a spell. The same spell Gantry used to kill Queen Cecily."

The vision pulls me in. Eleanor, a dark girl about Linnet's age, drinks from a cup. But it wasn't poison in the cup: the poison, the spell was on the cup. It latched on and began to eat away at her from the inside, like the Wasting.

Almost exactly like the Wasting.

Eleanor's youth and health have kept her alive, and the many protection spells the king has laid on her. The king's magicians have put her in a sort of stasis spell, until someone can Heal her. Peter is sending for Healers right now, but he's afraid of the kirche. Julianna is too far away. Someone heads for the castle…

I tell Hugh and Julianna as I cling to a chair, blinded by the vision. It fades slowly.

"My Great Lord," Julianna whispers. "That's what he's doing with his spell, all that power. He's creating death spells. He's creating death spells to use on … Hugh, we have to tell the king!"

"But someone told Alexander she'd been poisoned," he said. "So someone is either lying at the king's behest, or for another reason. We don't know whom, and we don't know which. I don't trust anyone that we haven't personally vetted, now. Someone could still make the case that a Healer would know how to create a death spell and tie you to that, too."

"Gantry is a Healer. A poor one, but a Healer nonetheless," Julianna says.

"We can't accuse him without proof – Montmoore is too powerful, and I know this is his doing. He wants Stephen on the throne." Hugh's face is grim.

"We don't know that Stephen ordered…"

Hugh closes his eyes. "We do know."

I sit heavily in the chair, letting the vision drain away, catching my breath. "Gantry means to use that spell on you. Soon," I say.

They look at me. "We took Orrin from him, which might disrupt things. But I will stay well away from him, don't worry," Julianna says.

Hugh doesn't look so sanguine.

I think of the demons – there are other ways to get power, if one is crazy and desperate enough. Demon power when you don't have the capacity – like my runes, or Orrin's – will drive you mad, if you can't barricade yourself. And if one wants that much power, I've learned from all my reading, barriers will get in the way.

I try to tell them, again. "D – de – de – d –" They watch me struggle, and I push myself to dizziness and nausea, but I can't say it.

Julianna stands before me, touching my face. "It's all right, just breathe. I know; there's something else, something he did that has you frightened. I promise I won't take any unnecessary risks. None of us will."

I regain my breath slowly, watching the gray edges recede from my eyes.

Hugh speaks to Julianna in low tones, and she leaves to join her mother for dinner. I look up to find Hugh watching me. We regard each other for a few moments. "He's called demons, hasn't he?"

Hugh's words punch a hole in my center, and I can't breathe again. I reach out to grab him, anything, falling from the chair.

Hugh hurries to me, pulls me upright, cursing and trying to help me. "Lords all damn the man! What can he be thinking? The danger to – to everyone! All right, all right, you were right, I should have just let you poison him. Except a demon spell is notoriously unstable, and I don't know if his death would stop it, whatever it is."

He pulls me to the couch and then paces in front of me. "Damn everything. I have to get him out of here without setting it off. Or get everyone else in the castle out. Or the town. I don't think I can move the whole town.

"Doubtless he's been experimenting on those poor souls in the Inquisitor's Building, as well. And the hospice. Damn him! This is monstrous."

He stops pacing at the far side of the room, looks back at me. "I'll get a message to my man, tell him he's to leave immediately. We'll lose an inside eye with Montmoore, but it can't be helped. Bugger his cover. Cardinal Robere must change his route and come here. We cannot wait any longer."

I slump back into the couch, curiously light. Someone knows. Someone who can do something knows. Hugh sits down next to me.

"We'll work on some alterations to our spells later, to keep the demon magic at bay. I hope. And we need to adjust your barriers and your flow. You let too much of yourself spin out in the thread of your power. You could do yourself serious harm, weakened like that."

He runs his hand over his face. "You were right, Rhia. I'm sorry I didn't catch on sooner."

I just shake my head. I can't speak still, but for once, I don't feel frantic about it.

"You should join Juli for dinner. Meet me in the library later, and we'll work on those spells." He stands and helps me up.

I feel that twinge as he takes my arm, pulling power

again. I cut him off as he showed me, but it's disturbing that I have to all the time. I sway a little. "Are you all right?" he asks as I waver. I firm my legs and brush his hand away, which helps.

"Yes, thank you." I take a deep breath, and slip out the door and into the chill, dark hall. Dusk falls earlier now than even a few weeks ago, and the lamps are not yet all lit. I head downstairs for the blue salon, and dinner with Julianna and her mother.

I excuse myself early from dinner. Tension and unease seem to flicker among all the ladies, as Julianna and her mother either have determined smiles or grim visages. She must have told the duchess about the letter.

I catch Julianna's eye, and she nods, so I quietly slip away as everyone is preparing to drink wine and play draughts, chess, or piquet. I am not in the mood for piquet.

There's a man I don't recognize in the entry hall, arguing with a young woman. When she turns, I see she's pregnant, and younger than I thought. Her hair hangs in a wispy braid down her back, and her cloak looks bedraggled.

"What is this?" I ask. Both of them jump and turn toward me, their faces flushed and anxious.

"You, you are Lady Rhia, yes?" asks the man.

"I am," I say, feeling confused and concerned. "Do I know you?"

"I know His Grace," he says, still gripping the woman – girl – by the arm. "I am bringing, that is, there's a situation I'm hoping you can help me with."

"Is there something you'd like to explain?" I offer, gesturing toward the shivering girl.

She looks down, keeps her mouth shut.

"She is...well. This is ... indelicate."

"Pregnant, you mean."

"Yes. Well." Silence.

"Well?"

"I was charged by Prince Alexander to bring her to the duke, and leave her with him. She is, that is, His Royal Highness...." he says.

I begin to see. "Her condition is -" I hesitate to say it.

"The concern of His Royal Highness."

I blink back dread. Julianna will be furious. "Is there anything else?"

"Her name is Mora, daughter of Sir Robert who was killed ten months ago at Serramonte. The prince tells his grace that she is to be settled quietly and not linked to the throne. He - asks that the princess not be informed." He releases the girl and bows to me.

"I see," I say, but he is already gone, turned and left without another word. I sigh. The girl looks at me with dread and heartbreak.

"I -" she breathes, then is silent, worried.

"Mora, I am Rhia. I will take you to His Grace, but we must go quietly. Hurry now," and I motion her to follow me. She stands hesitantly, then keeps quick to my back as I head back up the stairs.

We walk swiftly through chill corridors. At Hugh's door I hesitate, knock twice, and enter, motioning Mora to stay put.

"Yes?" Hugh looks up, wreathed in light from glowsand lamps at his writing desk.

"Your Grace, something has come up. I have a... delivery."

His brow creases. "Delivery?"

I open the door and usher Mora in. Her hair is revealed as dark blonde, and her slouch hides her belly until she stands straight under Hugh's confused gaze.

Then he stands, his eyebrows raised, stern. "What is this, Rhia?"

Mora's lips tremble, and her shoulders cave again. I put my arm around her. "This is Mora. She is the prince's concern." I borrow the spy's phrase.

Hugh's eyebrows meet his hairline. "Ah. Earlier than I was told, and not the girl I expected."

Mora visibly shrinks. I squeeze her arm for support, but she flinches.

Hugh walks over and circles us slowly, then stands before us, his face thoughtful. "Mora?"

She jumps. "Yes, my, yo-, your Grace?" She has a small voice, high and soft.

"Not to worry, girl. We'll sort this out. Now then, how far along are you?"

She turns pink, then white again. "S-seven months, about, sir. Your Grace. I, he, I mean -"

"Yes, yes. That's fine. Let's see. Seven months ago, where was I? Oh yes. I was in Jervaulx. Do you know it?"

"No, your Gr -"

"Fine. I'll tell you all about it. You're from there. Can you cook?"

"Some, y -"

"Sing?"

"A little -"

"Sew?"

"Yes, your -"

"Good. You're a seamstress then. A seamstress from Jervaulx. I'll hire you for fancywork, and you'll answer that the child has no father when anyone asks. We'll let everyone think the babe is mine. No mention is to be made of the prince. Ever. Is that understood?"

Uncertain whether the duke asks her or me, Mora nods, glancing at me in confusion.

"Fine. Good. We can show her to the servant's quarters in the morning. Tonight she can sleep in here."

"That's ridiculous!" We all turn toward the door. Connor stands in the doorway, framed by a black hall.

I feel a rush of relief that he is here, and fine. And a rush of other emotions to see him at all.

He closes the door firmly and stalks into the room. "We can't add another unknown girl to your household, on top of those here, and the other coming. Everyone's safety is compromised enough. You can't possibly expect to explain her, and her - condition."

Connor paces the length of the room, his lecturing tone causing Mora to become yet smaller. He doesn't even glance at me, which makes me happy and sullen together.

"Now, Connor," Hugh holds out his hands helplessly, "these are our prince's orders. She's his ... concern."

I wince. This won't go well.

Connor's pacing stops abruptly. When I open my eyes Connor stands in front of Hugh, his face hardening to stone and his hands twitching.

I flinch before the shouting begins. "Another? He sent another girl -"

"Now, Connor, you know how Alex is in a battle. And she's young, and pretty. I'm sure he only meant to comfort her, and -"

"And he's married to your sister! That rotten-! And how can you be so callous to Julianna?"

"How can either of you be so callous to Mora?" I ask through clenched teeth. "Here she stands while you talk as if she isn't in the room!"

The men stare, disconcerted.

I realize I'm almost shouting, and my stomach boils: I want to throw something. "Mora, come with me. We'll get you settled for the night in Connor's rooms."

Connor stands straighter. "What?"

"You can just spend the night here arguing with Hugh. You will anyway. And she's not sleeping seven months pregnant on a couch!"

Hugh backs from my thrusting chin.

"And if you do continue arguing, I suggest you shield the room, your Grace. I'm surprised they can't hear you in Jervaulx!"

I sweep toward the door, Mora in tow.

"I'd let her have the bed," Hugh says, bemused.

"It would make more sense for her to stay here," Connor snaps, irritated. "I suppose we are passing her off as Hugh's lover. She should stay here."

I look at Mora, who is shaking and starting to cry.

I spin to face him, Mora scampering behind me. "The pair of you are completely heartless. Can't you tell when you're upsetting someone? Don't you dare come back to your rooms before morning, my lord. This woman will be resting and you can be the one to sleep on Hugh's couch!"

I spin back around, hearing muffled snorts of disbelief - to find Julianna standing in the doorway.

"Why are we passing this young woman off as Hugh's lover?" she asks quietly.

I freeze where I am for a moment, remembering only when Julianna glances at me tug Mora into a curtsey with me.

"Your Highness," I murmur.

Julianna is not one for such formality, but her gaze demands it now. I glance at Mora, and see her face has gone a little gray. When I look over at Hugh and Connor, both of them look ill, as well.

"She just needs a place to stay, Juli," Hugh says, his voice quiet and placating. "She's very young, and made a mistake. You can't hold that against her."

Julianna's expression, when I meet her eyes, bodes ill for us all. "Young and blonde, and very pretty. How far along are you." She isn't asking.

"S-s-s-, your Highness, I beg– I–" Mora's voice quavers into nothing and I take pity.

"She's seven months along, your Highness."

"So many? It is a comfort he found companionship so soon after reaching the border. And she's staying here for her confinement."

Hugh takes a breath. "Juli, pet, we can't let Alex's child just disappear somewhere. I thought it best if–"

"You thought it best? Did you really? Or did Alexander ask you too sweetly to be denied, yet again? Might I remind you who his wife is, brother dear. He didn't marry you."

Hugh's face drains entirely at her vicious tone, and he spins on his heel and stalks to his bedroom without another word, slamming the door behind him.

Julianna lifts her chin and leaves, closing the door quite carefully. Connor, Mora and I stand still, afraid of explosions.

Connor's face seems carved out of rock, and I can

feel the rage roiling in him. It overwhelms me for a moment, and I can See his desire to strangle his cousin, the crown prince, with his bare hands. The vision of Prince Alexander growing purple under Connor's grip isn't pleasant for either of us. Connor releases a breath, and I fall out of the vision.

Mora whimpers: I realize I'm crushing her hand. "I'm so sorry, dear. Let's – let's get you settled somewhere…" I trail off, no longer sanguine about taking her to Connor's rooms. He looks at us both, and sighs again.

"I will arrange for a room to be prepared at the end of the hall. Wait here." He strides past us and out the door.

Mora and I both sag a little in relief once he's gone. I realize the girl is weeping silently. One hand on her lower back, her head lolls on her shoulders, and tears leak down her neck and drip onto her bodice.

I help her to the couch and sit next to her, patting her hand. "They're not always like that," I tell her. "I'm sure His Grace will find you somewhere inconspicuous, and you can start over." I don't know why I'm being so kind to her, except she seems so young and lost, and I know how that feels. Aside from the pregnant by the crown prince part.

When she breaks down and sobs, I understand why she feels so familiar. "Da is dead, and Mum died last winter, and I have no family. I have nowhere to go if His Grace turns me away. And I miss, I miss my mum. I miss her so much," she sobs into my shoulder. I find myself starting to weep, too.

"I know how you feel," I say. "I'm sorry," I say. And I see a vision of Mum, smiling at me, that almost feels like the Sight, like she's right here, and tears drip down my face, too. I haven't been missing her, or Da. I've been trying not to. But a wave of loneliness sweeps over me, and I long for home.

But there isn't any home any more. And when Linnet and I go there tomorrow, Mum and Da won't be there, humming or arguing or scolding me for slouching too much. I know this, but it hits me again. I let us both weep while we wait for Connor.

When Connor returns, we are quiet, but a bit soggy. He blinks at us both, but is solicitous in helping to settle Mora into the south boudoir, at the end of the hall. When we step out of the room and leave her to herself, I catch Connor's hand as he turns away. "Thank you for helping me," I say.

He looks down at our hands, and I snatch mine away. He takes a breath. "I'm sorry if I was insensitive, earlier. I lost my temper."

"I know," I say.

His mouth quirks, fighting a smile. I stare at his mouth for a moment, thinking, I kissed the king's nephew. The Duke of Torrence's son. I kissed him. That's probably some sort of treason of its own. His almost-smile widens, and I look up blushing. "Will they turn her away?" I gesture to the door.

Connor shakes his head, not smiling now. "Hers won't be the first child said to be Hugh's bastard, nor the last. One or two of them are even his. She will be cared for."

I nod, glad she won't be as lost as she fears.

Connor turns to leave.

"And Or-, um, about your errand?"

He looks back, nods his head. "The package is safe for now." He gazes at me moment longer, then turns away.

I watch him walk down the hall to his own rooms in the flickering dark. Shivering, with a dark spinning in my stomach, I turn to the stairs to head to my own room, and Julianna. There are more storms to soothe tonight.

As I stayed up till nearly dawn with Hugh, working on spells, I feel entirely justified sleeping in today. Linnet makes noises getting up and dressed, but I ignore her and turn over toward the wall. I will let her deal with everyone's chancy moods this morning. I'm not up for it.

Linnet wakes me in the afternoon. I groan, lift myself off of my side. My body aches from magic and sleeplessness, and I anticipate worse before the day is through.

She holds a lunch tray. "Her Highness wants you to attend her when Montmoore comes. So hurry up, you're going to be late."

"All right, all right, I'm getting up."

She swipes bread from the tray and snacks as I pull myself upright. I smile a little, happy to see her snacking, and shove myself out of bed to wash from the pitcher. The cold water shocks my head to throbbing.

The heavy air tells me, correctly, that there's a muggy and threatening sky. The trees in the garden outside shake their leaves in a sullen breeze.

I check my reflection in the mirror: my hair corkscrews and tangles in knots that stand up from my head. Sighing, I work my comb through snarls with little patience, missing the weight of my long hair. The tangles weren't better, but it stood straight up a lot less.

Linnet leads me to the great hall. When I walk in, the head table is covered in packages and jars, and Duchess Marguerite and her ladies are packing chests and rolling bandages.

"Good, Rhia, you're here. Help me over here with the jars." Julianna smiles and beckons me over.

Connor stands just below the dais, directing castle guards and servants to fetch full chests away. Hugh stands at the head of the table, speaking with the captain of his guard. I hear him say the chests are to be delivered to the hospice as soon as the carts are full.

Hugh and Julianna are pointedly not looking at one another. Connor's stiff stance and everyone's curious looks tell me that it hasn't gone unnoticed. I sigh and stand at Julianna's side.

I help pack simples into smaller chests, the stoppered jars cushioned by the rolled bandages and items of clothing the other ladies are rolling together. It seems a lot of bandages, but perhaps there is a higher need for them than I know. Sailors get in a lot of accidents.

When Montmoore arrives with Gantry, the bustle has reached its height. But everyone slows a little and lowers their voices when the kirche guard marches in, Montmoore and Gantry in their midst.

The archbishop is a medium man: his build is medium, as is his height and his coloring, but for gray in his brown hair. He's not dark or light skinned, not skinny or fat, but entirely unremarkable, but for the intelligence and watchfulness behind his eyes. His energy is all power and respect, as he strides into the great hall in his golden robes of office.

The kirche guards march smartly ahead and behind him in scarlet and black. Gantry beside him is an over-grown crow, his head cocking and twitching as he tries to see all the people in the room.

I let a little of my magic brush Gantry's mind. A whirlwind of anger and madness beats at me, and I retreat, afraid to See further right now. Curious, I test the edges of Montmoore's mind, but his is a steel trap, and I leap back before he catches me in it. I hold tight to the table to keep the leap from being physical as well as mental, and keep my gaze down, but I feel his eyes sweep across all of us, looking for the source of that brush. I hope my sweating isn't too obvious.

"Ah, your Grace, so good of you to come," Hugh says with a distracted and affable air. "I'm sorry we're in a bit of a mess here. These are just a few things we're delivering to the hospice. I know they run low so quickly these days."

"Your Graces," Montmoore says, his mouth pinching sour. His voice is a pleasant baritone. He nods to Hugh and Duchess Marguerite. "Your Highness, a pleasure to see you again. I offer you congratulations on your happy news."

"Thank you, your Grace," Julianna says.

Montmoore smiles in a pitying way. "My very best wishes for a happier outcome this time."

Julianna's smile is a parody of her usual warmth, and I feel her anger spike.

Duchess Marguerite steps in front of the table, blocking Julianna from the delegation. "Such kind concern, Your Grace, for my child. And my grandchild." Her voice is a low burr of warning.

Montmoore's smile does nothing to ease the tension. "I have great concern for all the people of the realm, of course."

"Is that so, your Grace? Because you don't seem to show it for all my people here in Haverston."

"To what can you be referring, your Grace?"

"To my hospice, your Grace. Where my people are dying. So many more sick than even a month ago, yet you will not allow other Healers to help."

"Ah, my dear Marguerite, you would force this discussion now?"

"It seems appropriate, Richard."

I blink at the sudden drop in honorifics. The chill in the room deepens. Gantry takes a deep breath to speak, but Montmoore puts his hand on his arm, preventing him.

"I will not debate kirche doctrine with you … Your Grace."

"It is not kirche doctrine, Richard Montmoore, it is rank greed, and you know it. That hospice belongs to this duchy, my duchy, opened with monies brought in by my people. If your priests turn one more person away, I will see every monastery in this duchy closed and your monks and priests turned out, and your bishop, as well.

"I've heard more tales from my people of their treatment at the hands of yours. And several of yours have come to me in despair, because they actually want to Heal. So do not speak to me of the kirche, or of Holy writ. I demand much more concern – your Grace – than you've so far shown for any people.

"I demand that you show a reckoning to us, in the form of money, and also in the form of returning our hospice, and allow oversight from our own Healers and physicians. This kind of hypocrisy cannot be allowed to stand."

Montmoore's face grows mottled as Marguerite speaks, although he doesn't try to interrupt. Gantry seems ready to explode into rage, but Montmoore's grip on his arm is an effective leash.

"Is this you speaking for your son, the duke?" Montmoore asks, his voice quiet.

"I agree entirely with my mother on this, your Grace. She is, as usual, completely right."

"That is unfortunate, your Graces. I do not dispute some in this bishropic have acted rashly, and without proper guidance. But it has been the declaration of our prophet Ashere that Healing is a holy magic, and must be therefore a holy right. I cannot allow your lay Healers to profane the will of the Star Lord.

"You do have my word I will look most carefully into the hospices, and who has been running them so poorly. No deserving person should be turned away."

All movement in the ballroom has stopped. No one even pretends to be working. Most of us stare avidly at the ground or table in front of us, glancing up from time to time, hoping to stay unnoticed. I am too frightened to venture the Sight around this man. I keep my mind locked tight.

"Are these the medicines from those trader ships – from Indranah, weren't they?"

Julianna answers, her voice bored. "Some are, yes.

We arranged for their shipment, as Indranah grows herbs we can't, that have worked on some plagues such as the Wasting for their own people. But to return to your last remark – who exactly is deserving, your Grace? And deserving of what, precisely? Because if you are implying that any of our citizens deserves to be ill and die, I will have to take great exception to that. As will my husband, and the king. That is not the doctrine we were raised with."

"You were raised as heretics by that blaspheming, pox-ridden -"

Montmoore turns slightly to Gantry and looks him in the eye. "That's enough, Theodore."

Duchess Marguerite regards them both with distaste. "I don't believe this bishropic is the right place for you, My Lord Bishop. I don't think you would be happy here. I expect you will find it far more comfortable in Corat, or perhaps your home county." She turns her back and walks behind the table. "Do find your way out, ny Lord, your Grace. And find your way home again, quite soon."

"Do not overreach, Marguerite," Montmoore begins, but Julianna cuts him off.

"What overreach, your Grace? I am sure, very sure, that you do not mean to threaten a duchess? I would think the other nobles would feel so distressed to hear of that. And kirche lands are so very attractive, aren't they? And so rich, and yield a good income. Of course, they aren't your lands, are they?

"It would be so terribly distressing if the nobles all decided they couldn't trust kirche promises all at once, and called your rents due. And so very many of your lands belong to, well, us. To my brother, to the king. I don't think you would be so impolitic to push a bishop on a duchy for which he is quite unsuited."

"You dare-" Gantry's face is nearly purple, but Mont-moore's grip on his does not ease.

"I would not be too sure of yourselves, your Highness, your Graces. But we will take our leave, and return to this – discussion – at another time." The kirche guards have been stepping closer to them, and surround them as they turn to sweep out.

Which they must do between a full phalanx of castle and royal guards, who have been entering and standing at attention in twos and threes for the past little while.

The essential truth of Haverston is: everyone loves the duchess. Most of us love her in a distant, doting way. But we do not take kindly to anyone acting the bully toward her. Not even the kirche. The guards and servants and minor nobles make sure these kirche gentlemen know it, glaring them out.

I let out a breath I didn't know I was holding. When we hear the great doors thud shut, everyone slumps a little.

Hugh turns to his mother. "That did not go precisely as planned."

She shakes her head and sighs. "No. That man always did make me angry. But he's a fool if he thinks the court will support him on this, or his other plans."

"Mother," Julianna says, warning her off.

Duchess Marguerite shakes her head again, shoots a look at her daughter. "Let's get this finished up, shall we?"

Everyone gets back to work packing chests. My hands shake. I know that whatever else happens, it will be open war from Archbishop Montmoore from now on.

The packing finishes with alacrity. Several guards mill by the stairs while Connor speaks to them. I brush at my skirt and run my hands through my hair as I walk slowly over. I try to lie to myself that I'm not nervous to speak to him.

"Spread the word," he tells them, "all kirche guards and persons are kept out until further notice. The gate is to be closed and guarded at all times. Tell captain Tand that I have business this evening, but when I return I will check in with him."

"Yes, my lord," the woman in front says, and bows. They turn and leave, and I stand behind Connor, my feet twisting in my shoes. I try to think of how to start.

He looks over his shoulder at me. "Good day, cousin."

"Good day."

He waits for me to say something else, but my mind races in circles while he stares. He sighs and offers me his arm. "Allow me to escort you to your rooms," he says.

I accept his arm, and we head toward Julianna's chambers.

"What did you want to say?" His voice is calm, but distant.

"About the package," I say.

"Ah. I told you,"

"I know. Safe for now. But where is it?"

He shakes his head. "Not far, but I won't tell you more. There are plans to move it tomorrow or the day after, to somewhere safer. You have other things to concentrate on. Don't think about the package. I'll give you information when I can." He stops at the door and looks at me, but doesn't release my arm. "About last night," he starts, and stops. "I...."

I shrug and smile a little. "Apology accepted."

That startles a laugh from him, and I step away and through the door, shutting it behind me. I try not to fret about Orrin for now, and focus on Connor's assurances. Tonight will be long, and I have preparations to make.

CHAPTER 25

Hugh greets me jovially from the midst of gay party clothes swathed about his chambers. He wears loose golden trousers, a bright purple sash at his waist, and nothing else so far.

I catch Linnet staring at his bare back. She sees me smirking and sticks her tongue out at me, turns back to sorting tunics.

I keep smirking until Connor walks into the room from the bathing chambers, similarly clad. Swallowing quickly I look at Hugh instead of Connor's dark skin.

"Rhia, you're late," Hugh calls. "Come meet Asa and Preyasi, they will help you to dress." He ushers me past Connor into the bathing room where four people fuss over stunning gowns of colors I didn't know existed. Such fabulous dyes are why Da wanted me to travel to Indranah: our dyes here in Talaria don't render colors of that intensity.

"Rhia, here are Asa, Preyasi, Bhanu and Zelig: the traders from Indranah. I think you've met Asa. Zelig,

Bhanu, come help Connor and me with these blasted tunics."

Asa smiles at me, and I offer her a nervous smile of my own. I can't help but remember our last meeting; I was less than gracious. She doesn't seem to care as they help us dress and place jewelry carefully on our too exposed limbs.

Preyasi gasps for a moment at my scars, and she and Asa trade glances, but otherwise don't comment.

I keep my eyes on the floor. This is the first time I have undressed in front of anyone on purpose. I can feel my hands shaking.

Asa quietly helps me with the skirts. I try to focus other things.

I admire the way both women move: as though always dancing. Hugh's plan seems impossible to me. No one will ever believe I am Asa, and Linnet is too darting and quick to ever be the languid Preyasi. Even with illusion laid over us, we are ourselves.

We enter the bedchamber for the spell casting. Connor struggles with his tunic. I bite my lips and try not to blush at the sight of his bare skin. Asa catches my eye and grins.

I smile back, feeling my blush deepen. She laughs and pulls his tunic straight, wrapping the end of it under the sash. Then we wait for Hugh to finish admiring the cut of his clothes in the mirror. I catch Connor rolling his eyes.

Standing in a loose circle, Linnet and Hugh and I chant the verse of the spell, joining hands. I spin my magic out to join theirs, and See green and blue light swirl around us. A tight, thin green line of power courses from me to them both.

The glow from our joined power fades as it drops around all of us. I feel dizzy as the chant ends, but blink and smile as Hugh and Linnet turn to us in triumph. And I realize it isn't them anymore. I see Bhanu and Preyasi in front of me, instead.

"It worked!" Linnet squeals out of Preyasi's mouth.

Behind her, the real Preyasi smiles at me. "I can't tell you from Asa!"

Linnet dances around me, gleeful.

"And these complete the vision," Hugh says as he lifts more jewelry from a wooden box on his bed. Necklaces hang from his fingers, thin silver chains. On each chain hangs an eight-sided star pendant that glows brightly to my Sight. The one I gave to Linnet already hangs about her neck. She looks under her lashes at me as Hugh gives out the others. I smile at her.

"Prophet's Stars," Hugh continues. "Many wear them in Indranah. Their blessing-spell will hide the power of the illusion. And … anything else." Hugh looks sidelong at me.

Hugh clasps the silver Prophet's Star about my neck, the pendant resting perfectly at my collarbones. He settles my hair back into place and turns me to look at him: but it isn't his face. Instead I see Bhanu's smiling visage, with his crooked front tooth and equally crooked smile. Behind that I catch a glimpse of Hugh's more perfect smile. The double vision dizzies me, as does the sea-colored glow about us all.

The spell rushes under my skin as we maintain it. As we spoke the words together, I felt the drain and pull, as though a river runs through me. The glow surrounds the four of us and shifts when we do.

I lick my dry lips and stare at Hugh. "Are you sure about this?"

He laughs and spins me toward the mirror. I see a grown woman, tall and bronze and graceful, showing more bosom than I'm used to. More than I actually have.

"Look at you. I'm sure. We've been over this. Try not to worry too much – the illusion is working perfectly." Before I can form my next question, he spins me back to face him. "And the Prophet's Stars were infused with a powerful blessing. They will hide the spell, and you."

I glance at Connor, or at whom I think is Connor. The Zelig who is dressed for a party. Still tall and dark, only a little darker, now his face is rounder, smiles more easily. But underneath I sense his concern. At least some of us are worried, I think quietly. But Connor nods at me: my thoughts must show in my face. In Asa's face.

The real Preyasi fusses with Linnet's gown. Shining a brilliant rose, it molds to her curvy torso and falls gracefully to her ankles. Her black hair cascades around her round shoulders and her teeth flash white against her red mouth when she smiles. Her beauty stuns me; but she is not my sister.

I blink at the aura from the Prophet's Stars and the illusion that blurs my vision.

"Ready?" Linnet seems eager for this evening. She never had her coming-out ball. And this is Francis' majority ball as well as an engagement. Everyone for miles will attend this event. Even if she can't talk to any of her friends, she knows they will be there.

My own coming-out ball was an unfortunate disaster. I managed to spill on my gown almost at once, and I tripped over my tongue the whole evening, trying not to say the wrong thing. So Mum and Da spent more time showing off the manor than they did me. I remember leaving as early as I could without offending anyone, and reading in my room. It wasn't as if I was trying to get a husband, I reasoned at the time. I was already betrothed to Francis.

And that is another thing, my head reminds me, as Hugh goes over last minute instructions whispered to the Indrani: the manor. The ball will be held at our home. Aman has taken that from our family as well. If Da hadn't been executed, if there had been a real trial, we might have gotten it back. But because of the disgrace and rushed circumstances, Aman took advantage, and stole our family holdings as well.

I exit Hugh's rooms on Connor's arm. Bhanu and Preyasi are married, and Asa and Zelig are Bhanu's siblings. We act our parts accordingly as Gervaise escorts us to the carriage we are to take "with his Grace's blessing and thanks." I smile Asa's smile at my "brother" and try to bite back the butterflies that threaten to fly from my mouth.

The carriage is sumptuous and as comfortable as a carriage can be. The walls, lined in dark satin, flicker with shadows as darkness falls and the outer lamps are lighted. I huddle in my wrap next to Linnet and hold on to her when we rumble over holes in the road. We ride through the town, mostly in silence.

The window shades are open, but the lamps swinging on their posts obscure the sights as we progress. Only well-lit houses and shops are easily visible, and tonight in Haverston there are few. The storm wind from this afternoon still howls eerily about the trees, but has not erupted into the rain we expect. Connor sighs, and I look at him. He peers out the window as well.

As the carriage pulls up to the brightly-lit manor, I am sure we will be recognized. The illusion itches my eyes, and everyone looks blurry. The Prophet's Stars around all our necks give off a fierce silver glow when I look at them, and I only hope Hugh is right and it will hide my power.

"It's like looking at the night sky through a lamp glow. The stars still burn, but the lamp hides it from you," he said when I asked him. Hugh smiles at me as he fingers the necklace about his own neck.

My swirly skirt unnerves me. The women of Indranah wear shorter skirts than we do. The material swirls about my ankles in bright aqua, the color of the sea in Indranah, Asa told me. I have never seen water this color; but she said the sun shines so brightly that Pavas, the ancient water goddess rejoices in it.

The shorter style is pretty, but years of outgrowing my gowns too quickly have taken their toll. I feel juvenile and awkward as I step out of the carriage on Connor's arm. The shoes – far too large – are of such thin material that the cobbles bite cold into my feet. Asa laughed when she saw how many rags I needed to stuff into the toes.

"My Papi always said I had longboats for feet."

Knives of jealousy: to be able to speak with such cheer about family. I smiled at her, anyway.

I feel grateful now for the extra warmth of the rags. But those sharp knives still tear my stomach as we approach the banquet hall through the garden entrance of my old home. The wind pulls at my skirts and my thoughts together, and I try to keep my mind on tonight.

The room sparkles and shines with couples who undulate gently like flowers in the breeze, as they dance to harp and flute: a quaint fashion popular with the guilds now. The air smells different than it should – sharp smells of wine where there should be flowers from Mum's garden. I nearly cough from trying to smell them and failing.

All the tapestries of generations of Owen-Weaversmith are gone. Aman-Weaversmith tapestries hang here now, and banners proclaiming the betrothal of Danwright to Aman, Francis to Melisande. I know months have passed since my parent's deaths, but this final sacking leaves me weak. I feel Linnet stiffen behind me as she enters, and I clutch her arm with my free hand.

Connor grasps my other and nods graciously to the footman. "Smile," he whispers at us, and we do, and enter. I let Connor's momentum carry me into this parody of my family home.

Bowing to the host and hostess, I try to glare only a little, and at the floor, not Jeffrey Aman. He stands in state with his wife, Giselle. Francis and Melisande mill to their right, the Danwrights to their left. The dais where they stand used to hold the first loom that great-grandfather made and used in this very home. Images of my father polishing it sting my eyes. I wonder what Aman did with the family things.

The Guildmaster and his family acknowledge our bows, then ignore our party, behavior no doubt inspired by Archbishop Montmoore, if the news of this afternoon has spread. It likely has, and traders friendly with the Duke of Haverston will not find warm welcome with allies of Montmoore. We slip to the sidebar and out of notice. The rest of the party takes their cue from Aman, and we are shunned.

I reach for a cup of wine on the table against the wall. The room is set up for dancing, and large banquet tables line the walls, covered with pitchers of wine, breads and cheeses in baskets, and platters of sausages and fruits braised in sugared wine. An enormous subtlety graces the head table on the dais at the top of the hall. It looks rather like a dog being strangled by vines, but I can't be certain it isn't supposed to be a stag in a forest, to represent Francis' virility.

The tall ceiling of the hall is festooned with ribbons and banners in the families' colors, which have been altered slightly so they don't clash. I had forgotten that Danwright colors are topaz and garnet. Aman colors are purple and blue.

I smirk at the played-down threads of violet stitching and edging on things. Green and gold, Owen colors, at least would have matched. I point it out quietly to Linnet, and we both stifle grins.

The mirror that has been here for generations still hangs magnificent on the wall across from me. Its huge golden frame and the enormous size of the glass itself explain why they didn't move it, despite the subtle Owen family crest stamped in the metal frame.

I catch a glimpse of a tawny woman, her dark eyes wary in her oval face. I recognize the dress before I recognize myself.

Hugh steps in front of me, his purple and gold tunic flashing in the lamplight. "Chins up, folks. These backwater Talarians don't know how to throw a party."

Dark looks pierce us from all sides. Connor casually picks up a meat pastry and inspects it. I try not to roll my eyes at Hugh.

In a low voice, Hugh reminds us of our instructions – at the first opportunity he and Connor will slip away to other rooms. Linnet is to stick close to me, and I'm to keep my mind open, use my Sight cautiously. If at any time the spell goes awry, quietly get out and meet in the carriage. If anything at all goes wrong, meet in the carriage. Linnet sniffs at this possibility.

"We have to stay until the second music break, to be polite. After that we'll leave. Get whatever you need by then." Hugh grins at us all, Bhanu's crooked tooth a mischievous gleam in his black beard. "Meanwhile, have fun! We're at a party, not a funeral!"

Around us the laughter swirls as couples dance to a morisque, my favorite of the modern dances. It looks so pretty: all those colors whirling around, the skirts like flowers blooming.

Hugh whisks Linnet onto the floor in a gap between dancers, and I find myself similarly pulled into Connor's arms. The heat of his hand on my waist startles me, but I fall into the steps easily. Looking into strange eyes, I see a familiar half-smile lurking. As we step with the rhythm of the dance, he inclines his head toward me.

"You dance very well," he says.

I grin; something is going right this evening. I feel lighter than I have in months. "It's the one thing about all the parties I actually liked. And since Francis and I were already engaged, we never needed to court or even talk. All we did was dance the first three dances and then he and our fathers would talk business, and I would either dance with polite young men my mother brought to me, or hide upstairs in the library, reading."

Connor spins me in a wide turn as the music ends. "Which would explain why you know General Sherron's speech at the battle of Kiras, but it doesn't explain why Francis is only coming to majority now, and not three years ago when he should have."

I look at him in surprise as we start the next dance, a slow pavanne. "Everyone knows that. It's because Francis is a terrible Jewelsmith. It took him two years longer than most to get his journeyman's badge. Da wouldn't pass any of his past projects for his master work.

"He and Master Danwright would get into furious fights about it. Francis may be a fine merchant when it comes to business: but he is not an artist, and Da would have nothing less for a Master Jewelsmith. Even if it meant ruining my betrothal into the family."

Connor's eyebrows rise. "Does it upset you, his marrying someone else?"

I shrug and perform my reverence, curtseying low. "It was marriage or the kirche, and I chose marriage, and marriage was supposed to be to Francis. But we were never friends. I don't think I was his first choice. I don't think he thought much of me at all."

"Then he was a fool," Connor says.

I stare at him, my mouth a little open in surprise, and I look down to hide a blush. When I glance up, that little half-smile lingers on Zelig's mouth, but I know whose mouth it truly rests on.

And what that mouth feels like on mine. I blush harder.

CHAPTER 26

The dance changes to a galliard and we spin with the music, jumping and turning until the last high jumps at the end. Laughing and out of breath, the dancers exit the floor as the musicians take their first break.

Connor and I join Hugh and Linnet near the wine. My pulse beats harder than even the athletic dance calls for.

"Oh dear, Francis. I hope the wine is not all spoilt." A familiar sneer greets me and I turn slowly to my left. Melisande and Francis approach us, looking past us as though we aren't here. A trick Melisande perfected when she was six, as I recall. Her topaz gown is not a good color for her, and the multitude of ruffles succeeds in making her look like a meringue. She sniffs petulantly as Francis steps toward Hugh.

"Don't worry, dearest. Southern winds can't spoil good, northern wine." Francis' voice is more nasal than I recall. He leers at me as they approach, his gaze fastened on my chest. The bright colors of his velvet tunic over-power his pie-like face and mouse-brown hair. He reaches past Hugh for a cup of wine.

Hugh grins in his face. "If it isn't the groom! Well met, young Francis Danwright. The Star Lord's blessing on you and your bride!" Hugh stares into Francis' eyes, grinning Bhanu's grin, until Francis starts to stammer.

Unable to repudiate a blessing from a guest, Francis pulls back his arm without taking any wine and stutters a thank-you.

"The Star Lord's blessing on you, Indrani," Melisande sniffs, more adept at the insult game. A mere blessing doesn't disconcert her. "I should think you need it more." She turns her back on the lot of us and pins the shrinking Francis with a pointed "Francis. My wine."

Francis winces and looks petulant.

Hugh hands her a goblet with a flourish.

She flinches back, unready for such gallantry in response to her snub.

"You are of course right, dear lady. A couple such as you needs no blessing for a good life. I see so many younger couples rush blindly into things: it is wise of you to start married life as an older woman."

Melisande flushes. I don't quite muffle a snicker. She glares at me, and I give her Asa's most beatific smile. Her chin comes up. "You're very forward for such a back-ward people. In our country, a guildwoman waits for her betrothed to reach his majority. Francis worked hard until he was satisfied with his masterwork. He's very particular." I hear a few snorts from the people around us, and she tosses her hair. "And anyway, he's lucky he did wait: otherwise he'd have married that witch!"

Silence ripples from her outburst over the gleaming crowd. Heads turn toward Melisande. Francis glares daggers at her as Hugh surreptitiously steps from the picture. Spice merchant Sandros speaks up from behind me. Connor pulls me close to hide my startled jump.

"Now, young lady, 'witch' is an inflammatory word to throw around. The guild council never did record the Owen girl so, since she died without trial. The Owen family didn't get a full hearing in front of the guild. Never sat well with me, that whole business." The burly trader's deep voice carries to Gantry, who has just entered to an unnoticed fanfare. White with rage, he flows through the stunned crowd like a storm.

"Do you question the validity of a kirche verdict, Master Trader?" His voice like ripped silk covers me with a sheen of sweat. Gantry's eyes flash over people and everyone shivers: I can feel his slipping control, and I think others can, also.

Sandros stammers an apology. "My Lord Bishop, I meant no disrespect. There was no verdict, is what I meant. You should have sat at their trial, my lord. I'm sure there was no mistake-."

"Mistake! Do you dare imply—"

A firm hand descends on Gantry's shoulder. Archbishop Montmoore steps from behind Gantry and smiles at the stunned crowd. "Now, Theodore, let's not discuss politics at a party, hmmm?"

Gantry stares straight ahead, his mouth closed like a vice.

Montmoore reins him hard – the knuckles on his hand stand out in stark relief against Gantry's fancy red robes.

"Of course the man meant no harm. We shall let

wine-sotted remarks pass, shall we not?" Montmoore smiles a diplomatic smile and steers Gantry away from the knotted statues of nervous people. "Let's greet our host, Theodore. No need for quarrels tonight."

I can hear my heart beating hard, and I begin to breathe again, trying to keep my gasping quiet. I realize I'm not the only one to have held my breath as I hear others do the same.

Melisande, cheeks flaming, flees the room. Francis follows her, glaring at everyone. The music starts up again, another pavan, soft and soothing. I see Aman with his head bent, furiously whispering to a servant as Gantry and Montmoore drift toward the food. The music break is over early – a diversion, I suppose.

———

The party continues despite dramatics. We all dance several more sets, laughing and eyeing the guests. I take a few turns with Hugh, and we analyze the mood of the room. People seem out of sorts and tired, fewer dancing, some leaving early, claiming illness.

Francis makes his return, and drinks his usual copious amount. Most who are left are the younger set, closer to Linnet's age, becoming more raucous and inebriated. Several people seem overcome by the wine and dancing, fainting and being carried off by their friends. The older traders and guildfolk stand at the wall, in the halls, murmuring to one another. They look wary and concerned.

Hugh jerks his head toward the stairs, and he and Connor make their separate ways toward them. Linnet stays with me, smiling and nodding to my non-existent chatter. Her gaze darts after them now and again.

The wine in my hand feels heavy suddenly, and the room sways as if I'd actually been drinking it. I set my goblet down carefully on the table and look at Linnet. Her face appears the same bronzed color – the benefits of illusion – but the glow around her fluctuates in time with the pounding in my head and the pull on my magic strengthens as she struggles for power.

I lean forward, smiling brightly.

"What's wrong? What happened?"

"I don't know. We've never held this spell for so long. I think I'm just tired."

I grip her hand in alarm. "Should we get out? Should we warn the others?"

She smiles a party smile, although her eyes are vague and wandering. "It's fine, Asa. I just have had too much wine."

I turn in time to catch Francis leaning close to hear us. I smile as wide as my mouth will go and pull Linnet closer to me. I back away from him and toward some chairs for the old, ignored, and weary. I feel I must be all three.

"Mistress trader, is there something the matter?" Francis at my elbow, hovering and in the way.

"No sir, my friend is just tired. I'll sit with her and I'm sure she'll feel better soon." I try to speak quietly, as near to an Indrani accent as I can.

Francis takes my hand as Linnet sits on the edge of a high-backed chair. His hand feels as clammy as I remember, but his eyes seem more aware of me than ever they were when we were betrothed.

"You needn't sit with her, mistress. She'll be fine here without you. Of course you will dance with me." His breath stinks of wine.

I sigh inwardly. Linnet visibly wilts, and I feed her more magic, even though I'm afraid of the consequences. Although overloading the spell is a worry, I find it far less frightening than the spell failing all together. There are spells to ward off overload. There are no spells against death.

Francis continues to tug my hand, saying something about wine, or dancing, or toes. Where is Melisande? I look around. "Where is your lady fiancé, Mastersmith? Shouldn't you dance with her?"

"Oh, we have danced the required dances. She's retired early. I am fortunate enough to have a stronger constitution, and a love of dancing. Especially with such pretty ladies."

Was he always like this? I also used to leave parties early. I sigh, pulling my hand away, and curtsey deeply to him. "My dear Mastersmith, I'm afraid I can't dance with you. I really must stay with my friend. Pray forgive me." I back fairly gracefully into a chair and sit, smiling with determination.

Taking Linnet's hand, I congratulate myself for disaster diverted, or at least aggravation, and try to open the link between my sister and me a little more. She looks into my eyes, startled and confused. Double images flood my brain; me looking at her, her looking at me. I See as if through her eyes for a moment, and feel her looking through mine.

Emotions wash over me – exhaustion, grief, some excitement, and fear that the spell is too powerful for me to hold. I realize that these emotions aren't mine, but Linnet's. I blink and the feeling recedes. She pulls away from me magically. The sharing is reduced to a trickle, and we stare at each other, concerned. That was too much sharing.

Francis hovers again. "You look pale, mistress. Perhaps you should get some fresh air." He holds out his elbow, but I ignore it.

"Preyasi. I'm going to get my brothers. Perhaps we should leave if you're feeling so poorly. Wait here for me."

Linnet nods slowly and I stand.

"Forgive me again, Mastersmith. I'm afraid my friend is feeling ill. I must find the rest of our party. Pardon me," I say as I edge past him.

He pursues me to the entryway, where I sweep up Linnet's and my cloaks. Francis follows. I hadn't remembered how much he resembled a sheep. "Surely one dance won't hurt. Your friend will recover," he insists, trying to grab my elbow.

I shrug away. "My concern must be with my sister-in-law, sir. We should leave as soon as I find my brothers. Really, I do hope you'll understand," and I sweep past his outstretched arm.

Annoyance flashes over his features, but it hardly matters. We'll be gone soon, and Connor will just have to figure out another way to get into the manor.

I head for my father's study, remembering that Connor was to check there last. I pass the ladies' retiring room, and the clumps of people in the hall have thinned out to nothing. I try to seem as though I might be lost, in case I do run into anyone. The hall is deserted, and I enter the study slowly, on the off-chance someone is in there. I can always claim I'm looking for the retiring room.

The light from the hall shines into the dark room. I open the door a little wider, and slip inside. The room still smells of my father's liniment and wool and old paper. The desk is an unfamiliar untidy mess. Da liked things in order, from wool to looms to papers to his children. But I used to come in here and sit with him, talk about books with him, in the evenings.

The light from the hall slants across the room, creating odd shadows. I don't see Connor anywhere, but the large closet stands partly open. I walk quietly over and peer inside. It's empty, but I think of the hidden safe, and walk in. The closet door swings almost shut behind me. Dim light peeks through, and I peer into shadows.

Shelves line the closet, and cloth and thread and yarn sit under dust covers. I bend down, run my hands over the mounds of cloth at the end of the lowest shelf, looking for the latch. The latch clicks and the shelf pulls out. The safe is full of a wrapped package: Aman never found it.

I unwrap the package to find three pieces of weaving. One I recognize as Linnet's first work: a lovely purple sash she wove when she was six, fine enough to be worn at her coming out. I remember Da putting it away and saying he would always treasure it. Another work I don't recognize – a small wall hanging, dark with what looks like stars in the form of a face. And the last I peer at, and finally know it. It's my own first work: a scarf I made for Mum. It's blue and green and gold – green and gold for Owen colors, and blue for her eyes.

She never wore it, and I thought it was because it wasn't good enough to wear.

I close my eyes and sit back on my heels. I hug the works tightly to me, trying not to cry. The wall hanging must be Keenan's. I remember the sash of Linnet's used to be in Mum and Da's chambers, in a chest Mum kept up there. I don't know why Da put these here, but I'm glad I found them.

There's also a letter, a ledger, and a bag. I tuck them all as lumplessly as I can in with the cloaks. Hoping I can keep from dropping everything, I clutch the bundle to my chest.

Voices in the hall, and I shrink into the corner of the closet behind a table stacked with cloth.

"Are you certain the man can be trusted? He seems unstable to me," a smooth voice says.

I hear the door to the hall close, and for a moment the room is dark. The lamps near the door light slowly as someone touches them.

"Be assured that Gantry can be trusted to do his job. He is here in Haverston for a purpose." I recognize Montmoore's scratchy voice. "Once that purpose is accomplished, he will no longer be a part of the plan."

"I won't be able to pull the other guilds or the merchants behind me unless they have some confidence that this will work, your Grace." I recognize the first man as Aman.

"You must get their support. The mission here is critical to the rest of our plan. Once we have enough money and support, we can proceed. The throne will fall."

My breath stops at this confirmation of Julianna's

worst fears. But the merchants? Why here in Haverston? What good would the guild do them?

Idiot. The guild controls the commerce, and all the goods and money that go through here. And Haverston is one of the few duchies the king can count on fully. If Haverston were against the king ...

They could outfit an army. A vision swirls over me, short and sharp and painful: battalions on the move. They mean to outfit an army. I yank myself back to the present.

"How many are with us?"

"Not enough. But pressure is being brought to bear on those who owe me money – and there are a lot of those. The people of Haverston are restless, afraid, and hungry. King Peter's mistakes with his son, and Julianna's supposed witchcraft are bandied about often. But the people here are behind the duchess, your Grace. They won't betray her easily. There must be proof of witchcraft and treachery before most will join."

"Not to worry, my dear Guildmaster. There will be proof a-plenty."

A frantic knock sounds on the door, and I hear hurried feet. "Guildmaster! You must come immediately to the ballroom!"

"What is it? Can't you see I'm with a guest?" Aman's voice loses some of its smoothness.

"Please come right away, sir. Merchant Sandros has fallen very ill!" The footsteps hurry away.

I wait what seems like an eternity, holding my breath. Distant sounds of raised voices, but no one comes near.

I creep to the door and peer out of the crack. The lamps are still on, the hall door open, and no one about.

Making sure my discoveries remain secure, I cautiously step out of the closet.

No alarm yet. I make my way to the door, and seeing no one, slip into the hall. I make my way further toward the party, starting to breathe more easily.

"And who might you be?"

Whirling, I find Archbishop Montmoore striding toward me from the east wing. I put my hand to my throat and think desperately of an excuse, or anything that might get me out of this. Silently yelling a prayer for salvation, and a message to Hugh, I manage a small smile.

"Your Grace is the Archbishop, yes? You gave me such a fright! I am looking for my brother, Bhanu. I've just come from the garden, but he's not out there. Have you seen him? I really must find him: his wife is ill."

During my too-fast speech Montmoore frowns, his neck growing as his chins draw back. At the mention of illness, he starts a little. I see sweat stains on his golden robes, and I notice sweat on his brow.

A hand snatches at my elbow from behind, and I clutch tight to the cloaks to keep the packages from falling out. To be caught a thief in this house would be almost as bad as being found out a witch.

"There you are, mistress. I thought you had been gone too long. Your friends await you in the ballroom. Shall I escort you?" Francis pulls on my arm, to guide me into the hall.

I shrug him off and back as gracefully as I may, and stutter something incomprehensible. I'm afraid to back into Montmoore, and I realize I'm cornered. I hear Asa's name being called, and we all turn to see Connor walking toward us. Relief floods my senses.

"Zelig! Thank goodness! I've been looking all over for you," I scold and march past the other men to his side.

He takes in the scene quickly and bows to Montmoore and Francis. "I am sorry, your Grace, good sir, but we must take our leave. My sister-in-law is very ill. Please convey our apologies to our hosts." And he bows again.

I curtsey clumsily, trying to hold onto everything.

Connor takes my arm and we head back toward the ballroom. Everyone seems to be leaving.

"Is the party over already?" I ask as he chivvies me along. "Not a successful celebration for the Aman family."

"The others are already in the carriage. Too many are suddenly feeling ill, and people are afraid it's the food. I'm afraid it's something else," he murmurs, as we make our way out the door.

Our carriage is further down the drive, waiting in a line with the others. Connor grabs my hand firmly and whispers "hurry," pulling me along faster than I can walk with such treasures filling my arms.

I pull on his hand and ask him to slow down, to no avail. The bag thunks to the pathway.

Connor stops and looks at me, and the things on the ground.

I feel a sheepish smile growing on my face. "I found something."

He scoops up what's dropped and hides it in his cloak. The wind blows his hair into his eyes. "What else have you got hidden in there?"

A giddy relief bubbles up my throat, and I try not to laugh.

He looks away and bites his lips, clearing his throat. "Shall we?" He gestures to the end of the path and our waiting carriage.

I clutch the rest of the cloaks to my chest and hurry to comply.

CHAPTER 27

Connor and I scramble into the carriage as it pulls up along the garden edge, out of the line of the others. The lights and noise of the manor quickly fade behind us as the driver urges the horses faster.

I lurch into Linnet as I try to settle myself. The carriage jumbles along toward the castle, and the ride is fraught with bumped foreheads as we all lean together.

"I have a note, and a ledger," I say, pulling apart the clothing and handing Linnet her cloak. "I found some things in the secret safe. It didn't look like Aman ever found it."

"That looks like Da's handwriting," Linnet says.

"I can't read it in here." The light from outside is too variable, and the ride too bumpy.

"Let me see," Hugh intones as he plucks them from my hands. He flips through the ledger, squinting. "We'll have to have a better look in good light, you're right. But this letter is addressed to Linnet."

"It's probably nothing," Linnet says, her voice quiet.

It's clear they realize I'm disappointed the letter isn't for both of us. But we can't release the spell until we're back in the castle.

I push away my emotions. "There's something else," I say, and I tell them about Montmoore and Aman talking. Connor swears quietly and Hugh sits back, tucking the ledger under his arm.

"If the merchants are already involved, then it's more serious than I feared. I had hoped they would be more loyal." Hugh's face is grim, even with Bhanu's genial features.

I sense a shift in his mood suddenly, and he looks at me, hope dawning. "Rhia, you actually heard Montmoore admit to treason?" Hugh grabs my arm as I'm jostled off the seat by a rut in the road.

Rubbing my bruised forehead with my other hand, I look at him in the wavering light and sigh at his excitement. "You can't have him arrested on what I heard, your Grace. I never saw him, only heard his voice. And technically I wasn't even there: it was Asa. You can't drag her into this."

He grips my arm harder, determined. "We don't have to mention you were in disguise, or that you have anything to do with the Indrani. We need only place you in the court to —"

"They'll never listen to me, especially since I'm supposedly dead twice: once as a witch and once in a fire. If I go into court someone's bound to know the Wolff cousins are actually dead. Who am I going to tell, my lord?" I try to sound reasonable.

His grip loosens and he settles back next to Connor, frustrated. Connor leans forward, careful to grip the handle next to the door so as not to fly from his seat.

"I think we should focus more on what he said, or what your Sight told you. Did you See an army? Did you See where, or when?"

"I Saw an army. But I don't know if it was now, or a possibility, or in the past. It was just a glimpse, my lord. I'm sorry."

He leans back, sighs. "I'll have to get back in there somehow. I was close to something, before all the chaos descended."

"Chaos?" I ask.

"All the people getting sick. It was getting a bit scary," Linnet says.

The carriage jolts suddenly to a halt, the horses whinnying, and we tumble into a heap against each other. I hear the driver curse.

"What is it?" Hugh calls, his Indrani accent perfect. He tries to extricate himself from the mess of limbs and clothing we have become.

I find myself sprawled across Connor's thighs, my cheek pressed into his side. Muffled in my wrap and his cloak, the driver's voice sounds far away.

"The gates won't open, sir."

I push myself off Connor's chest and look up. Hugh pokes his head out the door of the carriage as Linnet struggles to a sitting position.

"Star Lord preserve us," I hear Hugh breathe. He thrusts open the door and stands staring.

We're outside the gates, and I can hear shouting. Connor grabs my waist and helps me up, and I push him upright as the carriage rocks from Hugh stepping down. We peek out, and two guards are yelling down to the driver and Hugh.

A guard is marking the gate tower with a black slash

in charcoal. I stare in dismay – it's the symbol people in the town use to identify houses touched by the Wasting: a symbol of plague.

"Oh sweet Dorei, no," Connor whispers. "Seely Magan," he yells up to the guards, and they stare down at him in consternation. "Damn your eyes, Seely Magan! Open the gates!" He's dropped his Indrani accent, and they open the gates reluctantly. Connor and Hugh enter the barbican without the carriage, and Linnet and I follow.

"We're under quarantine, sir, we aren't-"

"I can see that, Sergeant. We have people here. We enter willingly. The driver can choose," he says, and breaks into a run. We all rush through the main gate and into the courtyard.

Guards rush around, and a few people are saddling horses, trying to leave. The guards are trying to stop them. Orders for plague marker is that no one leaves until cleared, but I can feel panic washing from people in waves.

We run to the castle doors. The front hall is deserted. Noise and voices come from the great hall. Rounding a corner, Connor almost runs Preyasi down. He stops short, and grabs her shoulders as we all stumble to a halt behind him. Preyasi gasps in surprise at our arrival.

"Zelig!" And then comprehension dawns in her eyes. "Quickly, you must change back before someone sees."

We have to end the spell somewhere. She pushes at Connor and shoos us all before her toward the stairs.

"The princess," Connor rasps.

"Is fine. This way, now, hurry!"

We run up the main stair and into Hugh's rooms.

Servants rush around, eyeing our own running with alarm.

In Hugh's rooms, Preyasi urges us to change into our regular clothes. The men are in Hugh's bedchamber, and we're in the bathing room. Preyasi stands in the doorwary, facing us.

Linnet calls out to Hugh. "I'm releasing the spell."

The river of power that runs through me cuts off suddenly, and I stumble, giddy from the backlash of power washing into a dam. I look up, and Linnet looks herself again. Grasping the sides of the bathtub gratefully, I heave a breath and struggle for equilibrium.

"Shortly after you left, my friends and I heard much commotion in the halls. We were left to ourselves in our chambers, as his grace assured us we would be, but we were concerned that perhaps you'd been found out. After awhile, Bhanu decided he'd better have a look.

"He found everyone in an uproar, with many falling sick and needing help. It came on rather sudden, and so many at once, no one knew what to do.

"The princess has gathered anyone without sickness to help, moved everyone to the great hall to monitor them, like a hospice. Some of the servants have fled. Anyone left who isn't sick is tending to those who are."

I rip the gown a little trying to get it off without help. Linnet unhooks the back for me and I shrug into my gray linen. Who is ill, and who has fled? I am glad Orrin is safe, although I feel guilty for thinking it. But now I'm worried – is he alone? Is this striking everywhere? People were ill at the manor, as well.

I hear Hugh cursing as I help Linnet with her shift. I try to breathe slowly and hear everything Preyasi says.

"My countrymen and I are helping as we can. Asa

can Heal a little, but her gift is not strong. The princess needs help." We finish dressing and join the others in Hugh's chamber.

"Who is ill?" asks Hugh, his face a mask hiding all emotion.

Preyasi breathes deeply once before answering, and I see Hugh's face pale. "I'm sorry to report, your mother and her ladies seem to be the worst off. I believe a lady named Geneve came down with it this evening first, and your mother was tending her—" but Hugh is gone, rushing out the door without another word.

Connor catches my eye as Linnet and Preyasi follow Hugh, rushing to the great hall.

I hesitate, watching the door close behind Linnet with a thump. I round toward Connor and gasp.

He's right in front of me, and he hasn't put his shirt on yet. His skin mesmerizes me for a moment.

I close my eyes and step back.

"What is it?" he asks.

"I, that's what I was going to ask you."

I open my eyes, and he's stepped back as well.

"You should go help the others. I'll be along in a moment."

I nod, turn to go.

"Rhiannon," he starts, and I turn again. "Be careful of Julianna. She will wear herself to nothing. You'll have to keep her from killing herself to save everyone."

I look away. He catches my hand as I turn again. "Be careful of yourself, too. Julianna's not the only one with that habit."

I open my mouth to protest, and his other hand comes up to touch my cheek. My protest flutters to nothing on my lips. He looks into my eyes a moment, releases me and turns away.

"And keep your eye out for anyone who acts strange," he adds as he shrugs into a shirt.

"What?" I'm having trouble keeping up.

"Stephen has spies, too."

Shaking my head, I try to think up reasons why he could be wrong. "Now? Here? Would anyone stay to their posts during something like this?"

He turns and raises an eyebrow. "You are."

I sputter, shake my head again. "Connor, I, that's different! Why would anyone stay in this kind of danger to spy on Julianna?"

"You don't know my brother," he says darkly.

I have nothing to say to that.

He looks up from contemplating his hands. "Go help Julianna. I'll be right there."

I stare at his back a moment, then turn and hurry away. I put my hand to my face, where the brand of his fingers still burns on my cheek. Remember whom it is he loves, and why he's concerned, I tell myself, and force my mind back to the catastrophe at hand.

If the Wasting did break out so virulently at the manor as well as here this time, then this is a much more dangerous strain. It usually takes days for so many to sicken, and this has only taken hours. If we can't Heal them, then the dead will add up quickly. If this is a demon spell ... I don't want it to be a demon spell.

The great hall writhes; guards and servants cross in front of me, carrying cots that must be from the guard house, linens, basins of water. Many of the cots have occupants: I see Samuel lying in a knot, clutching his stomach and moaning. And Christine, the kitchen maid, limp on one of the cots. It seems at least a third of the castle is pale and sweating, moaning, vomiting. Guards and servants and the highborn ladies and their retinues, all brought low.

Hugh hurries by me, heading toward the kitchens or the herbarium, Linnet just behind. The rank stink of the Wasting hangs heavy. Julianna bends over a cot near the head table. I make my way toward her, winding my way through people and blankets and stench. "Your Highness," I call as I near her.

She doesn't look up, but gestures to me to hurry. I reach her as she grasps her mother's hand, and I can see how tired they both are. Julianna's brow drips with sweat, and her dress sticks to her back. The Healing magic flows from her in a thin strand. I put my hand on her arm, worried.

With a start I feel power draining from me in great draughts. Julianna's power strengthens and she finishes the spell. She straightens, and looks at me.

"I think I've caught my second wind. Thank goodness you're back."

I worry at how easy it was for her to pull magic from me. Should everyone be able to do that?

"So many became sick so suddenly: I can't keep the disease at bay." She takes a breath, smoothing Duchess Marguerite's hair. "I'm so glad you all are here, and well. I've sent to the hospice for help, but no one has come. I'm about to send someone to the Inquisitor's Building, but I don't know who will get the message."

A commotion makes us turn. Archbishop Montmoore staggers into the hall, supported on either side by sweating monks. The room shushes quiet but for the moans of the sick.

"How did he get in the gates," I ask, but Julianna hurries toward the group. I follow, sending for Hugh in my mind.

"Your Grace, we are in quarantine; you should not be here," she says, but she motions the monks to help him to a cot. Everyone nearby looks nervous. Hugh is cursing in my head.

"Highness," Montmoore gasps, "I must ask for your help. It comes to my attention that Bishop Gantry has worked a foul spell, and we cannot control it. I have hope that you and your brother can."

Julianna looks at me, but I am no less surprised. She looks up at the monks, but they seem frightened and worried. And sick.

I push the shorter one to sitting on an empty cot. His cohort follows suit. I try not to glare.

"A spell, you say," Julianna murmurs.

Hugh has not told her, I realize. I wish she could speak in minds. I try to hurry Hugh along. Looking around for help, I see Connor entering the hall.

He glances up, his tunic crooked and his hair in a tangle. I wave to get his attention. He takes one look at our tableau and strides over to us.

"How does the archbishop come to be here," he asks. His voice sounds mild, but his eyes bore into Montmoore as though pressing for confessions.

"Your gate guards were good enough to let me in, once I explained I needed the – the good offices of your princess," Montmoore says, his teeth gritted in pain. "Please, Highness. Time is running out for us all. You should gather all your wit-, your spell workers and try to stop this spell."

Julianna frowns at him fiercely. "This foul spell you

speak of, that Bishop Gantry started. This is the cause of the Wasting?"

Montmoore winces, in pain, maybe. Maybe embarrassment. "Yes."

I send all of this to Hugh, to Linnet, goad them to hurry.

"And where is Bishop Gantry," Julianna asks.

"I wish I knew." Montmoore glares at the ceiling.

I hear running, turn to see Hugh and Linnet rushing in. I can feel a vision trying to break in, trying to wash over me. The magic pulls, and I push at it; not now, not in front of this man. I See a house near the docks, shadows, Gantry's face. I shove it all away as I feel a hand tug at my sleeve, grab my arm. Power slips out of me like a sip of water, another drain.

"You. You're the one," Montmoore says, as I yank free and back away. "I can feel your power now. Where did you get it?" He gasps.

"Your Grace, you are raving," Hugh says, pushing me further away as he steps up. "And as for a, what did you call it? A foul spell? Why is it you haven't stopped this spell yourself?"

I look around at everyone staring at us. My lungs cramping, I realize all our secrets are about to be revealed to whomever is nearby.

Asa calmly walks toward us from across the hall. Connor, Hugh, and Julianna stare at Montmoore, waiting for an answer. Linnet stares at me.

Montmoore glares at Hugh. "I need more power to unravel it. Nearly everyone at the Inquisitor's Building has come down sick – the healers especially. I am surprised you have been spared, Your Highness."

He spits, grimaces, and curls over on his side, panting. Sweat dampens his robes. "No one has the magic to spare to stop this out-of-control spell. Except you, as long as you have that –" he gestures to me.

I hunch away from his scowl.

"She was here before, I felt it – at the party." His breath hisses between his teeth. "Use that power. Dismantle the spell. The sickness will stop."

"Unless it's powered by demons," Hugh says.

Julianna gasps, and Connor chokes back a curse.

I can hear the people around us murmuring in fear. Connor turns and looks at me. I'm shaking, fighting, trying to force the words out, but I still can't break this spell.

"Demon spells are very dangerous," Asa says from behind me, and it is all I can do not to scream, although I knew she was coming.

Linnet takes my hand and squeezes. I feel a little more power bleed off, but I'm grateful now, it is overwhelming me.

"Demon taint," Asa says, "is something the government of Indranah takes very seriously, indeed."

"Bishop Gantry has fled," Montmoore gasps out. "The kirche will condemn him as a heretic for this spell. You must stop it."

"Gantry is your creature," Connor leans in to murmur, his voice still deadly calm. "Any spells he did or did not cast were at your behest, surely."

Montmoore swipes his arm out, to hit Connor, or to wave away such allegations.

Connor deftly avoids it.

"Will you stop this spell?" Montmoore says. "Princess, it will kill all your people. You must stop it."

His voice turns thready; he will likely pass out soon. Some people do, when the cramping gets strongest.

"Is the spell a demon spell, that sickens everyone?" Julianna's voice could cut glass.

Montmoore does not answer.

Asa takes my arm and turns me to face her. Draining, again. This is not a good sign. "What is he talking about – oh. I see. That is quite something, isn't it?"

I pull away from her, too, but her gaze is less kind than scrutinizing anymore. "Not scars from a fire," she whispers. She doesn't seem surprised. "Perhaps we should move this discussion elsewhere," she says in a more normal voice.

Connor nods to us all, gestures toward the hall. "The lesser hall will suit," he says. He walks a little ways away to have a word with a guard, his face closed and solemn. I wait for him, and Asa waits for me, and Hugh and Julianna wait for all of us. Linnet keeps hold of my hand.

"What are you going to do?" she whispers to me.

I shrug, magic burning in my veins, still pumping through me from the vision I don't want. My fear is a cold lump in my stomach.

Connor speaks to Bhanu next, and then turns to us. "After you," he says to Asa, but it is Julianna who leads us all to the room. She walks as though her feet hurt.

When we enter the room, Julianna sinks into a chair at the table with a faint groan and leans back, her arms around her belly. Hugh sits on the table, runs his hands through his hair.

"Rhia Wolff Fitzwellan," Asa starts, walking toward me, but Connor holds up a hand.

"Wait. How are you sure of demons?" he asks Hugh.

"Context," Hugh says. He wipes at his forehead, tugs at his hair. "It fits, doesn't it? The strange runes we can't read, the power, the death spells, Rhia and Orrin. He can call a lot of power, and quickly, and tie it up in very intricate ways with demon spells and power wells. They're unstable, but one can manage a lot of complexity with them – because they're almost alive. But almost alive means they change. This one seems to have changed from specific targets to general populace. And I don't know how to unravel it without knowing what went into it to begin with. Also there's the point that I won't be calling any demons."

"Not while I am here, you won't," Asa says. Everyone looks at her.

"Tread carefully," Connor says. "This is Talaria, not Indranah."

"I am always exceedingly careful when it comes to demons. My sovereign will not take lightly to news of demon spell and taint in Talaria," Asa says. "Is this young woman in thrall to Bishop Gantry?"

"No," Connor says.

"Not as far as we can tell," Julianna says at the same time. "He did try, but the spell failed, and he didn't finish it."

"May I see?" She addresses me now. At least she is asking.

"You don't have to show her anything," Linnet says from behind me, her hand clenched in mine. I can feel her trembling, in anger or fear, or both.

"Who are these traders from Indranah really,

Connor?" Julianna asks. Her voice takes on a very royal tone.

Asa turns to her. "I am who I have said, Highness. Trader, ship owner, magician. Spy. You knew all that already. But I am perhaps a bit closer to my sovereign than I indicated."

"How close?"

"Close enough. Connor is aware, as is your King Peter. I can help you dismantle this spell, perhaps. But I need to know more about it. What is the thrall spell the bishop placed on you? Please, let me see some of it." She turns to me again.

I let go of Linnet's hand, and pull up my sleeve. She takes my arm, and power slips from me again. She looks up, her dark eyes wide. "That is very interesting. Does it always do that?"

"More often lately," I say.

"Interesting," she murmurs, looking at my marked skin. The scars are all white and old looking anymore, but still recognizably runic symbols. Asa turns my arm without pulling.

"I don't think we have time for interesting," I say, hoping against hope that she'll know something, that she can fix me. Fix this.

Asa nods, purses her lips. "I recognize some of these. Some are ancient Indrani, and some – I don't know all of these. Are they all like this?"

"I have drawings," Hugh says. "But this isn't the spell that is causing the sickness. This is just a version of how he got the power to call them, to set it up. He used Orrin. The spell might still be going through him, I think. Connor, where did you put him?"

"Who is Orrin?" Asa asks.

"Another of Gantry's victims. He's in a safehouse in town. I couldn't get him any further away than that, and I had to go there a very roundabout way. He was – not in good shape." Connor's voice is very soft for the last sentence.

My eyes burn, and I pull my arm free from Asa, turn to look out the windows.

"He has this same spell on him? That Rhia does?" Asa asks.

"Yes. But on Orrin it's complete." Connor catches my eye in the reflection of the window. "We don't have time to analyze this spell."

"It does tell us what kind of magician this Gantry is." Asa says.

I spin to look at her. "Evil, maniacal, and insane." I spit. "He wants power, he wants death, and he despises everyone he thinks is in his way."

"Familiar with ancient Indrani, clever enough to be able to conceal his actions, and, at least to begin with, cautious about interacting with the demons. Or he wouldn't have created the spell on you and this Orrin. If he feeds demon power through other sources, it keeps him clean of the taint."

"So you're saying Orrin is likely demon tainted," Hugh says, his voice gravelly.

"If Gantry used demon power to control a death spell this large and intricate, and used Orrin to feed the power through, then yes. Probably. If Gantry called demons and fed them what they want, what they always want, air and life force and blood, it's probable he used Orrin's blood instead of his own. If he used his own at any time – he is theirs. Demons do not give up what they own. They only consume it."

"How do we save Orrin then?" I hate how wavery my voice is. I can't leave my friend to that kind of fate.

"I don't know." Asa's eyes aren't kind or comforting. She stares back at me, her face like stone.

"Let's try and stop the spell first. If we can break the spell, then maybe we can cure everyone. We'll work on a way to save Orrin, too, Rhia. I promise." Julianna says. She starts to stand, then grunts in surprise. "Oh…"

I stare at the spreading wetness on her skirts, and Asa curses. Connor and Hugh stare in confusion.

"What is it? What's wrong?" Linnet asks.

"The baby's coming, I say, and hurry to Julianna's side.

CHAPTER 28

We have been here for hours, it feels, but a glance at the water clock on the mantle tells me I'm mistaken. Sweat drips down my cheeks and back and when I breathe. I feel smothered in wet velvet.

The storm that was threatening finally broke, full of wind and rain and thunder. We've built the fire in Julianna's chamber high to keep her warm while she labors, but I long to stand outside and drown in cooler air.

Asa has taken charge of the birth. The midwife we should have is sick, and Julianna doesn't want anyone else up here. As it stands we need all hands taking care of everyone who's ill in the great hall.

Linnet runs back and forth between here and there, bringing herbs and linens and anything else we send her for.

Connor stands braced in the doorway, behind the screen. I can see his head and his arms, holding the door frame as if he could tear it asunder. He only leaves to issue orders to the guards or for a few minutes if we send him away.

Hugh knocks into him from behind. I only hear a few words. He's been working with Preyasi and Bhanu on a way to break the spell. Zelig has come down with fever.

Asa says, "This is it," and urges Julianna to bear down. "It is now, your Highness, now."

Julianna yells, and Asa cries out as she pulls the baby the rest of the way free. Asa hold the child for a moment, then cuts the cord and wraps the child in a towel, wipes at its face and back. The child is still and quiet.

We wait for a cry, but it doesn't come. Panting, Julianna collapses against the back of the chair. I look at Asa, whose eyes tell me what I fear.

"Give him to me," Julianna says.

Asa wraps the baby in a clean towel, her head down. There's no movement at all. My hand aches from where Julianna grips me.

I lean down to Julianna. "I'm so sorry, your Highness."

"Give me my baby. He's mine. I want to see him I want Alex to see him."

I close my eyes on tears.

"Oh, Juli," Hugh says, and comes around the screen. I arrange the sheets down over her legs. Connor's head drops, although he still holds up the doorway.

"Give me my baby." She sits forward and reaches for the child.

Asa hands him over, and Juilanna pulls the child

from the swaddling. I feel a pull on my magic as Julianna links to me, pulls power without even trying. I clamp down on the link, slow it to a trickle, try to stay upright.

I feel a hand at my elbow; Connor is behind me. He looks down at Julianna and her child, his face a mask of stone.

Julianna's face crumples as she views the baby. His bluish skin and limp tiny limbs tremble from her crying. She clasps his corpse to her and rocks. "This is Gantry's fault. His damned spells. He was perfect, perfect," she sobs.

"The body is demon-touched. I can feel it," Asa says. "You say Gantry cast a spell on your babe?"

"He cast a spell. I stopped it – I thought I stopped it." Julianna says through tears.

"Juli, pet, let me have it." Hugh tries to take the dead child.

"Him! His name is Absalom. He is my son."

Asa and I gather up soiled linens. Sweat slides down my sides, and I try not to look at anyone's face. Thunder booms close to the castle.

"Let me take him into the other room, pet. Let us take care of you." He pulls the tiny bundle from her arms and takes it out of the room.

I look back at Julianna. She shakes her head, then groans a little, grips the arms of the chair. "Your Highness, it's time for the afterbirth," Asa tells her.

"Not yet. There's another baby." Julianna bears down again, as we stare in shock.

Connor spins back from the hall where he was going after Hugh. "What? Julianna, you're not having twins."

"It appears I am. Get out." She pushes, and Asa

hurries to check the position of the baby. Linnet and I stare at each other, then rush to get things ready for another birth.

"You knew," Connor accuses.

"Of course I knew. What kind of Healer would I be if I didn't know? Shut up! Get out!"

"Your Highness, hold back a moment, I have the head," Asa says gently, and Julianna pants.

I hurry forward with a cloth to wipe her face. I glance up at Connor: he's gone back behind the screen, bracing the doorway with both arms, his head down.

This baby is born much more quickly, and Asa cleans it off. It – she – starts to yell and move her arms. A live girl, and all her limbs seem well-formed. I breathe a sigh of relief. Julianna laughs a little, with a sob in it.

"Oh, give her here," she says, smiling, and I reach to help, but the look on Asa's face stops me.

Connor shoves forward at our silence. "What? What is it?"

"Give her to me," commands Julianna, and after cutting the cord, Asa does.

I take a good look at the crying baby. Her eyes are tight closed, and she looks fine to me, pinking up already. Julianna looks her over, touching her face, her legs, her back, holding her close.

"I fear she is demon-touched also, your Highness. There is a taint."

Connor whips around. "Hugh! Get back in here!" He turns and strides to us. "Can you lift it?"

"I don't know. Please step back, my lord. Now it is time for the afterbirth."

"Yes," Julianna breathes, holding her baby out to me. "Wipe her down with warm water, Rhia."

The tiny baby kicks weakly, still crying, but too tired to do more. I let the blankets fall away and reach for a cloth, soaked in plain water. When I touch her bare skin, I almost drop her. I sink to the floor, carefully, trying not to clutch.

I See a child with white eyes, blind. But I know she can see, with a Sight so strong she uses the eyes of those around her. I gasp and the child in the vision looks at me with her empty eyes, smiles. It is not comforting. I break out of the vision and look down at this baby, trembling.

In the chaos around me, no one has noticed my stumble. The baby is quiet in my arms, starting to root. Her skin is cold. I wipe her down quickly, wrap her again, trying not to touch her skin. I feel a hole has opened up in my stomach. Asa is right; there's something wrong with this baby.

Hugh rushes in past Connor, looks at the scene. He sees me holding a live baby.

"Oh, Juli. Twins. May I see?"

"Stay behind the screen, your Grace," I say, and I stand to bring him his niece. "I – Asa says the baby is –" and I look over at her, cleaning Julianna. "She is d-" and I can't speak. I shake my head.

"I see. Let me have the child."

"Give me my baby."

"Yes, in a minute, love."

Julianna seems about to leap from the chair, but Asa warns her to take care with herself. She helps her to stand.

"I want my baby."

Hugh is looking over the child, who has started crying again. He sends out a tendril of magic, draws it back. He looks up at Asa. "Do you think we can reverse it?"

"I will try with you, your Grace."

"Good, because I don't know how much energy I have left. I will need the help. Rhia – I hate to ask it of you, but how worn out are you?"

My head aches and the channels of magic in my blood burn and chafe. I don't know how much I have left. "Pretty worn, your Grace. But I can try to help."

He takes a deep breath. "Don't kill yourself. I mean it. But link to me if you can. Let me know if you have to drop out. I'm going to try a spell that I've only read. Asa, have you ever removed demon taint?"

"Once. Not on a child. It was difficult. Demons don't give up what's theirs."

Hugh closes his eyes, opens them and walks to the side of the bed. He places the child on it and we gather around him.

Julianna stands beside him, tense. He smiles at her. "Sit down, pet. Don't touch her just yet, but stay here and watch, if you'd rather."

He reaches for my magic, and I wince and open to him. It feels like old, creaking doors, like my blood is rust, like I am an old joint about to break. I cling to the bedpost and shudder at the feel of the spell he begins to create; I didn't know there were such spells.

Asa and Hugh chant words that bite sharp and cut ties, bind fast to create new ones, push out a lingering taint like a mold on the child.

Wailing and chittering voices call out inside the magic, spinning across my power to cut me off from Hugh. The line between us stretches thin. Exhausted, I reach further into myself and send a burst of power along the flickering thread.

The voices build into a shriek and I wish for mental hands to clap over my mental ears. I lean on the bedpost and feel chills crawl up my spine.

Blinding flashes of pure white light flicker across my closed eyelids, and the spell fails as I hear a thin wail. I open my eyes and see Julianna reaching triumphantly for her baby, who is squirming and hungry and angry enough to command armies.

Julianna closes her eyes. "My daughter's name is grief," she whispers. She brushes the thin fuzzy hair back from the baby's forehead. "Atarah Kieran, I name you. Your father will give you another name, but this name you bear for yourself and your brother."

A hard burden for a child, I think, but I am not a princess, and I did not just lose a child. Tears fill my eyes, and I sag back into Hugh, who catches me. Everything shifts sideways, and Hugh's hands claw into my shoulders. I sit with difficulty on the side of the bed to gather my strength.

Julianna holds her child to her breast, and Hugh and Connor turn to leave. I stand to go with them, but I feel myself fading – Hugh has broken his link to me, but Julianna still feeds on me in a small current, and I am too tired to cut it off.

Connor catches me before I fall, and shakes me. "Rhia, for pity's sake, breathe!"

I look up at him weakly. "I am breathing. Tell Hugh to cut his sister off from me before she kills me." I have dropped the Grace. I don't care.

Connor blinks and puts his arm around me, walks me out of the bedchamber.

I remember when the sight of priest's robes brought me joy. I shudder in Connor's grip at the sight of a young priest in the solar, standing to greet Hugh. He looks over at us, bites his already raw lips and bows a little. His shaggy hair is medium brown, the same color as his dirty robe. Dark circles bag under his bloodshot eyes, and his young face looks haggard with grief. He clears his throat to speak.

"I must," and his voice catches. He tries again. "I must get a message to His Grace the Duke of Haverston, or her Royal Highness, Princess Julianna. I was told I could find them here."

"I am the duke," Hugh says, looking almost as haggard as the young priest. His clothes are nicer, but also stained now, and his face is pasty and sweaty from the night, now become morning. "What is your message?"

"Please, your Grace, I am Daniel. Cardinal Robere sent me – we arrived at the seminary to find so many sick with the Wasting. He sent me to beg aid, but I find you also under plague banner."

He turns away and clenches his fists. "Cardinal Robere asks you to come, your Grace. He says the spell is demon-borne. If you have any information-"

Hugh wipes his face, his shoulders sagging. "I have been working on something that may help. The herbs – Rhia, go and tell Linnet to get them for me."

Connor stops me and turns to call, but Linnet's voice stops us both. "Will we be back before dawn?"

Hugh turns to her, shaking his head. "It is dawn. And we won't be going anywhere. I will go with Daniel. You stay here and get some rest."

"What about you? You need to rest, too."

He closes his eyes. "I do. But I need to get to the Cardinal even more. I'll bring him back with me as soon as I may; he should be able to help us stop the spell." Hugh's voice is hoarse. Linnet's face is stubborn. "I'm perfectly serious, Linnet. I need you to stay here, and help everyone out. There's still so much to do."

She shrugs her shoulders and glowers, but leaves for the herbarium without further argument.

"Connor, you'll need to – there's …"

"I know. I'll take care of it."

I presume they mean Absalom's body. I lower myself to the chair. Connor leans back against the wall and rubs his hand across his face. "Take sergeants Gengler and Watson with you. There may be desperate people on the road. You can't let them stop you, no matter what they need."

"I know that."

"Also do it."

"Look after-"

"I will."

Hugh nods, and ushers the confused Daniel from the room. I hope he thinks to offer the poor man some water.

Connor looks down at me. "You should go to bed. Is Julianna still draining you?"

"I – no. I stopped her. Or leaving the room did, I think. I can't tell anymore."

"Stay out of her chamber for now. If they need you they can call for you."

I nod and get up to walk to my room.

Asa passes me in the hall, heads into the solar to speak to Connor. I linger in my doorway to listen.

"Where is Hugh?"

"He's gone to fetch Cardinal Robere from the monastery. He hopes he can help stop the Wasting spell."

There's a pause. "This will be a very long report to my sovereign. I'm not sure she will be happy with you. How ever did you allow all of this to come so far?" Asa's voice is harsh.

"Don't push me. I've done what I can to keep Stephen's plots from coming to fruition. I'm not the Star Lord, to know everyone's heart and mind. If I had known about the demons, I'd have taken care of Gantry months ago." Connor sounds as if he's pacing.

Asa sounds like a disappointed parent. "And what will you do, now your king's heir's heir has demon taint?"

"I thought you removed the taint."

"I don't know how successful that was, Connor. We did the best we could, but demons are slippery, and their magic changes as you handle it."

"But you think you removed it. I would take it as a very great favor if you would keep word of Absalom quiet, and not mention it in your report. And also report that the taint has been lifted on Atarah."

A short silence. I can hear outrage in it. "You are walking a very rocky path, my lord," Asa says. "You cannot command me to silence. And while I look upon this royal family as friend and kin to my own sovereign, I will not take orders from you, or do anything to put my country in danger."

"I am not commanding; I am asking. And keeping

this event to yourself does not jeopardize anyone," Connor snaps.

"Oh no? And what if this child is demon touched all her life? What if she becomes queen in her turn? Shall I keep silent about the taint that lives in her?"

I worry about that, too. How can we tell? How can we save her? Save Orrin? Save me?

"She's a newborn babe," Connor is saying. "Maybe your spell worked, maybe she's free of the taint. Time will tell us that. Who knows if she'll grow into a wise person or foolish, or if she's ever even named heir. It's not as though Alexander were wanting for bastards to claim, even if Julianna never has another child."

"Connor, Bansha, listen-"

"But the court will not allow her to have another child if this gets out. They might not let her live." His voice is bleak.

"The princess is more than a broodmare."

"I agree, but this is the world we live in. The court is already baying for her blood. Absalom must remain a terrible, and private, tragedy. And Atarah – give her a chance to live. Give them all a chance to live."

"And what if the demons have a toe-hold now? Can you sanction an heir with demon taint?" Asa demands.

"When will we be able to tell?"

She sighs. "Maybe tomorrow, maybe next year? I am not an expert. We should call in experts. There are others who can help this child. You should want that."

"I do want that, but quietly. I ask you for the sake of my mother-"

"I have already done much for the sake of your mother," Asa growls. "This may be going too far. But what will you do if I am not silent? Will you kill me, to silence me?"

That hissed question chills my skin, and I shiver. I hear him suck in a breath. "That you could think that of me, Mashee –"

"Is that not your duty, son of my sovereign's daughter?"

Sovereign's… I blink, shake my head.

"Lord of all Stars," Connor yells. "My duty is not to kill my kin!"

"And yet you have threatened to kill your own brother. You do come from a kin-killing family."

"Would you have civil war, then? Think what a Talarian civil war would mean for Indranah," Connor grinds out.

"I do think on it. And I think on what an unbalanced Talarian ruler means for Indranah. I think of it every day. And so do all our court."

I close my eyes and try to breathe as quietly as I can. The only sound is the wind, and some crying from the baby, and Connor's harsh breathing. He is the grandson of the Indrani Empress. He is nephew of the Talarian king, as is his brother. Who is trying to kill the people Connor loves. Whom Connor has sworn to stop. I taste ashes in my mouth.

"Do what you will, Mashee. I will not command you. But I cannot say what my king will say or do, if you reveal this."

"I cannot speak for my ranee, either. I do not yet know what I will do."

I hear her coming back this way, and duck in my door, but not quickly enough. She stares at me, then nods as she passes. I nod back, my eyes down.

"Rhia," I hear Connor say, and I look up. The door to Julianna's chamber closes behind Asa. Connor stands at the entrance to the solar. "You were eavesdropping."

"I – I'm sorry. It – I was …"

"Eavesdropping."

I shrug. "Yes."

"It has its uses," he says. "Did you learn anything?"

I swallow carefully. "That you are related to some very interesting people."

He laughs harshly. "That, at least, is very true. And what else did you learn?"

"I don't know, my lord." He walks closer, and I realize I'm whispering. I clear my throat. "I, I don't know."

"Don't you?" His eyes are deep and dark in the shadows of the hall, and I lean a little toward him. He stops across from me.

"I, we need to be careful about information…."

He nods. "That is always true. But the main lesson from that conversation, Rhiannon, is that I come from a kin-killing family. You should bear that in mind."

I shake my head. "She didn't mean it."

"She very much did, I'm afraid. And she isn't wrong."

"You are not your brother, my lord."

"Or my father, or my uncle, for that matter."

"Who is king."

He laughs again, without smiling. "Who is my king." He leans his head back, and I see there are tears in his eyes. I step forward, put my hand on his cheek, and he lowers his head to look at me.

"You are not your brother, Connor." Leaning in, I press my lips to his, then retreat to my room before has a chance to react. My hands shake, but I ignore them and very deliberately undress and get into bed. Exhaustion keeps me from thinking for very long, and I am grateful for it as I slide into aching sleep.

CHAPTER 29

I wake reluctantly to the sounds of a baby squalling. By the sullen light coming in the window, it is mid morning. Dragging myself out of bed, I splash stale water on my face. Someone hums in Julianna's room: it sounds like Linnet. I pad out into the hall. The baby still fusses, but less urgently. A sound behind me makes me turn.

A quiet groan and rustling come from the solar. I tiptoe warily into the dim room, the soughing wind and rain covering my steps. I think of rats, or desperate plague victims, maybe Gantry …. As I pass the fireplace, I grab the poker. Hefting it, I walk around the chaise and stand, mouth open.

Connor is twisted into an impossible shape on the chaise, his shirt half unlaced and his arms tucked close across his contorted body. His knees in his rumpled hose are pulled up to his chest, his head buried under several pillows.

I lower the poker as he uncovers an eye and blinks a few times. I step back a pace, and he slowly unfolds, sitting up. The wind sings a mournful counterpart to Linnet's muffled humming. His hair falls into his eyes.

I reach forward, my fingers trembling, and brush the tangled hair from his forehead. Of its own volition, my hand slips down to touch his cheek. He leans into my caress, his eyelids fluttering down. His cheek feels less bristly than I expected. Just behind the morning's growth of beard, in front of his ear, the skin is so soft. I rub it with trembling fingers, and a low moan escapes his throat.

Standing slowly, he reaches for my shoulders, his hands hot through my clothes. I remember all I'm wearing is my shift. I shiver, look down.

He lifts my chin with his hand. The rain on the window is a staccato beat in time with my pulse. He strokes my neck and collarbones, tracing the lines of my scars, my veins. I feel myself falling into his eyes. His fingers wind in my hair.

The door to Julianna's room opens, and we jump apart. I wince as I feel a few curls follow Connor. Linnet hurries into the room, a tray in her hands.

"Rhiannon! What are you doing out here in your shift?" I dither, my mouth pursing like a fish. Linnet looks at the two of us. Her eyes start to narrow.

"Clean clothes," I blurt. "The, the laundry never got done." Linnet closes her eyes in exasperation.

I wait for her to say something scathing.

"Laundry!" she says. "I forgot. I'll go find you something to wear. And something to eat. Are you hungry? I'm hungry. I'm getting a tray of food for Julianna, too." She raises an eyebrow at me, and runs off.

I start to go after her, then remember Connor. And my clothes, or lack thereof.

Connor stands awkwardly next to the settee, clutching at nothing. He cocks his head when I look at him, and smiles a little.

"Were you going to brain me with the poker?"

I look at the poker still in my hand. I decide to try for a light tone, as well. "Just in case of rogues, you know." His brow quirks up.

I return the poker to the fireplace and walk at a measured pace from the room. When I reach the safety of my room I close the door and sag against it. What can I be thinking? I have too much to do. I do not have time for dalliances with the grandson or the nephew of a monarch, let alone someone who is both. And in any case, his true heart lies with Julianna. I walk to the bowl of water and shove my face in it, hoping for clarity.

Linnet brings me clothes and bread, and I throw on the one and tear into the other, ravenous. Linnet heads downstairs again to help Asa and the others in the great hall. I plan to help them.

Before I head down, I peek in on Julianna. The baby lies sleeping in Julianna's arms. Julianna's eyes are closed, and I step back and close the door softly.

"Rhia," Connor says behind me.

I turn, heart pounding, and he holds a bundle out to me. Now my heart pounds for other reasons. Absalom's body.

He nods at my look. "I need you to take this to the tower stairs. I'll meet you there shortly. We have to burn the body. There's a ritual. Can you manage it, if I show it to you?"

I blink, draw in a shuddering breath. "I can try, my lord."

"Good. Please, take – him. I'll meet you there as soon as I can. I'll bring what we need."

I follow him out of Julianna's rooms, carrying the bundle cautiously. It feels wrong no matter how I carry it. I don't want anyone to guess this is a baby, but I don't know how else to hold it. Him. I needn't worry: everyone is in the great hall. I don't meet anyone as I make my way to the tower stairs.

The spiral stairs take longer than the main stair, with their old arrow-slit windows from centuries gone by, going around the tower rooms inside. Passing the ground floor, I feel a sharp breeze, hear a loud thump of the outside door closing, and footsteps. How did Connor get ahead of me?

I freeze where I am. It's not Connor. Backing up the stairs one careful foot at a time, I try not to make any noise. I turn to run when Bishop Gantry boils around the curve below me, yanking a vacant-eyed Orrin by the arm.

"Orrin," I gasp, almost falling.

Gantry looks up at me, his lips pulled back from his teeth, his hair a wild storm around his head.

I trip backward over the stairs and he looms over me.

"What's this?" He lets Orrin go to grab at my arms and I drop the wrapped body, try to push him away. A glance at Orrin shows him holding himself against the wall, barely able to stand.

Gantry raises a hand to strike me, and I grab at his arm, try to twist away from the blow. Stone grinds into my spine and sides as his hand glances off my cheek. He grabs my hair with one hand, slaps me hard with the other, and I feel my bones ache with the shock of it. I hang limp in his grip. His mind reaches for me, slithers along my barriers and finds my magic.

"Ah, what's this? The Star Lord gives me a gift of more power," he says, and starts to laugh. I bring my feet up and kick him as hard as I can in the knee, the groin, push him.

He staggers back, taking some of my hair with him, falls down several steps to his back. "Fiend! Invader! I'll have you burned!"

I lurch to my knees, reach for Orrin's hand, so close, so close. He looks at me but does not reach back.

"Run," he whispers, and throws himself into the Bishop, keeping him from getting up.

"Orrin," I shout, but Gantry starts chanting a spell. I feel it trying to pull from me as well as Orrin, and I don't know what all that power will do.

I slam up all the barriers I can and trip, scramble up the stairs away from them as fast as I can, weeping.

As soon as I feel far enough away, I lower them partially and scream out in my mind for anyone who can hear me to help, Dorei, help us.

I crash through the hall like a panicked animal, panting, scrabbling for footing that eludes me. I slam into a body. Connor catches me before I knock us both over.

"What is it? What happened?"

"Gantry," I gasp. "He has Orrin – he has Orrin, and he was coming up the tower stairs, and-"

"How? How does he have Orrin?"

"I don't know, I don't know, but he does, and he's, I don't know what he's going to do-" But I do. I do know. The vision washes over me and I sag against the wall, one arm on Connor's chest. "The spell – he called him back, called him and found him where you hid him. The chapel," I say. "He's going to – he's giving them a body. Orrin's body. With all that power. And now he has Absalom's body too, I dropped it, I'm sorry, I dropped him, and he's going to do something awful."

Connor swears, wipes at my face with his sleeve, and I see blood, my nose is bleeding, my face throbs where Gantry hit me.

I wheeze and weep and tremble.

"Dorei save us," Connor whispers. He kisses my forehead, shakes my shoulders. "Call for Hugh. Do you understand? He should be on his way back. Try to get him back sooner. Tell him to bring the Cardinal. Tell them to hurry." And he is gone, running toward the chapel, yelling for guards.

I lean my weight on the wall, gather my magic on the spindle of my mind. I push at my range, at the ends of where I've ever been able to go.

It hurts. My skin crawls with it, but I call up power and drop all of my barriers. I can feel Gantry's spell reaching for my power, but I'm using it, and it will follow my commands now.

Panting, I push past the castle, past the walls of the town, down the road, looking for Hugh. His mind meets mine as I call, try to find him. I feel thin and faint, but I hear him finally, and he hears me.

Rhiannon? What is it? How did you get this far?

Gantry has Orrin. Has Absalom. Spell. Bring the Cardinal. Hurry. It hurts to push so far. I strain, feel my head throb, all my magic burn in me.

How did this happen?

Just hurry.

A panicked call in my mind from Linnet. She heard my cry before and followed Connor to the chapel. They hide behind pillars outside the doors as blasts of raw magic rock the stones.

I shamble into a run. Down stairs, around corners, I feel the magic in the air. Everyone else appears to be wisely hiding from it.

Gantry's voice grates on the air in the otherwise silent castle. "All your guards can't save you from judgment! The night sky will swallow them whole! You are all tongues of evil – I shall cut you out!"

I round the corner beyond the great hall. I feel demons gathering at his calling, whispering and enticing him.

The wild power that breathes beneath the castle beckons me. The well is deep, viscous and bright with its gathered magic. I open myself to it despite the pain, relish the seering flash along my body, as I stumble down the corridor.

Magic pours into me, burning, blistering the overused pathways of power. I try to control it, but it sings as savagely as the demons. I send it to Linnet, who cries out too, burning herself on the heat of it.

Linnet flings power past the doors of the chapel in the form of a fire spell, but I hear Gantry laugh, Connor's voice ringing out, a clash and clatter, my own heart beating.

The wild power devours me. Clutching the power I have gathered in too full mental arms, I manage to sever the link to the well. Magic swirls in my veins like a squall. I find myself on my knees against a pillar, Linnet across from me. I grasp the cold stone and drag myself to my feet, peer into the chapel.

Connor dodges demon fire, slashes at Gantry with his sword.

Gantry stands in front of the altar, hurling his spells and abuse. Three guards lie motionless among the pews. Wisps of my sweaty hair cling to my eyes and nose. I drop to my knees, motion Linnet to keep behind the pillar, keep throwing balls of fire. Which I did not know she could do.

I start to crawl into the chapel, keeping low. I can hear hissed invective, see purple flashes of light like odd torches. I look around for something I can use to help, anything.

Fire from Linnet glances off the marble statue of Dorei above me in the balcony, and I see it rock on its mooring. Gantry stands close by. I cannot poison him. I cannot stop him with spells I don't know. But I think I have another plan.

I send to Linnet, tell her what I want her to do. Crawling through the pews, dodging bael-fire as best I can, I head for the gentry box.

Linnet runs past me, hurling her own insults and fire.

Gantry stands below and to the left of the balcony. His hoarse whispers grate around my ears, swirling with the invisible demons in the air around us. I can hear them, feel them feeding from him, and from Orrin.

Orrin lies behind the altar. From here I can see his face like ashes, his body limp. The demons whisper of power and righteousness, of the glory of their promised body, of death and destruction.

I look for a way to cut them off from him, but I don't know how. I only hope my plan works.

Connor sprawls against an overturned pew across from me. He dodges bael-fire, throws himself under a pew. When he looks up at me I motion with my head to the rocking statue. Connor glances toward Gantry, eyes slitted against the flashes of fire, demon and Linnet-made.

Gantry aims bael-fire at Linnet, and though she transforms what she can, it leaks through her barriers and scorches her. She yells and leaps away, and he laughs. At that laugh, I stand and scream at him, using all of my anger and pain and despair, and I overload his spell.

I let him have my magic – the magic he so desperately wanted. The magic he cannot control. I push all of the pulsing, wild power into Gantry's gathering skeins, and I break them.

Gantry screams, tries to fight me, but I am not trying to control demons and a rogue spell and hurl bael-fire all at the same time. I concentrate on stuffing him with all of the power I pulled from the power-well, and I watch him start to burn. The lines of power warp and snap and rebound on him, and I scream and send the message to Linnet.

"Now!"

Linnet sends magic fire overhead, to the statue of Dorei. To its feet, to the moorings. She sends more. I hear it groaning.

Connor springs into a shoulder roll, knocking Gantry to his back beneath the balcony. Gantry screams again, calls out for his demons.

The crack of the mortar as it gives way makes Gantry look up. He aims his bael-fire upward to the falling statue, but too late, and it lands heavily as Connor rolls away just in time.

Gantry's control of the demons is gone with the thunk of the marble. Free of the restraints of his fragile chains, they rise, glittering to my Sight, supple and gorgeous, turn their attention to Linnet and Connor and Orrin. Their forms coalesce into dusky smoke, half-rotted faces in the air, changing and malleable and deadly.

Connor stands, ragged and bloody, sword drawn. Linnet shakes, but raises her hands and her magic. I hang from the rail of the gentry box, try to get ready to add mine.

Hugh and a man in Cardinal's robes pound into the chapel, their boots muddy and their voices raised. The Cardinal's hands weave a silvery light in the air. The threads become a shimmering net around the angry, seething demons.

Cardinal Robere chants a spell and cages the demons: I can feel the hum of power as he pulls the spell tighter. The cage grows smaller. Shrieking in agony, the demons disappear with sounds of shattered glass and exploding purple starbursts.

The chapel grows dark and quiet, silvery light fading, with only dusk from the windows to see by. Connor and Linnet stand panting. Connor turns stiffly to offer Linnet his arm as she wavers on her feet, but she stands taller and waves him away.

I hang dazed where I am.

Cardinal Robere looks around at all of us. He walks over to Gantry and looks down at him. He still lives, I can feel it. But I don't think it will be for long.

"Orrin," I say, and I feel his fear like a weight in my mind. "Oh Dorei, the spell is still going," I whimper, and stumble to the altar.

Bare to the waist and bloody from a beating, from the teeth and fire of demons, Orrin looks far worse than when I saw him on the stairs. The scars on his skin look angrier than mine, as if they cut deeper. His eyes open, and he looks at me. "It is too late," he says.

I can feel the magic pulsing through him. Beside him is the still wrapped form of Absalom, still tainted, magic going between Orrin and the corpse.

Hugh and Cardinal Robere push me aside, and the Cardinal starts a spell.

I can See the darkness of the spells already on my friend, and I reach for his hand. "It is not too late, Orrin. Fight," I whisper.

Robere's spell breaks and the threads scatter. He closes his eyes, rubbing at his temples.

"It didn't work." I say.

"No. I don't have enough power left. I need help, Hugh. Link to me."

Hugh reaches to grasp Robere's left hand. I watch them meld their magic together — silver and blue — and wrap it in and around Orrin until he begins to glow.

The demons that tear him apart inside howl through his pores and rip at the spells they weave. I feel them weaken, and I add myself into the warp and weft of the spell, linking to Hugh.

My lungs burn, my joints burn, and I am inside Orrin. His wounds bind the demons to him; they drink his blood and enter his spirit. Absalom's body is still a vessel – his body carries the demon taint, and now I feel it, like a disease that can mar the very air.

If the spell continues, the demons will use Orrin as a conduit from their plane, wreaking whatever havoc they can. He is demon-torn: his spirit bleeds as they try to meld with him. Though he fights them, he can't hold out for long.

Neither can the others. I feel them weakening, the drain on me. I open to the well of wild magic under the castle again, feel it burn through me. My scars singe and sear, the air driven from my lungs with the pain. I wheeze and gasp, but the warp is full again and our spell sings strong.

Magic whispers in my mind. At first I think it is demons, but I see the shape of a spell, the shape of runes, the glorious arc and movement of words and shapes and color and power. I start to chant through the pain of it all, chant words that suddenly spring to life, on Orrin's body. On my body. I take control of all of the magic, Hugh's and the Cardinal's and mine, and I weave it all together.

I can feel the shape of my runes change with the force of the wild magic. I chant though my skin burns, my eyes burn, all I see is the white hot spell.

Voices cry out around me, but they are driven back. Orrin twitches, I can feel him cringing away from the flame that is me, but I reach my burning arms around him. His body crackles in my arms.

I feel the power rush out of me, rivers of power. It fills me, pours out of me in fountains of white so hot it is stars. I feel it enter Orrin and drive the demon-sickness from him, burning the reservoirs of his power until they boil away. The power encases us in a cocoon of light: Dorei protect me, I am fire.

I take hold of this power with charring mental hands, direct it inward and away from Orrin before I kill him. The magic answers my call sluggishly, whirls in my veins, along new runes seared into my skin. I cut myself off from the wild magic, let it drain away. I think it drains all of me away with it.

My eyes clear of the light. The heat of the magic has forced everyone back, and I see them staring, calling out to me, their eyes wide. They move as though slowed in time.

I look at Orrin – his body seems whole, I do not see the sickness or the spell on him. His eyelids flutter, and he looks at me.

I lie down beside him, so tired. It all aches. My cheek presses into cold and gritty stone. I reach for his arm. "No more demons," I say, and I breathe a laugh because I can say it. "No more demons, and no more demon spells. We are free," I tell him.

He lifts a shaking hand and lays it on my cheek. "Don't die," he whispers.

"You either," I whisper back.

Robere reaches Orrin at the same time Connor reaches me. Connor pulls me into his lap. It hurts, everything is pain. I gasp and shudder, try to speak again but I can't. I open my eyes to Connor patting my face. I can't hear him but his mouth forms words. "Breathe, Rhiannon! Look at me! Breathe!"

My ears fill with a frantic beating. I drain away in dribbles and I can't hold on any more. Darkness comes for me as Connor's voice rings in my ears.

CHAPTER 30

I wake to the sounds of water pouring, voices, someone weeping quietly. When I open my eyes, I find I'm looking at high pointed arches and white marble. The great hall. I turn my head and see cots lining the walls, much more organized than when I last saw it. Someone lies on the cot next to me, the blanket pulled up and cocooning. Turning my head to look the other way, I see much the same thing.

I spend some time trying to convince my body to move, but give it up as a bad idea after awhile. I only hope my bladder will hold out.

"Rhiannon?" I look back to my left. Linnet stands next to my bed, a mug in her hands. Her left arm is bandaged to the elbow, her sleeve rolled up to stay off of it, and her face looks sunburned. "Are you really awake?"

"Yes," I croak, surprised at the state of my voice.

"I mean it. What's my name?"

"Linnet," I cough, try to lever myself to my elbows, give up. "Don't be silly. Can I have that tea?"

"There you are." She smiles. "You've been either raving or asleep for days. Time you woke up for real."

"Days?" I cough some more. She has to help me sit up to drink from the mug.

"Orrin," I start to ask.

"Look for yourself," she says, and points to my other side.

When I turn my head, I realize it's him lying on that cot. He's turned his head to look at me. One side of his mouth quirks up a little. "Hello, sleepyhead," he whispers.

A weight I didn't know was holding me down lifts, and I feel my mouth widen and grin, my eyes close. I reach across to the edge of his cot, and grab at the blanket. "Hello, you."

"You sound terrible." I stick my tongue out at him.

"Your breath stinks, too," Linnet adds, and Orrin smiles a real smile and turns his face to his pillow to chuckle weakly.

"How kind of you."

"The rest of you doesn't smell any better," she adds.

"Shut up, Linnet," I say, but with no heat. She's probably right. "So help me get up. I need the guarderobe."

My head pounds and my body shakes like a newborn calf as she helps me to the makeshift privy in the corner of the hall. Blankets have been put up as a little tent, and old fashioned chamber pots for people to use. It's not pretty, but with what looks like twenty or thirty people still in beds in this impromptu hospital, the guarderobe at the end of the hall is too far. At least it's kept as clean as can be.

There's another blanket tent, with wash water warm from the fire, and several clean shifts and tunics on a bench. Linnet helps me wash and dress. All my scars are still there, but now there are new ones on my wrists – faint and white and more like filigree than the others. My magic changed the runes.

Linnet stares, and stares at me staring. "Don't ever do any of that again," she says.

I look up at her, wary. "Do what?"

"Almost kill yourself. Nearly burn down a chapel. Fall into a fever for days. But do try to stay awake for an hour altogether this time, will you?"

"Did you miss me?" I tease, but she looks sad.

"Yes."

I sit blinking, and she presses her lips together and pulls the shift down over my head, walks me back to bed.

I try to be careful of her arm. "What's the bandage for?"

"Your, uh, magic. Burned me. Us."

I take a breath. "Oh." She arranges the covers back around me, fusses with my pillows. "I'm sorry."

"It's nothing," she says. "Lie still. Do you want soup?"

I look over at Orrin, who stares up at the ceiling. He doesn't look back. "Who is – who didn't-" I take a breath. "Who has died, then?"

"Marla cook, Mary, Robert, Samuel. Lady Geneve. Gervaise. That new seamstress. Some guards. A lot of people in town." Linnet clears her throat. "Really a lot.

"And Gantry –"

"He's dead." Orrin's voice stays flat, and his gaze stays to the ceiling.

"And the demons?" I keep my eyes on Orrin, but I feel my mouth say the word, and I feel my breath even in my lungs, and I can't help but say it again. "Demons. He called demons."

"I know that," Linnet says.

But Orrin turns his face to me. "He called demons, and he killed the queen, and he tried to kill Princess Julianna, and Princess Eleanor," he says in a rush. "He is no true bishop. He is no true anyone anymore." He takes a deep breath, shudders. "He called demons."

"He's dead," I say, to confirm it. To let breath into my lungs. I reach my hand over to him, and he reaches back to grab it. We hold on for a moment, but we are both so tired.

"I'm getting Asa," Linnet says.

But I can feel myself slipping back into sleep, now I'm lying down again. I try to shake my head, mumble something, and the voices go fuzzy and far away above me as I fade back into darkness.

I jerk awake in the blurry half-light, lamps turned down and a rocking weight on my cot. I blink my eyes to focus them, see who sits with me. A spike of fear clears the sleep from my mind – that is Archbishop Montmoore.

"Well, see who joins us. Good evening, young lady," he says quietly. I try to cry out, but his magic is strong, and I am still so weak. His power ruffles through my mind, and I can't reach out while he keeps my magic quiet. "So much power here. I think you could share," I hear him mutter.

I can't do anything magical, but I can move. The cot lists already from him sitting on it, so I throw myself against him, which dumps us both onto the cold floor.

Montmoore shouts in surprise, and I hear other voices raised, people coming closer.

Montmoore extricates himself from the tumbled mess that is cot and blankets and me, and stumbles to his feet, swearing. "Cleverness can only avail you so much, child," he whispers. His magic releases me as he hurries away. I send to Hugh for help, wincing at the ringing in my head as I do.

We're coming, Hugh sends back. *Don't let him take you anywhere.* The message bangs in my head like drums, and I cut myself off from everyone. Montmoore is gone, out toward the barbican.

When I look up, Orrin's face peeks over the edge of his cot, his eyebrow raised. "You do seem to find yourself in trouble a lot, don't you?" he rasps.

I try to make a rude gesture, but the pain and exhaustion overwhelm me, so I give up in favor of a vague glare and wandering out of consciousness.

Arms lift me from the floor, arms that feel familiar. I squint up at Connor's face as he walks out of the great hall with me.

"Where are we going?"

He glances at me, his mouth pressed into a thin smile. "Somewhere a tad more private. And guardable."

"Tell Montmoore," I drop my head against his chest, "tell him sharing is overrated." Connor's chest shakes lightly with a laugh or something else, and I let myself drift away, feeling safe.

I rouse a bit when Connor lays me down in a bed – in my bed, in the room I share with Linnet. He pushes curls back from my face and looks stern.

"Did he get away?" I ask.

"Yes. I have people looking for him..."

"But there was a ship waiting," I finish. The vision of Montmoore on a deck slips sharp and painful into my mind. I wince away from it.

Connor sighs and shakes his head at me.

"I have to leave tomorrow for Corat. I have reports to deliver to the king, and Julianna needs to present the baby to court as soon as possible. Try not to get into any trouble while I'm gone."

"You either," I say.

He snorts at me. "Who in this room is currently laid low by immense over-use of magic?"

"Who told me himself he has enemies everywhere?" I retort. My voice is weak, and I can't focus my eyes fully. "When are you coming back?"

He shakes his head. "I don't know. Soon, I hope. It will take us a week of travel at least, with the carriages. And I may need to stay in Corat for awhile, to deal with some matters." He strokes at my hair. "Hugh sent the bailiff to arrest Guildmaster Aman and the others we know about, but it's likely Stephen still has agents in town, possibly in the castle. So do me a favor and be careful. Do what Hugh tells you. Mostly."

I roll my eyes. "Who gets to tell you what to do?"

"Almost everyone."

"Then do what I say, too. Stay safe. Remember you're not your brother."

"I am most decidedly not my brother. Be well, Rhiannon." He smoothes my hair again, kisses my forehead. Bending further, he touches his lips to mine, soft, gentle. A shiver runs through me and my hands spasm in fists in the blanket, then on his arms. I kiss him back, pulling him closer, dizzy from exhaustion, from him. When he draws away to rest his forehead on mine, we're both breathing harder.

"I'll look for you when I return," he says, his voice maybe a little rough. He stands and leaves the room, abrupt as ever.

"I bet you say that to all the exonerated witches," I rasp at the closing door. I see the gleam of his eye, a hint of a smile as he turns, and then he's gone.

The next few days I wander in and out of wakefulness, slowly regaining my strength. Julianna left instructions for me, as did Cardinal Robere, on what to eat and when I can stand up. Asa and Hugh check in on me, but Linnet is the one who spends her time making sure I follow instructions. I haven't seen Orrin since the night Montmoore escaped. Linnet says Orrin doesn't want to see anyone. She's the only one he'll speak to right now.

I walk across the hall to the guest room where they've put him. I knock and crack the door open, so he can't send me away before I peek in. He looks up from the bed, where he's propped against the large wooden headboard, staring at nothing. Afternoon sunshine dapples the woven hanging on the wall opposite the bed. The window looks out over the sea.

"Hi," I say. His curly hair is a little bushier, his skin less ashy, than the last few months. I think not being trapped in Gantry's spell agrees with him. I think magic scars that live on your skin is hard for both of us. I think he needs a friend. I know I do. He still says nothing. "I missed you," I say, feeling stupid.

He glances at me, then stares at his fingers picking at the rosy embroidered counterpane. "I didn't know how to stop him."

"I know. I knew. I wasn't – I didn't know either." I walk a few more steps into the room, biting my lips.

"You saved me," he says quietly.

"You saved me first. A couple of times. I wish I'd saved you sooner."

"So do I."

And we are weeping in each other's arms, arms scarred with runes that mark us, change us, make us different. Our skin is marred, but we own our souls.

"What's going on in here? Rhiannon, are you making people cry again?" Linnet stands in the doorway with a tray, frowning at us.

"Linnet, do you have a handkerchief?" Orrin asks. I start to laugh, and he smiles at us both, but his eyes are still sad. Linnet sighs and brings the tray to the side table.

"You both are so strange. Here, have a napkin. And I have letters for you." She draws papers from her skirt pocket.

"Letters? From whom?" I wipe my face and take the papers, look through them quickly. Julianna has sent something, and Robere for both Orrin and me.

"A certain Earl of Dorward has sent a missive." I look up; both Orrin and Linnet are smirking at me.

"Shut up." I fight my own smile down when I see his name. "Shut up both of you." I look at Orrin as he scans his letter from Cardinal Robere, his expression tense. "What does he say?"

"He wants me to come to Corat to work with him. He thinks we both should go."

"As an acolyte?"

"He doesn't say."

"Do you still want to be an acolyte?" Linnet asks.

Orrin shrugs, his face very carefully blank. "I don't know."

I press my lips together and work to keep my thoughts private. Orrin should get to make up his own mind. I don't know what I want to do now, either. I pick up the next letter, the one from Julianna, but a piece of paper falls out of it, folded smaller with my name – my full name, Rhiannon Owen, on it. It has no other seal, and no greeting when I open it.

"Who is that from?" Linnet asks. It doesn't say, but I know.

I can't wait to meet you, clever Rhiannon.

No signature, but I know it's from Stephen, Connor's brother. My stomach drops and my hands tremble, and I'm so very cold. Orrin reaches for the paper, and when his hand touches mine, the vision swamps us both.

An angry woman, a queen, tears up a treaty, calls it an insult. A dark eyed man smiles and makes her promises for when he is king. An army gathers in a mountain city.

We both drop the note and stare at each other, panting. Linnet picks it up.

"What is it? What does it mean?" she demands.

Orrin and I speak at the same time. "War."

ACKNOWLEDGMENTS

I have so many people to thank for this book happening at all.

Of course, thank you to my (first) publisher and editor Jak Koke, for reading the version I had put away for so many years. Thank you for liking it enough to say yes, and helping me to make this new version as good as it can be.

Thanks to Karawynn and Shannon, for copyedits, proofs, feedback, and asking "this is good," when I needed to hear it.

To Scott, who emailed that earlier version to Jak while we were at a party, despite both mine and Jak's consternation, when Jak said he was looking for manuscripts.

To my writing group pals, for reading version after version, for corrections, and ideas, for loving the story, and for believing it was good even when I flubbed whole chapters.

To my family, for cheering me on at a distance, or reading manuscripts and giving me feedback. (Especially Mom, who said, "I was surprised how much I liked it." Thanks, Mom.)

To my writer friends, many of whom read bits and pieces, had ideas to make it better, and wanted to see more. Thank you for being my tribe and my cheerleaders, thank you for kicking me in the butt when I need it, and thank you for patting me on the headband giving me cookies when I need that, too.

For all my friends, thank you for being your awesome selves, and for believing min me when I said "I'm a writer."

To Angie, for being my best friend and for making a kick-ass cover, because she is kick-ass, and so is this cover.

And again to Scott, for being who he is, for being there for me, helping me when I'm overwhelmed, and for loving me as I am, warts and all.

Hugh isn't entirely happy with our spy discovery plan, but he's gone along with it so far. I want to find everyone who could hurt us and stop them before they can.

"Rhia, I wish you wouldn't..." he starts, but sighs and reverses our arm placement to escort me instead. "I don't want you to risk yourself when Connor and I may have other ways of finding out this information. He's worried about you, too, you know."

I blush and look away. "Is he? He hasn't written lately."

Hugh clears his throat. "Ah, well, he's kept very busy in Corat. But he asked me to look out for you, which I'm trying to do. Searching for the minds of spies can be dangerous—you almost lost yourself in Montmoore's mind when you tried last year. You and Orrin are too..." he trails off again, searching for a word.

"What? Precious a resource? Useful as tools?" I sneer.

"No, Rhiannon. No." He stops and turns to me, his face so beautiful, so wounded. He cups my cheek with a soft, warm hand. "You are both too likely to be hurt, and I would be devastated if you were. Please be careful. If you must try, then I will help to keep you safe as best I can. Don't push too hard, don't get lost in the minds of others, don't get trapped or lose control. You are precious to me because you are precious. I want you to be safe."

He blinks at me for a moment, dropping his hand from my face. "Tell me, if you would. Can you hear my thoughts when I'm not sending them?" His voice is maybe a little nervous. I pat his arm.

"Your barriers are very good," I tell him. I don't tell him that those barriers aren't always good enough to keep me from hearing very strong thoughts. I don't want to worry him, and there's nothing he can do about it anyway.

We walk into the small castle chapel together, my arm through his. The morning light through the west facing windows, highlighting the golden wood of the pews and the lacy stonework, bright on the whitewash and the colorful murals. The smell of burning candles, an affectation since most of the walls hold glowsand lamps, wafts over the smell of perfumed people, sweating in their worship finery. The air is a little damp with the spring chill, the stones only reluctantly heated by the steam heat that moves through the walls, and a few braziers in the corners.

Hugh escorts me to the front pew of the gentry box and sits at my side, showing support. He often sits with me rather than up in the balcony with his mother, the Duchess Marguerite. He smiles at everyone around us – the soldiers off to our right in the main pews, a few servants with them, and the Duchess' ladies. The ladies head for the second pew of the gentry box and leave us on our own. Hugh reaches for the book of Dorei in front of us and thumbs through it, waiting for the pastor to begin. I take a deep breath and try to get comfortable on the hard, wooden pew. The sermons aren't terribly long, but it should be enough time to start my search.

Chapel isn't the ordeal it was when Bishop Gantry was leading it, but it still isn't my favorite. I don't feel close to either Dorei or the Star Lord. I don't feel that my prayers mean anything, and I don't like the way everyone looks sidelong at me. But Marguerite pointed out that my going makes me look normal, relatable, and safer.

I know—better than anyone—how people feel about us. That Marguerite supports us helps a bit because everyone trusts her. But what if she's wrong? I can hear them thinking it at me. What if she's wrong and this magic brings ruin?

Minds are like buzzing bees—a flower garden of thoughts, all whizzing around, some lazy, some with purpose, and far too few of them very important. As many minds as are in the castle, it's like hundreds of hives trying to pollinate the same garden.

When you're trying to hear just one set of wings amongst the swarm.

Often I hear thoughts from the people passing by, and even if they aren't physically making a sign against evil, inside their minds they're wondering if they should. Their thoughts are full of fear or disgust, certain I'm contaminated by what happened last year.

Contaminated by demons, or the demon-wrought Wasting plague that Gantry caused with his spells. Even though we've been declared innocent victims of his plans, we're still forever tied to Bishop Gantry, who everyone knows was working with the enemies of Talaria.

King Peter formally declared war against Fanthas, again, naming Archbishop Montmoore as a traitor to the crown—along with his nephew Stephen Valcourt, Connor's brother. Hugh, as the Duke of Haverston, placed Linnet and Orrin and I under the protection of Haverston Duchy. We live in the castle as ourselves, not pretending to be servants or hiding. Not pretending we don't have magic.

Sometimes I wish I were still pretending. People don't like us having this power, even if they don't exactly know what the power is. And the thoughts of people who are frightened of you are so tiring, even if you only catch them in bits. Sifting through those frightened fragments to find someone who is plotting to hurt you and not just thinking you're a monster is not a task I've excelled at so far. But I'm determined, even if Hugh thinks it's too dangerous for someone so...precious.

It's hard to match specific thoughts to a specific person, especially since I don't know who I'm looking for. But I do hope I'll know it when I find it...

ABOUT THE AUTHOR

Lindsey S. Johnson lives in the Pacific Northwest with her significant other and several fuzzy little monsters known as cats. When not engaged in day job or word tinkering, she dances, sings, bakes, and has been known to spend time staring pensively at nothing or randomly muttering to herself, although she claims that also counts as writing.

A Ragged Magic is her first published book, the beginning of The Runebound trilogy. You can find out more about the series online, at

www.lindseysjohnson.com